VENTURE INTO HORROR

TALES OF THE SUPERNATURAL

WORKS BY TY'RON W. C. ROBINSON II

BOOKS/SHORT STORIES

DARK TITAN UNIVERSE SAGA

MAIN SERIES

Dark Titan Knights
The Resistance Protocol
Tales of the Scattered
Tales of the Numinous
Day of Octagon
Crossbreed
Heaven's Called
The Oranos Imperative
Underworld

Forthcoming

Magicks and Mysticism
*The Resistance vs. The
Enforcement Order*

COLLECTIONS

Dark Titan Omnibus: Volume 1
Dark Titan Omnibus: Volume 2
Dark Titan One-Shot Collection

SPIN-OFFS

*In A Glass of Dawn: The Casebook of
Travis Vail*
Maveth: Bloodsport
The Curse of The Mutant-Thing

Forthcoming

Trail of Vengeance
War of The Thunder Gods
Maveth vs. The Swordman

ONE-SHOTS

Maveth, The Death-Bringer
Mystery of The Mutant-Thing
Shade & Switchblade
Retribution of Cain
The Mythologists
Ambush Bot
Kang-Zhu
Cheeseburger Man
Tessa Balthazar

THE HAUNTED CITY SAGA

The Legendary Warslinger: The Haunted City I
Battle of Astolat: A Haunted City Prequel (KOBO Exclusive)
Redemption of the Lost: The Haunted City II
Helper's Hand: A Haunted City Short Story
Consequences of the Suffering: The Haunted City III (Forthcoming)

SYMBOLUM VENATORES

Symbolum Venatores: The Gabriel Kane Collection
Hod: A Symbolum Venatores Book
Symbolum Venatores: War of The Two Kingdoms
Symbolum Venatores: Elrad's Chronicles
Symbolum Venatores: Mystery of the Magician (Forthcoming)
Symbolum Venatores: Twilight of the Gods (Forthcoming)

VENTURE INTO HORROR

TALES OF THE SUPERNATURAL

TY'RON W. C. ROBINSON II

CONTENTS

DOCTOR FORTUNE: THE SUPREME ENCHANTER

A young woman ran toward a small shack in the cold and wintry forests near the area of Nepal. She moved with haste, not bothering to make a simple stop or slow down near others who were in her way. She stopped at the shack door and knocked three consecutive times. No answer. She knocked again and no answer. She continued to knock until the interior lock clicked. She took some steps back from the door as it opened, revealing a man dressed in black clothing with a cloak and tunic. His facial hair stood out with his emerald colored eyes locked onto her.

"Why are you so far out here, Madame?" The man asked.

"Are you who they say you are?"

"Pardon?"

"Are you the Doctor?"

"Which doctor? There are many of them around these lands."

"Doctor Donald Fortune. Is that your name?"

"It is. Why have you come to my assistance, lady?"

"I need help. It's an urgent matter and I want them gone."

"Want what gone?"

"These demons. They continue to mock me about my past experiences. I can't take their voices no longer. I've heard you can cast them out."

"I've cast out devils in my time of service. I'm not sure if you understand the cost of what could happen to you when the casting takes its place."

"I don't care. I just want them gone. Out of my head, so I can have a full conscience. A clear mind that I can control."

Fortune nodded. Allowing the woman to enter his shack. Closing the door, she looked around Fortune's shack, seeing artifacts that pertain to mysticism and spiritualism. From his cloaks to his staff, which is said to have belonged to a powerful wizard during the early middle ages. His name unknown to the world, but known to Fortune and others like him. She went to touch the staff slowly with her finger.

"I suggest you keep your hands to yourself while you stand in here." Fortune said. "You have no idea as to the amount of power is withheld inside that staff."

"Sorry."

Fortune poured the woman some hot tea—which she drank, sitting down at the table in front of him. Fortune examined the woman, from head to toe. Searching her spirit through his mind. Within her, buried deep are the demons. Laughing and mocking her and her past actions. Fortune can hear the conversation between the demons. Their laughter itches Fortune—he starts to slightly rub his arms to remove the aura from his body.

"I can hear them." Fortune said.

"What?" The woman said, sitting down the teacup. "What can you hear?"

"I can hear them within your being. The demons. They're laughing and mocking you. Speaking of your past experiences as if it's only a show to them. They enjoy seeing you suffer from those moments and they relish it with all their power."

"Can you remove them?!"

"I can."

Fortune stood up from the table and walked into the middle of the shack. His hand extended out toward the woman. Looking at her eyes with caution as he can see the demons starting to manifest within her.

"I need to know if you are ready?"

"I am."

"Then come. Lay down on the floor and I will begin the casting out process."

The woman walked to the middle of the shack. Fortune removing the carpet, revealing a painted pentagram on the wooden floor. The woman jolted for a moment—seeing the symbol on the floor. She stood still, shaking and holding herself still. Fortune looked at her and knew it was the demons making their move to hold her back from the floor. She and the demons were playing a spiritual tug of war and Fortune could sense which side was winning.

"You'll have to be strong and fight against them. Only then will you make it towards the floor. Be strong and fight them within."

The woman struggled making her way towards the floor. She took several steps and the growls of the demons could be heard through her own voice. Fortune stood calm, awaiting to see the outcome of her determined will to lay down atop the pentagram. Fortune aided her with words, throwing out positive suggestions to give her internal strength to continue fighting the demons.

"Keep going, lady." Fortune said. "You're almost there."

She struggled constantly, slamming herself on the floor. The demons went silent as she looked around, seeing Fortune standing over her. He smiled and walked to the other side of the pentagram. Standing in front of her feet—Fortune grabbed and put on his other cloak. Different from the last one; a violet one and within the cloak was the Amulet of *Quirinto*, a mystical object filled with great power and vast knowledge used for such situations. Fortune stood in front of the woman as she looked up at him. His arms stretched out and his eyes closed. Standing next to him was a podium. Atop the podium was a grimoire which had the title of *'The Book of Durriken'* written on its cover.

"By the power of *Quirinto*, I bind the demons within the body of this young woman and command them to come out immediately!"

The woman began to scream as if she was in tremendous pain. The pain a woman would feel during labor. Fortune sensed and knew the screams were from the demons making their anger known from within her. She shook around on the floor, trying to stand up, but the mystical power of Fortune's enchantment held her down as if she was tied to the floor. Fortune continued to chant out the words to cast out the demons. Their screams had increased in both pitch and sound. From around her arose a cloud of black smoke and within the smoke were the demons themselves, hovering over her and staring at Fortune. Their eyes flashing from within the smoke and Fortune could only smile.

"You." The demons said in conjunction.

"Yes." Fortune said smiling. "It is me. I know of your kind. You're all soldiers, aren't you?"

"We do what our Master requires of us!"

"I can tell you this, your mission has been halted. You can blame me and my knowledge of the mystical."

"You play around with such power and use it on weaklings like this woman! You have no true knowledge of what great power is. Our Master will find you and he will end you!"

"Be that whoever your Master is, give him a message for me. If you will so, please."

Fortune raised his hands and appeared a glowing blue aura— which surrounded the demons and started pulling them into the pentagram. Fighting the pull, the demons screamed at Fortune, scratching and clawing at the woman to hold on. Finding themselves becoming transparent and losing their grip as they were almost pulled into the pentagram completely. One demon had raised its head up and roared at Fortune with a deep glare. Fortune looked in the eyes of the demon and laughed in its presence.

"We will find you and we will destroy you!" The demon declared with a deep pitched voice.

"You may try demon." Fortune said. "But, I am no ordinary man. I am the Supreme Enchanter and by the power of Quirinto through the Mystic Father, I now banish all of you back to your wicked kingdom! NOW!"

A powerful gust of wind blew throughout the shack, blowing the demons through the pentagram and within a split second—the demons were gone. The woman's eyes had opened, she slowly sat up from the floor. Looking around the shack, only see Fortune kneeling in front of her.

"How do you feel?" Fortune said.

"I feel… I feel clear." The woman responded with a smile on her face.

The woman stood up from the ground and thanked Fortune. A few minutes later, she walked out of the shack, smiling and full of happiness. She turned around to Fortune and hugged him.

"Thank you, sir."

"One more thing before you go, Madame."

"What is that?"

"Do not repeat the same actions as before. For if you do them, the demons will return with more than what was before and more aggressive in nature."

The woman nodded with a slight hint of fear in her being.

"I understand."

"You don't have to fear them." Fortune said. "Do not repeat

those actions and you will be fine."

The woman nodded, thanking him again for his help and she waved goodbye to Fortune. Fortune entered his shack and closed the door. He sat down at his table, raised up his cup of tea and took a sip with a slight sigh.

"We have to go!" He shouted. "We must leave!"

The man shouted continually as he witnessed his partner raping a young woman in an alleyway of an urban city. His partner relished in his actions. Shaking his head, he grabbed his partner by the shoulder, pulling him away from the woman.

"Didn't you hear what I said! We need to go. Now."

"Come on." His partner replied. "Why do we need to go? There's no cops nearby. Nonetheless anyone else near this alley besides the two of us and this hot spice here."

He glanced down at the woman, who's crying from the incident. The partner grinned. Loving her cries.

"Besides, I'm not done with her just yet."

"You're not listening to me."

"Why should I by the choice of your words, partner?"

"Because he's coming."

"Who's coming?"

"The one who collects the souls of the sinners."

"The what?" The partner questioned confusingly. "Who's coming?"

"The one who chases after the souls of sinners."

"You're talking about Jesus?"

"No. I'm talking about someone else. Something else."

The partner refused to believe him and went back to raping the young woman. He goes to pull his partner from her once again, by the touch of his hand to shoulder, the partner backhands him, knocking him to the ground.

"Let me have my fun!" His partner yelled angrily. "I want to enjoy this night."

The partner returned to the woman as his teammate arose from the ground. As he stood, watching he looked across the alley and saw what appeared to be a man. But it was not a man. He could tell by its eyes and the presence. He started to back away, seeing the entity coming toward them.

"He's here!" He yelled. "He's here!"

"Shut your mouth!" His partner replied. "Leave me be with your superstitious talk."

He ran from his partner and out of the alley. His partner looked up, sensing someone standing near him. Believing it to be his partner.

"I told you to lea-" He said before gazing the eyes of the Death Chaser. His head covered with a hood and his leather-type clothing standing out. Spikes on his shoulders and forearms. his eyes glowing with a burning fire. The essence of fear stroked the partner immediately.

"I have come for you." The Chaser declared. "Let the woman be."

The partner stepped back from the woman, who ran. The Chaser took small steps toward the partner as he began to plead for his life.

"Look, I was only looking for a good time. Not much was happening tonight."

"You do not know the deed you have done. You have deflowered a virgin. One that could've reach a great price to a worthy man."

The Chaser snatched the partner and rammed him against the wall. He held his head tightly as he screamed out for mercy.

"You want mercy from me?"

"Please! I'll go home, and I will forget this moment ever happened! I won't bother any other woman like this ever again!"

"I will give you mercy."

The Chaser stared his eyes, measuring his spirit. The Chaser nodded and stared at the partner.

"What are you doing?" The partner asked fearfully.

"Very well. I have searched the reins of your heart. Therefore, I declare you need the Cry of Repentance."

"The what?"

The Chaser breathed on the partner, endowing him with the memories and the pain of the actions he's committed, including the recent act done to the virgin. The partner yelled in pain, falling to the ground as the Chaser overlooked him.

"You are in pain." The Chaser said. "For the moment. Afterward, may you have learned you lesson. If not, I will return for you and that moment will be your final day on this Earth."

The Chaser walked away, vanishing through the dim light as if he was a physical ghost. The partner continued yelling in pain. Begging for help. No one came to his aid and he remained in the alley until the morning when he was found by police and taken to the hospital. There, it was seared into his mind, he met the Death Chaser, the Soul of Retribution and Chaser of Souls.

DOCTOR DARK: THE PURPOSE OF DARKNESS AND LIGHT

A group of untrained wizards meet up in secret within the bowels of a undisclosed location. Although, it's near a forest, not known which forest it could be. The wizards have agreed to meet up together to conjure up an entity of any kind to prove to their doubters that they are real wizards in the flesh.

"Are you sure we'll be unseen from this place?"

"I have to ask the same thing. What if that "swordsman" guy shows up and sees what we're doing here. He might toss us into Pegasus for all we know."

"What if that guy from Enigma City appears in the sky over us? If he shows up, we're as good as dead."

"No one is showing up to stop us. The only thing that will make itself known is what we conjure up from our ritual."

The leading wizard creates the surrounding landscape they will set up the ritual and the location for the entity to conjure out of the other dimensions before them. The wizards are prepared for anything to take place as the other two are in fear of who will show up during their ritual.

"Shall we begin."

"Yes." The wizards said. "Let us begin."

The leading wizard begins to recite a spell from a scroll, kept within his robe. Reading from the scroll, the area stars to shroud up with strange smoke. A dark smoke with a bluish hue to its appearance. The leading wizard continues reading, the language is Latin.

"Vobis hodie vocamus, olim domini de adumbration! Alterum nobis cum surrexerit Sabaoth!"

The ground vanishes around the wizards. They can't even see the ground through the dense smoke. The Wizard continues chanting from the scroll and they hear footsteps approaching them. Coming within a distance. The wizards shiver in fear and in excitement. Waiting for their master to make himself known unto their presence.

"Please greet us!" The wizard shouted. "We need your eyes to gaze upon us!"

Through the smoke appears a figure. Standing tall over the wizards. They crouched down to their knees, bowing before the shadow figure as it walks toward them and through the smoke. The smoke doesn't even make a touch to the figure's body as it flows through the figure. The wizards take notice and believe their master has come. The figure stood before them, gazing down at them with its white pupils.

"You have summoned me from my home." The figure declared.

"Yes. Yes, we have."

"For what purpose to you disturb me?"

"We desire to have your powers." The leading wizard said. "With your powers, we can change this world for the better. Get rid of all these folktale figures popping up across the earth."

"You believe you can do a better job than those who are already doing the work?"

"Yes, master. We surely believe that fact."

The figure nodded, and the wizards bowed their heads.

"Very well." The figure said. "Take heed of the words that I'm about to speak to you."

"Yes, Master. We will."

The figure raised his arms above hem and into the night sky. The wizards gazed upward, seeing before them one side of the sky covered in the darkness of the night and the other side shining in the brightness of the day. The leading wizard became confused by the message in the sky.

"What is this sign you've given us, Master? What does it all mean?"

"You seek to have the powers of the darkness. To do your work upon the earth. Yet, you have no knowledge of the light. How can you control the darkness without the intellect of the light? It is a shame for your kind to have such feats."

"You can teach us this mighty works. Please, teach us the things you can do, and we will grow in them and we will achieve our mission."

"I will not teach you these things you have seen this night."

"Why not?! We summoned you hear to give us knowledge of the shadows. To do things which no other humans could possibly comprehend."

"Yet, none of you can comprehend what the signs of the sky declared before you."

The figure waved its arm, removing all the smoke from the area. Clearing it out completely. The wizards took cover as the gust of wind blew away the smoke. After the gust settled, the wizards raised their heads up toward the figure and the could see it and they were frightened. More frightened than when it first appeared.

"You're not our master." the leading wizard said.

"I am not." The figure replied.

"Then, who are you? Who are you that can create the signs of the sky and reveal those feats before us?"

The figure stood before them closer. Revealing his true form. His form was of a pale man with long black hair and black facial hair. Dressed in all black, with a black trench coat, shining with the hints of royal violet. His eyes completely black with his white pupils shining from them. The wind blew around him slowly while snippets of thick darkness surrounded his presence.

"I am the Keeper of the Cosmos. I am Darkous of the Astrals."

"The Astrals. They can't be real."

"You're looking at one now and we are all real."

"Then, what will you do to us?" The leading wizard asked. "What could we have possibly done wrong this day to insult a true Astral entity?"

"Go home." Darkous declared. "Return there and leave this life of the mystic arts."

"Leave it?"

"Yes. Leave this life. Live a life such as a human should. You're not fit for this purpose."

"What purpose?"

Darkous turned away from the wizards, preparing to leave them. The leading wizard stood up and ran toward Darkous. Reaching out with his hand, he touched Darkous' coat. Darkous stopped and turned toward the wizard.

"What purpose?!"

"The purpose of darkness and light."

Darkous' pupils turned from white to red and within seconds a flash of light bolted from him. Blinding the wizards. They ran around, searching for the wall to lean on and while they were doing such–Darkous was gone. Nowhere to be found.

CREED: KNOWING WHO YOU SERVE

"I had a life. It was taken from me without notice. Without hesitation. That day, I learned there was another side to everything, and it was at that moment, I became who I am this day."

A figure cloaked in a dark blue cape. The cape extended far beyond average length to the human body. His body was covered in black and gold armor. Rough in detail and somewhat scaly to touch. The figure reached the top of a church and stood still. His eyes glowing as fine gold. A mouth could not be seen nor could ears and a nose. He watched the streets of the city move with cars. He could spot civilians walking along the sidewalks.

"This world, it isn't all it's talked up to be. I learned that day this world is temporary. People build up treasures on this earth, only to leave them behind after they're dead. Their treasures and possessions crumble underneath the weight of the dust and the homes of the moths."

The figure kept his gaze upon the city and its people. He remained there for hours on end. It wasn't until near daybreak where he was visited by an angel. The angel's name is Ananchel. The figure arose from his stance, almost as if he was a living statue atop the church as of the gargoyles.

"Creed." Ananchel said. "I need your help."

"My help? What for and what of?"

"Adrambadon is coming to this world in full force. He has an army behind him. Ready to take the orders he spews out."

"Do you know who may be in this army of his?"

"I saw those of The Cult. The hooded ones. I even glimpsed the demon Abacus, the beast known as Satanic, and I saw legions of tormented souls marching behind them. They're ready for a war on this earth."

"And you desire to have me find him and his army before things get out of hand?"

'As always. You're a different breed of character, Creed."

"I am no different than those who have come before me in this similar state. Humans can assist your causes better than I can."

"They don't have your strength. Your speed. Your reflexes. Even, your knowledge of the supernatural realms."

"Are you sure of that?"

"Very sure. Which is why I've come to you. Trust me, there are others who can help in this cause. But, they're busy with missions of their own. All of us are in this day and hour."

Creed removed himself from the top of the church, standing beside its giant cross. He thought to himself of Ananchel's motives and the words she spoke. It wasn't clear to Creed if he should take up the cause, yet, he could sense he was meant to prepare for something.

"If I take up arms in this fight, I don't do it for you, and I don't do it for this Madam who's been discussed by many."

"Then, you will you do it for?"

"The one who saved me from working alongside Adrambadon in the beginning."

"Ah." Ananchel nodded. "I see."

Creed walked over to the edge of the church, gazing down at the open road. The sun began to pour out from the clouds above him. He began to absorb the sun's rays. Ananchel could only watch the scenery.

"When will you start with us?" She wondered.

"You'll find me when you'll see." Creed declared. "Remember, I am not far away. As you have managed to find me this day."

Creed jumped from the church and in the air, he flew. His cape spread across the sky to where those on the ground could see him. The span of the flowing, shining cape was tremendous and it would confuse the people to a small plane moving through the sky. Ananchel flew off and Creed vanished like a shadow into the morning sky.

IN A GLASS OF DAWN: THE CASEBOOK OF TRAVIS VAIL

THE TALE OF THE HAUNTING

Occult Detective Travis Vail set out on his investigation to a mansion which is documented to be a very haunted location. Wearing his black coat with slacks, Vail arrives in the city of Hartford, Connecticut, where the mansion is located on the outskirts of the city. Vail gets to the mansion, known as the Rosebane Mansion. Outside of the mansion is its current owner, Lloyd Sharp. Sharp extends his hand as a greeting to Vail.

"Welcome to Rosebane Mansion, Mr. Vail." Sharp said.

Vail shook his hand in greet and allowed Sharp to invite him inside the mansion.

Within the mansion's interior is a beautiful structure for a century-year-old building. The walls are made of granite marble with historical paintings and picture frames across. The flooring was made of hardwood. Vail quickly examines the mansion's interior.

"What happened here that caused the haunting?" Vail said.

"The former residents were unaware of what was buried here centuries ago." Sharp said. "One day, their son was digging in the backyard and discovered a skeleton with Indian artifacts."

"An Indian burial ground, you say.' Vail said.

"Of course." Sharp said. "Once the parents discovered it, they had it taken away, which later became a regret to them as the poltergeist activities began to occur."

"Truly a mistake they made.' Vail said. "So, I've been brought here to investigate these haunting?"

Sharp brought Vail into the bedroom section of the mansion upper floors. Inside were a total of six rooms, the master bedroom belonged to the parents, another to their son, and four for guests. Vail walked through every bedroom, scavenging the entire location for anything resourceful. Sharp watched him as he went through every room like a focused individual. After Vail completed his search through the rooms. Walking through a corridor, Sharp took Vail out to the backyard. Once outside, Sharp pointed to the now buried sport of where the Indian burial was originally located. Vail walked over to the spot and rubbed the dirt on the ground. He raised his head, looking around the backyard. He turned to Sharp and thanked him for showing him the areas of the mansion,

"I take it you're ready to do your work.' Sharp said.

"Yes I am." Vail said.

Vail went to the nearest museum and did research on the mansion and the land. his hotel room and began setting up his equipment. From holy water to crosses to a book that is encrypted with proper ways to end curses or send spirits back into their world. After he left the room. He went back to the mansion to begin his investigation upon its encounters.

Later that night, Vail returned to the mansion, alone. He found the key to the front door underneath the movable block by the door. He entered the mansion and shut the door. No lights were on throughout the mansion, only the moonlight. Vail walked around the mansion, pulling out a book that contained previous reports and encounters inside the mansion.

"Very well." He said. "You have me here all alone. So, I would demand that you reveal yourself to me or at least give me a sign of your presence to start with."

The mansion is silent to the point where if a pen would fall onto the wooden floor, it would make a louder sound. Vail slowly walked through the corridor of the mansion, surrounded by frames of the previous owners of the mansion and the land of which it lies upon. He looked at the frames and walked over to one that resembled a English settler. Once he stopped to look, a banging sound was heard down the corridor. Vail paused.

"I see you're trying to get my attention."

He walked down to the end of the corridor. Once at the end, he sees nothing in sight. He heard another banging sound that came from the bedroom areas.

"I want to speak with the spirit of the burial ground." He said. "I know you're here inside this mansion with me."

Vail continued down the corridor as one of the picture frames instantly flew off the wall and down the other end of the corridor. Vail looked and ran after it. He reached the other end of the corridor and the frame was nowhere in sight. He turned back around walking upstairs toward the bedrooms. He heard a distant moan near the rooms.

"You're getting better at this."

The lamp on the side of the bed levitated and slammed itself against the wall. Vail walked into the bedroom, which was a guest room.

"Very violent I noticed."

"*Get Out.*"

The words caught Vail's attention as he heard the distinctive voice coming from the master bedroom nearby. He walked into the room and it was quiet, everything is the same as it was earlier in the day. Vail reached into his coat pocket and pulled out a cleansing artifact that he received during his research into Indian burial grounds.

"I suggest you prepare to see the other side."

Vail began blessing the entire mansion with the cleansing. As he walked through the mansion saying the blessing, more sounds of banging occurred along with moans and distant yelling. Vail ignored the sounds and decided to head into the backyard.

As Vail walked outside in the backyard, he noticed the wind beginning to blow. He continued the cleansing as he walked near the burial ground. Vail paused for a second as he seen what appeared to be fire coming from the burial ground. Vail kneeled in front of the burial and held the cleansing over it, blessing it once more. As he spoke louder while blessing, he looked up and seen an apparition of what appeared to be a Indian man, wearing Native American wardrobe. The Indian apparition stared at Vail, who did the same.

"I see you as you can see me." Vail said to the apparition. "It's time you leave this place and enter the afterlife."

The wind slowly calmed, and the fire vanished along with the apparition. Vail walked back into the mansion and he felt a sense of calmness. Vail walked through the mansion for a final time to double check. Every room he went into he felt a sense of calmness and peace.

Later in the morning, Sharp returned to the mansion as Vail began to leave. Vail walked up to Sharp as he wanted to know what he had encountered and experienced.

"What did you come across?"

"I came across a spirit that did not want to leave." Vail said. "However, he had no choice. He had his time in the world of the living, its time he entered the world of the dead."

"So, is the place safer to live in?"

Vail paused and looked back at the mansion.

"As long as they don't bother with the burial ground or bring in any type of spiritual items that may invoke a spirit, they should be just fine."

 "Sharp extended his hand toward Vail.

"I thank you for coming and solving this problem." "Believe me, we really needed it."

"I just do what I must." Vail said.

Vail walked toward his vehicle that resembled a 1970s car. He drives away as the sun started to rise above the location of the mansion.

PRAYERS FOR THE DEAD

Occult detective and paranormal investigator Travis Vail has been called in to investigate a series of haunting events that have plagued an old-century church. The owners of the church have told Vail that it was once used as a place for satanic rituals by Satanists. Vail understands the power that Satanists tamper with and what they can release if not careful. Along with Vail on this investigation is Dr. Galen Donovan, a middle-aged African American who's well-practiced in the fields of exorcism and paranormal investigation.

Dr. Donovan arrived at the abandoned church to speak with the current priest. As they talked and discussed the series of haunting that have taken place, Vail entered the church, walking inside calmly while observing the interior. Dr. Donovan stood up from his seat and walked toward Vail.

"Detective Travis Vail, it's an honor to meet you." Donovan said.

"Same here, Doctor." Vail replied. "I hear you're going to be investigating the church with me."

"I am. I feel it's better to do mainly because of my history with exorcisms."

"Just in case I end up being partially possessed supposedly, you'll find a way to help me." Vail said.

"Exactly."

Vail nodded.

"Fair enough then."

Vail walked over to the priest, greeting one another as they shook hands. The priest escorted Vail and Donovan throughout the church.

Walking through the church, Vail noticed some distinctive red smears on the walls. He asked the priest about them. The priest had responded by saying those markings are the previous locations where pentagrams were once painted. The smears were done by wiping them off the walls. Donovan shook his head, rubbing his chin.

"They really chose a place like this to do their worshipping." Donovan questioned.

"Tell me, these folks have to be led by someone." Vail said. "Any idea as to where their leader could've gone?"

"Their leader hasn't been seen for some time." The priest responded. "We hope to find him.

"Surely you will."

The Priest continued to walk them through the church. Vail looked at the site and studied every room inside. Donovan thanked the Priest for showing them around and for allowing them to investigate the haunting. After saying thanks, Vail traveled to the nearest museum to do some extra research concerning Satanism and the Occult. Once he had studied the arts of both. He discovered that the cult's leader might be lurking around the surrounding land of the church.

Upon returning to the church, with Donovan at his side, the sun started to set as they enter the church. The Priest said a prayer for them before he left. Vail and Donovan looked around the silent church, walking through the chapel and passing through the pews. Donovan told Vail to be very careful and to watch his surroundings. Vail turned to him, looking prepared.

"I did some research of my own to prepare for this night."

"Hope you put it to good use."

"I will."

Vail looked ahead of him and seen something glowing underneath some of the pews. Vail looked closer, squinting his eyes and what he seen were two red eyes in the distance. He ran after it, Donovan startled and followed. Vail ran through the aisle between the pews, chasing the red eyes. Vail stopped at the podium, not seeing the eyes anywhere. Donovan caught up to him, looking around as well.

"What did you see?"

"Two red eyes." Vail said. "Very distinctive."

"They're here now."

Vail walked down the left hall of the chapel, passing through the other offices. As Donovan followed, he heard a distinct voice in the distance of the hall that sounded like a woman calling him.

"I just heard a voice."

"Did it sound like a woman or a child?"

"It was a woman's voice. She was calling to me."

"I'm sure you're aware not to follow that voice. Could be a demon mimicking a woman to lure you into a trap."

"Of course."

Vail heard the same female voice coming from the end of the hall. He is tempted to follow due to its high pitch sound. Spotting the two red eyes again with a laughing sound. He chases after it again. Donovan is quickly able to follow Vail this second time.

Entering another room that appears to be a lobby area, Vail stopped Donovan as they both saw the full apparition of a demonic entity. It appeared as a female, but Vail noticed the horns coming from its head, only to be seen by its shadow against the stone wall.

Donovan pulled out a cross at aimed it at the demon. It slowly backed up against the wall and started to laugh. Once, Donovan took a few steps back, the demon vanished. Vail turned to Donovan, noticing that the cross barely worked. Vail took out a bottle of holy water. He also took out his small notepad, re-reading what he had wrote down in the museum regarding demons.

They continued to walk through the church with only six hours left before sunrise. Getting no responses of any kind. They stumbled upon a red pentagram painted on the wooden floor. Vail glances more closely at the symbol and turned to Donovan.

"It's still wet and its blood."

Donovan kneeled, looking at the symbol. He told Vail that the blood is indeed what he feared, human blood. He took a sample of the blood for further testing. Vail put his hand over the symbol. He felt the sense of heat coming from it, intense heat.

"Whoever put this here knows what they were doing and have summoned up something."

"What could they have possibly summoned? More demons? More malevolent entities?"

Vail slowly looked around him and Donovan and glanced at the pentagram.

"One thing. You would think the person who placed this here would still be inside this church."

"Certainly."

They suddenly hear footsteps behind them in the distance. From the sound, they appear to be coming closer. Vail and Donovan slowly turned around as the steps became loud enough for the echoes to become silent. As they turn, they see a man wearing a black trench coat with all black clothing. The man has long wavy black hair.

"Who are you, fellow?" Vail asked.

"Vernon Lance."

Donovan looked at Lance and started to take a few steps toward him. Pointing at him with a question in mind.

"I get the sense that you're responsible for the pentagram on the floor."

"Indeed I am. I'm the cult's Priest."

"Using human blood! What kind of man does such a thing?"

"A greater kind. One needs the blood of a human to gain knowledge of the hidden power that surrounds us all."

"He's the one responsible for all of this. The demonic haunting, the previous pentagrams that covered the interior of this church."

"I understand that average people such as yourselves couldn't fully understand to have taken this course to bring about the next civilization."

Donovan stared.

"Quickly, Vail!"

Vail quickly pulled out his notepad, setting up to recite a ritual to Lance. Donovan took out a bottle of holy water, preparing to toss it at Lance. Lance looked unworried about his current circumstance.

"I don't know why you're preparing to attack me. I'm only human with demonic intellect."

"We're not going to attack you, we're condemning you." Vail said.

"You're ready?' Donovan said.

"I am."

Vail began to recite the pagan ritual as he stared into Lance's piercing green eyes with Donovan preparing to toss the holy water into Lance's face. Lance stood his ground with his arms standing upward, open for Vail and Donovan's attacks. Lance smiled at Vail and Donovan.

"It's really taking a while for you two to finish your condemning."

"Shut your mouth!" Vail said.

Donovan glanced at Vail, knowing Lance's distraction is causing Vail's ritual to cease working.

"Vail, his distraction is ceasing the ritual."

"That can't be possible." Vail remarked.

Lance grinned.

"Anything is possible in this universe to be maneuvered. Besides, I have to say it again, I am human with demonic intellect."

"What can we do now?" Vail said to Donovan.

Lance quickly raised his arm above his head, covering his face from the light coming through the window. Vail and Donovan notice Lance's strange behavior and turn around, seeing the sun rise and its light causing Lance to hide. Vail turned around and Lance has disappeared. Donovan notices burn marks on the ground where Lance was previously standing. The marks are still burning as if Lance was pulled into the ground by an unknown force of energy.

An hour later, the priest returned to the church, seeing Vail and Donovan standing and waiting in the chapel, sitting on the back pews. The priest walked up to them both, shaking their hands.

"Appears you two have had quite an investigation."

"We did."

Vail pulled out his notepad, revealing that he had wrote down Lance's name and description. He showed the priest as he told him about their investigation and how they later ran into Lance. Vail also tells the priest that Lance suddenly vanished as the sun rose and its light shined through into the room. The priest thanked them for their investigation of the church.

As they walked off, Donovan told the priest that they will have someone to come over and clean the pentagram off the floor and give a cleansing of the room to avoid any contact with demonic entities and to close to possible portal that may lie inside the room.

Vail walked to his car as Donovan approached him.

"It was a pleasure to work with you, Travis Vail."

"Likewise, here, Doctor. Hopefully we can work together again."

"I'm highly sure we will."

They shook hands as Vail gets into his car and drives off the location and down the road. Donovan looked around the surrounding areas of the church to find any further evidence of Lance's disappearance. Donovan discovers a track of burn marks within the grass. He followed the tracks as they lead him to an open field. Within the field, Donovan noticed a marking on the ground. The marking was an enlarged pentagram carved into the field that was large enough for a small home to fit in.

A LOST GIRL

In the suburbs of Chesterfield, New Hampshire, Cooper and Janice Lawrence have contacted Travis Vail to investigate mysterious behavior of their nine-year old daughter, Carrie Lawrence. According to the parents, Carrie had been participating in some unusual behavior, talking and playing with an imaginary friend whom she calls Leta. Within a few days, Carrie began to act a certain behavior that appeared to be abnormal to her parents, speaking in an unknown tongue and drawing art that seemed to have an infatuation with death and fire.

Vail arrived at the suburb home of the Lawrence family. He walked toward the door and knocked three times. Cooper opened the door and greeted Vail, allowing him to enter his home. When Vail walked inside the home, he immediately felt a negative presence. He looked around the home's first room, which was a living room, next to a kitchen. Sitting on the couch in the living room watching TV is Carrie.

"Carrie, meet Mr. Vail." Janice said.

Carrie turned and looked at Vail. She stared at him for quite a bit before turning back toward the TV. Vail turned to Cooper and Janice. He asked them about Carrie's behavior when she began to speak about an imaginary friend. Janice told him that it stared when Carrie went outside to play with some neighbors before she saw a young girl sitting by a tree, who she claimed to be Leta. Vail told them that he will investigate their home later that night to find evidence of Carrie's friend.

Vail returned to their home and began his investigation. Upon finding no source that could trace to Carrie's imaginary friend. He started to doubt that he would find anything related to Leta. Though, Vail walked into the backyard to the site where Carrie came into contact with Leta. Vail noticed some form of objects buried in the dirt by the tree. What Vail found was a locket necklace. Inside the locket was a photo of a young girl with the name Leta under the photo. Vail took the locket and left the home, stating that more research had to be done.

The next day, Vail meets with Raynard Brown, a historian. Raynard greets Vail as he pulls out the locket and showed the picture. Raynard looked at the photo.

"I would like to see if you could tell me what century this photo was taken in?"

"Appears it dates to the late 19th century."

"The late 1800s you say."

"Indeed. Tell me, what about this picture intrigues you, Mr. Vail?"

"I'm currently on an investigation about a young girl's imaginary friend. This locket was buried by a tree where the girl first met the imaginary friend."

"So, I take it, you believe this young girl on the photo is the imaginary friend?"

"That's my current guess. Even though, when I walked into the home, I felt a negative presence that seemed beyond human."

"It is possible that a demon could have taken the form of this "*Leta*" and is using it to deceive and control the young girl."

Raynard handed the locket back to Vail, who placed it inside his coat pocket.

"I'm heading back over there immediately to do another form of test."

"Wish you luck on this one."

"Thanks, but I'm not an actual believer in luck."

Vail left the building, returning to the suburb home of the

Lawrence Family.

Vail returned to the home, he sat with Cooper and Janice to speak with them about Carrie. Janice request for Carrie to sit in her room while they talk with Vail. Carrie walked into her room and closed the door. Cooper turned to Vail.

"So, what have you discovered so far?"

"I found this buried in your backyard." Vail said, pulling out the locket from his coat pocket.

Vail handed the locket to them. Cooper opened it and seen the picture of a little girl. Janice placed her hand over her mouth as she saw the name "Leta" beneath the picture. Cooper pointed.

"That's the name which Carrie told us. That's the name of her friend."

"So, you're telling us this is who Carrie's been talking with?" asked Janice with fear in her voice.

"It's a possible theory. Not sure so far since I would like to speak with Carrie, if you don't mind."

"Sure."

Janice called out Carrie to sit with them. Carrie sat between her parents as she stared at Vail. Looking him in the eyes. Vail could feel the heavy presence from her.

"Carrie, I would like to ask you about your friend, Leta."

"She doesn't like you."

"How can you tell?"

"She told me that you're here to get rid of her. She says you won't be able to because we're friends."

"I know you're just a child, you shouldn't play around with things you can't comprehend."

"I understand enough, thanks to Leta."

Janice turned to Cooper, frightened at her daughter's words toward Vail. Cooper looked at his daughter, worried about her well-being.

"Honey, what has Leta told you?"

"Leta told me that we will be friends forever and no one can breakup our friendship. Not even this man here."

"Sweetie, this man is here to help you." Janice told her daughter.

"This man is here to ruin my friendship with Leta and I won't let him."

"Carrie, me and your mother have decided that you cannot be friends with Leta anymore."

"Leta is my friend and we will always be together. Whether any of you like it or not."

Vail looked into Carrie's eyes and noticed a slight change. Her eyes had shifted solid black for a quick second. He warned Cooper and Janice of this change and told them to stay guard of what could possibly happen.

"Carrie, where is Leta at this moment?"

"She's here with us."

Vail stood up and looked around the room, Cooper and Janice looked around, but saw nothing. They looked at their daughter with fear and confusion, not understanding what is happening to her.

"What is she doing?"

"She's plotting to kill you silly." Carrie said with a smile.

Carrie giggled as objects in the room began to levitate and throw themselves at Vail. He ducked the thrown objects that came his way. He yells to Cooper and Janice to take Carrie out of the house. They take Carrie and leave the home in a hurry. Vail is left inside the house by himself, seeing the objects in the room levitating and moving around with no natural explanation. Vail knew it was Leta's doings.

"Leta, I know it's you. If you wanted a fight, you have one with me."

The objects ceased moving and the room quickly turned silent. Vail slowly walked through the house, with a ritual notebook in his hands, equipped with a metal cross.

"Where are you, Leta? I know you're still inside this house."

Vail heard a set of footsteps coming from behind him. The footsteps become louder as Vail stood his guard. He turned to see what could be creating the footsteps and when he turned around, he sees Carrie's room and coming from the room is a young girl, the same girl from the photo. She is Leta.

"So, you're Leta."

"I am. Who are you supposed to be?"

"I'm Travis Vail, occult detective. My job is to find and solve cases that involve the paranormal, such as you."

"There's no reason for you to have ever come here. We were doing just fine before you came into our lives."

"First off, you don't have a life anymore. You're dead. Secondly, you're turning a young girl into a monster. Her parents are scared to death of their daughter because of your influence."

"Her parents are a thing of the past. Carrie is the future and I'm guiding her in the right direction."

"You're not guiding her in any direction but the paths of pain and death. You don't belong in this world anymore, Leta."

"What gives you the right to say so?"

"Because it's my purpose."

Vail took out the cross and held it toward Leta. She slowly backed away from Vail, her hands up, covering her face and screaming at him to drop the cross.

"I'm not dropping it." Vail stated.

Leta looked at Vail and smiled. She waived her hand toward the cross and it melted in Vail's hands. Turning into liquid ash. Vail stepped back, looking down at the remains of the cross.

"You know that stuff doesn't work on us." Leta smirked.

Vail had realized Leta isn't an ordinary ghost who's trapped on Earth. She is the negative energy that he felt, and he now knows she's a demonic entity posing as the young girl in the picture.

"What are you going to do, Spirit-Seeker?" Leta inquired. "Show me what you have to offer."

"It's time for you to go, little demon."

"You have no understanding. I'm not going anywhere!"

Leta raised her hand, causing a wave of energy to hit Vail. The wave was powerful enough to pick Vail off the ground and knocking him into a wall. He looked up and doesn't see Leta anywhere.

"This girl I tell you." Vail muttered to himself as he stood up.

Cooper and Janice walked back into the house with Carrie. Entering, they see the living room covered with shattered frames, vases, and other objects on the ground. Vail walked back into the room, seeing Cooper, Janice, and Carrie.

"Are you alright?" Janice said.

"I'm alright. Why did you come back inside?"

"We heard noises going on and we wanted to see what was happening." Cooper said.

"What did you find?" Janice asked.

"For starters, I seen your daughter's imaginary friend. She's a tough one to deal with."

"You're telling us that Carrie's friend isn't imaginary, but real."

"That's what I'm telling you. She wants the two of you to stay out of her way. She said she's influencing Carrie for the future."

"Influencing her? There's nothing wrong with our daughter."

"I thoroughly believe that your daughter is mildly possessed by Leta. That would explain the shifting eyes and her friend coming from her room"

"Why do we have to go through this." Janice stammered.

"Lot of people have these problems in a lot of different ways. I'm just here to help out."

Janice grabbed Vail's hand, looking him in the eyes with fear. Vail could feel her fear.

"You have to save our daughter. You must."

Vail nodded. Cocked his head with a nod and slight chuckle.

"I have one more solution that can be done."

"Name it."

"I'll have to exorcize your home and your daughter."

Later at nightfall, Carrie is sitting down on the couch in between her parents. Vail walked into the room with holy water. He dabs his thumb into the water and created an insignia onto Carrie's forehead. She screamed as the first touch of water burned her. Her parents held her tightly during the burning sensation that she felt.

"That confirmed she is mildly possessed." Vail said. "Thought you should know that. For the best."

"What are you going to do next?" Cooper asked.

"Read a ritual that will lift the essence of Leta from your daughter and send her to the other side."

Vail took out his book of rituals and began reciting the ritual of lifting Leta's essence. The home was quiet and there weren't any sounds to be heard.

"I, Travis Vail, read from the book of rituals, I hereby declare a cleansing of this home and its inhabitants."

Carrie started to shake, as if she was losing control of her body. Her parents held her down as Vail continued to do the ritual.

"I hereby command the spirit of Leta to leave this home and its inhabitants."

Vail looked at Carrie as she screamed in pain. Janice's face covered with tears as she held her daughter down. Cooper held in his emotions. Carrie looked at Vail with intense anger, now knowing that it isn't Carrie.

"You'll never take me away from here!" Carrie said with a changed voice. A deep-pitched voice.

"We'll see about that." Vail replied.

Vail continued reciting as black smoke started to emit from the house and from Carrie into the air. Vail ran over to the door and opened it as the black smoke swiftly flew out of the house. Carrie stopped screaming and fell unconscious. Janice called out to her for a response. The smoke left the home and Carrie. Vail shut the door and approached the parents.

"There's nothing to worry about. She's fine."

"Thank you." Cooper said.

"Thank you so much." Janice beamed.

Vail prepared himself to leave the home and was getting himself ready. Before he left, he was stopped by Janice, who hugged him for his help. Cooper stood behind Janice, smiling.

"Thank you again."

"It's my job to help."

"If I may ask, where did the spirit go?" Cooper inquired.

"Leta went to a place that she will feel comfortable, I hope. In truth, she was just a lost girl looking for a way out."

Vail left the neighborhood and Carrie awoke inside her room with her parents over here, smiling.

"What happened, mommy?"

"It's a long story."

LOCKED FOR ETERNITY

Travis Vail has decided to investigate a century year-old prison. The prison is called Desdemona Penitentiary. Its inner structure is surrounded with over thirteen cell blocks across acres of land. There have been notable deaths throughout the prison and through its existence. From murders, to raping, to riots, and suicides, there is no doubt that there are entities that reside within the prison walls.

Vail arrived at the prison, which is located on the east coast of London. Colton Levi, a close friend of Vail's comes to the prison's entrance. He joined Vail for the investigation as they are greeted by the owner of the prison and its land, Robert Leonard. A man in his middle age.

"You've finally made it here, Mr. Vail"

"I'm honored you've contacted me about this place. I've heard many stories throughout time."

"Who's the partner?"

"He's Colton Levi. One of my closest friends within the field."

"I take it he won't be afraid of what's inside."

"He shouldn't be. He's done this before in many places."

"Those places weren't Desdemona, my friend."

Leonard opened the gated entrance to the prison. They walked through the front yard, noticing gravestones that stand in a field on the side of the prison. Levi took out his camera, he began taking pictures of the outer structure of the prison and the gravestones. Leonard pointed toward the gravestones.

"Those stones belong to some of the prisoners that died here."

"I notice there's no names on them." Vail mentioned. "Just only numbers."

"Their prison numbers. Didn't matter what their names were. They were called by their six-digit prison numbers."

"That's a terrible thing. I suspect they're not at rest." Levi said.

"They aren't' They're still here in these walls."

They entered the prison, looking at its intense inner structure. Vail looked around, seeing many cells toward them. Levi continues to take pictures. Leonard walked them over to three cells. He tells them that's where many soldiers from World War I were kept after the war was over. Levi took pictures of the interior of the cells. He looked at one and noticed a black smog hovering off the ground. Levi was shaking, but calm.

"Vail, I think I found something already."

Levi showed Vail the photo, seeing the black smog inside the second cell. Vail walked inside the cell, standing in the middle, quiet and calm. Leonard and Levi stood outside the door, watching Vail.

"Whoever decided to manifest themselves as a black smog, I suggest you tell us your name and place, now."

Getting no response, Leonard continued to take them around the prison. They walked through different halls of the prison.

"The first cell block was famously known for murders."

"How many murders exactly?" Vail asked.

"Estimated over six hundred. At least."

"That's a lot of death and anger." Levi said.

"That's right. The second cell block areas is known for the large amount of rapes that took place."

"You're saying male prisoners raped other male prisoners?" Vail said.

"There were female prisoners, visitors, and minor female officers. So, it's possible they were the targets."

"Of course."

Leonard walked by the last few cells and pointed down the halls.

"Suicides apparently dominated this entire area."

"It seems each cell block carries its own kind of death." Vail said. "If you wanted to be murdered, you have the first section. If you wanted to be raped, you had the second section. Now, if you wanted to kill yourself, you had the third section."

"Choose your own fate, basically." Leonard said.

"They chose it well I suppose." Levi said.

After seeing much of the prison. Vail traveled to the nearest library to read up on more history of the prison. Levi went on an errand to gather a pair of digital cameras, digital recorders, and EMP device to catch frequency energy signatures. Finding the library, Vail discovered the origin of the prison. It was founded by a well-known millionaire during the late 1800s.

The prison was first used as a correctional facility for juveniles and over the years became a penitentiary during the start of World War I. Both during and after World War I, many of the soldiers, from either side were kept within the prison. The prison continued to stand even after World War II and the Vietnam War. It was used briefly during the height of the Cold War. Vail read on how the prison was shut down in 2003 due to low funding.

Vail returned to the prison with Levi, who was carrying the bags of the digital supplies. Vail looked at Levi and took a glance at the bags. He smirked.

"You love your technology."

"How else are we able to capture images and video of spirits."

Leonard walked out of the prison towards Vail and Levi. They walk back inside the prison as Leonard closes the gate as the sun sets. Vail looked back at Leonard and nodded. Leonard nodded back in respect.

"Hope you find what you're looking for."

"Don't worry, we will."

Levi began to set up the digital cameras on tripods across the hallways of the cell blocks. Vail recited a ritual that is known to protect both himself and Levi from malevolent spirits that may reside inside the prison walls. Vail approached Levi, who's finished setting up the cameras and recorders.

"You're ready for this?" Vail asked.

"How can I not be ready for this."

Once the moon glinted across the prison windows, Vail and Levi started their investigation. They first decided to check the first six cell blocks. They stood inside of the circular shaped room, seeing all the entrances of the cell blocks, Levi looked around as he noticed something familiar about the circular room.

"This place is a smorgasbord of spirits."

"You know, Vail, this room reminds me of another prison in the states. I've seen it on one of the paranormal shows."

"I hope they did a good job."

"They did. One of the best paranormal shows on TV to date."

They slowly walk through the prison. Levi, with a digital camera in his hands, looks around through the LED screen as Vail uses his senses to track his location.

"You want to start the conversations?" Vail said.

"Sure."

Levi walked by the cells and stood in front of the fourth one. He pointed the camera towards the cell, looking inside, seeing the bed spring, sink, and toilet. Vail walked towards the other cells nearby.

"Is there anyone inside this cell?" Levi said. "We want to know if you're here or not."

"They're here, Levi. Just be careful."

Walking slowly and calm through the darkness of the cell block, they began to hear sounds of knocking coming from the cell blocks.

Levi looked around with his camera at the cells, seeing nothing in the lens. Vail entered a few of the cells.

"Are you in here? If you are, I demand you say or do something now."

The knocking increased as Levi spotted a shadow that walked by the cell where Vail was standing inside of. Levi ran over toward the cell, telling Vail what he captured on the camera and how it passed by the cell he was standing in. Vail left the cell and continued to investigate the other cells.

"So, more deaths took place in this cell block." Levi mentioned. "The other guys would've loved to see this."

"I'm sure they would. Over six-hundred murders in this location. That's a lot of energy."

While walking toward the end of the cell block, Vail caught a shadow, which moved past the exit door. He looked back to see it, but nothing was there. Levi noticed Vail's behavior.

"What is it?" Levi asked.

"I saw a shadow. It walked past the exit."

"Let me try the digital recorder to capture their voice."

Levi pulled out the digital recorder. He talked into it, asking a series of questions to the spirits within the cell block. After a minute to a second, he received a response. Vail walked over and listened to the recorder. He hears the voice of an older man, threatening to kill them if they don't leave the cell block.

"It just threatened to kill us." Levi remarked.

"It can't kill us if it doesn't have enough energy to use. Don't lend them your energy. Block it all off. That includes the devices."

"I'll try."

"You will. There's no trying in here. We're in dangerous territory right now."

Upon getting no other signs of spirits within the cell block. They entered the second area of the cell block. While they walked in, they could hear disembodied screams coming from the cells. Levi looked around cautiously.

"You hear those screams, Vail?"

"They sound like women in pain."

"They're being raped!" Levi yelled.

"It could be just an irrelevant response. A sound that was once here repeating itself."

"We have to check to be sure."

"I am sure it's an irrelevant spirit."

Levi walked over to the cells, seeing no one inside. He looked through the camera to find anything. Seeing nothing, they walk further down the cell block. As they walked through the cell block, they heard a distant laugh coming from the left of them. Vail walked by the cells on the left, looking inside.

"Who's here with us?" Vail asked. "I demand you give us a

response of your presence."

Across from Vail, a small rock is thrown toward him from the cell block. Levi scouted and found the small rock on the floor nearby Vail's area. He looked around, showing minor signs of fear while Vail was calm and quiet.

"You want to throw things at us now. I see you want to play rough. We can play rough."

"What are you talking about, Vail? They just threw a rock at you."

"I've went up against worse than a small pebble."

Vail walked around the cell block. They began hearing more screams and laughs. Levi started to shiver as he sweated and stood against a corner. Vail stood in the middle of the cell block, both arms at his side, with no expression on his face.

"They're playing with us, Colton. We're in their territory."

"They're playing kind of tough." Levi muttered.

The screams and laughs had silenced, leaving the cell block to become completely silent. Vail told Levi that they're going to the third and last section of the cell blocks. They entered the third section, feeling their energy being drained and feeling signs of dizziness. They started to feel depressed as they could hear crying within the cell block.

"What's going on?" Levi asked. "I starting to feel drained and dizzy."

"They're using our energy to fill themselves up. That crying might be the start of it."

The crying continued as they walk through the cell block. Still feeling drained and dizzy, they looked around, seeing shadowed, disembodied figures walking around them. Levi tried to hold the camera up to capture the shadow figures. As he captured them on the camera, the camera froze and completely shut down, signaling the sign of a low battery.

"I just charged this camera." Levi shouted.

"They're using its energy." Vail said. "They're gathering as much as they need."

"So, what do we do?"

"We use our instinct to see and to touch. Not all the spirits are intelligent or benevolent. I'm starting to sense a malevolent spirit in here and it doesn't belong in this cell block."

"They're jumping cell blocks now." Levi blurted.

Vail felt a presence surrounding him closely. He could feel something on his back, he knew they were hands. The presence of the hands shoved him violently against the wall. Levi looked and went to help him up. Vail scanned the cell block, still dizzy and drained from losing energy. He continued to walk through the cell block and stood upon staring at a black smog. Levi also saw the smog and he pointed toward it.

"That's what I saw earlier on the camera."

"That's not a benevolent spirit. Its malevolent and belongs in the murder cell block."

The black smog didn't move. It only stood still in the air. Vail and Levi continued to stare at it. Vail reached into his coat pocket, taking out the book of rituals. Levi looked over at the book seeing the variety of rituals inside.

"What are you about to do?"

"I'm about to send this spirit to the other side. Where it can be judged for its sins."

Vail recited the ritual, making a way to send the malevolent spirit to the other side. As he recited the ritual, the black smog slowly evaporated before vanishing into the thin air. Vail looked around, not seeing any more shadow figures. Levi rubbed his head.

"I'm not dizzy anymore." Levi said.

"Neither am I. The ritual must have sent them over."

Vail looked toward the window above them, seeing the sunlight peeking through the cracks into the cell block. He and Levi walked toward the entrance. Levi gathered the tripods and cameras that sat in the hallways. Leonard returned as the morning started and thanked them for their investigation.

"So, may I ask what you seen or heard?"

"We heard a lot and seen a lot." Levi said.

"There are many spirits that reside in this place. I would only believe that they're locked in for eternity because of the path they chose to go.”

“I believe that very well. I guess they’ll never find a way out of here.”

“They’ll find a way to leave and enter the other side. It will take some time of course for it to be done.”

“Well, I want to thank you for coming over here and investigating this place. Not many would have done this.”

“It’s what we’re here for.”

Vail signaled to Levi to leave. Levi places the cameras and devices in the back of the car before getting in the passenger’s set as Vail drives away from the prison.

CASE OF THE WHITE LADY

Travis Vail is set to investigate Huntly Castle where legends speak of a spirit known as The White Lady resides. Vail had read up on the history of the White Lady and how she is involved with Huntly Castle. After arriving in the country of Scotland, Vail traveled to *Aberdeenshire*, one of the thirty-two council areas within Scotland. Aberdeenshire is also a lieutenancy area. As Vail arrived in Aberdeenshire, he traveled straight for Huntly Castle. Once on Huntly Castle's land, he started at the castle, scanning its structure as a twelve-century castle.

A man walked from the castle, he greeted Vail as they stood outside the historic structure. The man is Barclay Iomhair, the current tour guide and owner of Huntly Castle's property. Vail speaks with Barclay about the castle and its history. Barclay tells him that the castle was built by Clan Gordon in the twelfth century as an L-Plan tower house. Vail began to ask about the castle's former inhabitants as Barclay tells him about how it was formally named *Strathbogie* and how it was granted to Sir Adam Gordon of Huntly in the fourteenth century.

He told Vail that the castle was once burned down and later rebuilt. They begin to walk through the interior of the castle, seeing all its ancient structure around them. Vail states that he can feel the emotions of the people that once lived in the castle. Barclay begins to tell him about the well-known folklore that travels around the castle.

The folklore of the White Lady. Vail turned to Barclay, he showed a slight smirk.

"I'm curious about this folklore." Vail said. "What's the exact tale of this White Lady?"

"There are many tales of the White Lady to be exact according to my knowledge."

Barclay began to tell Vail about the case of a daughter of the Lyon Family. He tells him how she committed a folly that everyone else thought was heinous and how a male servant was involved in the folly. He tells Vail the daughter was banished to a bedchamber in the tower of the castle, which was believed to be over one hundred feet from the ground. He says she suffered from agony within her mind and later found relief from either jumping or pushed out of the tower's window and fell to her death. He continued saying the tale was passed from each generation that came afterwards. The room where she was banished to is now known as the Waterloo Room.

The second tale is the most well-known tale of the White Lady and how it's about the Countess of Strathmore who had entered her second ill marriage. Barclay tells Vail that the Countess has suffered greatly within the romance part of her life as she lived unhappy with the husbands who later turned another way. She wrote about her experiences as being wretched and her writing is still described today as the most damning indictment of a husband ever to be written by a wife in any age.

Barclay decided to tell Vail that the most-well known one is on the halfway of being the accurate story as he believes the Lyon daughter is the White Lady that haunts the castle. Vail tells Barclay he'll surely discover who the White Lady truly is during his investigation. Vail leaves Huntly Castle and heads toward a nearby library, where he will look up more of the castle's history and residents. He finds records of the castle being burned down and how King James IV of Scotland would come over and gave gifts to the stonemasons that worked on the castle. He also reads that in October of 1503, King James IV returned to play a shooting contest and later came the Huntly Castle every October after as part of an annual pilgrimage to the shrine of Saint Duthac of Tain, a royal bough and post town in the Highland area of Scotland.

Vail retuned to the castle grounds just before sunset as he spoke with Barclay. Knowing he couldn't be locked in for the whole night, he decided to stay on the castle grounds from sunset to sunrise. Barclay leaves the area as Vail stood and stared at Huntly Castle. He decided to walk around the area for a while until the sun had set. He examines the area twice as the sun starts to set. Smirking, while watching the sunset. He begins his investigation of Huntly Castle.

"The sun has set, and I am here on Huntly Castle ground. I am here to see the White Lady."

He walked through the ruined structure of the castle, calling out the legendary White Lady. Not receiving any sign of her in his presence, he continues his investigation. Upon walking through the ruined castle, he spotted a white mist moving from right to left in the darker parts of the castle. Vail takes out a flashlight and approaches the darker area.

"Who is here with me? I would like for you, whoever you are, to make some sort of contact with me, so that I know you're here."

Vail entered the dark area, not able to see anything in front of him without the flashlight. He begins to hear a distant cry coming from inside the dark area. Vail looked around the entire area, not able to see what the crying was coming from. He could still hear it while looking around the entire area. He does a double take around the area. Still seeing nothing, he decides to leave the area. As he approached the front of the castle, he sees a young boy dressed in a double-breasted sailing jacket. Vail approached the young boy slowly, staring into his eyes.

"What's your name, son?" Vail said. "You can tell me your name."

The boy gave no response to Vail. Vail continues to ask the boy about his name as the boy stayed quiet. After one last attempt to get a response from the boy, he walks away. Vail watched as the boy slowly faded away as he was walking away. Vail says to himself that he just seen a spirit, but it wasn't the legendary White Lady that locals and folklore speak of. The sun begins to rise as Vail takes one look back at

Huntly Castle before leaving Aberdeenshire.

The next day, Vail traveled to *Longforgan*, Perth and Kinross in Scotland. He traveled through Longforgan to find a prison that's known as Castle Huntly. Sort of the sane title as the ruined castle in Aberdeenshire. While during research the day before, Vail discover documents containing information about a fifteen-century year old castle with Huntly as a name. Like the other castle, this Huntly is currently an HM prison. HM stands for His Majesty's Prison.

Vail arrived at the prison castle, looking at its structure and seeing how it's been renovated and adapted to stay in modern times. Upon entering the prison, he discovers it's an open prison, with the capacity of two-hundred and eighty-five people. Not sure about how he could do an investigation throughout the prison, he decides to find a way. After speaking with officials within the prison and some of the prisoners themselves, he discovers that the White Lady has also been seen in the prison, including the same young boy that was seen at the ruined Huntly Castle.

Later that night, Vail decides to do a minimal investigation throughout the prison. He decided to leave two hours after midnight to avoid the prisoners. Once his investigation started, he began to hear prisoners screaming across the hallways. He ran down the hallways to find the prisoners. Once at the end, he sees prisoners staring at a woman, who's floating in the air. She's only wearing white with white hair and clear glowing white eyes.
"It has to be her." Vail said.
The prisoners run in opposite directions to avoid the lady. Vail walked up to the lady as she slowly turned toward him. They lock eyes as Vail has officially come face to face with the White Lady. Vail smirked as he stared at her. Her face showed no emotion as she continues to stare him down. Other prisoners look from across the hallways, staring at Vail and the White Lady.
"So, you the legendary White Lady." Vail said. "After all this time, I've finally got the chance to meet you."

The White Lady says nothing to respond to Vail. He continued to talk to her as the prisoners continued to hide across the hallways. Vail decided to reach into his pocket and take out his book of rituals. The White Lady glanced at the book, noticing its symbolic encryptions on the front and back. She vanished in seconds as Vail looked around, not seeing her anywhere.

"Dammit."

Vail ran through the hallways searching for the White Lady. As he went through each hall, he continued to only see prisoners standing or sitting down. He stopped to take a breath and he started to hear what sounded like prisoners fighting each other down the hall he just past. Vail returned to that hall and seen the prisoners fighting each other as the White Lady went passed them in seconds. Vail followed the white trail of mist that was made by the White Lady.

He continued to search for the White Lady as it was only thirty minutes before he left the prison. He walked into a room that resembled a museum of the castle's history. As he walked slowly through the museum, he finds artifacts that date to the origin of the castle's existence. As he looked at the artifacts, he starts to notice the room's temperature lower. He pulled out a thermometer, which signified the room's temperature was below thirty degrees. He turned around, looking around the museum. Vail raised up his left sleeve and looked at his arm, noticing the hairs standing up completely straight.

"I know you're here." Vail uttered. "You can come on out, so we can discuss your place in the future."

Vail feels a swift breeze on the back of his neck. He turned and sees the White Lady. She's standing on the ground, facing Vail. Vail stared at her, looking unworried about his possible safety. He glanced at his watch, seeing he only had fifteen minutes before his investigation was over.

"I only have fifteen minutes to help you before I leave this place." Vail said. "So, I am here to help you move on to the other side."

The White Lady shakes her head, disagreeing with Vail's wishes. Vail slowly reached into his pocket for his book. The Lady moved an inch closer to Vail. He stopped moving his hand and stared.

"I am here to help you, miss. There's no reason for you to stay in this place. Especially in today's time."

"You can't help me." The White Lady said. "You can even help yourself."

"Please, let me read from this book and I can send you to a better place. A wholesome place."

The White Lady giggled at Vail. He glanced at his watch and noticed he only had about ten minutes left before the investigation was over. He pulled out the book and turned to the page he was previously on before. The White Lady looked at the book.

"I only have about ten minutes left before I leave. I am sending you to the other side at this moment."

Vail read the ritual from the book as the White Lady tried to leave the room. In front of Vail, a white light shines through the entire room. The light begins to pull the Lady towards it as she begins to be pulled inside the light. The light later consumes her and vanishes. Vail placed the book back into his pocket and looked at the watch, seeing only six minutes left before he was done.

"There's nothing else for me to do here." Vail said.

Two hours after midnight, Vail leaves the prison castle. After the sun rose, he went back to Huntly Castle to speak with Barclay. Barclay sits inside his car as Vail approached him.

"I hear you visited Castle Huntly prison." Barclay said.

"I did."

"How was it? Going inside that place by yourself?"

"It was a worrisome task, but, I managed to get through it."

"So, I take it you saw something at both Huntly Castles?"

"I saw a young boy here. He vanished before I could get anything in place. At the prison is where I've seen the White Lady. It took a while before I could send her over to the other side to be in peace. It seemed to be that both places have been covered with the folklore of the White Lady."

Barclay smiled as Vail walked to his car.

"This means your case on this is officially done?"

"The case of the White Lady has been solved in my opinion."

Vail gets into his car before Barclay walked over to the car door,

"Give me a little insight on your next case?"

"I feel my next case will be in the States. Mostly to involve the legend of Salem."

Vail drove away as Barclay watched on.

SALEM WITCH TRIALS

Occult Detective Travis Vail has entered Salem, Massachusetts to investigate the historic tales of witchcraft and the possibility of it be continued in today's time. Salem is the key location to many historical accounts and records of witchcraft. The Salem Witch Trials took place between February 1692 and May 1693. Throughout the history of the years, paranoia and fear overtook Salem as many believed that The Devil was watching their every move. Anyone they saw or talked to that resemble unusual behavior was considered a witch or warlock.

Vail looked through the town of Salem. Knowing that it was a great effort to gain permission to investigate Salem's dark history. After a town council event, Vail was granted access to all of Salem and its historical records. Speaking with many of the town's residents, Vail realizes that witches still reside in Salem in modern day. Knowing they no longer hide and look just like the average person today. Vail traveled to the downtown area, asking many residents if they have seen any witches or if they are a witch themselves. Vail approaches two women wearing black cloaks, covering themselves from the cold light rain.

"If I may ask you ladies. Are any of you witches of modern day?"

"Why would you like to know? You're investigating the trials, aren't you?"

"Yes ma'am."

The women looked at each other and smirked. They turned toward Vail and shook their heads.

"I'll put to you this way, sir. Witches don't have a Jerusalem. They have Salem."

The women walked away, leaving Vail thinking about their last statement, saying how Salem is a witch's Jerusalem. Upon doing later research, Dr. Galen Donovan arrived in Salem and contacted Vail about his arrival. They later meet at the Lyceum restaurant, which sits on the land that once belonged to Bridget Bishop, the first woman who was hanged after being accused of practicing witchcraft.

"We're finally in Salem." Donovan said.

"It's been a long time coming. This one should be the one that's worth it."

"So, how was the town council meeting?"

"The meeting went great. Many residents agreed with what we're trying to do by discovering more evidence of their city's past and what truly happened."

"What's the current time that we head over to the Witch House?"

"Sometime this afternoon. I also plan to attend a play that resembles the trials exactly as the transcripts portray them. Once that's complete, we'll return to the house later tonight for the investigation."

Donovan nodded and looked down at his watch. Reading the time, he looked up toward Vail.

"Best we head over there at this moment."

"I agree."

Vail and Donovan arrived at the Salem Witch House. Looking at its old structure, Vail began to feel a chill coming from the house. Donovan noticed Vail's movement as if he's fighting something off.

"Is there something wrong, Vail?"

"I feel a presence of some kind. Not sure what it is, but it's coming from the house."

They approached the front door, being greeted by a woman named Fawn Verrucca. She greeted them as she allowed them inside the house. Once inside, they notice the historical artifacts the reside inside the rooms of the home.

"These are paintings that show the residents of this land. These are Elizabeth Gibbs' children. She had a total of four children. One of the children had died a year before she married Mr. Judge Jonathon Corwin. Her daughter, Margaret has passed away the second year she decided to get married."

"So, are all of these paintings portrayals of women?"

"Not these two on the wall."

Fawn pointed toward the wall, where two paintings were set. Vail bent down and looked at the paintings. He turned and looked at Donovan before facing Fawn.

"So, these two are paintings of young boys?"

"Yes, it is. They were known as Little Henry and Little Robert."

"So, they wore dresses in the late 1600s."

"Mainly until they reach around six years old. At least that age we know of."

"Fascinating." Donovan said. "You learn something new every day."

"If you have an open mind." Vail said. "So, what else can you tell us about this place?"

"Mr. Jonathon Corwin and the jury in the court had presided over the courses of the trials. Condemning many who were considered guilty, were put to death. Corwin even lived in this home."

"Was there a way that they could confess the truth to the jury, so they would be set free?" Donovan said.

"Their integrity was too prideful as they would rather die in this life and keep their integrity in the next. Instead of being what's considered a coward and just giving in to the Judge and jury's demands."

"So, this Bridget Bishop was one of the first women to be considered a witch." Vail said.

"She was first to be brought in as potentially being a witch due to her being an easy target. All the men would flirt with her as all the women would hate her and many of them condemned her as practicing witchcraft."

"So, this home belonged to Judge Corwin during those times of the trials?"

"Yes, it did. He lived in this very home."

"So, there should be much energy in this home." Vail said. "Maybe that explains what I was feeling before I entered."

"Also, in a way to find out if the women were witches, they would take their urine and mix it with flour, baking it into a cake. They would feed the cake to a dog and watch the dog for any unusual behavior or movements to determine if the women were witches."

"They fed dogs cake with urine baked in it." Donovan said. "Utterly disgusting."

"Horrifying at the most." Vail said.

Vail and Donovan later visited a location where they're going to watch a reenactment of the trials taken directly from the transcripts. As they enter the school, watching the young girls portray the historical figures of the witch trials. Donovan watches uncertainly with fear as Vail appeared to be in a trance, studying the words and movement of how the young girls portrayed the figures. After watching the reenactment, they decided to head back over to the Lyceum restaurant as they speak with residents who are currently sitting inside the restaurant. Vail and Donovan question as many as possible about Bridget Bishop. A few residents show Vail photos of a wedding that took place inside a banquet hall where in the photo is an apparition of a woman who they believe to be Bridget Bishop. After speaking with the residents, Vail noticed the sun is starting to set. He tells Donovan that they must head back over to the witch house to begin their investigation.

Once they returned to the witch house, Fawn allowed them back as she locked them within the home. Donovan began taking out equipment as Vail began to say a prayer over himself and Donovan, protecting them from any malevolent spirits that may reside inside the home or on the land itself.

"Much of the equipment is ready and set." Donovan said.

"I'll start once you're ready."

"I'm ready."

While Vail and Donovan walked into the living room of the home, Vain began to feel a chill as the room's temperature suddenly dropped. Donovan sees his own breath coming from his mouth. He turned over towards Vail, who appeared to be fighting off something again.

"What's the problem?"

"I'm feeling someone else's emotions. I don't know who this is, but I am feeling a little sad for some reason and it's not my emotions."

"Are you going to be alright?"

"I'm not letting this get to me. But, I can't ignore what I'm feeling right now."

Donovan reached into his jacket pocket and pulled out an EMF Detector to find any EMF energy. Noting the major temperature drop, the EMF energy stops itself at the number "*666*".

"The energy is at "*666*"." Donovan said.

"What the hell is going on in here, Galen."

"We know there's something here with us right now."

Vail took out a digital recorder as Donovan walked around the home with the detector.

"Who's currently here with us? Mr. Donovan and I would like to know."

Donovan continued walking through the home with the detector.

"Find anything yet?" Vail said.

"Nothing yet. The temperature's back to normal."

Donovan suddenly felt hands on his back. He jumped up and turned toward Vail, who looked at him uncertainly.

"What's wrong?"

"I felt hands on my back."

"There's nothing behind you, Donovan. I'll check around this area to make sure what's around here."

Vail walked through the area of the room, using the digital recorder and asking questions towards the spirits. While asking the questions, he hears a disembodied female voice in the room he's currently inside. He turned quickly, scanning the room. Noticing Donovan inside the other room.

"Who's inside this room with me?"

He didn't get a response. A few hours later of not finding any signs of any spirit, Vail looked outside the window and seen the sun rising from behind the clouds. He turned to Donovan, who approached him with the other digital recorder and detector.

"The sun is rising." Vail said.

"Looks like this investigation is about over."

They packed up their gear and awaited Fawn to unlock the doors. Around 6:30 AM, Fawn arrived and unlocked the front doors, allowing Vail and Donovan to leave the house. Fawn, showing curiosity approached Vail as he began to enter his car.

"Did you discover anything?"

"Some uneasy feeling. Though, we must go through our recorders to make a perfect statement. Thank you for allowing us into this home."

Vail and Donovan leave the home as Fawn walked inside. She closed the door and through the window was an apparition of a female looking outside at Fawn as she left the house.

Within a few days, Vail and Donovan spent most of their time dissecting the recorders, searching for any signs of a spirit's voice. While scanning the recorders, Vail noticed a distinctive voice. He quickly paused and rewind the recorders, going back to the voice. Donovan approached him, looking at the screen.

"Find anything?"

"I believe I just did."

Vail played the audio, listening to himself asking the question of who was inside the room with him when he heard the disembodied female voice. After hearing himself ask the question, he caught a distant voice inside the audio. After enhancing it, he played the audio once again and caught the voice.

"Is that who I think it was." Donovan said.

"Bridget Bishop was in the home with us."

Vail and Donovan later appeared at a City Hall meeting in Salem with the city council and residents of the city. Vail and Donovan showed the audience all the information and evidence that they discovered inside the witch house. The audience was sort of stunned by the evidence. The last evidence that was shown was the voice of Bridget Bishop. Upon playing the audio for the audience and council, they were quietly appalled. Afterwards the gave applause to Vail and Donovan. Thanking them for their visit and their investigation.

Upon leaving Salem the following day, Donovan asked Vail what his next investigation would be if he already knew. Vail, sitting inside his car turned and faced Donovan. He gave a small smirk.

"From what I can guess, my next case will probably be out of the ordinary."

THE FOG FROM WITHIN

Many areas across the middle of The United States have reported sightings of a strange Fog that arrives in their cities and towns and causing a great disturbance throughout neighborhoods and counties. Many reports speak of strange anomalies inside the Fog itself. Some resemble human beings, others see animals, or other types of strange things that basically live inside The Fog.

Travis Vail has now been contacted by many of the cities and towns to investigate the mysterious Fog. As Vail prepares himself to investigate the sightings, he begins to think to himself what he can back up on the mysterious Fog. The first city that Vail investigates is Boulder, Colorado. As Vail enters Boulder, he meets with a few of the residents that reside in Boulder that reported The Fog's appearance.

While speaking with the residents and listening to their view of The Fog's appearance for over several hours, Vail noticed many of the residents had particularly seen the anomalies moving inside The Fog. Upon further research about the mysterious Fog, Vail discovers that the Fog was seen centuries ago after the genocide of many soldiers and innocent people.

Vail contacted his fellow Historian, Raynard Brown to investigate the history of the mysterious Fog. Raynard suggests that the Fog was created by way of witchcraft, possibly due to Pagan rituals and celebrations. Vail takes those suggestions into his mind and keeps them there for further references later throughout his investigations. Vail continued to speak with many other residents who've seen the Fog in front of their homes. Vail declares to Boulder's Mayor that he will begin an investigation throughout the neighborhood that night, which the Mayor allowed with no problems.

The following night, Vail walked throughout the neighborhood, awaiting the possible appearance of The Fog. He doesn't feel anything unusual nor see anything that resembles paranormal. Though, Vail noticed the wind began to pick up slowly as the trees slowly moved along with the cold breeze. Vail walked through the empty streets in the neighborhood, following the breeze's whereabouts. As he walked closer to the breeze, he hears a sudden whistle. Vail turned and seen no one behind him.

"If anyone is out here, please state your name and purpose."

No individual makes themselves known before Vail as he continued to walk down the street. He continued to follow the breeze.

The following day, Vail continued to study on the Fog and its ghostly inhabitants. Raynard contacts him once again and they discuss the Fog and its possibilities of being conjured by a Pagan cult through Witchcraft or a possible supernatural entity that only appears during the Winter season of the year. Vail continued to take those suggestions to his mind and began focusing on the Pagan root of the Fog. Vail later set a return date to Boulder after he visit's the other cities that have been reporting The Fog.

Vail arrived in Topeka, Kansas, where The Fog had reportedly attacked individuals in the streets during a Christmas festival event. Vail speaks with Topeka's Mayor and the residents who were present during the Christmas festival. Upon listening to the residents and even the Mayor's own account of The Fog, Vail tells the Mayor that he will have an investigation of the location later that night. The Mayor allowed him to have his investigation and commanded police to close the whole area just for Vail to have complete clearance to proceed with his investigation.

Later that night, police gather around the entire area of where The Fog attacked the festival. Vail walked throughout the area, seeing its damaged Christmas lights and stands on the ground. Vail began to call out The Fog by yelling out names of Pagan gods and goddesses. Though, Vail had seen no signs of The Fog or anything that was related to Paganism or the paranormal.

The next day, Vail thanked the Mayor for his time in Topeka, yet having not seen The Fog himself, Vail continued his investigations across the other cities. Vail decides to head over to Tulsa, Oklahoma to discuss The Fog's appearance within their city. Upon entering Tulsa, Vail is highly greeted by the residents of Tulsa and their Mayor. Vail talked with all of them during an assembly as the residents each stood up and took their chance at telling Vail what they seen about The Fog.

Vail investigated Tulsa that night and begins to feel something unusual in the air. He looked around himself and turned toward the streets in front of him. Vail sees what looked to be three anomalies approaching him. As Vail decided to walk toward the anomalies, he sees a giant white mist behind them, which he cannot see through.

"There's the Fog." Vail said.

Vail stared at The Fog as it approached him. Through its path it knocked down street signs, destroyed windows on buildings and nearby cars and even made the ground itself tremble as if a miniature earthquake erupted in Tulsa. Vail did not run from The Fog as it approached him even closer. Vail stood his ground as The Fog ran right through him. As Vail was inside The Fog, he seen many spirits walking through The Fog. Vail quickly stared and studied the spirits that walked past him, noticing their outfits resemble the mid-1800s. Vail sees soldiers that appeared to have died during the Civil War and even sees innocent civilians walking through The Fog. Inside the Fog feels like a giant fan is blowing directly in front of you. Vail continued to stand his ground as the wind began to pick up as The

Fog was coming to an end.

While the Fog was coming to its end, Vail noticed six druids walking slowly at the end of The Fog. Wearing black and red cloak with their hoods on. They were silent and didn't even glance at Vail as they walked right past him. Vail turned and watched the druids leave as The Fog ended. The druids and spirits disappeared in the air along with The Fog.

"That was something I've never encountered."

The next day, Vail told Tulsa's Mayor about The Fog and said that he has no idea what could conjure it up, though it may have already been finished. Afterwards, Vail returned to Topeka, where he tells the Mayor and residents that he seen The Fog back in Tulsa and said that it might not return. Vail last returned to Boulder, where he has a conversation with the Mayor. After their conversation, Vail began to leave Boulder as the Mayor approached him.

"It's a good thing that you came in time before Christmas." The Mayor said.

"Hope the residents are happy with their Christmas."

"Do you celebrate Christmas, Mr. Vail? It's just a question because you seem like a man who doesn't have time for holidays."

"I celebrate certain days. Not Christmas."

"Why is that?"

"I'm not Pagan."

Vail walked away, getting into his car, driving away.

THE REVENANCY VOYAGE

The ship that's known as *The Revenancy* was one of the most graceful and respected ships that has ever sailed across the Atlantic Ocean. Its service ran for over three decades until its untimely demise after it was attacked and raided by pirates of the European Union. Now, the ship sits on a dock near the Atlantic Ocean where it is presented as a historical relic and used for tourism.

The ship is also known for its large amount of haunting after its demise. Many people who have went into the ship have reported paranormal disturbances throughout the entire ship. Some have reported footsteps, voices, moans, and even screams. One reported that a lamp was thrown toward them. Due to the increase of reports, the current owner of the ship has contacted Travis Vail to investigate the ship's haunting.

Within a few days, Vail arrived in Charleston, North Carolina to the dock where the ship is currently residing. Along with Vail is Colton Levi, his longtime assistance in the paranormal. They approach the owner of the ship, Clay Haskett. He approaches them as they greet each other. Haskett allows them into his office.

"It's a great honor to finally meet you, Mr. Vail."

"No worries, Mr. Haskett." Vail said. "So, what have you with these reports of the ship?"

"We've received many, if not dozens more of reports that contain paranormal incidents within the ship."

"What kind of incidents, if I may ask." Colton said.

"Voices, footsteps, moans and groans." Haskett said. "One report contained a lamp being thrown."

"Seems to me that these are spirits that do not want to be disturbed or have a darker history that what we were told by the officials." Vail said.

"What's your current plan, Mr. Vail?"

"Colton and I will walk through the ship and I will head over to your museum to do more research on the ship's history."

Haskett stood up from his desk and walked towards the door. He opened it and stood by, allowing Vail and Colton to approach the ship.

"May we enter the ship?" Vail said.

"Of course." Haskett said. "Just don't try to startle the tourists, please."

"Sure. No problem."

Vail and Colton enter the ship. Passing by tourists who are laughing and taking photos with each other.

"Try not to get distracted, Colton."

"No worries."

They entered the lounge area of the ship, noticing many tourists inside taking photos. Colton tells Vail to search another area of the ship before the lounge, due to the number of tourists within the lounge. Vail agrees with Colton as they approach the other rooms of the ship. After a left turn down a hall, they notice rooms that appear to be hotel rooms.

"This was used as a hotel facility?" Colton said.

"Appears to be so." Vail said. "This is new to me and I wonder what else will present itself."

They scanned the hotel rooms, searching for evidence. Upon approaching the other rooms, Colton heard a distant moan from deeper within the hall. Vail looked up and down the hall, seeing no one in sight.

"You heard it too." Colton said.

"I did." Vail said. "I suggest we take a look before we head out."

Vail and Colton walk down the hall, taking slow and quick looks in the rooms nearby searching for whatever the moan came from. They reach the end of the hall and find nothing that relates to the moan. Vail turned to Colton, suggesting they head to the museum for further research. As they walk back down the hall, a book is thrown at the wall in front of Vail. He stops walking and turns to his left, looking in a room where the book flew from.

"It seems these spirits are not too friendly." Vail said. "We better get moving and we'll return later tonight for our investigation."

They exit out the ship, seeing Haskett approaching them nervously.

"Did you find anything as of this moment?"

"There's something inside this ship and we'll find it tonight when we return." Vail said. "Nothing to worry about, Mr. Haskett. We will solve the problem."

Vail and Colton leave the dock of *The Revenancy* as Haskett looks at the ship with a little sign of fear.

At the Charleston Museum, Vail and Colton gather books containing historical records of *The Revenancy* and its historical tragic voyage. After reading through a few books and scanning their notes, Vail realizes that the ship was used in a cruise line and even in military use. He even finds a record that contains information of the crew being murdered by pirates near the European Union.

"This ship has some very dark history." Vail said. "Being used for military warfare as well as a cruise ship."

"What shall we focus on during the investigation tonight?" Colton said.

"We'll focus on the spirits that reside in the ship." Vail said. "Try to find a way for them to cross over."

Vail closed the books, placing them on their shelves before leaving the museum.

Near nightfall, they return to the ship where Haskett waits for them. He sees them and approaches them.

"You two sure you're ready for this?"

"We've done far much worse than this, Mr. Haskett." Vail said. "There won't be any problems tonight.:

Vail and Colton enter *The Revenancy* as Haskett leaves the dock. Once inside the ship, the silence air slowly brings up a chill to Colton.

"It's deeply quiet in here."

"Don't run off on this one, Colton." Vail said. "You've been inside a prison where hell basically took place. Don't let a ship scare you near death."

They approached the lounge. Now, it's not crowded by the tourists from earlier in the day. Vail looked around the lounge for any clues. Colton searches the other side of the lounge.

"See anything?" Vail said.

"Nothing yet." Colton said. "Sure, something will make itself present."

"It will make itself present." Vail said. "Maybe sooner than we're expecting it to present."

While searching the lounge, they hear a distant yell coming from the dwells of the ship. Colton turned to Vail, who tells him to walk down the hall near the yell's whereabouts. Colton slowly walked down the hall, somewhat a little startled.

"Is anyone here with me?" Colton said. "I'm just asking to be a little perspective."

A bucket had suddenly fell from a shelf in front of Colton. He stopped and looked at the bucket. Vail walked behind him and approached the bucket.

"You're not afraid of a water bucket, are you?" Vail asked. "Because it seemed to startle you."

"I'm doing just fine, Vail." Colton said. "No problems at all."

Vail continued to walk down the hall, passing by rooms that resembled a dining hall where many of the passenger had dinner and occasional parties. Colton looked in the room seeing the tables and banners which were inside the ship. Through a few turns down the right hall, Vail discovers a room that is packed with medical equipment.

"This must be the medical room." Vail said. "It's highly possible that many people died inside this room."

"It's sure able to have a pack of spiritual energy in here." Colton said.

"The energy is here, Colton, and it's getting stronger as we're in here."

Vail looked around the room. He told Colton to take out the digital recorder and place it on the table. Vail stood by the recorder on the table.

"I am Travis Vail, and this is Colton Levi. We are here to speak with any spirits who reside in this *Revenancy* ship. We're here to discover your existence and to send you over into the afterlife."

A sound creaked from the medical room's door. Colton turned and stared as Vail continued to talk by the digital recorder.

"Vail, looks like something is in here with us."

"I hear it Colton. Whoever has entered this room, please speak into this recorder device on this table next to me to respond to my questions."

Colton stood by the door, looking out down the hall as Vail began asking questions toward the spirits. Vail asked if the spirits worked on the ship during its military run or its cruise line run. They caught a voice that said military, which Vail believes it's a military Navy officer that must have died on the ship in the line of duty. Colton looked further down the hall and saw what appeared to be a silhouette of a man wearing a casual Ship Captain uniform walking into the dining room.

"Vail, I just saw an apparition down the hall. It walked into the dining room."

"I suggest you go and look. If you, please."

Colton walked down the hall and entered the dining room. Seeing no one inside the room, he turned back to the exit. Once he turned, he was staring a Ship Captain right in the eyes. Colton yelled and ran back towards the medical room. Vail paused and ran out of the room towards Colton.

"What's wrong?" Vail asked.

"It was standing in my face!" Colton said. "Right in my face!"

"What did you see?"

"I saw the ship captain staring me right in the eyes. A complete stare. I thought it lasted for eternity, yet it was a few seconds."

Vail looked out the window and saw the sun beginning to rise, signaling the end of their investigation. He turned toward Colton and looked down the hall.

"Seems our investigation is done." Vail said.

Vail grabbed the recorder as they left the ship.

The following day, Vail speaks with Haskett about the investigation and tells him about the Navy soldier that spoke about the military as well as Colton's sighting of the ship's captain. Vail says the spirits have claimed the ship their home. Haskett thanked Vail and Colton for their service. They leave the dock and Colton turned to Vail.

"This ship freaked me our more than the prison we've once visited."

"*The Revenancy* will continue to scare people towards the point of death."

"May I ask what's next on the horizon of the paranormal?"

"Whatever comes my way."

THE FOREST OF THE VANISHING

Within the outskirts of Seattle, Washington is a mysterious forest that many decide not to enter due to its intensive history of people vanishing without a trace. Animals walk through the area calmly and are not disturb. Only human beings are the ones that walk through with fear and paranoia who are later vanished. News reports have scattered across the nation with concerns of the forest being burned down to avoid any more people going missing. The debate is currently ongoing amongst the Washington State Governor and the US Government.

The occult detective known as Travis Vail arrived in Seattle as he prepared to do an investigation by himself inside the forest. While walking through downtown Seattle, Vail decided to meet with Seattle's Mayor to discuss his investigation into the forest. As Vail walked down the streets, he spotted the Mayor delivering a speech outside in the open with over a dozen residents standing and listening. Vail stood in the back of the crowd as he watched the Mayor talk about their city's future.

After the mayor finished his speech and the residents began to leave the area, Vail approached the Mayor. As he introduced himself, the Mayor instantly recognized who Vail was and they entered a small office inside a nearby building. While inside the office, Vail discussed to the Mayor of investigating the Vanishing Forest. After about an hour through the conversation, the Mayor gives Vail his blessing and Vail leaves the office building, heading towards the forest itself.

Vail entered the outskirts of Seattle and stands not too far from the highway. He began walking toward the tree and noticed a medium-sized sign sitting on his left side of the field, saying *"Do Not Enter! Forbidden Area."*. Vail smirked and started walking into the forest. As he proceeded through the quiet and smelly forest, he noticed ahead of him was a small shrine. As Vail inched closer to the shrine, he spotted it was built upon with bones of what appeared to be a buffalo.

"What is this." Vail said.

Vail began to step into the middle of the shrine, though being cautious. As Vail turned around, looking at the surrounds, he realized that there was more than one shrine. There was a total of thirteen shrines. The shrines were decorated with crosses, candles, bones, skulls of various animals and some even human, meaning there were possible animal and human sacrifices within the forest at some point. As Vail approaches each of the shrines, he knows that this is a site of a pagan ritual and burial ground. To his mind, he sees that as being a possible reason why many people have disappeared while inside the forest. Vail also spotted a few obelisks standing inside the forest as well that stood near twelve feet in height.

"Why would they choose a place such as this?" Vail said.

Vail continued to examine the surrounding shrines within the forest. As he studied each shrine and what it was built upon. While he was aware of the location of which he was standing in, he began to move very slowly. The forest began to grow a fog in the air, surrounding the shrines that Vail was studying. He began to write down every shrine that stood in the forest and the description of the shrines. While writing, Vail heard a distant sound coming from his left inside the forest. He stopped writing and walked over to the noise. Hearing a slowly dripping sound, he walked near the noise. Going through the fog that's growing larger and thicker. Vail stopped and looked down as he saw what appeared to be blood dripping from a tree nearby. As Vail looked up toward the tree, he finds an array of decorated skulls sitting and hanging on the tree.

"What did they do in this place?"

Vail backed away from the tree and decided to continue writing down the other shrines before leaving. As he wrote down the last shrine, he felt the wind blowing behind his neck, he turned as it began to pick up with the fog slowly evaporating into the air. Vail noticed that something was going on inside the forest. As The wind continued to blow, Vail spotted what appeared to be shoes laying on the ground. He ran over toward them and picked one up. Upon looking at it, the shoe belonged to a young boy. Vail looked around the spot for any other trace. Only finding the two shoes, he took them with him as he decided to leave the forest. As Vail walked through the forest, finding his way back. He begins to feel nauseous and drained. He placed his hand on his head, shaking it so he can focus.

"I don't know what you are. Now leave me be."

Vail regained his focus as he left the forest and returned to Seattle to show the Mayor the shoes and the shrines inside the forest.

Later that afternoon, Vail spoke with the Mayor about the shoes and the shrines that laid inside the forest. The Mayor began to call on a police force to head into the forest to search for the missing boy. Vail declined the force as the Mayor was running out of ideas as of who to send inside the forest. Vail looked at the Mayor and stated that he was returning to the forest that night to do a full complete investigation of the forest and the shrines. Believing that something might be going on during the night rather than the day. The Mayor paused as he returned to his desk and nodded. Giving Vail his answer to go into the forest after dawn. Vail left the Mayor's Office and headed toward Seattle's Museum of History and Industry to study more on the forest and its disappeared victims.

As the sun began to set and many of Seattle's residents were awaiting Vail's word of entering the forest, Vail approached the forest from the same direction as before, only this time, Vail carried a bottle of holy water and even his ritual book as he entered, which would only mean that something more was going on inside the forest with the shrines. Vail nodded to himself as he returned into the forest.

Now, walking through the forest in pitch darkness and only hearing the echoes of animals, insects, and the sticks and branches breaking and cracking underneath his feet as he walked, Vail focused on the shrines and the feeling of being drained earlier before he left.

A distant flutter approached Vail from his right side. He quickly turned, looking through the darkness of the forest. Not seeing anything unusual, he continued walking through. Knowing he felt uneasy inside the forest, he continued walking as he approached the area of the shrines. Vail stood in the middle of the location, where all the shrines were facing. He rubbed some of the holy water on his forehead and held his ritual book close to his heart.

"I know you're here. I know you're all here."

Vail held his arms out as he turned around, making a full circle, while holding the book in his hand.

"Whatever you are. Whatever you've done to these people. I declare that you stop your terrorizing and return to the other side where you belong."

Not seeing or hearing anything, Vail continued to call out whatever was lurking inside the forest, which is responsible for the dozens of disappearances throughout the years. As Vail continued, he felt that something was watching him inside the forest. He stopped talking and looked around.

"I can feel you watching me. So, why don't you come on out, so I can see you."

Vail stood still as the wind picked up once again. Vail could smell the evaporation inside the forest. As he looked around, he began to hear moans coming from each of the shrines. He looked at them as he seen druids from all over approach him. Vail noticed that the druids are all in different pairs, each pair is arriving from one shrine. Each pair was covered with six druids. Vail stared at the pairs as he realized it was seventy-eight druids that were approaching him. The druids slowly surrounded him in a circle with the leaders of the pairs approaching Vail inside the circle. The druids wore all black cloaks with hoods covering their faces.

"I demand that you tell me who you are and who you worship." Vail said.

The druids stopped and only faced Vail. None of the druids speak or make any sudden noises as Vail stared at them.

"I suggest you say something about the missing people."

The druids stood silently as Vail walked around them. He glanced at the druids that circled him as well as the leading druids. As Vail walked around, he glanced toward one of the druids that stood on the outside. Looking at its height and size, Vail realized that druid had to be a child. He ran over toward the druid as the others approaching him and shoved him back into the circle. Vail looked at the leading druids and glanced back at the child druid.

"Who is that child? Answer me! Who's the child?!"

One of the leading druids approached Vail and raised his head, facing Vail. Vail stood his ground as he took an extra step toward the druid.

"I will ask again. Who's the child druid?"

"The druid you speak of is the child that the common people consider a missing person."

"You're saying to me that the child is the one that I'm looking for?"

"Indeed. That child is one of us now."

Vail rubbed his head as he looked at the other druids that surrounded him. He turned back to the leading druid as he pointed out the surrounding druids.

"So, who are the other druids circling me? Are they the other missing or vanished people?"

"Yes. They are the vanished ones. They came into our forest, stepped onto our sacred land and decided to disobey the oath that stood on this land for centuries."

"You can't keep these people here. They need to return to their homes and families."

"Their families wouldn't accept them the way they are today. They have changed greatly and with a cost they can't turn away from."

"What are you saying exactly?"

"The people you see around you on this day are not the same people that vanished throughout the centuries. If they were to return to their previous grounds, they would only destroy not only the ones they loved and cared for, but also the land they lived upon."

Vail nodded as he raised his book and held it in the face of the druid.

"I'm sending you and these people back."

"If you know the words of which to say."

"I do."

Vail began reading from the book as the wind picked up again. The druids began to back away from Vail as he continued reading. The surrounding druids had disappeared and only the leading druids remained. Vail continued as each druid disappeared one at a time. As he read from the book, the druid he was speaking withstood still and watched Vail read from the book. Vail looked up toward the druid with energy flowing through him.

"Time for you to go."

"I will leave this time. But, listen carefully Mr. Vail, there will come the time that I shall not leave, and neither will you."

The druid slowly backed away and disappeared through the wind. The wind had stopped as Vail finished reading from the book. He exhales as he placed the book back into his coat pocket and proceeded to leave the forest.

The following day, Vail spoke with the Mayor and the residents of Seattle about the forest and what he had seen the previous night. Mainly frightening the residents, he told them about the druids and how they were all the people who reportedly went missing or vanished without a trace. Vail said they were in a better place and that no one should ever enter the forest again. The residents applauded Vail for his bravery as he and the Mayor left the stage. The Mayor thanked him for visiting Seattle and hoped he would return. Vail turned and nodded.

"I will make my return when the time is accurate to do so."

Vail entered his black 1970 impala and drove down the highway, leaving the city of Seattle.

THE ABANDONED HOTEL

During the early fall season and with heavy snowfall, Travis Vail traveled past Vancouver, Canada, heading towards an abandoned hotel named The Black Raven. The hotel is known for its prestigious setting as well as its number of floors. The floors of the hotel are a total of thirteen floors and all of them have a large majority of haunting that witnesses have suspected to be spiritual and demonic occurrences, some have even been attacked by the unseen forces.

Vail arrived at the Black Raven Hotel and found no one there but himself. While walking closer to the front entrance of the abandoned hotel, he heard a vehicle approaching him from behind. He took a turn around to see the vehicle and its driver. The vehicle parked next to his and the driver exited.

"I do not know who you are or where you come from, but you cannot enter this place." The driver said.

"Why shouldn't I enter?" Vail said. "Is it because of the spirits?"

"Yes sir. I'm giving you a fair warning here. I heard that some guy was going to go inside the place and try to contact those things in there. You make a mistake. You could release them out here."

"Judging by the way you speak, you do not understand the spiritual realm nor its duties." Vail said. "You are speaking with the Spirit-Seeker and there aren't many as I in this field. So, please do me a favor and return to your home in peace and leave the spirits to me."

Vail turned away from the driver and approached the hotel entrance doors. The driver, filled with emotions, ran over toward Vail and snatched him by his right arm, trying to pull him away from the doors.

"You need to leave this place, sir!" The driver said. "It is not safe to be here at this particular time and season!"

"Unhand me or I will suggest placing you inside this hotel and you can deal with those who are unseen to the human eyes."

"You wouldn't do that to me. I'm just an ordinary guy. I have a job, I have a wife, children, a home, a car. I have a life. I'm just trying to get you to understand that you must save yours before you make a mistake."

Vail stared at the driver and smiled.

"As always. Men like you aren't truly built for what awaits you after this life you're currently living in. Men like you will never fully awaken to understand what lies behind the scales that cover your sight. You and people like you are blinded to the truth and you never seek to find it nor the ones who hide it. Therefore, you are wasting your time trying to change my ways because I've already chosen my path as it presented itself before me."

"You must not enter this place! You cannot! Its suicide!"

"Suicide is what you do when you've given up your belief and strength in things beyond your comprehension."

Vail snatched his arm back from the driver and approached the hotel doors. He placed his hand on the door handles and pulled them back toward him. The hotel doors swung open as if a gust of wind had blown out of the hotel and into the open area. The driver panicked and ran to his car, screaming for his life.

"You've opened the doors! You've released the spirits!"

The driver pulled back and drove away as Vail watched him leave and gave a slight smirk.

"Now, let us see who's waiting for me in here."

Vail walked into the hotel and looked at its interior lobby area. Vail took a few more steps into the lobby area, the two entrance doors shut as if someone had closed them from the inside. Vail looked back and circled the lobby.

"I fully understand that there are thirteen floors in this place and I intend to search them all before the night is fully over. I hope those of you in this place can and will understand that."

Vail walked by an elevator, knowing there was no electricity operating inside the hotel since its abandonment. Vail walked past the elevator and as he approached the end of the hallway toward the staircase, a small bell rang behind him. Vail turned back and sees the elevator light blinking.

"Interesting and intriguing."

Vail walked back toward the elevator and the doors opened as if it was set up for him to enter. Vail nodded and entered the elevator. The door shut and the elevator operations as if it was still in use. The elevator goes up and stopped at the second floor, the door opened, and Vail exited the elevator.

"I take it that someone is on my side in this place."

Vail found himself in the hallway of the second floor and all that surrounded him are the rooms and the equipment which was left behind before its closing. He walked through most of the hotel searching for any signs of spirits. Not finding anything related to the spirits in the rooms on the second floor, Vail went toward the staircase door and the elevator dinged again. Vail turned toward the elevator and its door opened once more. Vail chuckled as he entered.

"Third floor I take it."

The elevator moved up and stopped. Its door opened, allowing Vail to step onto the third floor of the hotel. Vail stepped out and felt a gust of wind move past him. Vail quickly turned to his right and saw a shroud of mist hovering through the hallway, entering a room without the door being opened.

"Here we go."

Vail ran toward the room door and opened it. He gazed around and doesn't spot the mist which flew into the room, although he can hear what appeared to be people talking amongst themselves in the hallway, which doesn't startle him, but raised his awareness of his surroundings.

"There's more of you on this floor I take it. Proves very interesting."

Vail stepped out into the hallway and could still hear the voices speaking to each other as if they were having a conversation to themselves. Vail reached into his coat pocket and pulled out the book of rituals. He raised the book up above his head and circled in his steps.

"You see this book I hold above me, spirits? This book will send you into the Other Side, where you all will be judged for your actions here on earth and will prove your eternal place."

A form of wind began to pick up from inside the hallway, Vail continued to speak toward the voices and held the book above his head. Vail continued as he saw shady forms of humans, all appeared to be yelling at him in anger and hatred. Vail knew these kinds of spirits and raised his voice as he spoke to them.

"I will not repeat myself to you spirits of the demonic darkness!" Vail said loudly. "You will respond to me and you will enter the Other Side and be judged for your earthly account."

The spirits screamed toward Vail as each of them began to fly toward him and entered the wall behind him. Vail never flinched when the spirits flew pass him. He continued to speak to them and held the book continuously above his head.

Vail understood a few of the spirits had indeed went over to the Other Side while the remaining ones had decided to remain in the hotel to attack Vail in any shape they could.

"I know you've traveled to the upper levels of this hotel, spirits. I intend greatly to seek you out and to release you from this place you currently call your home."

Vail walked toward the elevator and it no longer worked. Vail shrugged his shoulders, taking the stairs up to the fourth floor. Upon arriving on the fourth floor, Vail didn't receive any communication or sound from a spirit of any kind. He searched every room on the floor to make sure there wasn't a spirit hiding amongst his presence.

"Fourth floor appears to be clean." Vail said as he checked the last room.

He went up into the fifth floor and all he could see around him was trash and left-over furniture sitting out in the hallway. The hallway had an odor resembling a dumpster, which would be sitting out back or on the side of the hotel, though there were no dumpsters near the hotel. Vail searched every room on the fifth floor, jumping over rugged and molded furniture to get into some rooms. Some of the rooms had a damp feeling and they possessed the smell of damp air after a rainfall.

"Fifth floor is clean. Spiritually clean I might add."

Vail arrived on the sixth floor and as soon as he took a step forward, a mist of cold air blew past him. He could feel the presence of a spirit, whether it be human or demonic. Vail smirked as he walked slowly down the hallway, which was much cleaner than the fifth floor.

"Finally, one of you has started to present yourself toward me and of all the floors you decide to pick the sixth floor. Guess six is your lucky number."

"We do not like your trespassing, hunter." A disembodied voice said from the hallway.

"I heard that very clearly and I would like for you to speak to me again, so I can get a sense of your character and afterwards send you to the Other Side." Vail said.

"We demand you leave our home." The disembodied voice commanded.

"I'm not leaving this hotel until all of you are gone from it and it becomes nothing more than an old building waiting to be crumbled down."

A loud scream shrieked through the hallway, Vail covered his ears quickly to avoid minor damage to his ears. The shriek had immediately stopped. Vail removed his hands from his ears and the entire hallway was dead silent.

"Whatever you are and where ever you've come from, I am here to send you to another place where you will never escape your fate."

After searching the entire sixth floor, Vail continued to make his way upward toward the remaining floors, seven through thirteen. On the seventh floor, during Vail's searching of the rooms, he found a note which was left behind by someone who was either staying or working in the hotel. Vail read the note as it had implied there was some otherworldly force that dwelled before he hotel closed. Vail placed the note in his coat pocket.

"Seems you've been here a while." Vail said.

The eighth floor possessed neither anything related to the supernatural nor were any spirits contacted by Vail throughout the entire floor. The ninth floor possessed very little furniture and a shortage of rooms, whereas the first eight floors were settled with a total of twenty rooms where the ninth floor had a total of ten rooms. Vail kept his patience in check as he noticed there were no spirits being found within the upper floors.

"I know you're here and you are waiting on me to find you, yes?"

Vail said. "I will find you and we will have our confrontation."

Vail stepped foot onto the tenth floor and spotted a difference in the air. A change of sorts which could only be caused by a weather effect, though it was continuing to snow on the outside, whereas the interior of the tenth floor felt a mixture of cold and heat. Vail had placed into his mind that he was dealing with a spirit or spirits that were unlike any he has encountered in his previous investigations.

"If you are on this floor with me, make yourselves known unto me." Vail said. "I heard one of you speak to me on the sixth floor and I demand that you speak to me now before I reach the thirteen floor and end this for good."

"Why have you come here, Travis Vail, the Spirit-Seeker." A voice said from the other end of the hallway. "You seem to be determined to eliminate us from our dwelling place and yet here we are."

Vail couldn't see the figure from the other end due to a dark mist covering its presence. Vail pulled out a flare and threw it toward the middle of the hallway. The flare lit up most of the hallway and all Vail could gather by his sight was a figure and on its hands were long sharpened nails and its eyes were like the cold sky to him.

"Come. Come Travis Vail. Follow me up to the thirteen-floor and you will receive what you've come for." The voice said as it disappeared.

Vail ran toward the other end of the hall, fanning away the dark mist that covered the end. Vail saw nothing and ran up toward the thirteen-floor, surpassing the eleventh and twelfth floors. Vail ran unto he reached the door that would lead him to the thirteen-floor. Vail kicked the door opened and looked around, realizing that the floor was a place where people would stay. The thirteen-floor appeared to be an office of some kind, apparently a secret office.

"What kind of place is this?" Vail questioned.

"This is our dwelling place, Spirit-Seeker." The voice said. "As is mine."

The voice appeared closer toward Vail as the entity revealed itself to him. The entity appeared to be a hybrid of both man and demon. Vail took a step back as he stared at the creature, never seeing a living being of that kind before in his lifetime.

"What in the hell are you?"

"I am known throughout the ages as Kamagrauto, servant of Dagor, the Soul Eater."

"Dagor? Soul Eater? What in the hell are you speaking about, demon beast?!"

"It seems you've never studied in the occult as deep as you thought. We're always hearing about what your work has done for many in the world. From your little stop at a mansion to that forest of druids. We know of you, Spirit-Seeker."

Vail stared at Kamagrauto, scanning the room for any others that might appear before him on the thirteen-floor.

"How have you been watching me? Why have you been watching me and for what purpose?"

"You are one of our enemies, Travis Vail." Kamagrauto said. "You and countless others all share the same goal of eliminating our kind from this earth to leave only the righteous alive to subdue it."

"There aren't others like me, demon. If there were, I would've already made myself known to them."

"The intriguing part of this meeting here is all of you mostly have encountered one another in the past at some point in time. Whether it was a small crossover or a passing by on the road. You've all met at some point in time and you all will meet each other again in the coming future, but that will be the moment where all of you get agree to join sides to face us."

"This isn't making any sense. I'm about to send you over."

Vail pulled out his book and raised it over his head. Kamagrauto laughed at Vail for doing the task. He even started clapping his hands and rubbing his sharp nails together to sidetrack Vail's focus.

"That little book isn't going to work on me, Vail. I am beyond an ordinary spirit. I was created by my master Dagor and only through him may I be put away."

"I won't let you leave this place alive and intact, demon." Vail said. "You must leave this place and take the remaining spirits with you."

"Why do you think I'm here?" Kamagrauto said. "I'm here on orders from Dagor to collect as many souls as possible and bring them back to him for observation."

"What is he observing them for?"

"Why to consume them of course and go gain as much strength as he needs to succeed in his plans."

"I will not allow such destruction to be cause in my presence!" Vail said as he ran toward Kamagrauto.

"You small pest."

Kamagrauto lifted Vail up off the ground and threw him against the wall as a frame that was hanging on the wall fell onto his head, cutting his forehead open.

"Very well, I will be leaving now, Travis Vail and we will indeed come across paths once again. But, that day will most certainly be your final investigation."

Kamagrauto vanished in a puff of smoke as Vail ran after it. Seeing nothing but an empty room, Vail leaves the thirteen floor and travels back down to the first floor. The sun began to shine down on Vail as he walked outside and sealed the hotel doors shut. He entered his car and drove away. Though, in his mind was Kamagrauto's words of what would come concerning Dagor and others whose work was similar to Vail's own.

MYSTERY OF THE MUTANT-THING
A DARK TITAN UNIVERSE ONE-SHOT

After a night out of investigating a series of demonic attacks across Washington D.C., Gabriel Abraham, known throughout the world as Abraham The Devil Hunter returns to his workplace called the Revelation Center. Entering his office area as his fellow partners have also went out into investigations themselves. Abraham reads through a series of files laid out on his desk, ranging from poltergeist activity in a suburban area to folkloric figures popping up in many areas throughout the country.

"This is just too much to deal with at one time." Abraham said.

He looks over to another files that is titled, "*The Mystery of The Mutant-Thing.*" Grabbing his attention, he opened the file and started reading the information within. He recognized some of the locations that were written down of the Mutant-Thing's possible whereabouts.

"This isn't too far from here."

Turning through the pages of the file, Abraham heard the front door to the building open. He raised his head, looking to see someone inside. Not seeing anyone, he leaves his office and walks out to the lobby area. Unable to find anyone standing around, he returned to his office. Abraham entered his office and seen a man standing behind his desk, reading the files of the Mutant-Thing.

"Who are you?" Abraham said.

The man looked up at Abraham and nodded his head.

"I'm Travis Vail. Some call me the Spirit-Seeker."

Why are you here, Mr. Vail?"

"I am here on the case of the Mutant-Thing mystery and I happened to hear your place was nearby. So, I figured you would have some information regarding the mystery and it appeared to be the truth. This file you have here gives much information."

"If you needed information, you could've went to some other place or even called in to let me know you were coming."

"That's not my style, Abraham. I appear out of nowhere as the wind blows and goes."

Vail placed the file back onto Abraham's desk and walked over toward him.

"For the best, I can ask that the both of us should work together on this mystery in order to discover its truth."

Abraham thought to himself while Vail waited patiently for an answer.

"I can assist you in this mystery, Mr. Vail."

"I appreciate it."

"So, we just go off to this dark wilderness?" Abraham said.

"No. We go to London."

"Why London?"

"I have a friend over there who could give us a helping hand."

Entering London, England at the brink of day, Vail and Abraham walk through London for hours on end with Abraham mostly following Vail around the big city.

"Why are we here exactly?" Abraham said.

"We're here to meet someone who can help us further this mystery. They're in the same field as the both of us."

They approach a Law Firm building and enter it. Inside Vail

walked toward the front desk, speaking with the receptionist while Abraham looked around the interior of the room and could sense the small presence of spiritualism around the building.

"Me and a friend are here to see Ms. Cindy Lawson. Is she here right now?"

"Sorry, but she left about an hour ago."

"She did." Vail said. "Thank you anyhow."

Vail walked over the Abraham, seeing him circling his head around the room. Vail tapped him on the shoulder to get his attention.

"I know what you're doing and its best to keep it to yourself for a little while. Until we find out partner here."

"You can feel the spiritualism in this place, and it isn't benevolent energy."

"I am aware of that. Which is why we have to leave this place now."

Leaving the Law Firm, the two walked down the streets of London, passing by the Big Ben. Vail stopped and stared at the tower for a moment. Abraham looked at him and looked at the tower.

"What is it, Vail?"

"Here."

"What about here? What's over here that's important to this case?"

"This is where she will be tonight."

"Who is she?"

"Our helping hand. We'll come back here at nightfall and our partner should be here."

They waited until the night had fallen over London and the moon shined its light brightly above the city. Vail and Abraham returned to the Big Ben with Vail looking upward to the tower, in the far distance, he could see someone standing up atop the tower, looking over the city.

"There she is."

"May I ask who this woman is?"

"Cinderella." Vail chuckled.

"Cinderella? As in the fairy tale Cinderella? Not a possibility."

Vail turned to Abraham with a smirk on his face.

"You hunt demons for a living. I send spirits to the Other Side and you mean to tell me that Cinderella doesn't exist. Yet the world doesn't have any belief in the things we hunt down and eliminate."

"I see your point there. But, how could this be a reality. How did she even get up there in the first place?"

"She has her ways, Abraham. She can tell you more about it than I can."

Up on the ledge of the Big Ben, Cinderella looked around the city of London, monitoring it for any threats lingering that night. She looked down and could see Vail and Abraham standing.

"What is he doing here?" Cinderella said.

She jumped down from the tower, using her coat to glide herself through the air before landing in front of Vail and Abraham.

"I never knew you could do that?" Vail said.

"The coat is made of some materials that allow me to do such a thing."

"I know you're going to ask me why I'm here. Don't worry, I will tell you."

"Tell me then."

"Me and Abraham here need your help on a small case that we're doing together."

"Abraham as in Abraham The Devil Hunter?"

"You've heard of me?"

"The words that surround your hunt for demons goes a long way. Inspires some to become just like you. Others deem you crazy and psychotic for doing such a thing."

"I've been told."

"What is this case that the two of you are working on exactly?"

"The Mystery of The Mutant-Thing." Vail said. "Ever heard of it?"

"I was mentioned once in the office as some kind of teenage joke, but the disappearances of many prove it to be more than just a joke."

"This dark wilderness location exists then?" Abraham said.

"It exists. I've been there before on some matters concerning the supernatural."

"Where is this wilderness, Cindy?" Vail asked.

"In Canada. Within the Ontario providence."

"Around some city called Retropolis?"

"That's right."

"Thank you for the information." Abraham said.

"I'm going along with you guys."

"I knew this would happen." Vail said. "That is why I agreed with it before coming to you."

"Why would you want to come along with us?" Abraham said.

"Because I only know where the wilderness is. Other than that, I know someone who lives around the city who can gives the three of us a better way of handling the area."

"Who is this person?" Vail said.

"Have the both of you ever heard of the Creed of Swords?"

"I've done some studies upon it. Only to know it's considered a legend."

"Once during an investigation." Vail said. "Why?"

"Because the one who's help we'll need is a mentor of mine."

They traveled across the Atlantic Ocean heading to Retropolis. Entering the city at the time of night, walking through the city, they see a police car chasing down a pair of criminals through the streets.

"Never been to this place." Vail said. "Is it like this all the time?"

"Pretty much." Cinderella said. "He should be here at any moment now."

"Who will be here?" Abraham asked with curiosity.

They gazed around the streets. From the corner appeared roaming, a black and silver vehicle pass them toward the criminals' car.

"What was that?" Abraham wondered.

"My mentor." Cinderella smiled.

From the car, jumped out The Swordman, dressed in his hooded cloak and Kevlar suit, latched himself onto the top of the criminals' car. Breaking the hood window and pulling the driver out of the car before jumping off the as it rammed itself into a tree near the sidewalk. Cinderella, Vail, and Abraham proceeded to walk toward the scene. Though not with much haste. Yet, they were in a hurry. Stepping closer, they witness The Swordman interrogating the criminal driver as the other one is laid out on the sidewalk. Unconscious from the crash.

"Where is Fear?" The Swordman said.

"I don't know." The criminal said.

"You work for her. You know where she is."

"She never tells us anything. Especially when it concerns locations."

"When you wake up, make sure she knows I'm coming for her."

"What? What do you-"

The Swordman head-butted the criminal, knocking him out. He turned around seeing Cinderella, Vail, and Abraham walking toward him.

"Cindy." The Swordman nodded. "Why are you here?"

"These two men need you help on a case they're solving."

"Travis Vail and Gabriel Abraham."

"How do you know about us?" Vail said.

"I've studied your works. I'm aware of what the two of you do for a living and how much you put into it."

"This is something I never expected to happen." Abraham said.

"Why do you need my help, Vail?"

"We're looking for a place known as the dark wilderness. It's supposed to contain the Mutant-Thing according to its legendary mystery."

"The Mutant-Thing is real."

"You know?" Cinderella asked.

"I've encountered the creature a few times during some of my novice investigations. It's a creature Man should not tamper with."

"We would prefer to see the creature firsthand before we come to our own conclusions." Abraham noted.

"I understand your meaning." The Swordman paused. "Very well, I will lead you to the dark wilderness. If you cannot handle the creature yourselves, I will accompany you."

"What are we waiting for?" Vail said. "Lead the way, Mythological Man."

The Swordman ignored Vail's sayings. "Get in the car."

"What car?" Abraham asked looking around the streets.

From behind The Swordman drove up the Assassin or the Swordmobile as it's called by the residents of Retropolis. They get into the car, surprise it fits up to four individuals. The Swordman drives off down the streets.

Entering the dark wilderness, The Swordman stood guard, removing his sword out of the sheath. Ready for combat. Cinderella was also prepared to fight if it became necessary. Vail walked through the wilderness, reminiscent of his past time of entering a similar wilderness, encountering an army of druids ranging from adults to children.

"Make sure you're on edge." The Swordman said. "Prepare yourself for anything."

From the trees, something moves past them, rumbling the ground beneath their feet and shaking the trees surrounding them.

"Earthquake?" Abraham said.

"No. It's the creature. It's making itself known."

"That's rather quick." Vail said.

The ground shakes and from beneath it arose the Mutant-Thing. Roaring toward them with anger. The creature was covered in roots, dirt, and grass. The Swordman and Cinderella were prepared to face the creature. Vail and Abraham stood by watching. Vail pulled out his ritual book, staring at The Mutant-Thing.

"Seems the mystery has been solved."

"If the creature makes any move to attack, you send it back into the ground, Vail."

"I will do so, Swordman. Trust me."

The Mutant-Thing roared as it swiped its arms toward Swordman and Cinderella. They moved out of its path quickly to avoid an attack. Swordman jumped above the creature, slashing it with the sword. Cinderella kicked the creature and delivered a small series of blows to its back and chest. Vail raised his hand up in the air.

"I got this." Vail said.

Vail started reading from the ritual book, slowing sending the Mutant-Thing back into the ground. The creature fought back, but Abraham attacked the creature with holy water and chanting words along with Vail. Working together, they send the Mutant-Thing back into the ground and leave the dark wilderness.

The following days, Abraham and Vail continued to meet at the Revelation Center, concerning cases that the two were working on. From the doors entered Papa Afterlife.

"What are you doing here?" Abraham asked.

"I am here on urgent information that concerns the two of you."

"What kind of urgent information?" Vail wondered. "We're listening."

"I have a plan to bring together people such as yourselves to combat a coming malevolent threat that will bring the earth to its very knees."

Vail and Abraham approach Afterlife. They nodded.

"Explain away." Vail gestured.

CREED: THE CRYPTIC CIRCLE

I

<u>THE BURNING</u>

Deep in the wilderness, afar off from any nearby city or town, The Cult, a group of worshippers cloaked in their black robes and hoods, stand in a circle, surrounding a strange pit that goes deep into the earth. They light incense and toss it into the pit and start chanting. Their chant is of ancient origin and of a language not spoken in modern civilization. From the pit, a fire roared and poured out of the pit, glowing a bright light. The Cult continued their chanting, until something had rushed toward them through the trees. They glanced around while continuing chanting.

From around them came a dark blue shadow, which knocked them from the pit. The shadow moved through the trees, attacking the worshippers. From the trees as the shadow came to a still, a figure arose from the trees. The figure's size was large, its golden eyes glowed in the darkness. Its body was dark as the night, except for a large white cross which covered his entire torso. Burnt bands on its arms and legs. Shining claws on its fingers. The shadow moving through the trees was the dark blue cloak it wore on his back.

"You will not succeed in this ritual." The figure said with a deep, graveling voice.

"Our master is coming." A member declared. "Not even someone of your nature can stop him."

"He can be stopped, and I will be the one to stop him."

The figure moved quickly as lightning and attacked the Cult. Beating them down, leaving them unconscious. Afterwards, the figure walked over toward the pit and looked down, seeing the fire still rising. He placed his dark hand into the flame and it did not burn.

"What is this?"

"Fire from the Cryptic Zone." said a figure behind him. "A place you are familiar with, Creed."

Creed turned around, seeing the angel Ananchel hovering above him. She came down and stepped onto the ground, walking toward him. Her wings were as bright as the sun, yet, a clearing came from them.

"Why are you here?" Creed asked.

"Because this needs your assistance. Adrambadon is near and his powers are growing at an hourly rate."

"And why has no one managed to stop him?"

"Stopping him isn't our task. It is yours."

"You're angels. You should be able to handle the might of the Cryptic Lord."

"Yes, we can. But, it isn't in our master's will."

"So, it's up to me to stop him."

"Yes. And you must do so quickly. As each portal is open, Adrambadon comes closer to stepping foot on the earth once again."

"Is that what this is? A portal into the Cryptic Zone?"

"Yes. They need to be closed."

"How many of them exist?"

"Six."

"How long do I have before he rises up?"

"A few days at most. Soon, his disciples will be upon the earth. Making way for his entrance."

"Disciples." Creed said. "Very well, I will handle them and if Adrambadon does rise from his dwelling place, I will deal with him as well."

Creed evaporated and vanished from Ananchel's sight. She glanced up at the full moon and sighed.

"His anger still kindles within him."

II

<u>THE GATHERING</u>

Creed went and circled the world, searching for every potential trail that could lead to Adrambadon and his rise. During his travel, he could feel within his being, Adrambadon's power growing. He would see the earth shake at every moment, signaling the Cryptic Lord's rise to power and reach toward the earth.

"His power is growing. Faster than even I could anticipate."

Ananchel appeared from behind Creed as he hovered in the air, overlooking the city of London. Where a portal was found in the outskirts of the city.

"He's growing in power." creed said.

"It will be only a matter of time before he surfaces above the ground."

"How do we close these portals?"

"By defeating those who he has placed upon the earth."

"Who's already here?"

"His allies. Forces from realms like his own. There is one that was sighted in Scotland. They call him Abacus."

"A demon?"

"Yes. One who is famous for his earthly appearances through Ouija boards. The generations of Man summon him continually without knowing the damage they're doing to the earth."

"Humans will never learn."

"Something we can agree on."

"I will find him out in Scotland. Summon him myself by using other means than a wooden board."

"And what will you do once he's in your sights?"

"Eliminate him from creation. It'll send a direct message to Adrambadon and his other allies."

Ananchel nodded. "I see."

Creed flew off and Ananchel hovered into the sky, vanishing through a quick sight of light. Creed traveled through the air at the speed of aircrafts, heading to Scotland. While flying, he concentrated his energy to discern nearby dark elements. Sensing nothing, he continued to make his move to Scotland to find the demon Abacus.

In Scotland, Creed flew in the night sky, as he flew, he caught a glimpse of a flashing light ahead of him. Keening his gaze upon it, Creed went toward it. Seeing it's the Callanish Stones. Upon landing on the ground, he discovered the flashing light was in fact a diversion. Only a strange crystal left unguarded.

"I know you're here." Creed uttered.

Behind him appeared a figure. Lean, toned, and dark as coal. Its eyes were white as the stars and it wore a cloak with a ripped tunic. Creed stood before the figure.

"I take it you're the one they call Abacus?"

"I am. I knew you would come. You're much bigger than he had told us."

"Where's Adrambadon?"

"He's on his way here. This world will be his. As will all others."

"A repetitive plan. It's been done before and it failed."

"Not with my maser, Adrambadon. He is aware of the goings of this world. The rising heroes, the change in the scenery, the loss of faith and the drive for individualism."

"The world will change once the end has come."

"Adrambadon is coming to bring the end. Just, not the way you are expecting."

From Creed's arms appeared an axe. The axe was made from his armored suit. Abacus was astounded by the quickness of the weapon's appearance. He gleaned closer to the axe and gasped.

"I recognize that material."

"You should."

"Oh, my. I didn't even notice."

"It's too late now."

"No, it's perfectly shown."

Creed lunged toward Abacus with the axe, Abacus moved from the attack and swerved himself around Creed, attacking him from all points. Creed's cloak swirled up the air around them, knocking Abacus into a set of the stones. His eyes brightened gold and Abacus smiled.

"Good. Good."

Creed grabbed Abacus by his throat and slammed him into the ground, denting the dirt. Abacus laid in a hole and rose up with a bigger smile on his face. Creed stepped back and grabbed the axe from the ground and slammed it on Abacus' left arm.

"Nice one." Abacus said, looking at the axe in his arm.

"Your head is next."

"I think not. This is only the start and I am needed elsewhere."

Creed swiped the axe across Abacus' neck. Slashing his head from his body. Abacus' body fell motionless and the head rolled over to the stones. Bouncing off of the standing mineral. Blood flowed from the body. Creed placed the axe over his shoulder and as he turned away, the stones glowed a neon blue. The ground started to quake.

"What is happening now?" Creed wondered.

From the stones, the ground had opened to reveal another portal. From the opening a bright light shot up into the air and traveled across the corners of the sky. Creed already knew it had just made a connection to the other portals and he could feel within himself Adrambadon was inching closer than before.

III

<u>THE CIRCLE</u>

Adrambadon's presence began to grow upon the earth. Creed could feel it at every second passing. Ananchel appeared before him with a sense of fear moving through her eyes, scattered from across the earth.

"Something's wrong." She said.

"He's coming. Creed replied. "But, I cannot have him reach the surface."

"What are you planning to do?"

"I will enter the Cryptic Zone and face him there. Defeat him at his own turf."

"You cannot. You alone won't be able to defeat him. Especially when he derives his power from the realm he resides."

"What other option do you have?"

"Perhaps we can wait on assistance and face him when he arrives."

"Foolish talk. If we were to take that chance, he would destroy much of the earth and kill those who he wishes. For an angel, you are surely a fool."

"I am what I am."

"You fear Adrambadon and yet, I don't recall you facing him in times past. Or did you?"

"I've seen what he can do firsthand."

"Then, join me in entering his domain and taking him out."

"It can't be just the two of us."

"Call one of your friends from the heavens. See which of them will assist us in this war."

"They're all busy at the moment. There are other things taking place right now."

"Then, while you wait, I will enter the Cryptic Zone."

Immediately in front of them, another angel came down from the sky. His height was tall, and he stood upright with a stature with his arms and feet the color of brass. His eyes kindling with fire. Creed looked up toward the angel. He nodded slightly.

"Uriel." Ananchel said.

"Ananchel, I received the call."

"That fast?" Creed asked.

"Yes."

"I would've expected you to come down here. Where are the others?"

"Michael and Gabriel are busy with matters throughout the cosmos. I came because of the need this quest requires. You plan on entering the Cryptic Zone to face Adrambadon. You will need some celestial assistance."

"This is good." Ananchel said.

"How many friends does Adrambadon have down there?" Creed asked.

"Other than Abacus, the one they named Satanic."

"It tells enough." Creed said.

"Not exactly. Unlike Abacus, Satanic is more animal than your standard demonic foe. Runs on all fours, equipped with bullhorns and a raging taste for blood. No matter where it's from."

"Good to know. The two of you can handle Abacus and Satanic.

Leave Adrambadon to me."

"Are you positive of your choice?"

"I am."

"How do we exactly enter the Cryptic Zone?" Ananchel wondered.

"We jump into one of the opened portals, a direct lead to Adrambadon himself. Or one of you can just open a doorway to his domain yourselves. If you possess the power to do so."

"If we were to do so, Adrambadon will discover us before we enter. Better we use his portals to our advantage."

"Good." Creed said. "Let's go."

They reached a nearby portal and lunged themselves in. diving down into a bright pit. It resembled a bottomless pit as they fell, nothing was dark and heat, instead everything was a bright violet with a cool breeze of air. Continuing their fall, Creed pushed himself further down as the angels followed.

"We're nearing the drop-off." Creed said.

"How do you know?" Ananchel asked.

"See that circle glowing ahead, it is the entrance to the Cryptic Zone."

From there, Creed and the angles landed. The portal above them still operating and they looked at their surroundings. Covered with orange crystal-like objects growing from the rocky walls. Emitting a strange energy. Creed felt the realm's own energy sinking into his body.

"Looks different than I can tell." Ananchel said.

"Keep your guard up." Uriel said. "They're not as far from us as you would believe."

"You know us well." Came a voice from around them.

They turned around, seeing no one, turning once more and yet there was still no one around.

"This way." The voice uttered.

They turned to its direction and there, they found themselves staring at Adrambadon himself. Besides him were Abacus and Satanic. Creed stared down Adrambadon. Abacus grinned at them and Satanic began to bark toward the angels. Adrambadon sat on a throne made from the same mineral that was seen growing in the walls. He was dressed similar to an overlord. Leathery armor from his neck to his feet. His long hair was in fact streams of fire. His eyes had no pupils. His face could be made out from its own shining streak. His voice echoed deep through the Cryptic Zone.

"Two angels in my realm!" Adrambadon said. "This is a good day."

"You know why we're here." Uriel said.

"Of course!"

"I've come to end you." Creed declared with anger. "Of all the things you've done."

"You can't blame me for the travesties that have grown upon the earth. For I know your true purpose and where your powers lie. Remember."

"I'm not here to discuss history. I have come to end you."

"Give it a go! Many have tried before your time and many will try after you've turned to dust."

Abacus warped and attacked Ananchel as Satanic rushed over against Uriel. Uriel grabbed the beast by the horns and slammed it against the wall, its scaly, burnt hide rubbed against the rocks. Creed stepped forward, facing the Cryptic Lord. Adrambadon stood up from his throne and stepped down its stairs.

"You will not succeed this day." Adrambadon declared.

"I will do what my purpose commands me!"

Creed raised his axe and lunged toward Adrambadon. He held his hand up, freezing Creed in mid-air.

"Then, you should be doing my will. After all, I'm the one who endowed you with the powers you possess. Have you not forgotten? I was the one who gave you this new life, gave you a portion of my own power. You were sent to the earth to do my bidding. The opening of the portals was your task."

"I am not your pawn!" Creed yelled, trying to fight against the hold.

"Oh, but, you are! Instead, you've chosen to help the innocent. Believing it will grant you repentance from your past sins and give you eternal life. What did you expect? You believe the Most High will save you?"

"He has all power in His hand!"

"I am aware. For this universe has so many secrets, not even I know them all. But, I will do what I must until the appointed time arises. For now, I will end you and find a new Creed to put in your place. One that will not disobey my commands."

Uriel flew over and swiped his sword against Adrambadon's chest. Creed fell from the hold and landed on the ground. Ananchel rushed over to him as he stood up.

"Where's Abacus and Satanic?" Creed asked.

"We dealt with them. But, they will be back soon."

Adrambadon grabbed Uriel's sword and kicked him toward Creed and Ananchel. Tossing his sword back to him, Adrambadon approached the three and gazed up toward the portal above them.

"How soothing it will be to have the three of you here with me for eternity. As this portal shall now be shut."

The portal began to close. Creed ran toward the Cryptic Lord, reaching from his back, impaling him with a spear made from his own power. Uriel and Ananchel flew up to the portal.

"Creed, come on!" Ananchel yelled.

Creed turned to Adrambadon and looked him in the eyes.

"Our war isn't over."

"Of course not!" Adrambadon said. "For we will have many battles and then, the war."

Creed pushed Adrambadon back and went into the portal. Adrambadon gazed up and smiled. Starting to laugh as he pulled the spear from his body and healed the wound with one of the orange crystals.

"Another day, my creation."

IV

<u>THE FUTURE</u>

Creed, Ananchel, and Uriel bolted from the portal and as they touched the ground, the portal shut. Its light vanished and the surrounding area silent. Creed looked around, feeling strange.

"This isn't where we last stood."

"The portal must've brought us somewhere else."

"We near a city. One the humans call Washington D.C."

"Why are we here?" Creed asked.

"I don't know." Ananchel said. "But, right now we need to be prepared for Adrambadon's next phase of attack."

"I had him."

"You did not." Uriel said. "Another day, you will."

Uriel and Ananchel hovered in the air above Creed.

"We must return to our domain." Uriel uttered to Ananchel. "We've been away long enough."

"Understood." She said. "Creed, I will return as soon as I can."

The two angels flew off into the sky. Creed sighed and turned around, only to find himself facing an elderly woman who was twice his height. She wore a dark blue dress with white linings throughout it. Appearing to be small crosses. Her hair was white as snow and her features were of a young woman, yet, old.

"Who are you?" Creed asked.

"I am known through the realms as Madam Age and today, I have come to warn you."

"Warn me of what?"

"The future. The near future."

"What of it?"

"A threat is brewing upon this earth. Adrambadon is not part of this. Neither are those you have encounter before. This threat is growing from a mortal man and it is near for his power to rise."

"I don't understand."

"Prepare yourself. Prepare."

DEATH CHASER SOULS OF RETRIBUTION

I

IN YOUR DREAMS

The Death Chaser, known in the spiritual realm as the Soul of Retribution entered the Dream Dimension to complete a task in defeating a demonic entity referred to as Nightmare. The Chaser entered the dimension on a device, appeared to humans as a hybrid between a motorcycle and a Cadillac. The Dream Dimension was surrounded by a dark-green hue as Nightmare arose from the strange clouds. A large demonic figure with long, dark wavy hair, a goatee, and malevolent glowing green eyes. The Chaser approached the entity without fear.

"Nightmare. Your tormenting is over."

"There is no one who can remove me from my domain." Nightmare declared as his deep voice went through the Dream Dimension like a wave.

"This isn't your domain, demon. This is the realm of the dreamers and you are no permitted entry into this place. It is time to go."

Nightmare roared at the Chaser and lunged out from the clouds to attack him. The Chaser raised up a steel whip made of Sinfire and swiped Nightmare's hands, pushing him back into the hue. Nightmare's size was of a large stature to the Chaser's own height and size. The Chaser was as a civilian to Nightmare who was near the height of a 10-stoty building.

The Chaser created a whirlwind of Sinfire that grabbed Nightmare from the hue and sucked him in at a quickening pace. The Chaser picked up the whirlwind and tossed it out into a portal, exiting the dimension.

"Nightmare has been removed. For now."

The Chaser left the Dream Dimension and returned to the physical realm. When he made his return to the land of the living, the Chaser reverted to his mortal form as Danny Logan. He took a breath and went on about his business.

II

A KNIGHT AND A WIDOW

Danny went on, walking down an empty and dirty alleyway. While, walking, he caught the scent of perfume. Yet, it was a strange scent. One of the dead with a slight hint of roses. Danny sighed.

"I just wanted sometime alone." Danny uttered.

Shaking his head, his hands twitching and within mere seconds, he transformed into the Death Chaser. A head cloaked in a hood, but his face a skull. Dressed in all black with spikes running down from his shoulders to his wrists. He looked around with a deep fire in his eyes.

"Show yourself!" He yelled.

From the nearby trash can arose a woman cloaked in all black. Her pale skin reflected with the light coming from the moon. A black veil over her face. She approached the Chaser with fear. He gazed upon her face, reaching to remove the veil. As he proceeded, the scent went from her to him. He stopped his hand in mid-air, inching from her veil.

"The scent is you!" The Chaser said. "Who are you?!"

"Just a widow." She replied, pulling out two medium daggers from her back. "And I'm not alone."

She gazed up to the rooftop of the building and from there, came down a man. Wearing an all-red uniform. Resembling a military outfit with shades of black with the exceptions of wings in the form of a trench coat. His face hidden by the shadow of his beaked hood. The two stood before the Chaser with weapons in hand.

"We have been searching for you. For your kind." The man said.

"You desire a challenge from me?!"

"It is why we're here." The woman said.

"Then you're as foolish as your ancestors!"

The Chaser whipped out his sin fire, swiping the walls around them. The two stood back, thinking of a plan. The Chaser was consumed with sin fire, flowing all around him and yet, not touching him.

"What shall we do?" The woman asked the man.

"We take him down. By any means."

"Don't be foolish. Surrender now and spare your lives for another day."

"We can't do that. We've been hunting down an soldier of Demonti for some time and we've finally found one."

"Demonti…?" The Chaser said with a pause. "What do you know of Demonticronto?!"

"You're his pawn! Just like all the others we've read about in the books!" The man yelled.

"Books. Have you ever seen Demonticronto? Have you ever faced him? No. Because if you did, you wouldn't be standing here. Now, tell me what you know about him."

"Strike him now."

The woman rushed toward the Chaser with her daggers. Attempting to stab him and as the daggers came closer, the Chaser grabbed them with one hand, ripping them from her hands. He threw them on the ground and snatched the woman by the throat. Staring into her eyes.

"Don't you hurt her!"

"Keep quiet!"

"Or what?!"

The Chaser released sin fire that snatched the man and slammed him against the brick wall. Holding him in place. He struggled to get free and as he did, the fire quenched tighter. The Chaser turned back to the woman, removing the veil from her face.

"Why have you chosen such a futile task?"

"We're only doing what's right for all creation."

"And what may that be?"

"Stopping you from unleashing Demonti's power upon the earth."

"You do not know who I am, do you?"

"You're the one they call the Hunter. The one who gathers souls for Demonti's use."

"Then you do not know me." The Chaser said, pushing the woman next to the man. "Allow me to tell the two of you who I am. I am the one sent by the Master to cause sinners to repent by the fear of the damned. I am the entity that is sent out to find lost souls and bring them to a dwelling place. I am the one spoken about throughout the ages as the Shadow, the Angel of Death, the Feared Fire. All of creation knows my name as the Death Chaser, the Soul of Retribution!"

"The Death Chaser?" The man questioned. "How?"

"Because your books were wrong, boy. As is your plan to stop Demonticronto. There is only one way to stop him and I am that way."

"Then, let us free from this fire and help us." The woman said. "Help us stop him."

"I can look at the two of you now and perfectly say, you aren't capable of entering such a realm of existence. You would do better to live like the humans. Live out your days in peace. Read the Psalms and the Proverbs. Place them in your hearts. Live and die. As your ashes return to the earth where it was taken."

The Chaser turned away and the woman screamed. He turned back and started at her with anger kindling in his eyes.

"Don't try something idiotic."

"Help us. Please. If not that, teach us. Guide us to understand the spiritual realm."

The Chaser walked over to them on the wall, swiping his hand across the fire to release them from its heated bonds. They were relieved when the fire was gone, and the heat stopped.

"Just help us out." The man said. "We only want to do some good in this world."

"What are your names?" The Chaser asked.

"John Clarkson." The man said." But, my codename is Robin Knight."

"And you, woman?" The Chaser asked.

"My name was lost when I was young. I have been called Widow ever since."

"Were you married in times past?"

"Yes. But, my husband at the time had died."

"How did he fall?"

"A demonic attack. We were only novices when we discovered the spiritual arts. We read much of Aleister Crowley's writings. Tried to imitate his works. We conjured a demon and my husband was killed in the process."

"Did you learn your lesson?"

"I have now."

The Chaser nodded. "Good. Next time do not bother repeating the works of a mage."

"I understand."

"What now?" John asked. "Will you help us stop Demonti?"

"First thing, how do you know Demonticronto is coming to Earth?"

"We came across a strange spirit. It mimicked the sins of the world. Used them to fuel its own power. The spirit told us the world's sins are increasing and Demonti will rise again. This time with all the world ion his side and it would mean the end of all things."

"We're already in the end." The Chaser declared. "Many just have not looked to notice."

"We have to show him where we came into contact with the spirit." Widow told John.

"I agree. We have to bring you to the site of the sighting."

"Very well." The Chaser said. "Go there now. I will meet you there."

"How?" John asked.

"I am not of this world remember."

"Oh. Yeah. I understand."

The Chaser vanished from their sight through a fiery whirlwind. John and Widow went about their way, going to the site of the strange spirit.

III

SIN IS TRANSGRESSION OF THE LAW

John and Widow's travels have brought them to an abandoned building just outside of the local town. There, they came to the entrance and behind them, the sound of a whirlwind came. They turned around, seeing the Chaser walk out of the whirlwind before it vanished.

"This is the place?" The Chaser asked.

"Yes." John replied. "However, we saw the spirit inside."

The Chaser examined the building. He could smell blood, vomit, feces, and gunpowder from its surroundings. He shook his head and rubbed his face.

"This was a slaughterhouse many years ago. Once a gun manufacturer, a prison for children, and a mental institution."

"How do you know all of this?" Widow asked the Chaser.

"The scent is still here. No matter how things are moved from place to place. Its spiritual touch remains. This place is a hell made on this earth and one that shut down for good purpose."

"Then, why was the spirit roaming around in here like it was its own?"

"Because of the activities that occurred within this building. Many deaths. Many lies. Many false hopes. Many sins committed.

Lawlessness ruled in this place."

"You can get all of that just by the scent of the building?"

"The grounds are polluted with sins. Man have come here and transgressed the Master's Law. Fortunately, they are all dead and have been grated passage from my wrath. But, that's the least of their worries from this earth."

"What did you mean by transgressing the Master's Law? Who's the Master?"

"Who do you think?" The Chaser said.

"I'm not certain. There are many masters. Many gods. Many rulers."

"Yes, there are. But, only one manages to outwit them all at their own game"

"How?"

"Because He created all things. This universe. This world. You. Her. Myself. Created all things for his good pleasure and his good pleasure alone."

"You're talking about God."

"Which one is God to you? Better starts using names for identification. Don't want to make an error in the future."

"And that is why we need you to teach us the ways of the spiritual realm." Widow said. "To give us a proper understanding."

'Then, you would have to find yourselves a pastor."

"That's difficult to do these days. Most of them are all prosperity speakers. motivation lists for a vain goal. A cost to live in this world without knowledge of the world to come."

"You know enough as is, woman." The Chaser chuckled.

The Chaser approached the wooded doors and kicked them open. Inside of the buildings was nothing. An empty facility. The three entered and the only thing seen was dirt, hay, scurrying rats, and dried remains of the blood, vomit, and tiny specks of gunpowder.

"This place reeks." John said.

"You couldn't smell it from outside." The Chaser said. "Shows just how much discernment you must learn."

The Chaser continued to look at the building and felt a tug in his spirit. He turned his head quickly, startling John and Widow.

"Something wrong?" John asked.

"Someone else is here."

"Here as in the building or outside? I didn't hear any vehicles."

"Someone not of this earth."

The dirt rattled from beneath John and Widow. The Chaser pulled them from the spot and the ground opened, revealing a strange spirit rising. John and Widow stared.

"That's the spirit we saw." John said.

The Chaser stepped forward as the hole in the ground sealed shut. The strange spirit had the eerie appearance of a man, covered in tattoos. Glowing yellow eyes and unkempt hair. The tattoos however were of wicked acts. Sins of the world. Lewdness, uncleanness, filth, and hatred for the spiritual. The Chaser pointed at the spirit.

"Speak your name!"

"Ah, how I've always wanted to meet a Death Chaser." The spirit said. "This is my day."

"You smell of swine's flesh!" The Chaser yelled. "What is your name, Spirit!"

"I don't have a name. I do have a title."

"Don't test me." The Chaser said.

"I am known as the Sin Phantom. I have been on this earth ever since the Flood. The washed sins of those of the past I have consumed and made my own."

"This spirit's been around since the days of Noah?" Widow asked.

"Appears to be so." John replied.

"What are your doings with Demonticronto?"

"You know? Good. Because, he desires to meet you, Chaser. As does he desire to meet every man, woman, beasts, and child upon this world. He wants to give you all what you truly seek."

"And that is?"

"Freedom. Freedom from the laws that bind you. You desire many things. To do as you wish. Demonticronto has that gift for everyone and is willing to grant it. Only by one request."

"What request?"

"You submit to his will and obey his every word. Look up to him as you would to the Most High."

The Chaser emitted sin fire from his right hand. It glowed with a passion. The Sin Phantom steppe back as did John and Widow.

"I do not like your kind, Phantom. That is why I was created. To destroy pests like you!"

"You may try."

The Chaser threw the fire toward the Phantom and it vanished from the building quickly before the fire to touch him. The chaser moved and ran outside, looking for the spirit. But, it was nowhere to be seen. John and Widow followed him.

"Where could it have gone?" John asked.

"It's close." The Chaser replied. "It hasn't gone far enough."

Somewhere in the mountains, the ground shook and opened. From the opening fire arose and within the flames were souls. Souls made of molten rock. A dozen of them came out of the hole as it shut. There, they stood until the Sin Phantom approached them.

"You sent them."

"As are my words, Phantom." A deep voice said from one of the souls. "These tormented souls are here to do my bidding under your command. Release them against the Chaser and his allies. Stall them until my coming is complete."

"Yes, master."

The voice echoed away. The Sin Phantom directed the souls toward the local town.

"Find the Chaser and his allies. Kill them by any means necessary. For Demonticronto!"

The Tormented Souls made their move toward the town with Sin Phantom overlooking them with a large smile on his face.

IV

AN OLD ENEMY

The Tormented Souls entered the town, frightening the locals. However, they did not harm them by any means as their objective is to find the Chaser, John, and Widow. The Chaser continued his search and came across the Souls. Widow also saw them and was immediately unconformable.

"What are they?" She asked.

"Souls." The Chaser said. "Tormented ones."

'Tormented?" John asked. "By what?"

"By he cares of this world and the cares of this life at one point. Now, they're only tormented by the things they should've done when they were on this side of glory."

John watched as they did no harm to the locals of the town. He felt a slight relief come over him. He chuckled.

"They're not harming anyone."

"They're not here for them." The Chaser said. "They're here for us and us they will meet."

"Do we have to fight them?" Widow asked.

The Chaser turned toward her, handing her the two daggers. She grabbed them and looked at the Chaser.

"You had them the whole time."

"You need them for this moment. The only way we get out of

here is to face the Souls. The Sin Phantom is among them. Leave him to me. The two of you take down as many Souls as possible. I will aid you. You do not need worry."

"Alright then." John said. "I guess this is what it's like entering the spiritual realm."

"You have no clue yet, boy."

One of the Souls turned its head, seeing the Chaser. It screeched loudly to the point of shattering the windows of the nearby buildings and cars. Signaling to the other Souls of their discovery. They ran like animals toward them.

"I'm not ready for this!" John said.

"Gird up your loins like a man and face them!" the Chaser yelled.

"I am prepared." Widow said.

"Spoken like a true warrior."

The Souls eased with speed, and the Chaser warped them with sinfire from his mouth. John extended his coat, transforming it into a pair of red wings. Widow twirled her dagger and they fought off the Souls as they came. The Chaser ran through the horde, grabbing the souls by their faces and slamming them into the ground. One of the Souls bit the Chaser on his shoulder. He only laughed as his shoulder turned to sinfire itself, burning the mouth from the soul.

"Now you know pain!"

The Chaser brought out the sinfire whip and swiped the Souls around him. As if they were lost cattle. The Chaser laughed as he done it. Taking pleasure in destroying the Souls of the damned. On the other side of the fight, Widow was impressive in taking out Souls with her daggers. John flew over them, diving down like an eagle to its prey and back up again. The Chaser scouted the area.

"Phantom! Reveal yourself unto me!"

From there, the Phantom arose from the ground. Staring down the Chaser.

"You called me."

"I want you to send Demonticronto a message."

"I am listening."

The Chaser rushed over like lightning, grabbing the Phantom by his jaw. He held him up as John and Widow took down the remaining Souls with a team effort. They fell to the ground in a pile of rocks. The Phantom struggled to get loose from the Chaser's grip.

"Tell Demonticronto, the end is here, and it begins with him."

The Phantom muffled under his breath. The Chaser laughed.

"And show him my mark, which I give unto you."

The Chaser emitted sinfire from his hand, burning the Phantom's mouth and jaw. Dropping him on the ground, the Chaser raised up the whip and the Phantom scurried away. John and Widow ran toward him, looking around. The Phantom was gone.

"You had him." John said.

"I did. For a intentional purpose."

"But, we need to know where Demonticronto is lurking." Widow said.

"It's taken care of."

"How?"

"My mark is all that was required. I will know where Demonticronto will be at every moment and he shall know as well."

A week later, John and Widow continued to meet with the Chaser to learn the spiritual realm. While on his own, the Chaser would revert to Danny Logan. There, his travels brought him to Washington D.C., where he learned of a strange occurrence of demonic activity taking place.

"The cleansing shall begin." Danny said, morphing into the Death Chaser once more.

TRAVIS VAIL, SPIRIT-SEEKER: FIRST SINS

I

WHAT CAME BEFORE

Reading through his past investigations and encounters with the otherworldly, Travis Vail, known in the occult circles as the Spirit-Seeker, is researching more of his past encounter with Kamagrauto, the demon who opened his mind to the larger world. After the visitation from Kamagrauto at the Black Raven Hotel and in finding the Mutant-Thing, Vail is curious about the world he's about to enter. A world where the supernatural comes into conflict with the rising heroes. A mixture that will only end in chaos.

Still studying, Vail's phone rang, and he answered with slight haste and ease of movement. His instincts were still kicking. His mind on Kamagrauto's words and his encounter with Abraham and The Swordman.

"Vail speaking."

"Trav, good to hear your voice."

"Ah. Dr. Galen Donovan." Vail said with a smirk. "Same here.

Why have you called?"

"I have a case for you. If you're interested."

"What kind of case if I may ask humbly?"

"From what I've learned, it concerns the first sins?"

"First sins? As in the first sins committed after the Fall?"

"Correct."

Vail nodded. "I'm on board. Send me the details and I'll follow suit."

"Will do." Donovan said. "You'll have the information shortly."

Vail hung up and within several minutes, the information was sent to Vail through his email. Reading the files, Vail learned the first sins were moving through the world in slow form. Unusual to his previous encounters in past cases, there was a map attached to the files which detailed the past locations of the sins' movements. Vail packed his gear, what was needed, grabbed his black trench coat and left his lair.

Following the map's layout, Vail went across most of the United Kingdom into France and into Germany. Vail has spoken with several witnesses to the sightings and they explained the sins appeared as one. Embodied to moving around single filed. Whatever it was, it had no motives other than to terrorize and to instill fear into the humans it came across. After each movement it made, the more aggressive it became. From startling humans to torturing them if came close.

"This is something else." Vail noted. "Something far more powerful is at work here than just some series of haunting."

Vail continued his investigations and interviews for the next several days. During those days, Vail began to come across what looked to be plague doctors. Crouched in the shadows to walking past him in crowds. Vail took nothing from it until he managed to see one staring at him from the distance. The plague doctor dressed in an all-black robe. Covered from head to toe with its doctor's mask sticking out of its hood. Vail smirked.

"You think that frightens me, lad? Tell you what, take off that beak and we'll settle this like men."

The plague doctor stood still. Vail waited, yet, nothing came from the doctor.

"Figures." Vail said. "I'm going on about my business. Don't try to follow or you'll end up somewhere you won't like."

Vail contacted Donovan concerning the case and the uprising of plague doctors. Donovan stated the doctors are probably the result of the sins' travels. The doctors are following the path of the sins.

"They may be, but, there's something more to all of this. Something sinister at work."

"Why don't we meet up and discuss our ideas on this case?"

"Sure. Where are you right now?"

"In Italy."

"Let me guess, Venice."

"I'm having a word with Ms. Belinda Grazio. You remember her I presume?"

"I can't forget a face like hers. Anyhow, I'm leaving Germany. I'll be there as fast as possible."

"Take your time. Belinda is patient of your coming."

"She would be."

II

<u>WHAT CAME AFTER</u>

Vail entered the city of Venice near nightfall. Vail had walked through Venice reaching the hotel. When Vail came closer, he could see Donovan standing outside of a door.

"There he is." Vail said walking.

Vail made his way toward Donovan and the two hugged.

"You came quicker than I expected."

"I was on the move right after our conversation."

"Good timing."

"Not my best, but I try."

Vail investigated the hotel room. He saw no one inside. He gazed his eyes toward Donovan while pointing into the room. Donovan looked back into the room and turned to Vail.

"Looking for something?"

"I thought you said Belinda was here?"

"She's at her home." Donovan said. "She will meet with us in the morning. In the meantime, you and I need to discuss this case."

"Sure thing."

Vail entered the hotel room and Donovan followed. Inside, they sat at the coffee table. Atop the table were files Donovan had brought with him. The same documents he emailed to Vail to begin with.

Donovan had passed Vail a bottle of beer and Vail drank.

"Plague doctors?" Donovan asked with confusion.

"I saw them at every location the sins had come across. They just stood there. Staring. I taunted one."

"Sounds like something you'll do."

"What would you do if you had a plague doctor staring down at you from across the area?"

"Where did the doctor go?"

"Not sure. I walked away afterwards. Warned it if it followed me it would end up in a far worse place."

"What is your conclusion so far?"

"These areas are connected. The sins aren't traveling by themselves. It's as if they're merged into one. Like they've become an entity."

"You believe the sins have become a living entity? Your presumption I'm assuming?"

"It would explain this more clearly. Besides, the only way for the sins to have merged into an entity, it would need to be brought together by someone of a darker power."

"What of that demon you encountered at Black Raven Hotel? Could he be responsible for this?"

"Wouldn't surprise me. However, he was keen on something else. Regarding myself and others like me in the field."

"How would it know of your future to start with? Demons aren't that intelligent when it comes to one's future. The past they're aware of."

"That demon was more powerful than our usual demons. This one claimed to be a lieutenant demon who worked for somebody called Dagor The Soul Eater."

"The Soul Eater?" Donovan jumped. "He hasn't been seen since the Middle Ages."

"Well, if his lieutenant is bumping around the world, he mustn't be hidden anymore."

"Your words are true." Donovan nodded. "Well, once we meet Belinda tomorrow, she'll tag along with us on this case."

"No offense, but, why is she interested in this case? I'm sure she has plenty of cases in this city."

"She wanted this case to work with you again. Though, not as I expect it to be. We're not going to Poveglia this time."

"Noted." Vail stood up from the table. "I'm going to get myself a room in this place. I'll speak to you in the morning."

"Sure thing, Travis. Good night."

"Same to you." Vail left Donovan's hotel room.

While Vail had obtained his own room, he walked down the hallway toward the room. Before he could put the key in, Vail spotted another plague doctor standing at the end of the hall. Cloaked in darkness. Yet, its' beak was glowing. Vail sighed.

"You choose to do this now?" Vail asked. "I would like some kind of answer here."

The doctor kept still. Vail shook his head and rubbed his hands together.

'Guess I'll have to make you."

Vail moved with haste toward the doctor and once he reached him, the doctor had vanished into a thin dark mist. Vail searched the surroundings and found nothing.

"This nonsense is something else."

Vail returned to his room and unlocked the door. He entered and went to sleep.

III

<u>WHAT CAME BETWEEN</u>

The following morning, Vail and Donovan entered a café and inside sitting was Belinda Grazio. They noticed, and Vail only sighed as they approached the table and sat down.

"I know." Belinda said. "You're thrilled to see me again."

"I know why you're here." Vail said. "Besides, that's not why I'm here."

"She's here to assist us on this case."

"I'm aware. So, let's get to it shall we."

"Fair enough." Donovan said. "We need your skills to help us solve this case around the first sins."

"The first sins? That's your case?"

"Can you help us is the question." Vail pointed out. "Can you?"

"I can help. Only if I can come along with the two of you."

"She would do this." Vail said.

"You can."

"*Prego.*" Belinda said. "Glad we can work together again."

"I'm sure you are." Vail said. "Now, can we discuss this case?"

"Yeah. What do you mean by the 'first sins'?" Belinda asked.

"Travis can give you the details. It is his case after all."

"Sure thing. I've come across a number of plague doctors recently and all pf them have some sort of connection to the first sins.”

“Like all of them?”

“Yes.”

“And you want to find out where these doctors are going and who could be leading them?”

“Precisely. Which is why Galen decided to speak to you. Believing you could be of service to solving this obscure case.”

“Well, I can be of service.”

“Excellent. Help us and you can go on your way.” Vail said.

“What is the plan for today?”

“Since I was visited by a plague doctor last night, I figured we make a trip back to the hotel and search the area. Perhaps, the quiet doctor left something for us to find.”

“Well then, I will gather my things and meet you there.”

Vail nodded as Belinda hugged Donovan and left the café. Vail turned to Galen, shaking his head.

“Is it always going to be like this with the two of you?” Donovan asked.

“As long as she focuses on the mission, everything will run smoothly.”

“And if not?”

“Then, we will have problems. Delays. Something this job doesn’t require us to have.”

Vail and Donovan left the café and as they walked down the sidewalk, they stumbled across a pair of street preachers. Dressed in bright colors with the menorah and the Star of David on their clothing. They carried with them signs and a chart, detailing locations of the earth. Vail approached them, glancing at the chart.

“And what is this?”

“What do you think, Esau.” The preacher said.

“Heh, Esau now.” Vail uttered. “Is that what you just called me?”

"Esau is the white man. You are the Devil!" The Preacher yelled.

"Me the Devil? Look here, fellow, the only one of us who's truly the Devil is you and your gang of deceivers."

"Deceivers?! Read the Word, Esau!"

The Preacher looked, seeing Donovan approaching them next to Vail. The Preacher's eyes glanced back and forth between Vail and Galen.

"My brother, you can't be hanging around with the enemy."

"The enemy? This man is my friend."

"You can't be friends with Esau, my brother. Look at this chart right here."

Donovan looked at the chart and nodded. Facing the preacher and his brothers-in-arms.

"I have a solution to the problem. Mind if I speak it to you?"

"Yes sir."

"If the white man is truly Esau, then he is your brother."

"What do you mean by that?"

"Esau was born from Isaac's loins. Thereby, Esau is in fact a Hebrew."

"That's not what we're discussing, my brother. The white man is the Devil and the white man is Esau."

"Then, if Esau is the white man and the white man is the Devil, you should get busy at casting the Devil out of him. Free him from the demonic troubles."

The preacher stepped back, grabbing a hold of the Bible in hand. He shook his head.

"We can't help those who's minds have been wiped by the white man. We can't. You're a lost cause, my brother. I am deeply sorry. But, I hope *Yahawashi* has mercy on you and grants you entrance when he returns."

"As do I." Donovan said.

"Heh." Vail chuckled. "Hmm."

The two walked away as the preacher continued his preaching. They turned, entering an alleyway. Vail laughed, and Donovan shook his head.

"Didn't think they would be here." Vail said.

"They're growing. Besides, it's part of the endgame."

"As are many things happening today."

From there, smoke arose from the ground, startling the two. A thick black smoke.

"What is this?" Donovan asked.

"I know who it is."

From the smoke came Kamagrauto, the lieutenant demon. Cloaked in its robe and hood. Its eyes visible from the shadow and its horns spiked out. Kamagrauto levitated over the smoke. His legs could not be seen.

"Travis Vail. Galen Donovan. How intriguing it is to find you both here."

"Is that the demon you talked about?" Donovan asked.

"Yeah. That's him."

Kamagrauto glanced at Vail and Donovan. Its hands held together with his long, sharp, and dirty claws.

"Alright, what do you want?" Vail asked.

"To warn you of your current mission. You will not succeed."

"Is that so?"

"Your future depends on this case and I already know, you will fail. The first sins alone are far too vast for Travis Vail to solve on his own. You need guidance. Guidance from the other side and I can provide such."

"I understand your nobility. But, me and Galen have this under control."

"Oh, you do?" Kamagrauto gestured. "Then, I will be watching your every move and when you desire my aid and you will, I will make myself known unto you and those who will be at your side when the moment comes."

"What moment?" Vail asked.

"You will know. You will know."

Kamagrauto vanished into the smoke by falling. The darkness cleared from the alleyway and there was nothing remaining.

"That demon is noble?" Donovan asked.

"He has honor. I know. Strange for a demon to possess such a moral trait."

"Well, there are things not even we can comprehend."

"True. But, someday, I hope we can. Right now, we need to go and meet Belinda."

Making their return to the hotel, Belinda waited for them. She saw the looks on their faces.

"What happened?"

"We came across a demon." Donovan said.

"Or the demon came to us." Vail added.

"What kind of demon?"

"The lieutenant kind."

"That's not making any sense, Travis."

"I'm afraid it is true, Belinda. It's the same demon Travis met at the Black raven Hotel some time ago."

"Kamagrauto? Here?"

"Oh, you know his name." Vail chuckled.

"I thought you were only seeing things. I didn't expect him to exist."

"Well, lass, he exists and trust me, he's not one you would like to meet. Ask Galen of the encounter."

Donovan looked to Belinda and shook his head.

"Kamagrauto is not the typical demons we face. He is something far more ancient and we could feel his power.”

“But, do not fret. He offered to help us.”

“I hope you refused.”

“Not the slightest. He told me whenever I needed his help involving this case, which he is aware of. So, I assume there are others in the spirit world who are familiar with this and aren’t giving us any help. Kamagrauto told me to call on him if I needed his aid.”

“But, you won’t. we’ll solve the first sins together.”

“True. But, then again, stranger things have happened in this line of work.”

Vail walked to the hotel room door.

“I’m going to return to my room and get ready for the work we have to do. I won’t be long.”

Vail left the room. Belinda turned to Donovan with uncertainty expressing from her face. Galen knew it and sat down.

“What’s with him?”

“What do you mean? That’s the way he works. Travis is a very different kind of occult detective.”

“Yeah. Not one I would assume to have help from a demon. An ancient one at that.”

“Why don’t you go and talk to him. See what he tells you.”

“He already doesn’t want me here.”

“And that is more reason for you to talk to him. Get through to him. I know it’s possible.”

“How so?”

“Because I am the one who trained him in this field. His mentor in a way. Anyway, go and speak with him. It’ll give us enough time to prepare to find these plague doctors.”

Belinda approached Vail’s hotel room door and immediately the door opened. Vail stared at Belinda and she did the same. No words.

“What do you want?” Vail asked.

"Can we talk? For just a second."

Vail sighed as he allowed Belinda into his room. Shutting the door behind, Belinda stood, and Vail walked over to the table and sat down. He gestured his hand toward the other seat. Belinda sat with him.

"What?"

"What's with you?"

"How do you mean?"

"I mean your demeanor, your attitude. What's the problem?"

"There's plague doctors roaming around with the first sins on their back. I have to find out who's causing this and way."

"That's not what I'm talking about."

"Then I'm confused."

Belinda sighed.

"Why couldn't it have worked between us, Travis? Why didn't you bother to give it a chance?"

"You are not seriously asking me about relationship details right now."

"I am."

"Women always want to talk."

"Only if the men would listen to our words."

"I'm not trying to build up bitterness in my heart, lass. Besides that, I've told you before. A relationship with me won't work."

"Why not?"

"Because when I was young, I was visited by an angel. The angel warned me not to get married. Otherwise, tragedy would follow. Now, I see what the angel meant. Me traveling on this road of life. Dealing with the supernatural daily. Heh, if I did have a wife, she would've most likely divorced me or been killed in the process."

"But, there's always a way."

"Even though you're in this line of work, tragedy still strikes. The fact of Kamagrauto confronting me, proves the angel's point."

"Well, did this angel have a name?"

"He did."

"What was it?"

"Hmm. Michael."

"As in Michael the Archangel."

"Correct. Funny enough, he's been overseeing my activities since I was a little boy. No worries. However, I am keen on the fact he hasn't intervened with my confrontations with Kamagrauto. Maybe time will tell this course."

Vail sighed. Standing up from the chair, he grabbed his coat from the back of the chair, putting it on.

"Now, let's continue this case of ours."

IV

<u>WHAT CAME WITHIN</u>

Vail and Belinda met with Galen, who found the two of them together somewhat odd, but never the case. They moved forward with the case and after studying the trail of the plague doctor that Vail saw, a clue was given. A name connected to a series of plague doctor sightings. Belinda had the name.

"What is it?" Vail asked.

"Here's the name of the recent plague doctor sightings. All from witnesses who've seen the doctors and later a man would come and visit them. Asking about the doctors before they ever went public with a concern."

"The man's name." Donovan said. "What was it?"

"Timothy Ellis."

"Timothy Ellis. I've never heard of him before."

"I have." Vail said. "It's familiar to my ears."

"What do you know of this man, Travis?"

"He's deeply into the spiritual arts. Mystic stuff as well. But, in the occult circles, he doesn't go by that name. he is known and referred to as Balthazar."

"Is this the mage Balthazar a few have talked about?"

"It is. Balthazar is a mage. A powerful one. Took the name from the biblical magi. Cloaked in his dark-orange hood and robe, he gained power from a deep malevolent force. One of which I am unknown to. But, in time I will find out."

"So, where is Balthazar?" Belinda asked.

"New York City." Vail said. "Which means we have some traveling to do and in little time."

"Yeah, but how long before he finds out we're on to him?"

Vail turned and noticed a shadow hovering in the distance. He stared, and it revealed its eyes.

"Not long." Vail said, staring at the shadow.

"What is it?" Belinda said, turning to also see the shadow.

"What is that?" Donovan asked.

"Balthazar sent him." Vail said. "He already knows."

Vail ran after the shadow without haste.

"Where are you going?!" Belinda yelled.

"I'm going to see what this spirit knows!" Vail answered. "Don't follow me!"

Belinda went to follow, and Donovan held her back.

"Travis can handle himself."

"That's not what I'm worried about."

Vail chased the shadow, leaving Belinda and Donovan behind. The shadow brought Vail to a spot which was filthy, and the ground was covered in feces and vomit.

"Smells like shit." Vail uttered.

From its appearance, Vail knew it was a spot for homeless people.

"Show yourself, spirit!" Vail yelled.

"In front of him, the shadow appeared. Yet, no fear within it as it morphed into physical form. It resembled a young man, yet he was covered in blood, and chewed on swine's flesh. Vail smirked.

"The hell have we got here. A sin entity."

"Balthazar will have your soul." The entity uttered.

"I think not."

Vail tossed a handful of salt on the entity, startling it. There, Vail began to recite a chant, commanding for the entity to be loosed from Balthazar's hold and to return into the void. The entity was powerful enough to break Vail's chant, forcefully shoving him to the brick wall behind him. Vail fell to the ground and quickly, Kamagrauto arose from the pavement, snatching the entity by the throat and biting it, ripping off its astral head as the body returned to shadow form and fell. Evaporating into thin air.

"I'm not understanding any of this." Vail said.

"You have a higher calling, Travis Vail and I will not allow anyone to turn you away from your cause."

"You know about Balthazar? And how he's behind these plague doctors scaring folks."

"Balthazar has risen up the first sins. Yes. But, there is another spirit lurking the world. One far more powerful than Balthazar and is on the run from another soul as we speak."

"I wish that particular soul the best in his endeavors. Could use the bit of the help every now and then. How come you didn't tell me all this before I went further?"

"I know many things. Things even the smartest man would tremble at the sound."

"Good thing, I'm not the smartest man. I'm just an exorcist."

"One with a higher purpose."

"Then, why don't you just travel onto New York City and stop Balthazar for me? That way, I can focus more on this 'higher purpose'."

'Because it is not my duty to finish your work. You started this case, you must finish it."

Vail chuckled.

"I'll be. You know your kind are some slick sons of bitches."

"Do not compare me to the common demons you've slain."

"I'm not." Vail asked. "But, you really are a strange demon, lad."

"I am not like those demons. I am Kamagrauto. Kamagrauto."

Kamagrauto vanished into the black smoke as before. Vail shrugged himself and scoffed.

V

<u>WHAT CAME ABOUT</u>

Vail returned to Belinda and Galen, who saw his tiredness and often slackly behavior after things have arisen. They approached him with concern and he only smiled.

"What happened to the shadow?" Donovan asked.

"It was taken care of."

"How?" Belinda wondered.

"Kamagrauto killed it."

"The demon Kamagrauto?"

"Yes, Galen. The same demon we met in the alleyway. I confronted the damn thing. By the way, the shadow was a sin entity."

"That can't be so?" Donovan said. "there hasn't been one of them since the World Wars."

"And yet, here it is and not out of curiously either. Balthazar conjured it up."

"What happened to the spirit, Travis?" Belinda asked.

"I nearly came close to casting it away, but it possessed a power that outweigh my voice and tossed me against the wall. After that, Kamagrauto appeared and decapitated the spirit. Good for me."

"The demon helped you?" Donovan asked. "It killed the spirit right in front of your eyes?"

"Yes. Afterwards we spoke, and he revealed to me he's been aware of this whole case the entire time. I scoffed and wondered how come he couldn't do the work for us. Said it wasn't in his purpose. However, Balthazar is the one behind all of this and there's another sin spirit roaming the earth. But, Kamagrauto confirmed to me that another individual is chasing that spirit right now. So, hopefully we won't have too much work on our hands."

"So, what is our current objective?" Belinda asked.

"Galen, call Colton, tell him to meet us in New York. We need to confront Balthazar now and fast before more of his little ideas manifest into reality."

Vail, Belinda, and Donovan made their travels and arrived in New York City. Prepared to meet Balthazar. Wherever he may reside.

VI

<u>WHAT CAME TO BE</u>

Vail, Belinda, and Donovan stood in Times Square. Seeing the crowds go by, walking about their business. Galen shook his head in shame.

"They're just coming and going."

"It's their nature, Galen. Besides, it proves we're not the ones trapped in Pop Culture and materialism."

"Now, where will Colton be?" Belinda asked.

"He should be around here somewhere."

Vail looked out, not seeing his ally. Later, he turned his head and from there, he managed to get a glance at Colton. He pointed.

"He's coming this way."

Colton Levi approached them and shook hands. Standing in the middle of Times Square mind you amid the roaming crowds.

"Good to see you." Vail said. "Now, why did you want us to meet you out here?"

"Because, the guy you're looking for oftentimes roams through here."

"Are you sure?"

"Plague doctors are seen continually here. It's looked at as just a cosplay show."

"Point us in the direction." Vail said.

They followed Colton through the Square, moving past the crowds. There, Vail and Galen noticed a group of street preachers, yelling at all the white men in the crowds. Vail scoffed as the argument escalated to a brawl.

"They're everywhere."

"It's part of the times, Travis." Donovan said.

"True one."

Colton had led them into a spot where they set shops. He pointed toward the spot which had a crescent moon carved on the door.

"Is this the spot?" Belinda asked.

"It certainly is." Vail confirmed. "Let's see what's inside."

They entered the shop and quickly, surrounded by plague doctors. They raised up their guards as the doctors stood quirt and still.

"Oh, this is the place." Vail said.

The doctors approached them and suddenly, took steps back. Moving in a fashioned line on each side, leading them further into the shop down a hallway. They walked down the hallway and they reached a room. In the room were images of occult symbols, sacrifices, and spells. A pentagram was carved into the wooden floor. Vail stepped forward, seeing a hooded man crouched down at the fire.

"Stand up, you're embarrassing yourself here." Vail said.

The hooded man stood up, removing his hood. Revealing himself to be Balthazar. Vail smiled. Pointing.

"You son of a bitch!" Vail laughed.

"Travis Vail. The Spirit-Seeker."

"In the flesh."

"I figured you would come."

"Had not choice, lad. I've come to stop your doings. Raising up plague doctors and spirits. The shit has to stop."

"It will not cease until my work is complete."

"Your work is done. Just let it all go. Quit working for the enemy and just retire."

Balthazar raised his hands, shoving Belinda, Galen, and Colton to the floor. Holding them in place with a sort of spiritual bind. Only he and Vail remained standing.

"Why are you doing this?"

"Because I have a master to praise. One who granted me these gifts. I must serve him with all my might."

"Then, your master has to deal with me. And others out there."

"My master's coming was already thwarted by someone. I will not allow the Cryptic Zone to remain shut. He will rise."

"No, he won't."

"And what will you do when he rises and comes for you?"

"Don't all malevolent forces come for me? It's my job to piss your kind off."

"How about a deal."

"A what now?"

"A deal. You leave me to my work and I let your friends live."

"Um, deal declined. However, I can offer you a deal."

"Like so?"

"Let my friends go or find yourself entering Hell a little early than you expected."

"You cannot kill me." Balthazar declared. "No man can murder me!"

"I'm not going to murder you. I'm simply going to offer you a trip. Besides, best you deal with me and not Kamagrauto."

Balthazar froze. His eyes went wider.

"Kamagrauto?" Balthazar asked.

"Yes. You know, lieutenant demon. Works for Dagor the Soul

Eater. That kind of guy. He knows of your work by the way. Told me of it. Raising the first sins and all. Plague doctors and such. He knows. And if he knows, who's the say the others know as well."

Balthazar shook, dropping the hold on Belinda, Galen, and Colton. Vail smirked.

"They will not have me." Balthazar said. "My master will protect me!"

"Then, let's see him protect you from this."

Vail raised up his hand, shoving Balthazar down. He began to chant and before he could start, a whirlwind of blue flames surrounded Balthazar. Taking him away. The room was silent. Galen approached the spot. Belinda and Colton were confused.

"The hell just happened?" Colton asked.

"His master took him." Vail said.

"What of the first sins?" Belinda asked. "What of the doctors?"

"We'll see if they still stand." Donovan said.

They returned to the entrance, discovering the doctors are gone. Vail knew Balthazar's fear had driven the doctors and the first sins away. He smirked as they left the shop. The case was done. Yet, Balthazar was somewhere in the world. Possibly in other realms of existence. Vail knew he would see him again down the road.

With everyone returning to their proper places, Vail sat inside his own domain, researching more on the sin entity Kamagrauto mentioned in their conversation. There, Vail discovered there's an ancient power had risen, which is the cause for the sin entity's presence.

"In my line of work, things happen for the worst. Usually the better."

He knew the power was far too great for himself to face. By that standard, Vail went to visit a friend. A friend in Washington D.C.

THE DEVILHUNTER: UNSEEN WORSHIP

I

A CROWDED AFFAIR

Strange worshippers rushed into an empty church during the night. Carrying books, candles, staves, and many other objects. Laying them around in a circle. They were cloaked in black, scarlet, and violet robes and hoods. One of the black hoods lit a fire in the circle of the objects. There were a dozen worshippers in the church as they went down on their knees and began to pray.

"Oh, Great Lord. We call upon your name this night. To guide us to your magic's and to your mysteries. Reveal unto us your truths and your words. Grant us the power we so crave. For it is our sole duty to serve you."

Immediately, the church doors bolted open, revealing a man of an Eastern descent. He entered the church, raising up a shotgun and began shooting at the worshippers. The ran throughout the church as he fired at them. Killing them with every shot. He took a moment to reload the weapon and one of the hooded ones attacked him from behind. Stumbling, he caught himself and faced the attacker.

"Tell me." The man said. "Where is your lord?"

"For he is here. He is everywhere."

"You have me all wrong. He's not with you. You're speaking of someone else. Someone from another realm."

"You know." The hooded one said. "Then, our task is complete."

"What do you mean?"

"A sacrifice. A blood sacrifice had to be made of our lives and you've delivered it to our master, who is near."

"Who is your master? Tell me?"

"*Sit laus Festinatio.*" The hooded one said before the man blew his head off.

The man sighed. He searched the church, only to find the objects the hooded ones brought in and the circle of fire. Pouring dirt from the outside atop the fire to put it out, he discovered a pentagram was carved into the wooden floor and the fire was lit above it. He scoffed.

"I knew you were the ones."

This man is Gabriel Abraham. Known to the supernatural community as Abraham The Devil Hunter or simply The Devilhunter. Abraham walked out of the church with the ringing voice of the hooded one's words. Spoken in Latin. Abraham knew what he said and what he told him was, "*Praise Hastur.*"

Abraham returned to his facility, called the Revelation Center. Inside, he entered his office, where could be seen the document containing the mystery of the Mutant-Thing, and his writings of the encounter with Travis Vail, Cinderella, and The Swordman. Moving those aside, he grabbed an old history book from the shelf and sat down to read. There, flipping through the pages, he came across a page dedicated to a ancient demon known as Hastur.

"Why bring you here?" Abraham questioned. "A blood sacrifice he said."

Knocking came from the front door. Abraham heard it and walked over. Opening the door to reveal a man and a woman. They were startled as the door opened, seeing Abraham with the book in hand. The man was in his late 20s. A handsome one, dressed in slacks and a buttoned shirt with his sleeves up. The young woman was in mid 20s, an modest looking woman in jeans and a low-cut shirt. she wore little makeup, which intrigued Abraham.

"Are you Gabriel Abraham?" The woman asked. "The Gabriel Abraham?"

"Who's asking?"

"You might not remember me." The young man said.

"Tell me your name." Abraham said.

"Evan Wyatt. We've spoken once before concerning science and religion. Before your tragedy."

"Oh. Well, it's been a very long time."

"It has, sir."

"And who is this woman accompanying you?"

"Andrea Coralline."

"Ah. Hispanic descent. It truly shows. Yet, the name doesn't fit the credentials of your nation."

"It's what happens when foreigners come and raid your land."

"Duly noted." Abraham chuckled. "Come in."

Evan and Andrea entered the Center, seeing the number of statues and artifacts sitting within its walls. Abraham shut the door and stood toward them, closing the book in hand.

"Tell me why you've come to seek me out."

"There's been some strange activity going on in the world." Andrea said. "Stuff that hasn't been seen for centuries."

"And how do you know of this?"

"I am a paranormal investigator and part-time occult detective."

"Evan, what of yourself?"

"I'm new to all of this. I met Andrea after she rescued me from a group of Satanists. They ganged up on me and I couldn't defend myself."

"Pulled into a world you're not familiar with."

"Yes. Is the reason you're doing all of this because of losing your wife and daughter."

"I know what attacked them that day. Took them away from me and now I have the means to fight back."

"By making sure no one else has the same experience."

"Yes. It is a task I must do."

Abraham walked over to the statue of Baphomet, which sat in the front of the Center, yet it was scarred ad burnt. Appeared to be the case of someone attempting to destroy the statue by any means and failing to do so.

"Why are you here?" Abraham asked again.

"We need your help in stopping these activities."

"There's plenty of occult detectives roaming the world. Why didn't you contact Dr. Galen Donovan or the Spirit-Seeker? Why me?"

"Because we believe you would be the one to help us and equip us in this life."

"You want me to be your teacher."

"Something like that."

"Then, you have an even bigger concern. I had a group of pupils once. Until we lost a member. Beth Grasslands. A young girl on the verge of presenting the existence of demons to the public. But, she was taken from us and the pupils ran. Never to enter this job again."

"Was she killed?" Evan asked.

"I don't think so. Few of the pupils claimed she vanished into a wormhole. Probably trapped in another dimension or another world. However, she is lost to us. Lost to me and I will not allow such an act happen again to anyone under my wing."

"I'm sorry for your losses." Evan said. "Truly."

"Don't be. Just be certain others will not share in such a tragedy."

"Then, teach us. Help us in this matter."

Abraham sighed. "What are you seeking?"

"We discovered a succubus that lives in this city. We know how to find her, and we need your help in killing her."

"A succubus?" Abraham said. "Intriguing. Besides demons, there's more entering the land of the living."

"What do you mean?" Evan asked.

"I will explain on the way."

Abraham grabbed his coat and approached the door. He turned back, seeing Andrea and Evan just standing there. Lost for words and movement. Abraham chuckled.

"Are you going to show me where this succubus dwells?"

"Oh, yeah." Andrea said. "Right."

"Of course, sir." Evan said. "Andrea knows better than me."

Leaving the building and entering Abraham's vehicle, dating back to the 1970s, Abraham drove off from the Center.

II

SEDUCTION OF THE HUNTER

"What is your goal once this is all done?" Andrea asked.

"My goal?" Abraham said. "The only goal is to make sure no one else suffers in such a way as I. Besides, I am aware my job will be done once I'm dead."

"How many things have you encountered since you began this role as a demon hunter?" Evan wondered.

"I've come across many strange things. From ghosts, ghouls, demons, myths and legends. Hell, I've met a fairy tale figure and the Mythological Man."

"Never heard of a Mythological Man." Evan said.

"What fairy tale figure did you meet?" Andrea asked. "I'm curious."

"A famous one."

"But, which one? You'll have to be specific with me."

"Glass slippers. Fairy Godmother. You know."

"Oh. That one. So, does she really wear a nice dress and glass slippers?"

"No. Her dress is far from what the stories tell."

Abraham continued to drive, nearing the outskirts of Washington D.C. He looked around, only seeing the wilderness.

"Now, where does this succubus dwell? Where's the location?"

"In these woods." Andrea said. "Truly, she stays there mostly."

"Are you sure?"

"I am. Came across her during a walk."

"You were walking out here? By yourself?"

"Yeah. I wasn't harmed. The succubus wouldn't attack me. I'm a woman."

"Gender doesn't matter to a succubus. Believe me. They will take whatever they can get."

Abraham stopped the car. They exited and walked into the wilderness. Rarely any other vehicles passed by, which he noticed immediately. Walking deeper into the forest, Abraham spotted a shrine. Gesturing his hand toward Andrea and Evan quickly.

"Stop."

"What is that?" Evan asked.

"It's hers. And from where it sits, she's very close."

The trees behind the shrine rustled and from there, arose a woman wearing a blue silk dress, her wavy black hair mixed with the colors of the forest and the dress. Her eyes glistened with the moon as did her red lips.

"You've come." She said. "Beautiful."

"That her?" Abraham asked.

"It is." Andrea said. "She's the one."

Abraham nodded, turning his focus toward the woman.

"What is your name, succubus?"

"Those who damn me call me whole, prostitute, cunt, bitch, and anything else you wish to harm me with. But, those who love me and desire my fruits, they call me Sierra."

"Well then, Sierra. I am Gabriel Abraham. The Devilhunter and I am here to grant you leave from Washington D.C. and its surrounding neighbors."

"Oh. I just came here and I'm not going anywhere."

"What makes you say that?"

"Because, I'm here on orders from someone higher than my rank. Someone who knows what you did to his worshippers in that church."

"You work for Hastur?"

"Does it make you feel unconformable?"

"No. but, it gives me all I need to know about you."

Sierra turned her glance toward Evan. She smiled, gesturing him to come forward. Evan moved toward her without noticing. Andrea looked at him strangely. Unaware of his motive.

"What are you doing?" She asked.

"Evan, fight it!" Abraham yelled. "She's luring you with her power. Don't submit to it."

"Honey, it's all right. I will not hurt him. Only pleasure him in ways the human woman cannot do."

Evan moved closer to the point where Sierra's fingers rubbed his cheek. Abraham moved forward, knocking Evan to the ground. There, he raised up his gun, aimed at Sierra.

"Step back, demon."

"You wouldn't shoot me." Sierra laughed. "I'm only here to give a love unfamiliar to humanity. The love of your dreams. Love that will make even the toughest man wet himself of relief."

"Don't try it." Abraham gestured; gun aimed closely.

Sierra laughed, backing up into the shadow of the forest. As she backed away, her eyes glowed and from there, she jumped out with a screech. Her beautiful face was gone and had transformed into one of a monster. Long, sharp fangs came out of her mouth. She didn't appear human anymore. She was no what she truly is. A demon.

"Andrea, get Evan out of here now!" Abraham yelled, firing at Sierra.

Andrea grabbed Evan and ran out of the forest to the car. Behind them, they could hear the gunshots firing mixed with Sierra's screeching. In the forest, Abraham moved and dodged Sierra's claw swipes. He shot her in the shoulder and hip, but she kept moving. Shaking his head, he kicked her to the ground and stepped on her right leg.

"I'm finishing you off."

Sierra's screech turned into another sound. One of a calling and Abraham knew it. He backed up from her before shooting her in the leg. She couldn't stand up and the screech grew louder. Andrea and Evan were in the car. Andrea turned, seeing Abraham running from the wilderness.

"Take the keys." Abraham said, tossing the keys to Andrea.

"What are you doing?"

"She called some of her friends. I'm going to hold them off."

"You can't."

"I can. Take Evan back to the Center. I will meet you there once I'm done with these things."

"How will you get back?"

"I'll find a way. Now go."

Andrea paused and nodded. Entering the car and driving away. As soon as she went forward, she could see a horde come from the forest. A horde of demons. They rushed toward Abraham and he began to fight them off with his gun, later pulling out a silver sword from his coat. Last thing Andrea could see was Abraham cutting down the demons with the sword as she was more distant from the spot, returning to the Center.

III

ALL FOR ONE

Abraham battled the hordes around him with his gun and sword. Slashing towards any of them who stepped closer. He looked around the area, no sign of Sierra. He figured she remained in the woods to keep herself from further harm. The horde suddenly froze in motion. Abraham was dumbfounded as he walked past them, their eyes did not blink, nor did they breathe. It was as if a switch was turned off within them. Abraham sighed.

"The hell is going on?"

The horde went back into motion, walking backwards into the forest. Abraham slashed the ones closets to them to avoid more entering, however, they did not harm him and as the last one entered the forest, the trees closed together.

"Something's not right about this." Abraham breathed.

Meanwhile, Andrea and Evan returned to the Center, only to find it covered with Worshippers of Hastur. Andrea stopped the car near the entrance and froze. Evan began to wake up from the hit by Abraham and saw the hooded figures surrounding the building.

"Holy shit!" Evan said.

"Damn it!" Andrea responded. "Keep your voice down."

The worshippers stood still. They were chanting Hastur's name. all in motion and quietly. Their hands were to their side and their heads down. Faces couldn't be seen due to the hoods. Andrea and Evan remained still.

"What are we going to do?" Evan asked.

"I'll call Gabriel. Hopefully he's still alive."

"What happened with him?"

"After you succumb to Sierra's charms, Gabriel knocked you out to keep her from killing you. There, a horde of Hastur's kind came out of the forest. Gabriel fought them off for me to get us out of there."

Andrea dialed on her cell phone and it rang. Across the city, Abraham was walking down the sidewalk, leaving the forest. He can feel his phone vibrating in his jacket, he took it out.

"Yes."

"Good, you're still alive. I have some news to tell you."

"Same here." Abraham said. "What's yours?"

"Hastur's worshippers are at the Center."

"Seriously?"

"Yes."

Evan tapped her, pointing to the worshippers, she gazed as she saw them entering the Center.

"Um, Abraham, they're entering the Center."

"Who left a door open?"

"No one. It looks like they're being guided in. Someone else is inside."

"Hastur." Abraham uttered. "I'm on my way. Stay put!"

Abraham hung up and started running. Andrea and Evan remained in the car. Once the worshippers were in, they exited Abraham's car and crept up to the windows. There, they could see who else was inside and it was Hastur himself. Standing in the spot where the Baphomet statue was once placed.

"I didn't know he looked like that." Evan said.

"Me either."

Hastur's appearance was of a full demon. Had to be around ten or twelve feet in height. He had wings on his back, he wore a tunic and he had ram horns on his head. His eyes were red as blood and his feet resembled goat's hooves.

"What do we do?" Evan asked. "He's too strong for us to take on ourselves."

"We wait on Gabriel."

"Are you sure he's coming?"

"I'm positive."

IV

FALLEN'S WAY

Within the Center, Hastur's worshippers began to bow down to him. He stood tall, savoring the scenery. Andrea and Evan continued to watch through the window from the outside. Abraham was inching closer to the Center as he continued moving.

"This place is covered with symbolism." Hastur said with a deep voice. "A haven for my enemies."

"What are we going to do?" Evan asked.

"We wait here for Gabriel to come."

"What if Hastur leaves before he makes his way back?"

"I don't know. But, I have something in mind."

"Like what?"

"It may be stupid. However, I believe it's worth a shot."

"Tell me what it is."

The doors bolted open and Andrea and Evan entered with weapons in their hand. The worshippers all turned their heads toward them at the same time. Hastur glared at them with a smirk.

"This part of your plan?" Evan uttered.

"Not really." Andrea said. "But, we're inside."

Who are you two?" Hastur asked. "You're not native to this place."

"How do you know?" Andrea asked.

"Your scent comes from another place. Another field. This building isn't your home. It's someone else's"

"He's on his way here." Evan said. "He's the one who took out your worshippers in that abandoned church."

Hastur took a step forward toward Andrea and Evan. They stood their ground, yet, Evan took one step back out of fear of the tall demon.

"What is his name?"

"My name is Gabriel Abraham." Came a voice from the entrance.

Hastur looked, along with Andrea and Evan. Abraham stood at the door and behind him, a blue car had vanished from the entrance. Driving away with speed.

"How did you get back?" Andrea asked.

"Someone gave me a ride."

"You killed my worshippers?" Hastur asked.

"Yes." Abraham replied. "Your kind are a cancer to the world. I am one of the few who is determined to put you back in your place."

"A demon hunter." Hastur scoffed. "I've met many throughout the eons of this creation."

"Abraham raised up his silver sword. Pointing it toward the demon.

"Let's see who survives this day."

"I'm not here to kill you, demon hunter." Hastur said. "I've come to mark my territory for the coming war."

"What war?" Andrea asked.

"The war of the heavens. This city is only one of the spots upon the earth that will suffer from its cause. You've chosen a bad place to dwell, demon hunter."

"I'll take my chances."

Abraham rushed over, swiping the sword against Hastur's leg.

The burning flowed through him as he roared in pain. The worshippers rose up from the floor, coming towards Abraham. Hastur extended his hand, stopping them. He stared at Abraham.

"No battle is worth much bloodshed and tragedy this day. Yet, I give you this warning. I will return soon and when I do, it will be our battle. One of us will not live to tell the story."

"I intend on waiting and I will win."

Hastur grinned and warped into a fiery wormhole, sucking in the worshippers as well, including the Baphomet statue. The wormhole shut. Evan approached its spot and sighed.

"So, can we stay?" Andrea asked. "You can teach us as we asked."

"Fine." Abraham said. "I'll teach you."

Sometime later, while Abraham worked in his office, a knock came from the door. Abraham rose up to answer it and as he stood up, he saw a man standing at the office door. Wearing all black besides a white buttoned shirt. The man had his hands in his coat pocket. Abraham was staring at Travis Vail, the Spirit-Seeker.

"Too soon." Vail said with a grin.

THE MAN CALLED FABLE: THE MAGE AND THE
CON

I

<u>WANT TO HAVE A CONVERSATION?</u>

In the rift between the natural world and the magical realm, Pandora, a cloaked and hooded woman powerful within magic has summoned Kurt Wesker, who's known in the magic realm as The Man Called Fable. Fable, decked out in his brown duster coat, slacks, boots, and open-buttoned shirt stares at Pandora with confusion. His scruffy hair and facial hair moved with the brushing of the wind between the rift. The rift was warped with many colors, flowing up and down and around. Looked as if one could be hallucinating.

"You know why I summoned you." Pandora said.

"I'm familiar with the setting and all, but, I was in the middle of a card game. I had it won."

"Meaning you would lead the magical creatures out into the open as you've done before?"

"Not exactly. See, what happened that day was not my fault. Just a troll and his friends having some emotional issues. That's all."

"Then, what happened to Erkac the satyr was just a coincidence?"

Fable shrugged his shoulders and cocked his head with a smile.

"He wanted to go for a job. I spoke to him only a word and he took off. Exercise helps even the satyr kind."

"Never mind the past, Fable. I have called you because of a dire concern."

"What concern would have me involved?"

"Your thoughtless actions, moving between the natural and magical realms has sent out tears between the realms. Due to that, we've discovered an entity of the magical realm has returned and is looking to make the natural world his own."

"Does this guy have a name? Something that I can keep track of?"

"His name, we do not know."

Fable approached Pandora, looking her in the eyes. Her glowing warped eyes. They warped as the walls around them.

"No name?" Fable asked. "Hmm. I'll figure something out. You won't like it, but it will be done."

Fable walked toward the rift, preparing his way out.

"Tread carefully, Fable." Pandora commanded. "For this foe could be anywhere at any time."

Fable turned to Pandora and grinned.

"I'll be fine." Fable said as he walked through the rift, vanishing from Pandora's eyes.

Back in the natural world, Denise Kira, a reporter has been tracking down evidence of many cases since the rise of the heroes across the world. Kira searched the city of Manchester for any heroes of its own. After three months of searching, she's found one. In Fable himself.

II

<u>GREETING A CON ARTIST WITHOUT MAGIC</u>

During the night in Manchester, Fable entered a peculiar bar. One in the middle of the city. A bar full of magical creatures. As he stepped in, a troll sitting at a table in the center, waved his hand in the air.

"You've shown up."

"Of course, I would." Fable said. "Why wouldn't I?"

Fable went and sat at the table. Being surrounded by more trolls and a goblin. Fable smirks at the young woman at the bar, sipping her drink. The troll sitting down shook his head in disgust.

"Your kind have that problem deeply rooted."

"What problem?"

"The deep attraction for the opposite sex. It clouds your judgment."

"You believe that doll at the bar will cloud my chances of winning tonight?"

"Absolutely. Because I will leave here the winner and a richer man."

"Em. I wouldn't go around calling yourself a man. You're a troll, dude."

"You get the fucking point!"

"Sure, man. Sure. Figure of speech. I get it."

They began to play. Gaining a larger crowd by every hit. The bar door opened and Denise entered. She cannot believe what she is seeing, a place full of magic beings. She walked past satyrs, elves, fairies, and she looked ahead, seeing the crowd surrounding Fable and the troll during their card game.

"It's him." She said to herself.

Fable and the troll continued their game of cards. Rallying on the crowd. Full of beer and cheers. Fable laid on the table, a set of yellow cards with a large red circle in the middle, surrounded by four black circle and a triangle in the center of the circle. A connected double dash was also on the cards. The troll stared at the cards, gazing toward Fable with confusion.

"I've never seen those before."

"There's a rare type. I'll let you have them if you can beat me."

"Then, you've already given them to me."

The troll laid his cards on the table. The crowd startled. Fable looked concerned as the troll laughed. Fable showed a faint grin, placing one of the strange cards on the table. The troll bounced from the table with anger.

"You bastard! You cheated!"

"No." Fable grinned. "I won. Fair play."

"Son of a bitch!" The troll yelled, jumping over to the table, attacking Fable.

The crowds broke the two apart as Fable reached, retrieving the strange cards. Placing them in his duster pocket. Fixing his coat, he raised his hands in the air.

"It's cool, guys. It's cool. I won and now I'm going to leave."

"You better leave, boy." The troll uttered. "Don't think me one like Erkac and his goons."

"Why does everyone know about my situation with Erkac?"

"Shit travels."

"Well played." Fable laughed.

Fable turned to leave, bumping into Denise. He stared at her and she stared back. Their eyes locked onto one another.

"Hello." Fable said.

"Hi." Denise replied.

The two continued to stare until Fable nodded and left the bar. Denise took a moment to take in the scene and she too left the bar. Outside, she looked around, spotting Fable ahead.

"Excuse me!" Denise yelled.

Fable turned around, seeing Denise approaching him.

"What have I done now?" Fable asked.

"Nothing. Nothing at all."

"Then, what do you want?"

"I have to ask. Are you the man they call Fable?"

"Heh. The Man Called Fable. Nice ring to it. Um, what do you think? Do I look like The Man Called Fable?"

"I don't know. I've never seen him before. But, back in the bar, your actions and your dress suits what I've read about him."

"Wait, read? Where?"

"There's many sightings concerning Fable." Denise said.

"People are writing about me?"

"So, you are Fable."

"Spotted. Yes, I am Fable. The Man Called Fable."

"Then, the rift between our world and the magical realm is true."

"How do you know so much about this world and the magic realm?"

"I've done a lot of studying."

"Like, how much studying? Did you get any sleep from all of this discovery? A revelation deprived you of sleep?"

"One thing I must ask, have you ever considered traveling to

London to assist their vigilante?"

"What vigilante?"

"The woman."

"Oh. We both know fairy tale figures do not exist."

"Then, why have I just left a bar where you were fighting a troll. A bar surrounded by magical creatures."

Fable paused. He nodded with a wink.

"The world isn't what the general public believes it to be."

"Please, I want to know more about this magical realm. What lies in it? How much of magic are we to know is true?"

"Enough to live without a crisis."

"I have more questions for you, Fable."

"Then, you know where to find me." Fable smiled, walking away.

Fable turned a corner with a smile on his face. As he turned, Pandora was waiting for him, startling him.

"Don't do that."

"What were you doing?"

"What do you mean? I wanted to have some fun at the bar. Probably a little too much fun."

"I'm not talking about your little scuffle in the bar."

"Then, I'm lost."

"Speaking with a human woman concerning their world and the magic realm."

"She already knew."

"Yet, you were present for her to continue asking questions. She already knew of your existence."

"About that. How did she know?"

"Erkac."

Fable sighed. "You can't be serious."

"It is true."

"That little incident couldn't have traveled such far lengths."

"Well, it did. Your actions are causing much more harm than good."

"Is that what the growing power is all about? My actions? Speaking of which, what of this force you warned me about?"

"We've discovered his name."

"That's a start. What is it, Pandora? The name."

"Emblem."

"Sounds like a necklace."

"This is no joking matter. Emblem is a powerful magician. A wizard from the ancient past. He has returned with malevolent intentions in mind. As for now, do not speak with those outside the magical realm. We don't need any more innocent lives in danger."

Fable nodded.

"I understand."

"I will speak to you soon."

Pandora vanished in a rift between the worlds. Fable stood there and nodded.

"Ok." Fable walked off.

Behind him, Denise stood by the corner of the building. She has seen and heard everything.

"What the fuck?"

III

SURROUNDED BY FOUR CORNERS

Fable returned to his home, a shack in the Cheshire Plain. Upon opening the door, Fable stopped and stared, seeing four hooded individuals standing in his home. Dressed in gold-and-white robes. Their faces hidden by the hoods. Fable entered the home, slamming the door.

"Figured you guys would show up."

One of the hooded ones approached Fable slowly, standing before him with a greater height.

"You guys are much taller than I originally remember."

"Pandora has spoken to you about Emblem?"

"Yes. She told me about the guy. I haven't seen him."

"But, you will assist us in stopping him from gaining strength from the rift."

"Yeah. About that." Fable said, walking toward the kitchen. "This whole thing isn't part of my job. Remember, I'm a con artist. One who touts magic as his weapon."

"We know of your persona here in the physical realm. But, what shall you do when the realms merge by Emblem's growing power?"

"Look, four hoods, I have been doing this life since I was a lad, now, I am positive there are others out there who know about the magic realm that can assist you in taking out this Emblem guy. Not me."

"Emblem is already on this plane. His powers are growing and very soon, he will warp this reality and merge in with the magic realm. Afterwards, all of life will be in his hand."

Fable grabbed a beer bottle from the refrigerator, approaching the hooded one. He opened the bottle and took a sip with a grin on his face.

"Then, you don't need me."

The hooded one turned toward his brethren as they stood around Fable. He glanced around, seeing the four standing and staring at him. Fable took another sip of the beer and held it out.

"You guys want a beer or something?"

"Soon, you will understand there is more consequences to this world than you've been led to believe."

"I'll take my chances."

The four vanished through a sudden rift. Leaving Fable's home. He drank the beer and sighed.

"A visit from the Hidden Four is always a means for another drink."

Denise arrived at her apartment, shutting the door and turning on the light. Putting down her bag, she turned around, only to find Pandora standing in her apartment. She started to yell, but, Pandora waved her hand, muting the sound of the scream.

"Keep quiet." Pandora commanded.

Denise nodded, Pandora removed the mute from her mouth. Denise moved over slowly, towards the table as Pandora continued to stand in place.

"I saw you. Speaking with Fable near the bar."

"I figured you did. Which is why I'm here in your domain."

"What do you want with me?"

"I have come to warn you."

"Warn me of what?"

"Fable."

"What about him?"

"He's a dangerous man."

"He didn't seem so bad during our conversation."

"The more you interact with him, the more the magical realm learns of your existence and your knowledge of its presence. I am giving you a chance to save your life before you place it into further harm."

"So, it's all real." Denise breathed. "All of it. The rift. Fable's magic knowledge. Placing within this world where the magical creatures dwell. It's all true."

"Yes, and it is for the better you do not entertain the idea of entering such a world. Your life among the humans is enough for one such as yourself."

"But, there is so much to learn about the magical realm. How it was formed. Who formed it and why does it exist? Questions much of the world should truly know."

"The rising heroes have already gained your world's attention. They do not need more details into the true reality of this existence. For it may bring damnation into your lives and eventually take you away from it."

Denise nodded with confusion.

"I don't get this. Why keep such a large secret hidden?"

"None of your concern." Pandora said. "Do not interact with Fable. Heed my words."

Pandora snapped her fingers, within a blink of an eye she was gone. Denise lost for words once more. Shaking her head, rubbing her hand across her forehead.

IV

<u>ONLY A CON COULD BREAK THIS STORY</u>

Above Manchester, the clouds began to roar with thunder. Lightning flashed across the sky. Through the clouds, came down a man with the appearance of a general. Dressed in gold and red armor with a hint of white in the lining. He wore a golden helmet with only his glowing white eyes to be seen. He hovered in the air, looking down at the city.

"This is what they've managed to construct? This is what they perceive to be civilization! I have done much more and thus shall I do again."

He extended his arms and lightning poured out from the clouds onto the city. Striking the buildings and the streets. Cars drove off the roads to avoid the crashing bolts. The man laughed as he continued to maintain the bolts coming down. Elsewhere, the thunder could be heard, and Fable felt it from his home, going outside, he looked out, seeing the lightning bolts crashing.

"The hell is that?"

"That is Emblem." Pandora appeared from behind him. "And he has already begun his purpose."

"Then, why aren't you and the Four stopping him?" Fable wondered. "You have the power to do so."

"It is not our place."

"Not your place? But, it's mine?"

"This is your world. Your domain. You reside here. It is of your concern to deal with the Fallen King before he takes this world and merges it with the magical realm."

"I think you're all forgetting who I am. I'm a con artist who happens to know a lot about magic. I've lived in the magical realm for a time. Yes, I am human. This is my world. Yet, I am not the one who's set to take down some ancient dictator."

"But, you are. For I've seen your future. Standing side by side with others like yourself, taking on threats far greater than Emblem alone. This is only the beginning of your fate, Kurt Wesker. Do not throw it away out of the spirit of fear."

Fable sighed. Walking over to the table, he drank the remainder of the beer in the bottle and grabbed his duster from the wall. Putting it on, he approached the door before turning to Pandora.

"I'll see what I can do. But only on one condition?"

"Such is?"

"You stand beside me and face him."

"I can do that."

Fable nodded.

"Finally. Something she can do. Great."

Emblem continued to decimate Manchester as he glanced up into the air, seeing a tear forming in between the realms. He yelled as the rift began to open. The physical world and the magic realm meeting. Inching closer together.

"I will create the perfect utopia. One many of which have yet to witness. A new world for all creatures. For all creation."

A quick blast came from the ground, hitting Emblem in the chest. As he felt the attack, the rift slowly closed. Emblem looked down toward the ground, where he saw Fable and Pandora. His eyes locked on Pandora.

"You live!"

"End this treachery, Emblem." Pandora commanded. "This is not the ancient time anymore."

"Still abiding by the rules! After all these eons, you have yet to learn the truth about independence."

"I know much. Though, I am not a traitor to my own kind or to my people!"

"Such folly coming from your mouth. Have you forgotten the lives you cost after the first failing?!"

"No. I have only learned to move on."

Fable glanced between the two. Confused and uneasy.

"What's going on here?" He asked.

Emblem came down to the streets. Standing before Fable and Pandora as the lightning bolts continued to fall.

"You managed to gain another apprentice." Emblem said.

"Apprentice? What does he mean?"

"This man is not my apprentice. He is here to stop you."

"A human? You've brought a human to stop me? Do you remember where we're from? The things we can do. The worlds we can shape and the lives we can destroy? We are gods among men, Pandora!"

"He's dissing me, isn't he?" Fable asked.

"Don't get distracted."

"I have an idea. Hold on."

Fable walked toward Emblem. No fear, though to be seen. Emblem stood still as Fable approached him. Pandora didn't make a move, only watched on. Fable stood up to Emblem, raising his head as Emblem's height far surpasses Fable's own.

"You're one tall dude."

"Have you come to kneel at my feet, human?"

"Kneel? No. I've come for a different reason."

"And what may that be?"

"Well, since this is our first encounter, I only have to ask one question."

"A question?"

"Do you like fireworks?"

"Fireworks?!"

"Yeah. Allow me to demonstrate."

Fable stepped back and from his side, he pulled out a smoke bomb. Tossing it into Emblem's face. Emblem fanned the smoke from his sight as Pandora rushed over, grabbing Emblem by his arms and slamming him into the pavement. Fable ran over and pulled out his revolver, loaded with magic-infused rounds. He aimed the gun toward Emblem's head.

"Over that fast?" Fable asked.

"Over?" Emblem said. "This is only the start of things to come!"

Emblem snapped his fingers and the storm ceased. A rift had opened as Emblem kicked Fable and Pandora from him. He jumped into the rift as it shut. Fable and Pandora looked around the spot, no sign of Emblem nor the rift.

"Aw man." Fable said. "I thought this would've gone much longer. I had him."

"No, you were toying with him."

"Trust me, I did more than just toy with the guy. Gave him something to remember me by."

"And what is that?"

"The smoke. wasn't exactly smoke. They were nano-sized fairies. Grabbed them from a pack of neo-witches. See, the fairies will place a tracking signal on Emblem wherever he goes, and the fairies are magic-resistance."

"That doesn't make any sense." Pandora said.

"I know. That's why it's not true."

"What?"

"Just highly-concentrated pixie dust I picked up from a card game."

Pandora shook her head in utter disgust with some shame, walking away from Fable.

"I will find Emblem. You have much to learn, Kurt Wesker."

"You're welcome. And Uh, it's Fable, Pandora. Fable. Remember. F. A. B. L.-"

"I know your name!"

Pandora disappeared from the area. Fable looked around, only to see some scared civilians and crashed vehicles. He nodded.

"Oh, well."

Fable went away and within the crowds of frightened people, Denise was there. Writing down everything she saw with every inch of detail possible.

CINDERELLA: MIDNIGHT STRIKES

I

<u>TREACHERY IN THE FAMILY</u>

A pair of well-armed men gather goods from a facility used by one of the top criminal organizations in London. Their faces covered with masks, dressed in black uniforms, wearing bulletproof vests, cargo pants, and boots. While packing up the boxes into the black van, three of them stand to the side, keeping watch of the area.

"Don't think any officers will come by tonight?"

"Nah. It's not the officers that concern me."

"Then who?"

"You heard about that figure that took out the guys at the warehouse some time ago?"

"Yeah. Thought it was just a made-up story."

"No. It happened. Guys in the group thought The Swordman came here to do some work. But, one of the men said it wasn't a man. But, a woman."

"Pfft! A woman?! I'm not falling for such a story."

"Why not? He told the officers it was a woman that took them all out. By herself."

"That's where I draw the line. No way a woman can take out that number of men on her own. Not possible. Science says so."

"That's the thing. There's something else about her. Something different."

"Only one thing different, she doesn't have balls. Simple math, boys."

Within the shadows, each of the men are taken out quickly and with sharp succession. Only leaving the three men speaking to one another. They turn, seeing the other men on the ground. Unconscious.

"What the hell?"

"What happened to them? I didn't even hear a thing."

"That's the whole purpose." said a voice from around them.

They turned around, scouting the area. Finding no one.

"Who said that?"

"I don't know, man. But, it's strange."

"Why is it strange?"

"Because it was a woman's voice."

One of the men turned back to the van, seeing something crouched atop the vehicle. He knew who it was. Aiming his gun.

"Shit! It's her!"

He began firing toward her as she dodged the rounds, moving from around the van to into the bushes nearby. The other two men looked around, not seeing what their ally has seen.

"She's here."

"That woman you spoke about?"

"Who else would I be talking about?"

"Nothing to worry yourself about. We'll take her out. End her little vigilante business quick, fast, and in a hurry."

They walked into the waist-high bushes of the field around them and quickly, she took out two of the men, leaving the one who did most of the disrespectful talk. He held his gun tightly, before it was grappled from him, falling into the bushes. He ran near the spot before being tripped. As he fell, he shook his head and rose up above the bushes, only to see the woman his ally spoke of.

"You have to be shitting me."

"Should've listened to your friend. He was telling the truth."

"You were the one who took out those guys at the warehouse? You?!"

"Who else did the man describe. From what I've heard, he said it was a woman. Don't I fit his description?"

"We don't need people like you in our country."

"Too bad. Besides, I'm from this country and I was born in this city. Technically, you're terrorizing my home."

"And what now? You've chose to stop it? Protect your city like those fools over in the West?"

"You could say that."

She kicked him in the face and he fell back into the bushes. Dazed.

"Remember to tell them my name when you wake up."

"Your name?"

"Yeah. You already know what it is."

She punched him as hard as she could. Knocking him out. Later, she searched the van, discovering the organizations involved in the operations. She shook her head reading the names listed on the file sheet.

"I'm closer to stopping you."

Folding the file sheet and placing it in her trench coat pocket, she left the area during the night. Leaving only the trail of unconscious thugs.

II

A NIGHT OUT

The next day, Cindy Lawson went walking with her close friend, Charlotte Queens. The two were out for a social call, grabbing a cup of coffee as they sat inside the coffee shop. Charlotte is mostly known for her red attire. Always dressed in either a red cloak or red scarf. A trademark of her own making. Her own dark hair matched even Cindy's. Cindy's apparel was one of a dark blue skirt and a black t-shirt. She also wore a scarf over her hair, reaching to the middle of her head.

"I have to ask. What happened with the case?"

"The case went well. Unfortunately, they didn't see things my way. But, it all worked out for the better."

"And what of your other duties?"

"What other duties?"

"Your sly ones during the night. Scouring around London like you're its Swordwoman."

"Funny."

"Speaking on that. Have you ever considered aiding those other heroes who have risen across the world?"

"I rather not. London is my territory."

"But, imagine the great things you can do. Like for example, you could travel to Manchester and aid their hero."

"The Fable guy? Not likely."

"He's nearby!"

"Not likely."

"Fine."

"What of your business?"

"Oh, I'm just cruising along. As always. Finding what fits me best."

In an office, Hale Prince, a fellow advocate for all Londoners prepared for his upcoming speech to the city. Most of the city has aligned themselves with Prince, while the others have agreed to the ideals of Cindy's Stepmother Anne. Prince and Anne have had disagreements for the past few months, leading them toward a political war to determine which one the city of London will side with.

During the fall of night, Cindy went out once more after gaining more information on her stepmother's plans for London. Leading her into the wilderness of Suffolk. While moving forward, she came across a strange odor. Covering her face from the stench. A rustling came from the bushes and quickly bolted out a shade, shoving Cinderella to the ground. Cindy looked, only seeing the shade's strange face and glowing red eyes.

"I've heard of you." Cinderella said.

Cinderella shoved the shade off her, standing up to face the strangeness. The shade morphed into a woman, wearing a dark cloak and ripped clothing. She carried a wooden staff with her.

"The Cannibalistic Witch." Cinderella uttered. "Never assumed you would be in Suffolk."

"I have a purpose to be here and I sensed your scent."

"Comforting. Why seek me out?"

"I have my orders."

"You're taking orders? From who?"

"None of your concern, Cinderella. All I have been assigned to do is to take you out. Kill you and your flesh shall be mine to consume."

"Not today."

Cinderella tossed a smoke bomb toward the Witch and tackled her to the ground. The Witch rose up and slammed the staff into the ground, causing a small tremor. Cinderella stood still as the Witch levitated and rushed toward her. Grabbing her by the throat. Cinderella began pounding the Witch's arm from her neck. Not knowing the full strength of the strange woman, Cinderella kicked the Witch in the face and stomped her into the ground.

"Who sent you?!" Cinderella yelled.

"Your theatrics will not work on me!"

"Maybe not. But, I know something will."

Cinderella pulled out a blade and sliced the Witch's arm. The Witch screeched with agony as the blade burned her skin. Cinderella held the blade over the Witch's head, set to strike.

"I know your weakness. Silver blade."

"I will never tell."

"Then, you leave me no choice."

Cinderella slammed her arm to kill the Witch, but she vanished into a portion of green mist. Cinderella searched the nearby areas and did not find her. Uncertain of the mystery, Cinderella continued her trail.

Hale Prince sat in his office reading a newspaper article titled 'The Cinderella Effect'. The article mentioned the existence of the rising heroes as well as Cinderella herself dwelling within London.

Unsure of the article's facts, Hale set himself to discover the famed Cinderella after he has dealt with Stepmother Anne and her plans for the city.

181

Anne gathered her two daughters and arranged a plot to foil Prince's plans for the city. She sent out her daughters to meet with Hale secretly as they dressed in scandalous clothing, resembling such garments of a harlot. Anne's plan was simple. To have her daughters seduce Hale in the exchange of his downfall, giving her free reign to make the final decisions of London and Cinderella was closer to discovering the full truth.

III

<u>YOU HAVE A GIFT</u>

Hale continued to work in his office. A knock came from the door and he looked up, only to see Anne's daughters, Angelina and Alexis. They shut Hale's door and approached the desk.

"Excuse me, ladies, why are you in here?"

"We were told you were expecting us." Angelina said.

"Then, you were misinformed. I wasn't expecting anybody. Now, please leave my office as I have work to do."

"He doesn't want us in here, sister." Alexis uttered.

"I can see. We'll have to force it on him."

"You're not doing anything. Now, please leave my office."

"No wonder our mother will take over this place." Alexis said.

"Your mother?" Hale questioned.

"You know her. You call her Anne."

"She's your mother? And she sent you both here? To do what?"

"What do you think, genius?" Alexis giggled.

"Look at us and admit the truth. You wouldn't mind it."

"Your own mother sent her daughters to seduce her competitor? Strange days indeed. But, there's nothing new under the sun."

"You would not deny us!" Alexis yelled.

"I just did. I am asking as politely as I can for the two of you to leave my office. Before I call security.”

Alexis stormed out of the office with Angelina following. She gazed at Hale, rolling her eyes before slamming the office door. Hale chuckled as he sat back down to his desk.

“Strange days indeed.”

Cinderella continued moving and found a place near Suffolk. The location was small, but unexpected by Londoners. She saw Anne speaking with a man. He was dressed in a trench coat and a fedora. She couldn’t hear their conversation, but she saw a stack of boxes in the back of the man’s van as he shut the door. He and Anne shook hands as he left the area.

“I will figure this out.” Cinderella said to herself.

Cinderella made a return to her home and she sat down to meditate. During the meditation, she began to hear the voices of her father and mother. Her hands were held out and open. While the voices of her parents continued, a glow emitted from her hands as she began having visions of her past. Flashbacks with her parents to her training with the Creed of Swords. She opened her eyes, now glowing along with her hands. She balled her hands up in a fist and the glow decreased as did the glow in her eyes.

“You have a gift.” Her mothers’ voice echoed.

She stood up and checked the clock, seeing it’s close to midnight. She grabbed her coat and hat, leaving her home to confront her stepmother.

IV

<u>MIDNIGHT STRIKES</u>

Cinderella returned to the very same warehouse as before. When she arrived, she saw not only her stepmother present, but her daughters as well. Cinderella chuckled before making her entrance into the warehouse. As she opened the doors, she found herself surrounded by armed men. Anne turned around, seeing her. Angelina and Alexis were confused to Cindy's choice of apparel.

"Hold on." Anne said. "Cindy?"

"Anne."

"What are you doing here and why are you dressed like that?"

"I have my reasons. I know what you're planning."

"Wait. The guys that were attacked in this place sometime ago, that was your doing?"

"Who else?" Cinderella smirked. "I'm doing what others refuse to do."

"Cindy is the Cinderella?" Angelina asked.

"Not possible." Alexis said. "She's too soft to do such a thing."

"I'm more than you realize. This city has suffered enough harm from people like you. I've come to bring a balance."

"You're treading on some dangerous waters, girl."

"Danger helps the cause."

Anne stepped forward, approaching Cindy. The two stood face to face. Anne was several inches taller than Cindy. Anne smirked.

"Don't follow this path. Being a hero. It won't end well for someone like you. You know better than this."

"True. But, I also know right from wrong and what you're plotting is beyond such natural evil."

"Hmm." Anne uttered.

She glanced at her watch, stepping back from Cindy. She signaled the armed men to approach Cinderella as she and the daughters prepared themselves.

"This isn't over." Cinderella said.

"I know. This should give you a fresh start."

The daughters left the warehouse. Anne looked back at Cindy and shook her head.

"I'm going to miss you very much."

"Touching."

"Midnight strikes, Cinderella."

Anne signaled the men to attack Cinderella and they rushed her. She attacked their legs and arms. Elbowing a few in their neck. She looked up and tossed a shuriken, breaking the light bulbs. Placing the warehouse into darkness. There, she began using stealth attacks to knock out the guards one by one. Cinderella exited the warehouse, only to see Anne and the daughters leaving in a car. Cindy could only stare and she watched closely.

While returning home, Cinderella was confronted by a strange force. Unseen by the natural eye as it grabbed her and tossed her into a nearby wall. She stood up, looking around. There was nothing. She returned to her home to receive a phone call. A call from Travis Vail, the Spirit-Seeker. Something urgent has happened and it requires the Sly Detective's skill set.

I

AFTERLIFE VISITOR

Gabriel Abraham turned around in his office, staring at the door. Where Travis Vail, the Spirit-Seeker stood. Vail had his hands in his coat pocket with a stern look on his face. Abraham was confused to Vail's unknown and sudden visit.

"Too soon." Vail said grinning.

"Why are you here?"

"Something's happening, and I can't handle it on my own."

"What do you mean?"

"Something huge. There's a powerful force that's rising beneath the earth. Preparing to make an entrance into our world. One that will certainly end all on this world."

"Demonic force?"

"Stronger."

"Good to see you two here." A voice said, coming from the lobby area of Abraham's Revelation Center.

Vail and Abraham left the office to find the stranger, standing in the lobby. He was of African descent and was dressed modestly. Brown slacks, shoes, with a long-sleeve shirt and vest. He also wore a black fedora. Vail and Abraham have never seen the man before in the fields.

"Who are you?" Vail asked.

"How did you get in?" Abraham questioned.

"Front door was open. Figured I would make myself in and on serious purpose."

"Your name, lad?" Vail said.

"Name stays with me. But, those in our field of work call me Papa Afterlife."

"Papa Afterlife?" Abraham said. "What kind of name is that?"

"Afterlife? As in the magician Papa Afterlife?"

"That would be me."

"Hmm." Vail said. "Funny, you're different that I thought."

"You know this man?"

"No. but, I've heard of his work across the Atlantic. Done some things in Africa, India, places as such."

"Good. Then, you have an idea as to why I'm here."

"Something of the sort."

"Now, what is this thing of serious purpose?"

"There's a dark force coming. Almost near the physical plane of this existence. I was planning on paying you both a visit at your residence. But, given the tow of you here now, makes the message all easier."

"And the message is?"

"This force is ancient. Very ancient. You came across the sin entity during your mission overseas, Vail. You've already sensed the power. Plus, there's a stronger entity roaming around called the Sin Phantom. The Phantom was already chased down by the Death Chaser and is still on the loose."

"Death Chaser?" Abraham said. "There's no such thing as one of them."

"You haven't been studying much have you." Afterlife uttered. "The Death Chaser has been around for ages. You'll need his help in stopping this coming threat."

"You're here to tell us to form a team?" Vail smirked. "Like the heroes over after the Retropolis incident."

"Something along those lines. Because, this threat cannot be stopped with just the two of you. You'll need a unit. One made up of detectives like yourselves, and other forces at work. Spiritual assassins, cryptids, anything you can get to muster up enough power to send this force back into the prison where it belongs."

"And will you be a part of this team?" Abraham asked.

"I'll be watching. An overseer if you so ask."

"Great." Vail said. "Watching from the sidelines."

"I can do more when I'm invisible to the enemy. Soon, you may find that out."

"One can only dream, sunshine."

Afterlife turned away, approaching the door. He stopped, turning back toward Vail and Abraham.

"Unify your members. You do not have much time."

Afterlife exited the Center. Vail turned to Abraham, who was confused about the entire scenario.

"You think Cinderella will be of use to us?"

"We'll have to ask her." Vail said. "Right now, we need to gather some information on possible recruits. If what Afterlife is saying is true, we will need all the help we can get."

II

CALLING THOSE THAT ARE ABOVE

Vail and Abraham set out on their journey to recruit the members possible for their unit. After doing some digging, Vail came up with a list of names. Through much research and sightings across the world, the names he chose were the ones felt closest to the possible unit.

"Where are we headed first?" Abraham asked.

"Chicago. There's a man out there who calls himself the Spiritual Assassin. Figured giving him a look will determine much more."

"His name?"

"John Terror." Vail said. "Supposedly, he's a nubreed."

"One of them. I see."

"Plus, he was in Retropolis during their incident. Means he's in good company with the rising heroes. Maybe he knows more than we do."

Vail and Abraham traveled from D.C. to Chicago. There, they came across a place in the outskirts of the city. Away from the public. They looked around, it's quiet and still.

"He's here?" Abraham asked.

"Said to be. Might as well knock on the door."

Abraham knocked, the door opened. They didn't see Terror, but

189

they saw his ally.

"Who are you guys?"

"We're detectives." Vail said. "Looking for John Terror. Heard he resides at this place."

"And how would you know that?"

"Like I said, lad, we're detectives."

"Then, you're pretty sloppy." A voice said from behind Vail and Abraham.

"Shit." Abraham said.

They turned around to see terror himself standing behind them with two guns pointed at their heads. Vail smirked while Abraham was unsure of what to do. Terror looked at the young man standing at the door.

"Carl, go inside. You two, follow him."

"Sure thing." Vail said.

They followed Carl into the hideout of Terror. They were placed at the chairs near the working table. Terror approached them, removing his black trench coat and sunglasses. He sat in front of them, measuring them from their size to potential skill set.

"I know what you're doing." Vail uttered.

"Good." Terror replied. "Now, tell me, why are two strange detectives suddenly at my door?"

"We're not ordinary detectives." Abraham said. "We're occult detectives."

"Occult detectives?"

"Yes." Vail said. "He is Gabriel Abraham. Known as the Devilhunter of Washington D.C. You've heard of the Revelation Center, haven't you?"

"Once or twice. And you are?"

"Travis Vail, the Spirit-Seeker. I travel much."

"Ok, so why are you here? Why come to me? And what for?"

"We are recruiting possible members for a team. There's a supernatural threat coming, and it could very well-"

"Not this shit again."

"What?" Vail asked. "What shit?"

"I've done my team shares with those heroes."

"The Retropolis Incident? We know all about it. That tells us, you aligned yourself with those major heroes. Swordman and the like. I have to ask, was this before or after The Swordman confronted the Mutant-thing in the woods?"

"How should I know?"

"Then, how did the two of you meet?"

"We had some similar business. Taking down the same crime lords. We had an early scuffle, but, we're on good terms now."

"Splendid to hear. Then, you don't mind joining yourself with us."

"I'm not a team player. I did what I had to do in Retropolis for those who couldn't defend themselves."

"I get that." Vail said. "But, I have to ask, if the opportunity arose once more, would you take it?"

"Instead of just a city, it's the world." Abraham said. "Much larger than what you're accustomed to."

"How large of a threat are we talking?"

"One that could wipe out all life on this earth and perhaps breach the spiritual planes."

"That bad, huh?"

"It is." Abraham said. "So, what do you say?"

Terror nodded.

"When the time comes, I'll be there."

"How can we be sure of that?" Abraham asked.

"Lend some trust my way. You'll see I'm telling the truth."

"Fair enough." Vail said. "May we leave now?"

"By all means."

Vail and Abraham left Terror's hideout. Returning to Vail's vehicle. They sat inside as Vail looked over the other names. Vail circled Terror's name.

"Who's next?" Abraham asked.

"A friend in London. Figured she would help us out."

"Off to London. Again."

Traveling to London, they waited near the Big Ben once again at night. Abraham looked around for her as he did before.

"She's not here yet?"

"I gave her a phone call." Vail said. "She knows we're here."

Sliding down the walls of Big Ben was Cinderella. She landed, standing in front of the two occult detectives. They hugged each other with smiles. A rare thing to see in their fields.

"I got the call." Cinderella said. "What is it this time?"

"We need your help. Again. Only this time, it involves a more powerful force."

"How powerful?"

"Strong enough to wipe out all life and enter the spiritual dimensions."

"Well, this all sounds like a lot to handle. I'm still in an ongoing investigation."

"If this force rises, you won't have any investigations to cover. Cindy, please, you have to align with us and take out."

"That bad?" Cinderella asked.

"It is."

"Confronting the Mutant-Thing was fun. I guess I can add in the spare time."

"Great." Vail said. "Now, we wait."

"For what?" Abraham asked.

"Cindy wasn't the only one I contacted."

"Who else is in London besides me?"

"An old soul."

From the ground erupted a white mist. Surrounding Vail, Abraham, and Cinderella. The mist turned, morphing into itself, forming an astral body. The body formed and stood before them. Wearing clothing from the Victorian era. The body was of a man. Vail applauded the entrance.

"Abraham, Cindy, meet Robert Shaw. Or as the folktales call him, the Ghost of England."

"The Ghost of England?" Cinderella said. "I thought that was only a story."

"It's more than a story, lass. See, you're looking at him."

"Travis Vail, Spirit-Seeker." Shaw said. "Gabriel Abraham, the Devilhunter. Cindy Lawson, known as Cinderella. I stand before the three of you this night to declare my allegiance to your cause."

"That was easy." Abraham said.

"I figured you may know this we don't." Vail said. "Is there anything we don't know?"

"Best for you to meet with the Unholy Knight called Creed and the Death Chaser, a Soul of Retribution."

"Creed and the Death Chaser?" Cinderella asked.

"Me and Abraham were already told about meeting the Chaser. Trust me, that is soon to come. But, about this Creed fellow, where can we find him?"

"I will guide you to him. But, beware of his aggression. For he is keen to discovering the rising force that threats this world."

"Duly noted." Vail said. "Then, let's get going."

III

THE UNHOLY KNIGHT AND THE SOUL OF RETRIBUTION

Returning to the States, Vail, Abraham, and Cinderella are guided by the Ghost of England toward an old church in the Northwest counties. Reaching near the city of Hartford, Connecticut. The Ghost of England signaled a peculiar church building. One with a large black cross standing atop the structure.

"I've been there before." Vail said.

"What for?" Cinderella asked.

"Exorcism of a old man. However, Connecticut is filled with much paranormal and demonic activity. I know from experience."

"And is this where we find this Creed?" Abraham asked Shaw.

"Yes. He will be here soon. Trust my words."

"How soon?" Vail uttered. "I'm just curious is all."

"Soon."

"Tonight? Tomorrow morning? Next week? When? You must have a particular clue."

"You'll see."

"I guess I will."

The Ghost turned to face the group and his eyes shined upon the cross. Yet, he caught movement atop the structure. Vail caught his glimpse and gazed up himself.

"What is it, Trav?" Cinderella asked.

"We've found him. Or, he's found us."

The moving object lunged down toward them, landing on its feet in front of them. They stepped back as the dark blue cloak edged itself back to reveal Creed himself. Creed raised up from his bent position of the landing. Standing tall, facing the unit. His golden eyes gazed at them. His cloak echoing the sound of a chilling wind.

"Who are you?" Creed asked.

"We're detectives." Vail said. "Besides the Ghost here."

"We have no intention of bothering you." Abraham declared. "But, we need your assistance with a dire cause."

"The world is full of causes. Mine aren't sealed in the natural realm."

"Which is why we're here." Vail said. "There's a powerful force rising from beneath the earth. If we don't stop it soon, it will wipe out all life. Everything. Humans. Animals. Plant life. All of it."

"Where is the origin of this threat?"

"I... I don't know."

"Then you are wasting your time."

"Please, listen to us." Vail said, grabbing a hold of Creed's arm.

"Best you remove your hand before you have it no longer."

Vail pulled back his hand from Creed. Smirking.

"You must have some knowledge of a powerful force. Something."

"You speak not of the cryptic Zone."

"Don't think so. I thought that place was sealed."

"It is sealed." Creed said. "I and a fellow angel closed its portals from opening across the world."

"Then, it can't be someone from the Cryptic Zone." Abraham

said. "Vail, what do you think it could be?"

"I'm working on it."

From behind them, a spiraling flame emitted from thin air. Causing them to turn around, startling them without haste. Creed stood in front of them, his cloak flowing roughly, his claws sharpened and his gaze keen.

"The hell is that?" Cinderella asked.

"I've seen such a thing before." Vail said.

"Where?" Abraham wondered.

"It's the entrance of the Death Chaser."

The Death Chaser walked out of the spiraling flame and shut its door behind him. He stood face to face with Creed. Two opposing forces of the supernatural realm.

"The Unholy Knight." The Death Chaser said.

"A Soul of Retribution." Creed remarked.

"What's going on here?" Vail asked.

"I should ask you the same, Travis Vail." The Death Chaser said. "I have been tracking all your movements since you were visited by Papa Afterlife."

"Seriously?" Abraham asked.

"Don't feel too bad. It's his job."

"Death Chaser." The Ghost of England said. "Tell us of your purpose here. What do you know of this rising power?"

"More than all of you combined."

"That's good to know." Vail uttered.

"The rising force is a malevolent entity known as Demonticronto. My sworn adversary. Me and my liege were dealing with a soldier of his. A sin phantom."

"Sin Phantom?" Abraham asked. "The hell."

"Don't be too shocked. I know what he's speaking of. I came across this sin phantom during my investigation in Italy. It's a powerful foe. But, a lieutenant demon protected me from its wrath."

"What demon?" The Death Chaser asked.

"Kamagrauto. Heard of him?"

"I have."

"Who is Kamagrauto?" Abraham asked with confusion. "What is going on here?"

"We can explain later, Abraham. For right now, we need to focus on how to stop this Demonticronto demon from rising."

"Creed, Death Chaser." Shaw said. "Align yourselves this day with them. Aid them in stopping Demonticronto and the Sin Phantom."

"I will aid you." Death Chaser said. "Only to stop Demonticronto from causing much harm to this reality."

"As will I." Creed said.

"Excellent." Vail said. "Now, all we need is some guidance on finding a place where Demonticronto's power is growing."

A great flash of white light pierced through the air. Causing a rift between realms. Everyone covered their eyes from the great shine except for Creed and Death Chaser, who are immune to such power. From the rift appeared a man dressed in black with a midnight blue cloak, white gloves and a hat. His long white hair stood out amongst his white facial hair and shining eyes. His pupils could not be seen.

"Who are you supposed to be?" Vail asked.

"I am the Visitant Outlander and I have come to guide you all in this quest you have taken upon yourselves.

IV

THE BROTHERLESS ONE AND THE WRATH OF *YAH*

"Visitant Outlander?" Vail asked. "My, I thought you were just a myth. Hidden away by the ancestors of old."

"I am very real as I stand here before your very eyes."

"I can see that. Which means the other guy exists as well."

"He does."

Vail nodded.

"This is great."

"I don't get what's happening here?" Cinderella asked. "Why have you come to help us? We have Creed and the Death Chaser for that."

"All of you combined together cannot stop Demonticronto's grown power and with the Sin Phantom at his side. I have come to grant an offering to you."

"What kind of offering, lad?"

"To lock away Demonticronto."

"Lock him up?" Abraham asked. "What on earth for?"

"There is no prison that can keep the sin fire from burning Demonticronto." The Death Chaser said. "I will kill him when it comes."

"You shouldn't" Outlander said. "For Demonticronto's existence serves a much greater cause."

"I thought the greater cause was to take him out." Vail said. "Eliminate the evil. Put away the evil. Not imprison it so it can break out."

"Killing such a powerful force will only cause more tragedy than peace."

"And how would you be aware of such causes?" Creed asked. "What happened in the past to alter someone's mind such as yours of a simple cause?"

"I've been around for ages. Much longer than this physical realm. I know what happens when the greater plan is thwarted or tapped."

"Now, I get it." Vail uttered.

"Get what?" Cinderella asked.

"Why the other guy doesn't like Outlander here. He's too into the whole justice motif."

"What other guy?" Abraham wondered.

"He's here." Vail grinned, looking up.

Like a falling cloud, he came down from the night sky. Cloaked in a dark violet cloak and hood. Only his red eyes were visible unto the shining of his presence caused his face to appear. Brighter than Outlander's light. His amulet glowed like the sun. he approached Outlander, standing toe to toe with him.

"Dark Manhunter." Outlander said. "The walking embodiment of the Wrath of Yah."

"Visitant Outlander." Manhunter said. "The Brotherless One. Looking for a way to assist all humanity in its endeavors."

"This is good to hear." Vail said. "Now, we don't need a scuffle between two cosmic forces. Not yet anyway. Manhunter, may I get your view on all of this?"

"Demonticronto must be killed. Execute him before more

damage is done."

"Killing him will only bring more harm into this world." Outlander said. "You're speaking tragedy upon their lives."

"Their lives will only find peace when those like Demonticronto and the Sin Phantom are eliminated from existence. Permanently."

"Then, it's settled." Vail said. "We take down Demonticronto."

"As we should." Chaser said. "I will give the final blow."

"Oh, will you and Outlander be joining us on this journey?"

"We will be around." Manhunter said. "Right on time."

"I'll take your word for it."

Manhunter and Outlander vanished from their sight. Vail looked around, seeing everyone else still standing by. He nodded. Impressed.

"Now, all we need is one more member."

"And who is that going to be?" Cinderella wondered.

"A fellow friend from Retropolis."

"Come on." Cinderella said. "He's not going to stop what he's doing just to help us out."

"I'm not talking about him. I'm speaking of the other guy."

Cinderella thought for the moment. Abraham sighed and Vail grinned.

"Oh. Him."

V

THE MUTANT-THING RISES

The unit traveled to the city of Retropolis. Upon arriving, they noticed the city was under a minor form of martial law. Streets were still and quiet. There was hardly anybody along the sidewalks or outside.

"What's been happening here?" Vail wondered.

"I guess he's cleaning the city faster than I would expect." Cinderella said.

"Hmm." Vail replied.

"Whatever happened to John Terror joining us?" Abraham asked.

"Fumy you mention that. I called him as we were headed this direction. He said he would meet us in the wilderness."

"Meet us there? Why not here?"

"Out in the open I guess."

"We must reach this forest soon." Shaw said. "I can sense Demonticronto's power surging from below our feet."

"Understood." Vail said.

Entering the dark forest near Retropolis, they traced their steps from before, coming across a large crater-sized hole in the ground.

"This was the spot." Abraham said.

"I remember." Vail replied.

"How do you plan to conjure him?" Cinderella asked.

In the distance, motorcycle sounds entered the forest. They turn back, seeing Terror getting off his bike, walking toward their direction. Vail waved his hands for Terror to see.

"Good thing he's here." Abraham said.

"We'll see for sure."

"I told you I would come on my time."

"Yeah. Right after I called you."

"Seemed like the right moment." Terror grinned. "Now, why are you all out here in the woods? At night?"

"Here to find an old friend." Vail said.

"I wouldn't call him a friend." Abraham gestured.

"Then what is he?"

"A monster." Cinderella said. "One of cryptid origins."

"Nice to know."

Death Chaser started to move around the area. His eyes gazed on the surroundings. As he turned, facing the city. He pointed with great intension. The unit wasn't sure to what he was seeing.

"The Phantom." Chaser said. "He's in the city."

"Are you sure?" Vail asked.

"I know."

"Well, I have an idea." Cinderella said. "Why don't we split up."

"How so?" Abraham questioned.

"Me, Shaw, and the Chaser go find this Sin Phantom while you, Vail, Terror, and Creed summon up the big creature."

"I'm not for this, Cindy." Vail said. "But, since what Chaser said is true, best be going, lass."

Cinderella nodded as she, Shaw, and the Chaser went back into Retropolis. Vail sighed, turning back to the crater in the ground. He stepped into it. Stomping the soil, twisting his foot.

"What are you doing?" Terror asked.

"Waking the big fellow up."

"And he's just going to pop up out of that hole?"

"I hope so. Otherwise, I'm dirtying up my shoes." Vail smirked.

Cinderella, Shaw, and the Chaser walked on he road within Retropolis. Still no one outside. The Chaser moved faster than the two, walking near an alleyway. Cinderella and Shaw followed him. Discovering him coming to a stop, where they saw the Sin Phantom himself.

"You've found me." The Phantom said.

"I'm sending you away." The Chaser said.

"You're not supposed to be here." Cinderella gestured.

"Then, where can I go?"

"To the pit!" Chaser yelled.

Chaser emitted sin fire from his hands and threw it at the Phantom, who dodged the flames. Cinderella ran toward him, trying to grab him by his throat. The Phantom morphed his body into a transparent form, causing Cinderella to slip as he snatched her by the coat and tossed her against the Chaser. Shaw levitated toward the Phantom. Both entities staring down.

"You have violated the natural law." Shaw said.

"And you are going to lecture me on law? I know your history, Robert Shaw. Don't assume yourself as one of the helpless."

"My past is dead. Just as your soul!"

Shaw went to touch the Phantom, but the Phantom grabbed him by his head and his hand glowed like a blue flame above Shaw. He shook himself, trying to get free and as he reached for the Phantom's arm, he was let go.

"Shaw?" Cinderella yelled.

"He's currently occupied right now." Phantom said. "You will have to wake him up."

Shaw's ghostly body arose from the ground, facing Cinderella and the Chaser. The Chaser stepped forward, sensing something odd with Shaw.

"Stand behind me, Cinderella."

"What's wrong?"

"The Phantom, he's done something to Shaw."

"Like mind control?"

"No. he's awoken the once living nature when his being. Sin has crawled back into his soul. Wickedness is consuming him."

"What can we do?"

"We can beat it out of him. He's only a spirit. Not living flesh."

"Do well with such." The Phantom said. "I must be going. See you all soon when my master arrives!"

The Phantom vanished. Shaw's sin-filled spirit rushed toward the Chaser, grabbing him by the throat and holding him close. Cinderella attended to punch Shaw, but him as a spirit, she was powerless.

"Poor girl." Shaw said. "You're no help once more."

"You leave the woman out of this." The Chaser said. "I will cleanse your spirit of the sin that has entered you!"

"Why? I've never felt more alive."

"You're not alive. You're dead."

Vail, Abraham, Terror, and Creed stood around the crater. Vail reached into his pocket, pulling out his ritual book. Terror was confused, standing amongst a group of men he's never met. He gazed toward Creed, looking at his flowing cloak.

"How does that work?"

"It works with my mind." Creed said.

"Is that so." Terror replied. "I guess it works wonders."

"When it needs be."

"I'm going to read this ritual in Latin." Vail said. "It should summon the big fellow."

"Why Latin?" Terror questioned.

"It works for circumstances like this."

"What of Hebrew, Greek, Arabic, or Persian?"

"I've dabbled in it before. Best be careful with those if you ask me."

Terror nodded. "I see."

"Are you sure this will work properly?" Abraham asked.

"You were with us last time, remember?"

"This isn't like last time. He knows who we are."

"He doesn't know Creed or Johnny boy. We'll be fine."

Abraham shook his head and Vail grinned. Opening the book, turning the pages. He stopped and looked at the three around him.

"Ready?"

"Sure." Abraham said.

"Proceed." Creed said.

"Go for it." Terror gestured. "I'm curious."

Vail stood steady, gazing into the crater. His eyes focused on the page within the book. One hand stretched outward over the crater.

"Voco super te, qui habitas in terra ejus qui creavit elementa. Ergo surge, et sta in conspectu nostro."

The crater began to glow a bright green. They stepped back as the dirt flew into the air, falling upon them like heavy rain. After the dirt had fell and settled, their eyes were focused on who was standing in the middle of the crater. Vail smiled.

"You rose!"

Vail approached the Mutant-Thing. Standing in the center of the crater. His appearance hadn't' changed since their last encounter. Mutant-Thing looked around, seeing Abraham, Terror, and Creed. He looked down toward Vail.

"Travis Vail." The Mutant-Thing said.

"Listen, bog fellow. We're here on important notice. Not like last time.”

“Why have you truly come? Why disturb my slumber?”

“Because there’s a powerful force preparing to rise from beneath the earth. If it does, it has the potential to destroy everything.”

“What is the destroyer’s name?”

“Demonticronto apparently.”

“Hmm.” Mutant-Thing uttered. “His power is great. He was defeated ages ago by those such as yourselves. But, I see you’re missing several warriors”

“They’re currently busy finding a sin phantom. Working for Demonticronto it seems.”

“And you require my aid in taking Demonticronto down?”

“Yes.” Vail said. “That is why we’re truly here. Honestly.”

Mutant-Thing turned, seeing Creed. He pointed toward him, letting the others look and see.

“He is unholy. Made of malevolent origins. How can he be trusted in such a time?”

“I rebelled against the one who formed me in such manner.”

“I smell the stench of the Cryptic Zone on you.”

“I was chosen as an apprentice to Adrambadon, Lord of the Cryptic Zone. His demands were dire. But, over time, I broke from his grasp and chosen to make a better change with this curse he has bestowed upon me.”

“No matter. He has power over you as long as you’re connected to the source.”

“Not to cut off this contact.” Vail said. “But, we’re going to need Creed in order to stop Demonticronto and his little sin lad roaming on about.”

“As you say. I will give my aid to this cause. Only to help the earth remain in its current stead.”

“Understood.” Vail said. “How will this work now? When we

find the phantom and Demonticronto, how will you help us? Am I to summon you once more?"

"When the time comes, you will know of my help."

"That's it?" Vail questioned. "A tight, but small riddle."

"Take it for what it's worth, Spirit-Seeker. Now, leave this forest. I must return to my slumber."

"Fair enough."

The Mutant-Thing burrowed himself into the crater as the dirt covered him completely.

"Now what?" Terror asked.

"We find the others. Tell them it's time we come up with a plan."

"Hopefully, they've captured the Sin Phantom first." Abraham said. "Save us all some time."

"Let's find out."

The Chaser and Shaw fought one another with Cinderella giving slight aid to the Chaser. A ring of sinfire had surrounded the sin-corrupted Shaw. Cinderella moved over, standing next to the Chaser.

"You must be purged once more." The Chaser commanded.

"You can't take away such a feeling. I can feel pleasure again. Lust. Greed. I can sense them all."

"That is why I must do this. Only for the purity of your soul."

The Chaser balled up his fist and quickly, the sin fire had rose from the ground, consuming Shaw. The others arrived as they saw Shaw within the flames and chaser with Cinderella standing back.

"The hell's going on?!" Vail yelled.

"The Sin Phantom planted a seed within Shaw's mind. He became consumed with sin. I am purging it from his spirit form."

"Is he still in there?" Abraham asked.

"Yes." Cinderella said. "Chaser is burning the sin seed out of him."

Shaw continued to burn, and the Chaser opened his hand, ceasing the spiral sin fire as it returned to the ground, only leaving Shaw's spirit remaining. They ran over toward him. Chaser placed his hand upon Shaw's head.

"How is he?" Cinderella asked.

"He's still in there. The sin is gone."

"Just like that, you burned it out of him?" Terror asked.

"Yes. This is my line of work."

"Would be nice to have all humans enter this treatment."

"It would kill them." The Chaser said. "They're still in their mortal forms. The human body cannot handle such pain from sinfire."

Shaw's eyes opened as he arose from the ground, looking at his body.

"You purged it from me."

"As I only could."

"Now, since that's out of the way, we need to make a plan and quickly." Vail said. "I fear Demonticronto's is not as far away as we assume."

"He isn't." The Chaser said.

"And how are you aware of his whereabouts?" Abraham asked.

"I can sense him. He's walking upon the earth right now and he isn't far from our location."

"Then, you can track him."

"I can."

"Then, let's get going." Vail uttered.

VI

THEY HAVE BEEN CALLED

The unit followed the Chaser out of Retropolis and have stumbled upon a cemetery near the United States border. The cemetery was calm, quiet, and still. Vail shrugged his shoulders walking past the headstones on the ground.

"What is it now?" Cinderella asked Chaser.

"He's here." Chaser said. "He is here."

"Where?" Vail wondered. "Is he under the ground or standing in front of us? Just invisible?"

Dirt kicked up from a grave as the Sin Phantom made himself known once more. The unit stood their ground toward the Phantom, who did not move past the gravesite.

"You've come." The Phantom said.

"No shit, lad." Vail replied. "You know why we're here."

"I do, and he is proud to have you here. To bear witness to his uprising."

"Then, where is the bastard?"

"Where's Demonti?!" The Chaser yelled.

"He's right here."

He grave turned into molten lava within seconds and created an opening in the ground, a deep pit. The Phantom moved from the grave as lava flew up in the air, yet, not falling back toward the ground.

"You see what I'm seeing?" Vail asked Cinderella.

"Yeah. I do."

Within the lava, the unit could see something moving. Hovering within the lava. As the lava settled its pouring, the figure could be seen. His red-skin, torn tunic, and long fiery hair. He landed on his feet beside the Phantom.

"There you are!" The Chaser said.

"Yes. I am here."

"Demonticronto I presume." Abraham gestured.

"In the flesh as they say."

"You've come to the wrong place, fellow."

"Oh, have I?"

"We're sending you back into your prison." Abraham said.

"I give you the opportunity to try."

The Chaser grunted, running toward Demonticronto with his arms covered in sin fire. The Chaser went for an attack but speared to the ground by the Phantom with a quickening force.

"You and I have a score to settle, Retributor."

"You've forgotten me." Shaw said, tackling the Phantom.

The unit began their battle with Demonticronto. Creed went for the aerial attack as Demonti's height was near thirteen feet tall. Demonti's strength from his arms, knocked Creed from the air, as well as his dragon-like tail, swiping Vail, Abraham, and Cinderella off their feet.

"This is depressionaly easy." Demonti grinned.

"*'Depressionaly*'?" Cinderella said. "Is that a word?"

"Doesn't matter." Vail said. "We're not here to learn new words."

Vail chanted out a binding spell, causing the air around Demonti to constrict him. Holding him steady while Creed attacked him from his head to his torso. Abraham also chanted a spell to keep Demonticronto still. Meanwhile, the Chaser and Sin Phantom battled it out through the cemetery. Chaser snatched Phantom by his neck and tossed him against a headstone. Phantom dodged an incoming punch from Chaser with sinfire dripping from his fist. Shaw went for an attack of his own yet tripped by the Phantom.

"This is sad for your kind." Demonticronto said. "I assumed humanity had learned the means of working with such magic feats."

Demonti increased his strength, breaking the spiritual bonds around him, knocking down Vail, Cinderella, and Abraham. He grabbed Creed's cloak and slammed him into the ground. Terror ran up, firing shots with his pistols. Demonti grabbed the pistols, slapping Terror with them and stomping on his back. Demonticronto savored the moment.

"You're no match for me. I am above such primitive feats."

"I've heard that before." Cinderella said.

"Haven't we all."

The sky quickly opened above the cemetery and from there, Visitant Outlander and Dark Manhunter appeared before them. Standing in front of Demonticronto. He moved from the downed team and stepped forward to Outlander and Manhunter.

"The two of you, working as one? Impressive."

"Don't take this lightly, demon." Manhunter said.

"You have trespassed upon a realm you have no authority."

"Spare the reasoning, Eidolon. I have come for my purpose only."

"And your purpose shall be?"

"To rule over Man. As the others should have done eons ago."

"That is where you're wrong." Manhunter said, raising his hand.

"You cannot end me." Demonti said. "I am still needed. I know the end of all this. I am not a fool."

"Yet, you know the end and continue to act as such." Outlander said. "No, we will send you back to your realm until the opportune time arises according to the Word. However, this team of outcasts have revealed they're just as a match for you when the time comes."

"Look at them! They're not a match for me!"

"So, you truly do not know the end of all things." Manhunter said. "Go home, demon."

Manhunter conjured up a portal beneath Demonti's feet and he fell into the deep lighted pit. The Phantom also was pulled from the Chaser's grasp and dragged into the pit. Once they were inside, the pit closed at the command of Manhunter. Then, the area was still once more. The unit returned to their feet, approaching the embodiments of justice and vengeance.

"I'm confused." Vail said. "What's happened here?"

"Demonti knows of his end." Outlander said. "This day was not such."

"The end?" The Chaser uttered. "I know his end for I have seen it."

"You have, Soul of Retribution." Manhunter said. "But, this is not the day."

"Hold on." Vail said. "When is this end you're speaking of?"

"Soon." Outlander said. "Sooner than the world will know. For the end is near and it is right at the door."

"As in the days of Noah and such like?"

"You know the details, Spirit-Seeker." Manhunter said. "For a dark force will return to this world and claim it as his own. Many will fall at his feet in opposition and will rise once more. For now, continue as such and you will succeed."

"Fair enough."

"Best you all go your own ways." Outlander said. "Demonti will not return quickly as you will imagine. For there are other threats that pose damage to this world and the realms. When the time comes, you all will be united once more. For you all are *Heaven's Called.*"

"Yet, you will not know the day, the time, nor the hour." Manhunter said. "We bid your farewell. For now."

Outlander and Manhunter disappeared from their sights. Vail looked back at everyone and chuckled.

"Well, shit."

Afterwards, they each returned to their domains. Creed and Death Chaser continued their spiritual work, Cinderella and Shaw returned to London, Abraham made it back to the Revelation Center in D.C. and Vail continued his work across the world. Yet, somewhere secretly, a stash of grimoires had been taken by an unknown group. A group led by a priest who has a past with Vail.

I

<u>THE WANDERING IMMORTAL</u>

A plethora of murders have been committed across the earth grounds. The victims vary between men, women, children, animals, and the environment. The murders were detailed to have begun months prior, although many ignored the early signs that came before it. It was not until sometime later when the humans began to cry out for help concerning the murders. Many are now parentless, brotherless, sisterless, husbandless, wifeless, childless, petless, homeless, and now they call for help. They want the help and they want it now.

"So, I will go into the searching to find out what has taken their possessions and why. A matter such as this cannot go unchecked or underhanded."

Darkous, the Keeper of the Cosmos, also known as Doctor Dark and Randolph Dark to humanity, travels through the earth to every location where a murder has been committed. From various street alleys to city parks to construction sites to day cares to neighborhood homes to animal shelters. While searching, Darkous looked at humanity and what they are doing at the sites. Most simply are minding their own business, particularly have forgotten about the murders and are now busy with the cares of this world and obsessed with celebrities and self-indulgence.

While looking into a museum that was closed down due to a murder, Darkous found a unusual fabric on the wooden floor. The fabric was covered in the colors of dark violet and gold. It shined throughout anything else on the floor and inside the museum. He picked it up and analyzed it from the other fabrics throughout the history of Man. Darkous sniffed the fabric, sensing it to be soaked in magic.

"It must be him again. I can feel his aura."

Darkous took the fabric and evaporated from the museum and into the Astral Dimension realm. He travels through the dimension, through its various color changes from violet to green to blue to white and repeating itself. Walking through, Darkous comes across Beatrice, one of the Astral Entities, such is Darkous. Beatrice greeted Darkous as he walked through the dimension.

"A pleasure to gaze upon you once more, Darkous."

"I am here on duty, Beatrice. I found this inside a museum on earth. Its soaked in magic and immortal magic."

Darkous handed Beatrice the fabric. She sniffed it and rubbed it with her hands. Sensing and feeling the magic flowing through the fabric. It was somewhat of a cinnamon scent to her.

"It is something powerful. Good that a human didn't come on to this. There's enough magic in this fabric to cause a great catastrophe."

"By the way the magic surges through it and the power it possesses. It has to be Mazakala."

"Mazakala? I thought he was imprisoned in the deeper realm beneath us."

"His imprisonment expired some four hours back. I believe it was kept under wraps from causing a concern amongst us."

Beatrice put the fabric in her pocket and walked over to Darkous, hugging him and kissed him on the cheek.

"Very well, you must go and seek him out. I will remain here unless you contact me to aid you down in earth."

"Understand you well, Beatrice. I will call if needed."

Darkous teleports out of the Astral Dimension as if a gust of wind had picked him up and took him with it.

In Toronto, Ontario, Canada during the day, Supernatural Reporter Carol Hunters, a young attractive woman, who's countenance has brought about the wrong attention is investigating the series of murders. She has concluded the murders were done by a paranormal matter and the murders were caused by either ghosts or demons. Carol has been studying the paranormal for almost five years with some experience in the field. She has also come face to face with spirits and demons.

She is well known by sight from her long red-orange hair and her casual attire of a brown jacket and skirt with a white or black shirt at times. She also avoids wearing makeup, stating she doesn't like to wear animals on her face.

Carol searched the park, the downtown locations, the day cares, the schools, and the neighborhoods. She also spoke with some of the people that loss something in the murders and could barely get anything out of them.

"What do you know about the exact cause of your child's death?"

"We don't know. He was with us and we placed him to bed. We woke up the next morning and he was dead. Laying down in his bed peacefully."

"So, you do not know what if could've been?"

"We have no idea what could've done this. Maybe God decided it was the right time to take him."

"Only the matter will tell."

"They have no idea about the paranormal. Neither do they insist to know if it's a factor. These people are lost to themselves. Not understanding that something bigger is taking place all around us."

In the other parts of the world, particularly in Damascus, Darkous searches the ancient sites to find anything that will give him a signal to Mazakala's current whereabouts. The residents see Darkous searching the ancient grounds, they do not appear to be afraid of him, due to the awareness of the spiritual nature that surrounds the earth and the understanding of Darkous as a spiritual entity going about his business. Not finding anything with the wind blowing through his black hair and his dark violet trench coat and cloak.

"You are not this intelligent, Mazakala. No matter how much you perceive yourself to be knowledgeable."

"Darkous, I need to have a word with you."

Darkous heard the voice and understood its speech pattern. He shows a faint smile as he turned around and faced Michael the Archangel. Standing in front of him with glory beaming from his armor and wings. His skin glowing a dark bronze, his eyes appearing like a raging fire, and heavenly energy surging from his body.

"Michael, what is the word you have with me?"

"I know where Mazakala is located. But we must talk with each other someplace else. Not on earth."

"Where would you have us speak?"

Michael raised his head and gazed up above the clouds toward the clear sky. "Meet me in the Second Heaven and we can have our discussion there."

Michael flew up in the air with Darkous watched him on. He teleported from Damascus and into the Second Heaven.

II

<u>SEARCHING FOR THE WANDERED</u>

Michael and Darkous meet in the Second Heaven. The stars and worlds encamp around them. Darkous looked around seeing the sun in the distance and moon not too far from him. Darkous also glanced at the planets that were nearby and the meteors that moved on past them as if they were missiles.

"What is the word you have for me, Michael?"

"Mazakala is operating from various locations. He will make an appearance on the earth and will vanish. Afterwards, he'll show up in the dimensions and disappear, making a turn toward other places that exist in this universe."

"He's causing havoc and moving swiftly to avoid any kind of confrontation."

"What you'll have to do is outsmart him. He has been around for an eons time. But not as long as you have existed."

"Is he taking orders from someone or is he doing this all on his own?"

"He is taking orders. Small ones it appears from the ha-Satan."

"They're collaborating with each other? The two of them?"

"Satan gave him two allies. Their names are Kabra and Maba. They're demons who have committed a few of the smaller murders in the earth. They'll most likely have to be taken out before you can reach Mazakala. They appear to be his guards as well. When someone confronts him, Kabra and Maba are there for the attack and for the kill."

"I have some allies back on earth and in the Astral realm that can assist me on the two demons."

"As you are aware, Satan will need all the help he can get this day. He doesn't have much longer."

"You're right about that. I have been counting the hours that pass more so than before."

"The Elohim of Yisrael insists you find him before he causes something more troubling than murders in earth. Find Mazakala and defeat him for his imprisonment will be much longer than the last."

"I will do what I can to find him. I have a few places I believe he will make his way."

Michael nodded as he flew away like a flash of light. Darkous turned back toward the earth and evaporated like smoke, diving down toward earth and entering the atmosphere reaching the ground with the smoke coming together slowly, reforming Darkous in his physical form.

"I will need to speak with an ally of mine before I do this task."

At a meeting in Toronto, Carol stood by the wall, listening in on the men that are discussing various mythologies. The men insist the murders were caused by a mythological being. They vary in between mythologies, not knowing if the murderer is from the Greek and Roman, the Norse, the Hindu, the Japanese, the Chinese, the Celtic, the African, the Aztec, and other ideas. During their discussion, one of the men turned around, spotting Carol by the wall. She noticed his glare and tried to leave.

"Where are you going, lady?"

Carol stopped and turned to face them. The man waved his hand, insisting her to come to the table. She walked over to the table as the men turned and looked at her. She was somewhat fearful of the men as they appeared visually to be the mafia or some sort of crime mob due to the attire they wore. Traditional suits and coats with fedoras. Even smoking cigars.

"I take it you're some kind of reporter, huh?"

"I am."

"What are you reporting on?"

"The murders that have taken place over the few months."

"Oh. Really. So, what have you come up with on your investigations?"

"I believe the murderer was a paranormal entity. Like a ghost or a demon."

"I don't think so."

"What makes you say that?"

"There are many things which exist in this world, outside this earth, and throughout the universe and the dimensions that vary across it. We only know so little and it's the little that we should remain. But, there are those who seek more knowledge. Increasing our minds to fully understand the purpose of this world and universe."

"I did hear you gentlemen speak of the mythologies being the cause."

"Yes. We have a firm belief that the murderer is one of the various gods in the mythologies. We're not sure if its Thanatos also known as Mors in the Greek and Roman myths, Hel from the Norse, Kali from the Hindu, the Shinigami from the Japanese, Emperors of Youdu from the Chinese, Donn, the Dark One from the Celtics, the Ogbunabali from the Africans, Xipe-Totec from the Aztecs. Hell, it can even be some magical being like the Morrigan or it could be

Azrael or some spirits traveling around."

"It could be the Evil One." One of the men said.

"Yeah. You're right. It could be."

"You guys know your mythology."

"Yes, we do. We know it so well for a singular purpose that most people seem to lack."

"Why would they lack it?"

"Because they don't study. They have too much time on their hands and what do they waste it on. The latest fashion trend or some low prices on items at a store. You've seen the Black Friday crowds and what they can do when it comes to buying materials. Imagine if they put that much effort into shaping their own minds and growing more in knowledge and wisdom. So much potential wasted on junk."

"Are you guys from around here?"

"We're natives of Canada of course. But we all were raised in different cities. We came together because we have a common mind and a common goal. To learn more and to grow in knowledge of the knowledge that is secret but can be grasp with much endurance and patience."

Carol looked at her watch, signaling for her to leave the building. She prepared to walk away, but the man called out to her again. She turned and approached him. He took a puff from his cigar before looking at her.

"Hopefully we'll see you again and maybe you can join in on our little conversations. Seems to me you have knowledge and soon it'll need to be spread out. Mainly among us."

"Another time then."

"Of course. Whenever you decide is the best moment for you. We won't hesitate. We'll wait patiently."

Carol left the room while the men continued with their conversation. Outside of the building, Carol walked down the sidewalk, looking through her phone to find information on the men she spoke with. Not finding anything connected to them, she placed the phone into her pocket and continued walking.

Out in the wilderness, Darkous stumbled upon an old large cabin. He walked up the stairs and approached the door. He knocked three times. He waited, and the door opened. Standing at the door was Darkous' apprentice. He bows to Darkous in servitude. A sign of respect.

"Master."

"Good to see you, Malach HaMavet."

"You here alludes to something that must be done."

"May I come in?"

"Sure."

Malach allowed Darkous to enter his cabin. Malach is a man after the African countenance. His physical appearance shows his potential in a battle. The interior of the cabin is a mixture of a home and a dojo. Darkous sat down in one of the chairs and Malach walked over, sitting in front of Darkous in the other chair.

"What is it this time, Master?"

"An immortal sorcerer known as Mazakala has been released from his imprisonment and is out causing havoc amongst the humans."

"You need me to assist you in taking him down?"

"I can handle Mazakala on my own. I need you to assist me on confronting his two soldiers that are in the way."

"Are they humans or something else?"

"Their demons. Kabra and Maba are their names and it appears they were given to him by the ha-Satan."

"So, he's involved in this as well."

"In a way. Just a small dose. I don't expect him to show us fully during all of this."

"Give me some time to prepare myself, Master and I will be ready to head off with you on this quest."

"Take your time to prepare, Malach. We have some time to spare."

Malach stood up and walked to his room to prepare his clothing and gear. Darkous stood by the window staring outside, looking at the sky and the trees and the grass. Out in the distance, he could see a strand of horses.

"They stand and eat. They stand and drink. They run when needed. They speed when applied."

Darkous turned and seen Malach prepared with his warrior clothing on and his sword at hand.

"I'm ready, Master."

"Let us head out toward our first place of business."

"Which is?"

"Finding Kabra and Maba."

"Won't we need a location to find them? I mean, they'll be somewhere I'm sure."

"The closer we get the Mazakala, the closer they'll be. Straightforward, they'll come to us."

Sitting in her home during the night, Carol sat at her desk reading books on the various mythologies. Most of them are the ones the men were spoke about. She read through the Greek and Roman myths, the Norse myths, the Hindu myths, the Japanese myths, the Chinese myths, the Celtic myths, the African myths, and the Aztec myths.

"There's so many possibilities that are around these murders. If only there was a single trail that I could trace it would make all of this easier than it could be."

She closed the books and placed them at the side of her desk while reading a paper that contained information on cosmic entities and astral dimensions. She rubbed her hand through her hair while reading and writing down notes.

During the night, Darkous and Malach walk through an abandoned town. Nothing in sight except fro debris and abandoned vehicles. Malach walked slowly while looking around his area. Darkous kept walking straight making no turns to look.

"What brings us here?"

"I can sense Mazakala's power here. Its strong."

"So, I can take the guess that he's here."

"He could possibly be or it is his residue that's left behind. Either way, he's closer than he was before."

Out in the distance, Malach saw a golden light flash. Malach pointed toward the site and Darkous looked toward it.

"I just saw a strange light appear from over there. Right by that building."

"Let us have a look."

They walked over toward the building. The building appeared to be a torn down church. They entered it and could find nothing in sight. Malach searched the place all around with his sword in hand. Darkous stood in the middle of the church and brought in the aura that was around. Malach walked back inside the church toward Darkous.

"Nothing. I couldn't find nothing."

Darkous stood still and silent.

"Master, what have you found? You seem to have found something."

"I've found…… I've found him."

"He's here?!"

"He is."

"Where is he, Master?! Let's finish this quest now."

"We will. But we have to face his company first."

"Where are they?"

"Right here."

From out of the air in a swivel of smoke, Kabra and Maba appeared before Darkous and Malach. Malach moved over avoiding a quickening slashing swipe from Maba. The two demons were disguting in appearance. Their eyes were like the sun and their smell was of sulfur. Their clothing appeared to be ripped and burned by a blazing heat. Even their rough skin appeared burnt with boils on their arms. Kabra lunged toward Darkous, grabbed by the throat. Choking him, Darkous stared him in the eyes. Showing the dominion between the two.

"So you're who he gave Mazakala. I expected more power."

"Don't underestimate our physical appearance, Shrouded One. We have to protect our general and protect him we shall."

"Very well. Protect him now. From me."

Darkous threw Kabra against the church's unsteady wall. Malach and Maba were having a swordfight amongst themselves with them going back and forth with attacks. Kabra got to his knees on the ground, seeing Darkous walking toward him slowly.

"You're taking this slowly. You're taking us for granted!"

"You don't possess the power to face someone like me. You've only been around for about a century. I have been around since the beginning."

Darkous kicked Kabra in the head and stomped his head into the wooden church floor. Kabra screaming with blood coming from his face. Darkous picked him up by his neck and tossed him against the wall once more.

"I expected Mazakala to give you a portion of his own power. Yet, he did not. Still selfish as he was before."

"Mazakala promised us much when he succeeds. He promised us power, lands, kingdoms, and servants."

"The typical materialistic nature of humanity has been washed upon demons. How oddly things have become."

Malach slammed Maba down on the ground with his sword and cut off Maba's left arm, dropping his sword in the process. Maba screamed in pain, holding his arm as his dark red blood gushed from the wound. The blood even smelled of sulfur and would burn the ground it touched.

"Didn't know demons could scream like that." said Malach. "Now to finish you off."

Maba pushed Malach away with some form of magic. Kabra began to use the magic against Darkous, attempting to consume him with a thick blanket of darkness. Darkous stood still as the darkness consumed him. Kabra smiled as Malach looked over seeing it happen.

"Master!"

"Now we know who is stronger than the other in the arts of darkness. I can consume you, Keeper of the Cosmos, I can consume anyone who gets in the way of Mazakala."

Maba ran over to Malach and punted him in the head, knocking him down. Maba picked up Malach's sword and started to walk toward him. Malach gazed his eyes on Maba approaching him, but also seeing Darkous covered in a thick darkness.

"Master?" Malach said with concern in his voice.

"With this newly received power, I will become the new Keeper of the Cosmos."

"You think so?" Darkous said softly. "I do not."

The thick darkness immediate boasted away from Darkous and toward Kabra, who tried to keep it away from him with a magic force. Kabra pushed and pushed with all of his might. Maba looked on at Kabra pushing the darkness.

"You demons are all the same. You're all arrogant, proud, boastful, and selfish."

"Keep quiet!"

"You should understand something here, Kabra. Something that your general will soon come to understand as well."

"Get back! Get back!"

"Those who fear the darkness will dwell in darkness. Those who fear the light will succumb to the light. Either way, you'll fear."

Darkous raised his hand slowly and the darkness became like a beast and consumed Kabra, bringing him into total darkness to where he could neither see nor hear. Maba ran toward Darkous and Darkous turned to him and raised up his hand, pushing Maba against the wall and through a stake. Kabra's screams began to turn into silence. Darkous released Kabra from the darkness and it vanished into thin air, leaving Kabra on the ground motionless and silent. Malach retrieved his sword from Maba and walked over to Darkous.

"I didn't know what was going on, Master. I thought he had you for a second."

"I am the Keeper of the Cosmos. I control the darkness in this universe. I was created solely for that purpose."

They left the church, returning to Malach's cabin. While walking, Darkous stopped and gazed into the night sky taking witness to the stars above. Malach looked at him, sensing something taking place within the unseen realm.

"What is it, Master?"

"I am needed back at the Astral Dimension. I will speak to you again when it is time."

"Yes sir." Malach said with a bow.

Darkous disappeared into the night, appearing like dust flowing up above the air.

229

III

THE PLACE OF PURE DARKNESS

Darkous entered the Astral Dimension and sought his eyes on the person he seen standing in front of him. He levitated over toward them with anger in his eyes, which his while pupils are beginning to turn a dark red. He stopped and stared at who he was looking at. Lilu, one of the chief demons.

"Do you even want to test me in this dimension?"

"I do not wish to test you, Doctor of Mystics. That is not the purpose of why I'm here."

"Then why are you here, Lilu? I sensed trouble here and I come to find you here."

"I have come to bring word of Mazakala and what he has planned."

"Speak the word."

"Mazakala is making his move toward Sheol. He intends on using it for one of his plots."

"Why would he intend to use Sheol? How would he ever enter the realm."

"He has some help from the inside."

Darkous stared into the astral space, thinking to himself, silent. Lilu can only look at Darkous and wonder what is going on inside of his mind. Darkous returns to his conscious and glares at Lilu.

"I thank you for the information. Now, leave this dimension before I have to make you."

"I will leave at my own will, Darkous. But first I must tell you of an event that took place not too long ago on Earth."

"What kind of event have I missed that you have seen? It couldn't have been a major one."

"You remember Death? The young woman who's the sister of one of the Dark Gods?"

"I cannot forget such a twisted face. A face that humans would love and fear. A face that we dislike and destroy. She is all that they fear and love. Sad for the humans."

"She was apprehended in the city of Retropolis by some man wielding a divine sword. He brought her to their prison, and she is currently being held inside."

Darkous stood quiet.

"What do you want me to do about it?"

"What do you think I want you to do? Go and bring her back to where she belongs. With all of us."

"She made her choice to live amongst the humans and now she is paying for it. The man with the divine sword is no threat to us. I have known and seen the myths and legends of the sword he carries and the power it possesses. I have nothing to fear in him. But your kind surely should fear him."

"Here me out, I do not intend on freeing Death myself. But, she doesn't belong on the earth alongside the humans. She belongs with us here. On the Other Side."

"She made her decision. Besides, her goal is to free her brother from divine imprisonment. She already has the knowledge that he will be release when the imprisonment has been completed, and she can rejoice all she desires. Until then, Death is on her own. If I have the time, and I have the time to speak with her, I shall."

Darkous turned away from Lilu, he looked down and seen the pit toward Sheol. Preparing himself to jump into it, he glared at Lilu with his pupils glowing a dark gold.

"Now is your time to exit this dimension, Lilu. Return to your master."

"So, I can see. You'll be seeing me again sometime, Darkous."

Lilu warped into a wave of fire and flew out of the dimension. Darkous watched her leave before he took a leap down into the pit leading to Sheol. Diving down into the deep darkness to where no one can see or feel anything. Darkous' pupils turned to a dark blue, giving him the ability to see through Sheol's deep, thick darkness. He could also feel the darkness due to him being an Astral entity. Darkous landed on the grounds of Sheol with the dust rising The first thing he noticed are the cries and weepings of those that are trapped in the thick darkness. He looked around to see if anything was unusual than it should be.

"Why would you come to Sheol, Mazakala? What would be here for you that would enhance your already wasted power." Darkous said to himself.

Darkous walked through the darkness as he is the only one there to be able to see through it clearly as if the sun was shining above him, showing him the steps. Darkous suddenly felt the pressure of the spirits that are trapped surrounding him. Their emotions were sad. Their tears could be heard dripping from the faces onto the ground like a faucet left turned. Their fear could be felt as well, consuming them that were around the other.

"I have a proposition for your spirits." said Darkous. "Have any of you heard or felt a magic unlike any other? A magic that's pressure was strong and heavy? An immortal magic?"

The spirits screamed out their answers and responses. Darkous listened to them very carefully. Trying to point out the ones that referred to magic and Mazakala. Darkous kept listening closely to the spirits.

"I need more than that. Do any of you know about Mazakala the Immortal?"

"I do." said a voice from behind. "I know about the Immortal Mazakala."

Darkous turned and seen the spirit of an elderly man approaching him. Darkous noticed the way he walked as if he could see where he was going.

"How have you learned to walk such a way in the thick darkness?"

"I have been here for a very long time, Cosmos Keeper. I have also seen the feats that you can do with this darkness and how terrifying it can be when you put it to its full potential."

"What do you know of Mazakala and of his supposed business down here?"

"Mazakala did come here not long ago, Darkous. He came seeking information about cosmic power. A power that he intends to use against you and all the universe. He is angry of his imprisonment. Being set free will not heal that kind of bondage."

"I am aware. Mazakala put that bondage on himself and he knew the risks of his actions. Now he is repeating himself on a larger scale."

"Yes, he is. From what I could decipher, he was granted what he came for and is preparing for his full assault. Primarily against you and the others up there."

"That is his plan you say."

"That is his plan."

Darkous looked up toward the dim purple light that would lead out of Sheol and back into the Astral Dimension. He looked back at the elder spirit.

"Where is Mazakala headed now? If you know of it?"

"He's making his way toward Earth."

Darkous nodded to the man.

"Thank you for your pleasant conversation. Maybe you can be redeemed at the appointed time for your loyal help."

Darkous flew up in the air toward the dim purple light. Inching closer he flew through the light, returning to the Astral Dimension where he sees Beatrice standing by, waiting for him.

"Where have you been, Darkous?" She said with some curiosity.

"I've just returned from Sheol. Had a conversation with an elder spirit about Mazakala."

"Mazakala went into Sheol? For what? Information of some kind?"

"He went there to gain information on some sort of power. He apparently now has that power and is fully prepared to eliminate all of us from this universe from the lowest of us to the highest of all."

"What do you need me to do around here?"

"I need you to prepare yourself and anyone else around here to combat Mazakala if he makes his way here. The elder told me he was heading for Earth and I'm going there to confront him myself."

"Funny enough, I was about to tell you that you might need to go there for a small quest."

"What small quest is taking place?"

"Someone is trying to open up a portal in the city of Retropolis. If they open the portal, they will have entrance to the other worlds in the universe. This dimension as well as Sheol and possibly the Heavens."

"Be that as it may. I will handle this novice of a warlock in Retropolis and afterwards, I will find and confront Mazakala and end all of this. Period."

"Make sure you'll be careful if you come against him, Darkous.

There's no telling what kind of power he now controls."

"You have a good point there, Beatrice. A good point."

Darkous vanished from the Astral Dimension, flowing through the air toward Earth.

Late in the night, Carol entered a nightclub, seeking possible information on spiritual events taking place inside the club. She witnessed men grouping on women and women grouping on men. Couples kissing in the corners of the club to almost having sex inside the club.

She could also see others sniffing cocaine and shooting themselves up with morphine to get high. She decided to stand in the back corner of the club, near the back-exit door. She watched the dancing take place with the loud music and the flashy light effects. Someone entered the club, everyone stopped dancing and stood still, getting Carol's attention, she also looked. The man who walked in was Malach with his sword in hand.

"I know you men work for Mazakala and I am here to kill you."

Six men stood out from the other clubbers who began to run out of the club. The men snarled at Malach and lunged toward him. Malach began to slice the men up with his sword, killing them one by one and some in pairs. Fighting the remaining two with kicks and elbow attacks. He impales one through the heart with his sword and chopped the head off the last one. The club is quiet when Malach sees Carol trying to exit the club through the back. From the bar corner, a man ran and grabbed Carol, trying to bite her. She screamed for help as Malach ran toward her and impaled the man through the back and cut off his head. He helped Carol to her feet.

"Are you hurt, Ms.?"

"I am ok. I don't know what's going on around here."

Malach noticed she carried notes and he gazed by, understanding her notes contained information of mythology. Uncertain of her place being inside some nightclub pass midnight hours for starters.

"Why are you here with notes on mythology?"

"I have… I have been on the study case of the recent murders in the past few months and I was aware that this club had contained some insight to the supernatural."

"Appears your insight was correct. These men work for the one who committed the murders."

"Wait. You know who the murderer is?"

"I need to take you to a safer location to avoid confronting him."

"Why would confronting him be a problem? By the way you fight, you can handle a simple murderer."

"The murderer is that simple. Besides, my Master is currently tracking him down."

"Your master?"

"I have the feeling you two will meet soon enough. I hope you're prepared for it."

"Doesn't look like I have any choice."

"From your notes, you don't have a choice in this matter."

The cold air blew through the city air of Retropolis and so did Darkous. Moving in the air faster than the vehicles below him on the streets. He looked around, sensing the located of the proposed portal opening. He turned his head to the left and looked, seeing a large prison. He senses the magic from inside the prison.

"There is the site of the magic."

Darkous landed on the ground and walked through the gates of Pegasus Prison. He walked slowly through the entrance of the gates, surrounded by their gardens and see some of the inmates sitting outside the place surrounded by Retropolis police officers. Darkous walked through the door and entered the prison. Inside he could feel the magic surging through the place from all corners. He concentrated and focused on the strongest place where the portal was trying to be opened.

"Third floor." Darkous' eyes glowed with light. "Seventh cell."

Darkous evaporated into specs of dust and went up through the floors to the third floor and flew toward the seventh cell. The dust formed back into Darkous' physical body as he looked inside the door, seeing the man playing around with magic trying to open up the portal.

"This has to stop now."

Darkous walked completely through the cell door as if he was a ghost. The prisoner turned, seeing Darkous inside the cell with him. Confused and uncertain, the prisoner pulled a knife from his cot and stood up against Darkous.

"You think I'm open! Not a chance pale boy."

"Enough playing around with magic, Cartavious Cage. I demand you cease your actions now."

"I am getting my ass out of this prison and there's nothing anyone can do about it."

"This is your final warning. Cease the magic."

"I will not. Who are you to tell me what to do? You're just a man. I can kill you right now and mark you as my next kill. Afterwards I will do wonders to your body to where not even the security will find your body. Your blood will be drained from this toilet here. I have my ways."

"And I have mine."

Darkous conjured up a dark hole that appeared behind Cage. He turned and tried to cut through it with his knife. Having no kind of effect period, Cage turned to Darkous and lunged at him with the knife. The knife hit Darkous in the chest, breaking in half. Cage looked at the knife and to Darkous who backhanded him against the wall, knocking him unconscious. Darkous walked over to Cage's magic spot, looking at what he was dealing with.

"A red gem, some crystal sand, and a grimoire. Where did you receive these items from inside of a prison?"

Darkous took the items with him and left the cell. While leaving, he could feel the presence of Death nearby. He continued walking until he appeared at her cell door. Looking inside, he could see her. Sitting in the corner laughing and giggling.

"You will never learn the rules, woman."

"Dark... Darkous....... Is that you?!"

"Get yourself in gear, Death."

"Gear. Ha. Gear."

Darkous teleported from the prison with the last thing he could hear was the laughter of Death.

IV

<u>MATCHING CLUES</u>

Malach and Carol returned to her home. When they enter, Malach noticed the table covered in books of many mythologies, some books are references for demonology, ancient religions, and modern religions. He walked over to the desk to have a closer look at the books. Carol locked the door and took off her jacket.

"You can make yourself at home."

"I will do that, ma'am."

Carol went to her refrigerator and pulled out a glass of water to drink. She looked at Malach going through her books.

"You want anything to drink?"

"I will take a small glass of water please."

Carol grabbed a glass and poured some water for him. She placed the pincher in the refrigerator and handed the water to Malach. He took a sip.

"Thank you."

Malach sat down at the couch with Carol sitting in the seat facing him. Carol looked around her home, checking the windows and the door again.

"Is this place safe enough?"

Malach looked around at the surroundings. Mostly the windows and the door. He nodded while taking another sip of water from his glass.

"It will do for the time being."

Malach looked at Carol for a moment. Finding the whole situation somewhat strange to her. Although it is a normal day for him.

"I know it may seem crazy to have a stranger in your home. Right now, we need to have a discussion. Primarily concerning you digging yourself into this field. Why did you choose this field to work in?"

"I have always been fascinated with the paranormal and the supernatural powers that shape our world. I've always known them to exist. I just, I just never had the opportunity of doing it in my earlier days."

"You don't appear to be as old as you're talking about."

"I'm only thirty-three and I wanted to start in this field right at twenty. Things don't always go the way you planned them out."

"They never do."

"So, why are you what you are? If that makes any kind of sense. I'm strictly speaking of you wielding a sword and battling foes of the supernatural. I've heard of such things, but I've never come to believe they were true."

"My name is Malach HaMavet. I am a warrior in the supernatural and I obey the Father above all."

"So, Malach, how did you come to entering the supernatural field and becoming a swordsman?"

"When I was a young boy, I witnessed demons come from the shadow and kill most of my friends. My family thought I was nuts and called me a crack head, cook, cult leader, and a fantastic because of my testimony in confronting demons. They weren't exactly believers in the supernatural, but they went to church every Sunday to worship a supernatural deity. It wasn't until I decided to search the supernatural myself to understand what the demons were and where they came from."

"I take it you found out."

"I did. One day, I summoned the demons, the same demons who killed my friends. They came before me and we fought roughly. I was near-death, unable to combat them because of my ignorance in the supernatural. Suddenly, the room went dark and I couldn't see a thing, surprisingly neither could the demons see and I could hear their screams. Screams of fear and torment. I heard what sounded like a gust of wind had blown in from the windows and doors of the place and gathered them up and tossing them to the outside. Once the darkness had evaporated, I found myself staring face to face with the one who created the darkness. He told me I had courage and I had the Spirit to combat the demonic entities. So, he brought me in and trained me, taught me the supernatural realms and what is and what is not. Now, he is my Master."

"Who is your master?"

"My master in the art of the supernatural is known as Doctor Dark. He is the Keeper of the Cosmos and he watches over all of the darkness in the universe."

Carol showed a faint look on her face. Trying to understand how an entity of darkness could possibly help someone in need and even train them in the process to prepare their own selves.

"I always thought the darkness was evil and the light was good. Is there something I don't know?"

"There is a lot you do not know. I would hope that you could speak with Doctor Dark about it. He can answer all of your questions. Even the ones you haven't thought to ask."

"Where is he right now?"

"He's currently looking for Mazakala."

"So, he's the murderer?"

"He is and he's a very powerful warlock. He's basically immortal."

"An immortal warlock is responsible for the deaths that have taken place in the last few months? I would've never believed that to be the case."

"Mazakala has lived for eons and was temporarily imprisoned for his last actions in trying to open up the portals to the Heavens."

"Was he successful in trying to?"

"He could barely make a mark in the realms. Doctor Dark is on his trail and will eventually find him and put an end to his troubles."

"Will he need you to assist him?"

"If he contacts me, I will be needed. He hasn't spoken to me since we stopped Mazakala's demons in an abandoned town."

"He had demons under his control."

"They were given to him by Satan. Mazakala somewhat works for Satan at this point. It explains how he's constantly getting away from confrontations in all parts of the universe."

Carol stared at Malach. Trying to put all this information in her head and to keep calm and relaxed.

"This is too much for you isn't it?"

"Right now, I could use a small break of the mind. You know. Let my brain rest for a bit."

Carol drank all her water and walked back to the refrigerator and grabbed a bottle of wine. She poured the wine in the glass and drank it.

"You know, if I may, I spoke with a group of men earlier and they had much knowledge of all this."

"What kind of men? Did they look like the ones in the nightclub?"

"No. They were well-dressed men. Not clubbing men. They would be the ones you would consider that would run the club from behind the scenes."

"You're saying they're businessmen type. Suits and hats. Smoking cigars probably."

"They were all of those. They spoke about various mythologies and who could the murderer be. They had spoken their opinions on who it could've been."

"I've heard of a group like that. I believe they call themselves the Mythologists. They work underground. Away from the rest of society. Keeping all the information they gain to themselves."

"They invited me back for another talk whenever I wished. They were very interested to know what I know."

"Best you let myself and my Master accompany you on your next visit to see them."

"I shall do that."

Across the world, Darkous roamed through the cities and towns and counties and jungles and valleys and mountains searching for Mazakala. All Darkous had found are fragments of Mazakala's fabrics laying around at scattered locations. Darkous has collected the fabrics and remembers the locations of where they were placed.

"This is a set-up. He knows I'm looking for him and he's leaving behind nothing but breadcrumbs for me to pick up. Like I'm a dog to him."

Darkous traveled to Cairo, Moscow, Ethiopia, Jerusalem, Damascus, the Sahara Desert, Sydney, Australia, Scandinavia, Ukraine, Germany, Turkey, Palestine, India, China, North Korea, South Korea, the Amazon Rainforest, Tokyo, Mecca, the remains of Ur, Mount Ararat, London, Paris, New York, Chicago, Los Angeles, Miami, Little Rock, New Orleans, Houston, Dallas, Phoenix, Newark, Enigma City, Retropolis, Seattle, Vancouver, the Northern Mountains. All of those places is where Darkous had discovered the fabrics of Mazakala.

"He intends on invading these places to attack them. To turn them into nothing but rubble where he will be the only one to rise them up from their ashes."

Darkous collected all of the fabrics he could find and was not unaware of what he needed to do next. Uncertain of his next move, Darkous decides to return to the Astral Dimension to uncover more clues as to where Mazakala is heading next on Earth. Darkous vanished out of thin air and went to the Astral Dimension.

Upon arriving there, he discovered the place was attacked. He looked around and found Beatrice laying on the ground.

"Beatrice!"

Darkous levitated with speed over to her and held her up. Rubbing her face with his glowing hand.

"I can sense you're still alive. Wake up for me now, Beatrice. Wake up now."

Beatrice awoke and looked around, gaining back her conscious. Immediately she noticed Darkous in front of her, holding her.

"Darkous. What are you doing here? I thought you were supposed to be on Earth."

"What happened here is the real question. What happened here, Beatrice. What took place here for me to find the place in ruin and you lying on the floor unconscious?"

"I... I... I don't remember. All I can recall is me searching for the whereabouts of Mazakala and this bright light appear and that was it. Next thing I saw was you holding me."

"Someone must have invaded the realm. We need to be on guard."

"They could still be in here, Darkous. Somewhere around here."

"That is what I'm telling you. I can sense some form of energy in here and it isn't native to this place. It's something else entirely and I will purge it out of this place."

The bright light returned and knocked Darkous and Beatrice to the floor. The light inched closer toward them and dimmed down. Darkous looked toward it to see who was in control and he knew who was in control of the light. Darkous showed a small grin on his face as his pupils turned a dark red.

"It's about time we meet again."

"Yes, it is time."

The light dimmed, and it was Mazakala who invaded the dimension. He stared down Darkous. Mazakala's hairy structure showed off its golden color and his golden horns. He levitated off the ground holding two daggers in his hands. Darkous stood up and stared at Mazakala. The anger surging through him.

"All the mess you have caused on Earth, you bring here."

"This is your place isn't it, Keeper of the Cosmos. I fully intended on paying you a visit when I was released from my imprisonment."

"You understand that one of us will die on this day."

"I do, Darkous. I do and we both know who will survive this bout and it certainly won't be you. I will kill you by snapping your neck in two. I will absorb your darkness and become the new Keeper of the Cosmos and I will rain down darkness upon the earth and after that the universe and lastly, the Heavens. When that is done, I will be the new God. The new Elohim."

"You're finished now, Mazakala. There's no turning back for you now. You are living in your last moments. From this moment forward, when I get my hands on you, you will wish that you were still imprisoned. For the beating that I will give you will be unlike any attack you have felt in the eons of your days. Are you ready for it, Immortal One?"

"I am prepared for what may come of this battle and I am ready."

"As am I."

V

<u>DIMENSIONAL WARFARE</u>

Darkous and Mazakala clashed one another with their power. The power of darkness battling it out with the power of magic. Mazakala used his daggers to create a wave of magic beams that attacked Darkous. Darkous turned toward him and raised his arms, creating a dark ball and threw it toward Mazakala, knocking him back. Mazakala looked and seen Darkous flying toward him with a punch. Darkous punched Mazakala and backhanded him against the illusionary wall of the Dimension.

"You are strong as you've always been, Darkous."

"Enough words."

Darkous kicked Mazakala in the head and rammed his fist down on Mazakala's skull, imprinting a hole in the floor. Mazakala kicked Darkous back and grabbed him by his coat and threw him against the wall and slammed him on the floor. As Darkous gets to his feet, Mazakala flies up in the air, trying to escape and Darkous chased him. They fly and battle through the wormhole. Punching and kicking one another.

"Seems we're heading to Earth, Darkous! Ready to see what I have prepared down there?!"

"You have nothing down there!"

"Oh! We shall see if your words are as true as you believe them to be!"

Meanwhile on Earth, Carol and Malach are walking down a sidewalk in Toronto when suddenly a pair of black-clad soldiers appear from a portal in the middle of the street. The civilians run with fear as the soldiers began to tare apart cars with their strength.

Blocking traffic, the soldiers began destroying the cars and killing the people inside of them. Malach put his arm in front of Carol. The soldiers' eyes glowing red as they slowly began to walk toward Malach and Carol on the sidewalk.

"What are they?!"

"Don't run Carol! I may need your assistance on this one."

"How would you need my assistance?! I don't have a sword in my possession."

Malach reached down over to his side and pulled up his sheathe and handed it to Carol. She looked at it confusingly as the soldiers spotted them and started walking toward them.

"Give me your sheath?! This won't do anything."

"Hold it outward and turn it to the right."

"Why?"

"Just do it and see what will happen."

Carol held out the sheathe in front of her and turned it to its right. The sheathe began to shake and from it formed a sword of its own. Now, Carol had possession of a sword. She smiled while looking at the sword she was holding.

"That was? That was very unusual."

"Now, I need you to help me stop them before they kill more people. Can you do that?"

"I can now."

Malach and Carol run toward the soldiers who do the same. They collide with Malach impaling and cutting the heads off many soldiers. Carol blocked the attacks from the soldiers and stabbed as many as she could in the chest toward their hearts. They kept fighting as more soldiers began to show up through portals opening in the street.

"Just keep fighting, Carol! We can handle these soldiers!"

"Why can't you just call your master down here to aid us?!"

"He's busy with greater matters. We have to deal with the problems here!"

"Sure."

They continue fighting the soldiers. Swiping, impaling, and cutting off the heads of the soldiers they combat against. From the air view, it looked like there were over a dozen or so soldiers standing in front of Malach and Carol.

Above them, Darkous and Mazakala continue to brawl with punches and kicks. Darkous grabbed Mazakala by the throat and started pummeling him in his face. Mazakala shot some form of magic in Darkous' face. Blinding him for a small time. Mazakala laughed out loud.

"You can't see what I'm about to do next!"

Mazakala kicked Darkous, ramming him into the grounds of the desert. Darkous rubbed his eyes and could barely make out anything with his sight. What he could make out were a set of pyramids in the distance. He knew where they were.

"We're on Earth. We're in Egypt."

"Yes, we are, Darkous. We're in Egypt. One of the places where I will destroy all that sits here only to rebuild it in the image of Mazakala."

"I will not allow this to happen."

"What can you do, Darkous. You can't barely see what's going on. What can you really do."

Mazakala punched Darkous and grabbed him by his long black curly hair and slammed in in the dirt. Mazakala started to stomp Darkous deeper into the ground. Stomp after stomp after stomp, Darkous goes deeper into the ground as if Mazakala is stomping him into his own grave.

"Have you ever been buried alive, Darkous. I would think you have but it wouldn't affect you. The darkness wouldn't bring fear to you. You would use it for strength and would eventually burst from the grave, stronger once more. Not this time, Darkous. This time, you will die, and I will be the one to have killed you."

"I will not easily go down to you, Mazakala. No matter how much stronger you've become because of your allegiance with the ha-Satan."

"Satan. Oh! He's helped me very well. Gave me some power I could never have possessed if it wasn't for me opening up the door to my anger and rage. He helped me and I'm helping him."

"Figured you would say something like that. Still the weak immortal that you are."

Mazakala kicked Darkous in the face and started to stomp him in the face into the ground.

"This is where you truly belong, Keeper of the Cosmos. Underneath my heel."

Darkous pushed the foot of Mazakala off of his face and punched him. Slowly getting to his feet, Mazakala rammed him with a spear and summoned cobras with his magic. Mazakala directed the cobras to Darkous.

"Feast upon him, my creations! Feast upon the Darkness of the Darkness."

Darkous fights off the large cobras as the circle around him. He grabbed one by the head and ripped it apart. The other cobra slithered around Darkous and was able to snatch him and constricted him.

"You're weakening, Darkous. Looks like your time is about to be up. No more Darkous."

Malach and Carol continue to take down the remaining soldiers. Slicing them apart and impaling them as they fall to the pavement. Malach chopped the heads off of the ones that laid on the road while Carol impaled them in the heart. Malach looked ahead seeing the last remaining soldiers running toward him.

"There's three left, Carol. Let's finish this."

"Sure thing, Malach."

They ran toward the three soldiers and instantly Carol impaled the three together on the sword. She took a few steps back from them. Malach looked and saw what she had done. An idea had come to his mind.

"I can finish this."

Malach walked over and chopped the heads off the soldiers. Their bodies fall to the ground and Carol retrieves her sword. She looked around and all she could see was the bodies of the soldiers. Dead. Civilians started to show up from around corners and peeking from buildings and doorways.

"It's done. We did it."

"Yes, we did."

Carol handed the sword back to Malach.

"Here."

"Thank you. You're not bad with a sword."

"I had to learn very quickly. Never used a sword before for anything."

"Always a first for everything they say."

As they talk with one another, behind them is the museum and through the windows, stand the group of men that Carol spoke to. They stand, looking outside toward her and Malach. Smoking cigars. The leader shook his head.

"The woman knows something we don't. We'll have to get her back in here somehow and as soon as possible."

Back in Egypt, Mazakala is overpowering Darkous as the cobra is sucking the breath from Darkous' body. Mazakala is conjuring up more magic and throwing it toward the cobra, giving it strength and squeeze Darkous even more.

"Not much longer, Darkous and you'll be out of breath."

"I… still have….the fight… within me."

"No, you don't! Your time has come, and you won't accept it. The time is here and there's nothing that you can do about it."

"Maybe I can."

Mazakala heard the voice and was blown back by a wall of energy. The cobra was hit and flew across the desert. Darkous fell to the ground, regaining his breath. He raised his head and seen Beatrice standing in front of him, holding up a green gem.

"Good to see you here." Darkous said.

"I figured you'll need some assistance with this one. Besides, I want some payback of my own."

Mazakala rubbed the sand off his face and seen Beatrice walking toward him. He smiled and stood up to his feet. He pointed at Beatrice with anger behind it.

"If you think me laying you out on the dimensional floor wasn't enough. Prepare to witness what I can do with the power I know possess."

"Show me what you can do, Mazakala." Beatrice said with a smile. "Prove it to me, you bastard."

Mazakala forms a cloud of magic above them. The cloud is intense that lighting is forming from within it. Beatrice stared at the cloud and so does Darkous.

"He's stronger than before, Beatrice. It will take the both of us to combine our power to match his. That appears to be the only way that we'll have to defeating him."

"When we do defeat him, are we imprisoning him again or can we just kill the guy?"

"You know that's not up to me."

Beatrice shrugged.

"Meh. You're right."

She raised the gem, holding it high above her and Darkous. She smiled toward Mazakala. He could see the smile and it was sending him into a rage, thinking they were taking his power as a joke.

"This isn't a game, woman!"

Mazakala throws the ball of magic toward them. The lightning sparking and surging within it as it moved through the air.

"Feel the power of the Immortal One!"

Darkous raised his hands up toward the ball. He looked to see what Beatrice was doing and she was only standing still with the gem still above their heads. Darkous was confused about what she was doing.

"What are you plotting, Beatrice?"

"Trust me on this one, Darkous. Just wait for what you're about to witness here this day."

The magic ball inched closer toward them with Darkous slowly creating a shielding to protect them. Beatrice noticed the shielding and turned to him.

"If you're going to shield us, do it and leave the gem in the open."

"Why would I do that?"

"Because this gem isn't no ordinary gem, Darkous. Once the ball hits, you will find out what it is made of."

Darkous shielded them except for the gem as the ball slammed against them. The magic ramming against Darkous' shielding. They could hear the laughter of Mazakala coming from behind the shielding. Darkous, still weakened, holds up his strength against the ball. Beatrice holds her own against the ball in the shield.

"You two are finished. You won't be able to stop that much power. No matter what your positions are in the universe."

The ball touching the gem. The gem glows and absorbed in the magic ball completely within seconds. The area is quiet as Darkous released the shielding and looked toward the gem. Beatrice held the gem closely. Mazakala is confused as to what happened to his ball of magic and lightning. The gem continued its glow.

"Where did you get retrieve that object?"

"A friend gave it to me, and I know what it's for."

"What has just happened?!" Mazakala yelled. "Where is my orb of magic?!"

Beatrice looked up toward Mazakala and held up the gem. She smiled.

"Right here."

The gem shook and from the gem came forth the orb of magic, heading straight for Mazakala. Fearful for what has happened, he tried to hold it back with his strength. Yelling and pushing.

"This is not happening to me!"

The orb of magic consumed Mazakala as he yelled in pain. Feeling the lightning striking him. The orb evaporated and Mazakala crashed to the ground. Darkous and Beatrice walked toward him as he shook the disturbance of the lightning from his body. He glared toward them with anger.

"I feel somewhat different. But that will not stop me from killing the two of your right where you stand."

"Go ahead. Kill us, Mazakala. With all of your powerful might."

Mazakala held his hand out and began to recite a spell. The spell became intense that his hand started to glow. With the final words of the spell, a bright light came from his hand and immediately dimmed out like a light bulb. Shocked, Mazakala looked at his hand and tried again. Still no effect.

"What has happened to me?"

"Your power has been zapped away from you. The power you once had is stored inside this gem. I know. It hurts."

"This cannot be possible."

Beatrice turned to Darkous. He looked at her and smiled.

"You can finish him off now."

"As I may."

Darkous raised his hands above him and the sky immediately turned into darkness. Mazakala looked round and could only see Darkous and Beatrice. He tried wiping away the darkness that surrounded them.

"What is going on? What are you doing, Darkous?"

"This is your final end, Mazakala."

"It is not."

"Yes, it is, dumbass." Beatrice uttered. "Deal with it."

"You whore of an Astral!"

From the sky came down a blanket of thick darkness, falling directly over Mazakala. He stared, swiping it away from him. But the blanket is so thick it cannot be moved. Its touch is rough, yet, warm and cold. A mixture of the strangeness.

"I will not allow this to happen to me! I am Mazakala! I am the Immortal One!"

"You are Mazakala. Yes. But I am Darkous, the Keeper of the Cosmos."

The blanket consumed Mazakala as he tried to fight back against the darkness.

"I will give you comfort in the blanket of darkness. A comfort that you will not enjoy. A comfort that will eat you alive for all of eternity. This is my immortal gift to you."

"NO!"

"Now, accept your comfort."

Mazakala instantly goes unconscious in the blanket of darkness. Beatrice hugged Darkous.

"Now what do we do about him?"

"We'll take him to the Council. See what they will do with him."

"I'm with that."

Darkous and Beatrice disappear along with the darkness blanket and Mazakala in tow from Egypt.

VI

THE ATMOSPHERE ABOVE US

A sentencing was held for Mazakala as he was sentenced to the pit of Sheol until the appointed time for his releasing, which will be his final time. While leaving the sentencing, Darkous received a message from an anonymous messenger. He opened the letter and read it. The letter only said,

"Darkous, you are hereby to appoint to The First Heaven for discussion of Mazakala's actions on Earth."

"I have to pay him a visit. Should be interesting."

Darkous vanished and entered The First Heaven. Looking down at ground, seeing people going to and fro of their business. He continued to walk toward the throne room. The guards moved as he entered. They closed the door afterwards and Darkous stood there, staring at the chair.

"You wanted me."

"I did."

The chair turned and Darkous is staring at the ha-Satan. Tall and strongly built. He signaled Darkous to approach him. Darkous slowly moved toward him, being cautious of his surroundings.

"Still see you're here."

"Where else can I go to get a good view of humanity. The Father's most precious creation."

"That still bothers you doesn't it."

"I am the favorite creation. I am the greatest of all creations and yet, I was cast out and banished here on Earth. Yet, your kind, you Astrals, continued to go around doing your own business at your own risks."

"We do what we are created to do. We were all created for a purpose and you ruined yours."

"I did not call you here to start an argument about our places in the universe. I called you here because of what you've done to Mazakala."

"It is a shame that you brought him into your inner circle and look where that has placed him."

"No. No. No. Mazakala's own actions placed himself into the pit of Sheol. There are others in this universe, Darkous that are stronger and more cunning than Mazakala. Hell, they're even smarter than he is."

"I'm surprised you didn't call one of them up to do this line of work for you. Going around killing innocents."

"You know none of them were innocents. Do any of them keep the truth and the Law in their hearts. You already know the answer to this."

"Get to the point of why you called me here."

Ha-Satan nodded with a grin.

"Sure. I called you here to thank you."

"Thank me for what?"

"For showing me that Mazakala wasn't the right one for the jobs ahead. You've shown me there are more out there willing to do the jobs and succeed in doing them. I love your way of working."

"Whatever you intend on plotting next, I will be there to stop it."

"I'm counting on it, Darkous. You may leave now."

The doors opened and Darkous leaves the throne room and flies out of The First Heaven, going down toward the Earth.

After about a week, Darkous walked through Retropolis during one of their rainy nights. The thunder cracks above him in the night sky with lightning clashing against one another across the sky of the city. Darkous could hear the sirens of the police cars zooming down the streets. He could also hear them on their communication speakers.

"We have a suspect in tow." said an officer.

"Why don't we just let The Swordman deal with them?"

"Because he's a myth. Been reading folklore have you."

"Always they argue over what they don't understand. Humanity." Darkous said to himself. "They never cease to amaze me."

Darkous entered one of the alleyways and stumbled upon Death. Who's standing in front of him wearing her black trench coat. her face as pale as it could ever be with her black-colored lips and her green eyes. Confusion ran through the head of Darkous. He wondered to himself but decided to ask her of the situation in order to comprehend the meditation of what is taking place.

"How did you get out of the prison?"

"I have friends all over the place, Darkous. You know how I operate things. How did you know I was in the prison?"

"Lilu told me about it. You do understand that I will have to take you back there, right?"

"I'm not going back to Pegasus, Darkous. I am not going back. I have business to do at this moment."

"Does this business contain information about your Dark God of a brother?"

"It does a little bit. But, you see, Darkous, I want revenge against the man who put me in that prison to begin with. I also am aiding others that insist on taking down these heroes that have risen over the past three years. We are prepared to do anything to stop them."

"Very well. Just know that I will not interfere with your little task of causing chaos. But if it does become a larger threat than will threatened the universe, I will come for you and I will stop you."

Death laughed at Darkous. She walked over toward him and patted him on his shoulder.

"You are funny."

Darkous stared at Death with uncertainly in his eyes. Death continued to smile at him and giggle a bit.

"I'll be seeing you around, Death. You can guarantee that."

"I will surely do so."

Darkous evaporated along with the rain and vanished. Death looked around and walked away down the alley, laughing to herself.

"The time is right. The time is right. Hope your prepared for the fight is pared."

THE CURSE OF THE MUTANT-THING

I

DETECTION OF THE ELEMENTS

With Demonticronto defeated, the newly formed team of Travis Vail, Gabriel Abraham, Cinderella, Creed, Death Chaser, John Terror, Ghost of England, Visitant Outlander, and Dark Manhunter head their separate ways. Amongst them in the battle was the Mutant-Thing, whom left the area, returning to its own estate deep into the wilderness. While mediating, the Mutant-Thing sensed something sinister and it made its move east, toward the border of Manitoba.

Sometime later, a series of strange murders were committed within and outside the city of Winnipeg. Entering Winnipeg are two detectives. Keen in their skills. Detectives Cole Yeager and Lewis Knight enter the police station to learn more about the murders. Greeting the two is Chief Bill Thompson, who walked them to his office.

"Good to have you guys here." Thompson said.

"We got the call and figured it was something worth doing." Lewis replied. "Now, what is truly going on?"

"Where to start? Ah, we've been receiving several reports of bodies being found out in the woods. Apparently, they add up to a series of murders. Are they committed by the same suspect? We don't know and that's why you two were called up."

"Wait a second." Cole jumped in. "You called us here to find the suspect? Without any evidence to the case?"

"Only evidence we have are the bodies in the woods."

"How many bodies are we talking?" Cole wondered.

"A dozen. Maybe more."

"Ah shit." Lewis said. "Sorry, I wasn't sure it was that many. Thought it might've been five or six at the most."

"Who's at the sight now?" Cole asked.

"A few of our patrolmen. Keeping the place secure from prying eyes. You know how people are these days. Always filming something for social media."

"Generational things." Lewis scoffed. "They come and go."

"One more thing I must ask." Cole said.

"Speak it."

"How come you didn't call one of those 'risen heroes' to solve this case?"

"We don't have no heroes in Winnipeg."

"I see."

"Anyway, while you two deal with the case on the outside, we have a reporter who's already on the case speaking with possible witnesses."

"A reporter for what?" Cole questioned. "Lewis and I can talk with the witnesses."

"I agree to that." Lewis said. "Why bring in someone else when we're already here?"

"To broaden out the case. She will go around and question those who may have some insights to the murders. Be it family members of the deceased or those who might have seen something strange these past several days. You'll probably bump into her on your way around the city or when you return back here."

Yeager nodded, standing up from his seat and walking toward the door. Knight turned to him and looked over to the Chief. The Chief only pointed at the door to which Knight shrugged his shoulders with a nod, standing up and walking out of the office with Yeager.

"You could've said you wanted to head out now." Lewis said.

"I went to the door." Cole replied. "What other signal is there to add on?"

Traveling out near the wilderness of Winnipeg, Cole and Lewis stepped out of their vehicle, seeing several officers surrounding a pile. From their perspective, the pile appeared to be only mounted trash. Until they walked closer and saw arms and legs covered in mud and blood. Lewis covered his nose without hesitation while Cole continued walking closer. No expression showed or appeared. Cole was collected as he stepped toward the officer.

"You guys must be the ones they talked about."

"We are." Cole said. "We'll take it from here."

The officer nodded and stepped away as Cole kneeled toward the bodies. Their stench strong as Lewis knelt down as well, covering his face with a cloth. His eyes went in several directions. Both from the bodies and toward Cole. His eyes locked in on Cole for a second as he shook his head.

"This smell ain't bothering you or something, eh?"

"No. The smell does not command my body to respond to its own concerns."

"The hell that's supposed to mean?"

"Means I have ultimate control over my body than the bodies we see in front of us."

Lewis scoffed.

"Oh, good for you."

Cole searched through the bodies, seeing arms and legs of men and women. Cole leaned in closer and caught a glimpse of fur. Confused, Cole stood up and walked toward one of the nearby trees, looking down on the ground as he picked up a stick. He returned to the pile, using the stick to move the bodies.

"What are you doing?" Lewis wondered. "Cole, what's the stick for?"

"There's something else here. Something other than people."

Using the stick, Cole moved the bodies, uncovering a smaller pile of dead animals. Lewis stepped back, covering his face even more as Cole leaned in further. Looking at the animals, Cole nodded.

"Elk." Cole said. "Looks like some beavers as well."

"The hell's happening out here?" Lewis said.

"We're dealing with something that shares no discrimination between human and animal. This thing kills whatever it desires."

"What kind of person does this." Lewis replied.

"I don't think it was human." Cole added. "Something else."

II

LAW OF NATURE

A young woman stepped outside of her car in front of a home which appeared to be separate from the nearby suburban area. The woman carried a journal as she approached the front door and knocked. She waited and the door opened, revealing a woman similar to her age. She glanced at the woman and the journal.

"Who are you?"

"I'm Cassandra Day. I'm here to speak with you concerning the murders."

"And why would you speak to me about murders?"

"I was informed you might know what's happening here. What may have caused them."

The woman went silent. Her eyes moved left and right before she sighed, allowing Cassandra to enter her home. Once Cassandra had entered, the woman took a quick glance around the front of the home before shutting the door. The woman led Cassandra to her dining room table, where Cassandra sat down. The woman walked over to her coffee pot, pouring a cup.

"You want a cup?" She asked.

"No thank you." Cassandra replied. "I'm well."

The woman picked up her cup and sat down next to Cassandra.

"I never got your name." Cassandra said.

"My name's Morhana."

"Morhana." Cassandra said. "That's an intriguing name."

"It's foreign in many parts."

"Forgive me, but, that name sounds like it would belong to a witch."

"I am a witch."

"Oh." Cassandra paused.

"No need to be afraid. I'm not a sinister one."

"Well, I'm here to see if you may know what's been happening here."

"Regarding the murders?"

"Yes."

"I will tell you for starters, the cause of these murders are not only natural. They are also the cause of a supernatural force."

"A supernatural force?"

"You can't believe all of those murders were caused by a simple serial killer."

"There's records of it occurring in many places."

'Is that right?"

"Yes." Cassandra said. "I've been across this country and a few others to realize that murders such as this have happened before."

"Did you ever find the cause of the murders? The suspect?"

"Only for a few."

"What of the others?"

"The suspect remains a mystery."

"To the natural eyes."

Cassandra sighed, writing in her journal. Morhana raised herself up in the chair to get a glance. Cassandra spotted Morhana's movements, glancing at her from the journal.

"Just curious as to what you're writing."

"I'm writing what I need to solve this mystery."

"And I guess I'm a helper to your cause?"

"A minor one at the moment."

"Still good enough."

"Quick question." Cassandra said. "Your witchy tactics? How did you become one?"

"I was born this way."

"You were born a witch?"

"I was born into a coven. My mother was a witch as was my grandmother. They taught me the ways of sorcery and one I was of age, I was welcomed into the coven with open arms."

"Where is this coven now?"

"Underground. Although, we move around in the open secretly."

"How come?"

"Because, there are forces out there who seek to rid the earth of my kind."

"Let me guess. Witch hunters?"

"More than hunters. Sorcerers. Spiritual forces."

"And how do you face them?"

"By using what I've learned in my youth. They primarily use magic as their resource of power and I use it against them."

Cassandra closed the journal. Morhana's gaze was set on the journal.

"So, if I were to go by what you've said, I should be searching for the supernatural element to this case?"

"That would be your best bet."

"And what if you're wrong?"

"I'm never wrong." Morhana scoffed.

Cassandra nodded as she stood up from the table, grabbing her journal.

"Thank you for your time."

"No. Thank you."

Elsewhere, Cole and Lewis travel to a laboratory in the areas of Winnipeg. After gaining information from the officers and forensics, they make their way to speak with a scientist who may have some details concerning the suspect to the murders. Lewis parked the car in front of the laboratory and Cole stared. Lewis noticed Cole's silence and his stillness. Looking back between Cole and the lab.

"What's the issue?" Lewis asked.

"Something's not right about this place."

"Where are you getting this from? The door or the surroundings?"

"Both."

"Look, let's just go in there, speak with this guy to see what he knows, and we'll be out of this place before the sun sets."

"I know." Cole said.

"You know."

"I know."

The detectives enter the laboratory and quickly, they get the glimpse at the scientist who's operating at such a quick speed. Moving back and forth between desks. Lewis looked at the scientist's attire and scoffed.

"He sure dresses the part."

"The part?" Cole questioned.

"You know. The white coat, glasses. The whole gear set."

"Ah." Cole sighed.

Cole stepped forward, knocking on the desk nearby. The scientist jolted, turning around to see the detectives. He glanced toward them, looking at their attire. He raised his finger, pointing at them in a frantic fashion.

"Are you two students?"

"No." Lewis answered. "We're not students. We're detectives."

"Oh. But why would detectives be here in my lab on this day?"

"To ask you some questions concerning the murders." Cole replied.

"The murders? What murders?"

"You aren't aware of the murders in this city?" Lewis wondered.

"I'm afraid not."

"The hell you've been this whole time." Lewis asked. "Stuck in this lab or something?"

"What my partner is trying to say is how do you not know?"

"I keep to myself. Mostly."

"What's your name by the way?" Lewis asked.

"I'm Dr. Larry Grint."

"Grint?" Lewis said. "What kind of name is that?"

"A unique one."

"Sounds like one." Cole added.

Grint turned back toward his desk, Cole stepped forward looking atop the table, seeing nothing but papers and folders. Lewis looked around the lab, nothing interest him nor gave any indication that

Grint may know something. Lewis shrugged his shoulders.

"I think we hit a dead end."

"You're certain?" Cole asked.

"I am. The guy's not giving us anything. Hell, he's not even paying attention to us."

"Oh. I almost forgot!" Grint yelled.

"And that is?!" Lewis asked loudly.

"I saw trails leading into the woods several days ago. I wasn't sure what is what or where it came from."

"Trails of what?" Cole asked. "What were the trails made of?"

"It looked red. Like a bright red."

"You're talking about blood?" Lewis said.

"I assume so. Because the trail led to the pile of bodies."

Cole turned toward Lewis, a still expression. Lewis only let out a sigh and shook his head, turning toward the exit.

"Anything else?" Lewis asked, rubbing his eyes.

"Nothing so far."

"There is it." Lewis turned away.

"Thank you for your time." Cole said.

"Sure thing, gentlemen."

Lewis and Cole exit the lab and stand on the sidewalk next to their car. Lewis placed his hands on his side, shaking his head while gazing down. Cole was still. No expression. He turned toward Lewis.

"What now?"

"Let's give the site another glance."

"A glance for what?" Cole wondered.

"Humor me this once."

The detectives returned to the body site to find more details. Upon arriving, they discover they're the only ones there. The officers who were previously in place around the site were gone as were the forensic scientists. Lewis began to worry and Cole only walked closer to the bodies. Lewis, feeling uneasy placed his hand over his holster.

"Something off about this place." Cole said.

"You're just now realizing it." Lewis answered.

"No. I mean there's someone else here."

Lewis looked around. Only seeing the trees and the road. He

tossed his arms in the air.

"I don't see anyone out here besides you and me."

"Not a human being." Cole said. "Something else."

Cole stared into the wilderness, Lewis could see Cole was focused on something. As he turned toward the tress, he saw what Cole was staring at. A tall figure, shrouded in the shadows of the trees. Yet, the figure stood over nine feet in height as its presence brought sheer terror over Lewis. Cole's eyes were set on the figure as Lewis went for his gun, raising it up toward the figure.

"The hell is that?!" Lewis yelled.

"Don't shoot!" Cole screamed. "We're not sure why it's here yet."

The figure did not move nor make any noise. It only stood still, staring at the two detectives. Lewis was shaking as his hands began to sweat. Cole kept Lewis calm as he stepped forward toward the woods.

"The hell are you doing?!"

"Trying to get a better look."

"You see how tall that son of a bitch is?!"

"I do and I'm not concerned."

"Cole! Get your ass back over here!"

"Just calm down, Lewis." Cole responded. "I got this."

"You don't got shit!"

Cole had stepped close enough to reach the trees and he stood still. He raised his head to get a better look at the figure and what he saw he couldn't understand. Looking into the figure's eyes, Cole nodded and began to step back slowly. Lewis watched on as Cole returned toward him and only nodded at the forest. Lewis looked at Cole and turned back toward the trees, seeing the figure had vanished.

"The hell'd it go?"

"Deep into the forest." Cole said.

"How do you know?"

"It's hard to explain."

"The ride back to the station is long enough for you to explain."

Cole sighed, opening the car door.

"Hope you'll comprehend."

"Comprehend what?"

They left the site, returning to the base. Once they entered, everyone inside could hear Lewis ranting on about the incident. Lewis continually screamed toward Cole and Cole stayed silent as they entered the Chief's office. The Chief saw the commotion, standing up from his desk.

"What's this all about?"

"We went back to get a better look." Lewis said. "For more information. Little did we know we were being watched."

"Watched? By who?"

"Not a who. A what."

"Some… thing." Lewis answered. "It was strange."

"Cole, what's he talking about?"

"We went back to the body site after our visit with Dr. Grint."

"You spoke to Dr. Grint?"

"Yes sir."

"And what did he say about the murders?"

"Hardly a damn thing." Lewis responded. "the guy's a crackpot. He wasn't even giving us attention. Just busy with whatever the hell he was doing inside that lab."

"And the stalker in the woods?"

"It wasn't human." Cole said.

"What's that supposed to mean?" The Chief questioned. "What do you mean by 'not human'?"

"The thing was tall." Lewis said. "Had to have been over nine-feet at least."

"Is this true, Cole?"

"It is. I got a closer look."

"Yeah. This jackass decided to step forward near the thing. Go ahead, Cole. Tell him what you saw."

Cole sighed.

"I saw the figure in its full form. Its body was made of bark. Leaves growing from its limbs. It carried the stench of dew and its eyes were bright like the sun. It didn't speak, but it communicated in my mind. Like it spoke to me true some kind of brain wave."

"You talking psychic stuff?" the Chief asked.

"I am."

"Well, I guess I'll break it to you guys. I've heard of this being before."

"You have?" Lewis asked. "Seriously?"

"Yes. I only thought it was just some kind of joke to scare away tourists or to attract tourists. Either way, it gained some attention several months ago."

"What is the thing?" Cole asked.

"Some of the locals call it the Environment Man."

"Environment Man?" Lewis said. "Like a man who monitors the environment?"

"Not a man. A spirit. A ghost. Whatever it is, it's not human nor was it born human. The legends state the Environment Man was created and designed to watch over the environment at all cost. No matter the location or the scenario. Some incidents recall the being always present near deceased animals or humans. The fact that you two saw it at the body site only confirms there's something strange going on in this city and we need to get to the bottom of it."

"I agree to that." Lewis replied. "But, what are we going to do next? The doctor was a dead-end. Where's that reporter you spoke of?"

"She already made her rounds. She spoke with a witch apparently."

"No shit?" Cole said. "Does she know about the Environment Man?"

"Who's to say. But the witch told her there's something supernatural involved with the murders. So, if that's enough to go on."

"This shit is getting weird." Lewis said. "Definitely for me."

"Well, you can start at another site."

"Another pile?" Cole asked.

"Not exactly. The site is presumed to be a residence for the culprit. Perhaps, the murderer left something behind. I'll let the two of you head out there to find out."

The Chief handed them a map and on it was the detailed location of the second site. Lewis nodded, wiping the sweat from his forehead as Cole folded the map, putting it in his pocket.

"We'll come back with the details." Cole said.

"I'm sure you will. Also, be on the lookout just in case you run into him again."

"We will." Lewis said. "Armed up this time."

III

EVERYTHING HAS A SEASON

Cole and Lewis made the drive up to the secondary site. They see the location and the ruins. Lewis shrugged his shoulders, turning to Cole. He pointed toward the building.

"Is this what I believe it to be?"

"Another lab." Cole answered.

"You're sure this is the spot?"

"I'm sure. Chief marked it on the map clearly."

Lewis stepped forward near the laboratory door. Seeing a padlock, he sighed.

"Someone wanted to keep this place shut."

"And who do you have in mind?" Cole asked.

"A crazy scientist. As always."

Cole pulled the lock as Lewis took a gaze around the area.

"Would be better if we had the key."

Lewis' attention quickly turned toward the tree line behind the lab. Cole looked on, hearing some rustling. Lewis reached for his gun with speed, aiming it toward the woods.

"Something's watching us again."

"It's not the Environment Man." Cole said.

"How do you know? You see him?"

"No. Because the rustling is multiplied."

"Meaning?"

"There's more than one person in those trees staring at us."

From the trees walked out over a dozen figures. Shrouded in black robes and hoods. They stepped forward slowly toward the

274

detectives. Lewis yelled, holding his gun steady. Cole only glared, slowly going for his weapon.

"The hell's going on in this city?!" Lewis screamed.

"Who are these people?"

"How should I know!"

"Their apparel." Cole noticed. "They look to be part of some group."

"More like a cult if you ask me!"

The hooded one moved toward the detectives, their arms stretched out. The fingers shaking as they reached closer. Lewis kicked one in the chest and backed up. Cole only moved away from them. It reached the point where the two were backed up against their vehicle as the hooded ones circled them. Corning them in full. Lewis shook his head with the gun in hand. He was ready to fire. Cole only shut his eyes and raised his head.

"What are you doing?" Lewis asked. "Praying?"

"You could say that."

Once the hooded ones had their hands on the detectives. Lewis screamed and fired a shot, killing one of the hooded ones. The death didn't not shake them nor stop them. They kept coming. Lewis went for another shout, however, the ground began to quake. Cole's eyes open as he looked toward the trees. The hooded ones ceased, turning around to the woods. What they saw was a large crack emerging from the ground, separating the grassy plain from the concrete ground of the driveway. The crack stopped directly at the feet of the hooded ones. They glared down at the crack as Lewis and Cole slowly stepped back. The ground shattered open as the detectives saw the mutant-Thing attack the hooded ones. Snatching them by their heads and tossing them into the woods. The hooded ones all went in for the attack. Circling the Mutant-Thing, climbing him due to his immense height. Lewis looked on, seeing the Mutant-Thing was as tall or taller than the Environment Man.

"That's not the Environment Man." Lewis realized.

"It's something else." Cole said.

The Mutant-Thing exploded himself, impaling the hooded ones through their heads and chests. Their bodies dropped to the ground as the Mutant-Thing glared toward the detectives. Lewis slowly lowed his gun and Cole only stared.

"What is that?" Lewis wondered.

"Something beyond our understanding."

The Mutant-Thing nodded and turned back, bellowing into the crack and it closed itself as the Mutant-Thing disappeared. Lewis looked down, noticing the crack was gone.

"The fuck's going on here?"

Elsewhere, Cassandra made her next stop at Dr. Grint's lab. Surprisingly, Grint allowed her inside his lab. While there, Cassandra questioned him on the recent findings involving the bodies. Grint laughed, confusing Cassandra.

"You know, some detectives were here earlier. They asked me about the same thing."

"Did you tell them anything?"

"Not much."

"Why not? You're not aware of it?"

"I am aware. However, it is not any of my business."

"But, you live here. What happens here must certainly be on your mind when you're out in the public."

"One would believe such. Yet, it is better to keep your mind on your own affairs. Leave the others to their own concerns. Otherwise, you might cause trouble that shouldn't never have been."

"Well, I'll ask you this one question. What are you working on?"

"Ah. Something which will be used in the near future."

"For what purpose?"

"To make Winnipeg better. The environment better. Hopefully, once it's revealed, the countries of the world will accept it and my work will be spread across the world."

"You want to make the world a better place?"

"Doesn't everyone to some extent."

Cassandra nodded, putting her journal into her bag.

"So, you're not aware of anything. No strange sightings of any kind?"

"Nope."

"Thank you for allowing me to speak to you."

"Same to you, madam."

Cassandra had left the lab with Grint continuing with his work just as he did with Cole and Lewis. Back at the department, another detective had arrived after a call with Chief Thompson. She walked in and went straight for the Chief's office. She knocked on the door to get his attention and as he saw her he welcomed her inside the office.

"Go you've made it, Detective Salvatore."

"You called. Said something major was happening and I couldn't miss it."

"Yana, what's happening here, will need as much attention as possible."

"Where do I start?"

NEW FACES

Cole and Lewis returned to the office. Walking through the lobby toward the chief's office, they stop and see the new detective in the interrogation room with a suspect. Lewis confused, pointed while gazing at the other officers passing by in the lobby.

"Who's she?"

"That's not the reporter." Cole answered.

"You're sure?"

"I'm positive."

Lewis shook his head and waved his hand.

"I'll ask the chief."

"By all means. Oh, you're going to tell him of what we saw out there?"

"Which part? The druids or the monster from the ground?"

"Better to tell both."

Lewis sighed as he entered the office. While Lewis spoke with the chief, Cole watched Detective Yana interrogate the suspect. The suspect in general appeared as a mid-sized man. Cole watched his movement as Yana spoke more questions. The thing which fascinated Cole was the calculator sitting on the table. Why a calculator instead of a Smartphone Cole wondered. However, he approached the door and opened it. Yana turned around, seeing Cole.

"I'm sorry to interrupt." Cole said. "Me and my partner didn't know there was another detective here on similar work."

"I'm Yana." She extended her hand. "Yana Salvatore. I come from a town nearby."

Cole shook her hand with a nod.

"Nearby. Are you here to help with the murder investigation?"

"I am. Which is why I'm questioning this man."

Cole turned toward the man, seeing the calculator up close and the man's apparel. Which was only red buttoned shirt and black slacks. His hair was medium length, passing his ears and his facial hair was kempt to a degree. Cole pointed at the calculator.

"Don't have a phone?"

"I do. But, the calculator has given me much freedom."

"Noted."

"This man is Waid Givens. Calls himself the Calculator Man."

Cole stared. His eyes going back and forth between Yana and Waid.

"Calculator Man?"

That's what he said." Yana said. "He seems to know something greatly about the investigation."

"Knowing what?"

"He states he calculated the true suspect."

"Calculated?" Cole asked. "With the calculator?"

Yana sighed.

"Yes."

"And where do we go to find this suspect?" Cole asked Waid.

"You don't know?"

"How can I? You're the one with the answers today."

"My calculator estimated the suspect is always centered around the cemetery."

"Cemetery?" Yana said.

"What cemetery?" Cole asked.

"The one where the eeriness is always welcomed."

"Huh?" Yana said. "What's that supposed to mean?"

"It means the environment feels very, very strange. Like beyond this world. Beyond nature."

"How can we take this for face value?"

"You can't. Only you can estimate the numbers to calculate the location."

Cole took a moment of thought. He nodded.

"I'll track down which cemetery presents this eeriness you're talking about."

"Are you going out there?" Yana asked.

"Me and my partner will head on out there. It's what we do mostly."

Cole exited the room and as he shut the door, Lewis approached him from the chief's office. Lewis wiped his forehead and took a moment to breathe.

"What happened in there?"

"What happened in there?" Lewis said, pointing at the interrogation room. "You spoke with the new detective?"

"I did."

"And the suspect in there?"

"Waid Givens. He calls himself the Calculator Man."

Lewis stared.

"The fuck's that?"

"I don't know."

"He calls himself the Calculator Man? Seriously."

"Yes, he does."

"This case is getting stranger by the hours. How long do we have to keep this going?"

"Right now, we focus on getting it done. Now, he said he knows the location of the true suspect."

"Does he now? Where is this spot?"

"A cemetery."

"You're kidding me."

"I'm not."

"Ok. What cemetery?"

"He didn't say."

"And you believe him?"

"He only gave a small detail."

"Like what? Find the cemetery where the bodies raise up from the dead?"

"Not exactly. Said the cemetery where the suspect is presenting a form of eeriness."

"You're joking right now. Please tell me you're joking?"

"Afraid not.

Lewis nodded, glaring at the interrogation room. He saw Yana and she moved to the side, revealing Waid for Lewis to get a look at him. Lewis stared, seeing Waid holding up the calculator.

"What's with the calculator?"

"It goes with his name."

Lewis silenced himself and turned away.

"Let's just find this cemetery." Lewis said.

"Agreed."

While Cole and Lewis headed out to every cemetery they could find in searching for the eerie one, another detective had arrived at the office. Chris Harper. The chief contacted him in helping Detective Yana with their part of the case.

Cassandra traveled out into the wilderness after receiving another word from Morhana about a spiritual occurrence deep in the forest. Cassandra stopped her car and walked into the wilderness just as the sun was setting. With the surroundings growing dim, Cassandra took out her flashlight and searched the area. Unsure of what to find, she pulled out what appeared to be a compass. However, this compass was glowing. The colors reminded her of the northern lights only instead of the green, there was violet.

"Now, where do I go?" She asked herself.

She continued walking in the wilderness as the snow fell over her. The ground was covered in snow as she began to pick up her feet to continue walking. Nightfall had come and Cassandra was still in the forest. She looked around, seeing nothing but trees and snow. With that moment, she heard a loud breathing sound coming from the trees.

"Who's here?"

The breathing continued, followed by rustling snow and low thumping sounds. The thumping could be felt under Cassandra's feet and they began to grow in volume and feel. The compass ringed loudly as the violet colors transformed into a dark red. Right at the moment, the breathing had ceased. Except for the one huff of breath which was behind Cassandra. She slowly turned to see the source of the breathing and found herself staring at a colossal figure. She could only point out the horns, the legs, and the eyes.

"What are you?!" she screamed.

Cassandra started stepping back as the figure huffed once more and dragged its feet into the snow. Its breath could be seen through the chilly air. With the moonlight, Cassandra was able to get a better look at the figure. Seeing it's a hybrid of a man and a bull.

"A minotaur." She said softly.

The beast began to charge toward Cassandra and before the horns could touch her, the beast was pulled back by a larger entity hidden in the shadows of the trees. Cassandra moved herself to see and she saw the minotaur struggling to get away from the Mutant-Thing. The Mutant-Thing was covered in snow and was nearly camouflaged in the wilderness. The minotaur went to fight back, punching the Mutant-Thing with his man-like hands and rammed the Mutant-Thing with its horns. The horns went for another strike and the Mutant-Thing grabbed them, breaking one of the horns. The minotaur screeched as it trampled away. Cassandra stood still, gazing at the Mutant-Thing in awe.

"Who are you?" she asked.

"Leave this place." The Mutant-Thing commanded.

"Leave?"

"Go now."

"But, what should I tell everyone else? You saved me."

"Leave." The Mutant-Thing said once more.

Cassandra took in the words ad nodded before returning to her vehicle. Once she entered her car, she looked back at the trees, not seeing the Mutant-Thing. She sighed as she drove away from the woods.

V

HYBRID OF MAN AND BEAST

While Cole and Lewis were away from the office, Detective Harper had met with Yana and they began to question another suspect, who dimmed himself only a witness. The man claimed to have the ability to control the weather and brought with him a suit. A sleek uniform decorated in the colors of silver and red. He stated it was made of nanofibers, which the detectives quickly tossed away. He also included goggles and a wristwatch. Although, the wristwatch was not an actual watch. It was the source of his theory to controlling the weather.

"How is this possible?" Harper asked.

"Simple! You put on the suit and the watch. Afterwards, you have the power to change the weather to whatever you so desire."

"We're not buying this guy's games." Yana said. "He can't be a witness."

"Listen, Mr. Marston."

"Um. Mr. James Marston. But, call me… The Climate Control."

Yana looked around and shook her head in shame and let out a depressing sigh. She fanned away Marston as she approached the door.

"I'm done for the night." Yana said, exiting the room.

"Can I go now?" Marston asked.

"No." Harper replied boldly.

Dr. Grint continued working in his lab as the snowfall began to increase. The chill in the air didn't faze the scientist or interfere with his work. It in truth, enhanced it. Grint continued working more during the snowfall than the early hours where there was only calmness in the air. Grint stood over a large vertical table. Pulling tubes and cords from the surrounding walls, attaching them to a larger object on the table. Grint walked over to the desk and flipped a switch. There, a peculiar fluid moved though the tubes and entered the large object. The object itself appeared as what some would call a cocoon.

"In just a matter of sure moments. My work will be finished. A creation between man and beast."

VI

<u>A VISITANT STRANGER</u>

Cassandra returned to her apartment. She laid down her belongings on the table and as she walked toward the bedroom, she flipped the light switch and the lights flickered. Strange to her as the lights worked well earlier in the day. Unsure as to the occurrence, she flipped the switch again, turning the lights off. Flipping it again, the lights turned on and she paused herself, backing up against the closet door.

"Who are you?" She asked.

"Do not fear me, Cassandra Day." The visitor spoke. "I am here on your behalf."

"But, how did you get in here?"

"I have my ways. Ways beyond the borders of the natural realm."

"Are you a ghost?"

"I am not. I am known across the realms as the Visitant Outlander."

"I've never heard of you."

"Many have not. Few have encountered me. Now, you are one of the few."

"Why are you here?" Cassandra asked. "Why visit me?"

"Because of your reaction to the Mutant-Thing."

Cassandra relaxed herself, walking out of the bedroom to the living room of the apartment. Within seconds, the Visitant Outlander was standing in the living room, startling her. He understood and gave a slight nod, showing his understanding.

"You know of the creature?"

285

"I do. I was around before it even existed."

"How old are you exactly?"

"Far older than the world you see today."

Cassandra nodded.

"The creature did not attack me." Cassandra noted. "I'm not sure why. It looked like it was trying to save me."

"The Mutant-Thing did not harm you because you have not been tainted."

Cassandra paused, glaring at the Outlander.

"What do you mean?"

"You are a virgin. The Mutant-Thing cannot harm a woman who has not yet been married. It's a balance of nature."

"So, why come to me?"

"To tell you you're in danger if you continue down this path."

"It's my work. My job is to find out who's responsible for the murders."

"And what have you come to?"

"I believe there's something supernatural happening here. It explains you standing in my apartment right now, doesn't it?"

"Does it?"

"How can I know?"

"You spoke with Morhana earlier."

"Yes. She seemed to know something others did not."

"She knows more than she's letting you on."

"What do you mean?"

"Morhana is a witch. As you are already aware. Yet, you do not know her place within the confinement of this world. Morhana is currently hiding from others beyond even her control."

"I'm not getting what you're saying? Who's beyond her control?"

"Powerful entities outside of the borders of humanity."

"I have to ask. Are they responsible for the murders?"

"No."

"So, since you know so much." Cassandra said. "Then, you know who the murderer is."

Outlander grinned.

"I know who's responsible."

Cassandra approached Outlander, seeing his height was far over her own. She sighed, taking a step back. She sighed.

"Can you tell me who it is?"

"You've already met him."

"Him?" Cassandra jolted. "Who?"

"Take the moment to meditate. Then, it will come to you."

Cassandra walked over to the table, grabbing her journal. she turned back and the Outlander was gone. Without a noise or sudden movements.

"And he's gone."

Cole and Lewis traveled across the regions of Winnipeg to the cemeteries. The trail led them toward the last cemetery. They parked the car and walked through the gated entrance and out into the field of graves. Lewis held out the flashlight to keep a look around. Cole walked slowly behind him with no flashlight. He only wanted the moonlight to show him around. The field was covered in snow which annoyed Lewis.

"Didn't expect this much snow out here."

"Snow was said in the forecast."

"Oh good. What's the name of this one?" Lewis asked.

"Elmwood."

"Elmwood, huh. The place looks closed."

"Well, to the public it is."

"And us?"

"We're here on business."

"Good point. The place is giving me the creeps."

"You just now noticed?"

"Yeah. You don't appear to be a little shaken up out here."

"Because I sensed it as we drove up here."

Lewis scoffed, shaking his head.

"Figures."

Walking through the cemetery, they looked at all the headstones, seeing the names of the deceased. Lewis continued searching around as Cole showed his respect to the graves around him. While walking,

Lewis stopped in front of one headstone, seeing no inscriptions. The grave was also set next to a tree.

"Hey, Cole. Come look at this."

Cole walked over, seeing the unnamed headstone. His eyes focused and he sighed. Lewis was uncertain. Waving the flashlight around the headstone and the grave. Lewis spotted several spots of fresh dirt in the mix with the snow. The appearance seemed to indicate to Lewis the grave had been buried in recent hours.

"I wonder who's grave this is?" Lewis said.

"Don't." Cole said. "Don't bother with it."

"Why the hell not? This don't seem strange to you?"

"Oh, it does. Very."

While Cole stepped back from the grave, Lewis bent down, moving the snow from the grave, finding the dirt. Lewis grinned as he started wiping the dirt. Cole went to grab him and a decaying hand arose from the dirt, snatching Lewis by his tie.

"The fuck is this?!" Lewis screamed.

"Move back!" Cole yelled. "Move back!"

Cole grabbed Lewis and pulled him from the hold. They moved back with their guns in hand as the hand rose from the ground, exposing the body. The figure which came out of the grave looked decayed from head to toe. Lewis was terrified and Cole was intrigued. The figure was dead, but it's behavior was as if it was not dead.

"There's zombies now." Lewis asked.

"How would I know." Cole replied.

"I wasn't asking."

Lewis fired a shot and it had no effect. The deceased one screeched and behind the detectives emerged a disembodied spirit, which was visible to their eyes. The spirit grabbed the deceased one and returned it into the grave, sealing the dirt over its body without a fight.

"What is that?" Lewis wondered.

The spirit turned back toward the detectives and nodded. Lewis and Cole were unsettled. Both frozen in place and hesitant to move for their firearms.

"What are you?!" Lewis yelled. "The hell are you here for?!"

"I saved your lives."

"Saved our lives?" Cole said. "How and why?"

"You were trespassing on the grave of the Restoration Man. I am the one who keeps those such as himself in line to the natural order."

Lewis waved his finger back and forth between the spirit and the grave. The sudden appearance of a spirit made Lewis feel unsure to his surroundings this night. The snow and the chilly air did not help. The spirit kept its composure in a unusual way toward the detectives. Cole only stared in a creepy awe of the spirit. Questions began to linger in his mind. What should he ask and what does the spirit know.

"Restoration Man?..." Lewis said while catching his breath. "You're dead too or something?"

"That man is called the Restoration Man?" Cole asked.

"He is. He cannot be killed. If he's every brutally harmed, he will rise once more. It is his nature and his curse."

"And you're not like him?" Lewis questioned. "Like, if I were to shoot you, the round wouldn't harm you?"

"How can it? My body isn't made of this natural world such as yourselves."

"But, you were once human?" Cole said. "Weren't you?"

"I was once alive like the two of you. Now, I am a spirit who wanders and protects."

"Your accent." Cole said. "You're not from around here are you?"

"I was once known as Robert Shaw. Now, I am only known as the Ghost of England."

"You're from England?" Lewis asked. "Like London, England?"

"I am."

"So, why are you here in Canada? In Winnipeg?"

"I was summoned here by the Restoration Man's rise. You interrupted his sleep."

"The dead don't sleep." Lewis replied. "He was, is dead."

"I see you're not keen on the workings of the land beyond. No matter, leave this cemetery and continue on with your case."

"You know we're on a case?" Cole said intriguingly.

"Yes. Who you're searching for is not here. In fact, you've already spoken to them."

"What are you saying, ghost?" Lewis asked.

"Go and the answer will come."

The Ghost of England disappeared into the night sky. Lewis placed his gun back into his holster while looking at Cole, who was only focused on the sky. Trying to see if he could catch a glimpse of The Ghost.

"You see all this shit?" Lewis asked.

"Yes."

"And you're not bothered by any of this? Anything we've encountered these past hours?"

"Not really."

Lewis shook his head and shivered from the cold air.

"I'm going home." Lewis said. "I need some sleep after all of this nonsense."

VII

<u>THE TRUTH OF ACTIONS</u>

The following morning after the events which transpired, Lewis and Cole returned to the office and as they walked in, Cassandra was standing at the chief's door talking to him. Lewis pointed.

"That must be the reporter he told us about."

"Who else could it be."

Walking past them was Yana and Harper. They moved with haste toward the interrogation room. Cole wondered what the purpose for their speed was. He approached the interrogation room door as it closed and inside he saw the two detectives questioning another possible suspect. Only this time, the supposed suspect was very active and seemed a little shaken. Lewis walked over next to Cole, glancing through the door window.

"Another one?" Lewis asked.

"No. This one's different. He's not responsible."

"After what we were told, of course not."

Lewis rubbed his chin, trying to get a clear hearing through the window. He stopped himself and sighed.

"You wanna see what they're talking about?" Lewis asked.

"After you."

Lewis opened the door as Yana and Harper turned around to see him and Cole walking in with Cole shutting the door stealthy, even though the other detectives can see him. Harper stood up, pointing toward them and giving a glance at the door. He scoffed with a smirk.

"Trying to be ninjetic?"

"*Ninjetic?*" Lewis said. "Is that a word?"

291

"It is now. I'm not sure why you two are in here. But, this is myself and Yana's operation at the moment."

"Well, we came in to see if you needed a few extra hands." Lewis replied.

"Extra hands aren't needed if you're just questioning a potential suspect."

"I'm not a suspect!" The man said at the table. "I'm a witness. A clear witness."

"A witness to what?" Cole asked. "What did you see?"

"I saw everything."

"What's your name, son?" Lewis asked.

"Pablo Lopez."

"Pablo." Harper said. "Tell us how you know everything?"

"I worked for the government for a time. Saw some things they were operating on and I couldn't partake in it no longer."

"What kind of stuff?" Lewis asked. "Give us something."

"I worked in the scientific field. I saw tests. All kinds of tests."

"You're gonna have to give us more than just tests, Pablo." Harper said.

"I agree." Cole added.

"Ok. I was working alongside another scientist. His last name started with a G. But his first name was Larry. That I remember. we worked on hybridizations."

"Hybridization?" Cole said. "What kind of hybrids were you working on?"

"The mixing of man and beast with certain elements of nature."

"Like plants?" Lewis asked.

"Yes."

"Wait." Cole said. "You said the scientist you worked with was named Larry?"

"Yes. I can't remember his last name. We usually went by first-name basis in the lab. It was his protocol."

"You know a scientist named Larry?" Yana asked Cole.

"In a matter."

Cole turned toward Lewis and Lewis nodded. The two exited the interrogation room, standing by the door. Lewis gazed around at the other officers walking past them through the lobby area.

"You know who he's talking about." Cole said.

"Yes. I know. What are we going to do about him?"

"We could pay him another visit."

"You think he would allow us back in after our first visit? The bastard didn't even pay us any attention. Why would he listen to us now?"

"Because we have evidence of his involvement."

"The kid never said he was involved."

"But the Ghost did." Cole noted.

"The Ghost didn't give us much to go on."

"He gave us enough. Dr. Grint is the killer."

"So, what's our next move?"

"Let's dig up whatever we can on Dr. Grint. Find out what he's been a part of."

"And how are we going to do that while working on this case?"

Cole looked over to the chief's door, seeing Cassandra. Lewis noticed and nodded.

"Let's see."

They approached Cassandra as she was finishing up her conversation with the chief. She turned around just as they stood next to her. Lewis extended his hand.

"Detective Lewis Knight. We haven't had the chance of meeting."

"Oh. You're the two detectives working on the same case."

"We are. I'm Detective Cole Yeager."

"Nice to meet the both of you. So, what have you uncovered so far?"

"We believe Dr. Grint is the killer."

"How did you come up with that conclusion?"

"The two other detectives are speaking with a witness in the other room." Lewis said. "He told us the scientist he worked with is named Larry. Dr. Grint's first name is Larry."

Cassandra nodded.

"Then, what's your next move? Interrogate Dr. Grint into admitting to murder?"

"No. we need to check Dr. Grint's background to make sure the witness is telling us the truth."

"And you want me to dig into the history books?"

"You read out mind." Lewis grinned.

"Very well, I'll go see what I can find. Once, I do, we'll meet up back here then?"

"Sure." Cole replied.

Cassandra headed out and went into extensive research. Gong as far as to travel to libraries to research the scientific history surrounding Grint as his name was featured across various articles all speaking on hybridization and the proposed future of humanity becoming more than just human. Cassandra found little, but nothing with much weight. After she traveled to laboratories settled across Winnipeg and discovered old files and documents which were labeled *confidential* by the government. Inside the files were photos and documents speaking of a hybridization project. The names she read on the files were many, only one stood out in bold."

"Timothy Fegan?" Cassandra said.

The file documented Timothy Fegan being the test subject for the hybridization project overseen by Grint and his team. In the file was an image of the team and Pablo was present, only referred to as an intern. The remaining files detailed Fegan's disappearance from the public eye and the project went into darkness. There was nothing else available to the public concerning the project or Fegan. The team was broken up and Grunt was fired from the project and went into hiding, presumably finishing up the project on his own. Cassandra placed the file in her bag as she left the laboratory.

VIII

<u>THE HIDDEN BEAST</u>

Cassandra returned to the office where Cole and Lewis waited. She approached them hastily, pulling out he file she found. Lewis grabbed it and opened it, seeing the details. Cole glanced over, seeing the black and white photographs.

"Where did you find this?" Cole asked/

"I did some looking around. Came across one of the old labs in the city and discovered this in the archives."

"This states Dr. Grint was involved in some crazy shit." Lewis said. "Does anyone else know about this?"

"If they do, they're keeping themselves very quiet and very hard to find."

"Grint isn't hard to find." Cole added. "We should go and ask them about this."

"Yeah."

"Wait." Cassandra said. "I'm going along too."

Lewis scoffed with a short laugh.

"Look, I know you want to come with us and record all of it, but, this might get deadly and we don't need someone caught in the crossfire."

"You saw what was in that file. There's not telling what Grint is working on right now. He could be finishing what he started. You'll need all the hands you can get."

"She has a point." Cole said.

"Don't help her." Lewis grunted. "Very well. Just do not get in our way."

295

"You'll barely know I'm even there."

They went toward the door as Yana and Harper were walking back inside. They stopped, seeing them. Yana was uncertain of their motives and called out to them. Cole turned back, nodding to Lewis and Cassandra to head to the car.

"Where are you three going?"

"We have a lead on the case. We're going to pay someone a visit."

"And that's why the reporter is tagging along?" Harper questioned. "You sure she can take care of herself?"

"We'll see once we're there."

The three left the office and made their return to Grint's laboratory. Immediately, they noticed a strangeness in the air as soon as they pulled up. Exiting the vehicle, Cassandra looked around in the air, Lewis noticed her movements and glanced upward.

"What is it?" Lewis wondered.

"There's something in the air. Something's watching us."

"Like what?"

"I'm not sure."

"What does it feel like?" Cole asked.

"It feels… it feels evil."

The energy in the air communicated with Cassandra, turning her attention toward the door of the lab. She pointed as Cole and Lewis looked in the direction. With a nod, she knew for certain the energy was coming from within the lab. Lewis nodded and reached for his gun, rushing toward the door and kicking it open. Cole and Lewis had their guns up, aimed at Grint while Cassandra remained behind them. Grint was working on the table as he was prior.

"Put the tool down." Lewis said. "Turn around."

Grint stopped, holding the tool in his hand. He turned around slowly to see the detectives. What Grint held in his hand was a large kitchen knife. Lewis' eyes enlarged as he stepped forward with one foot. Cole glanced at Lewis' movement.

"Put the knife down." Lewis said.

"What's going on here?" Grint asked.

"The knife." Cole said. "Put it down."

"But, why? What's happening here?"

"Put the fucking knife down!" Lewis screamed. "I won't ask again!"

Grint nodded. Putting the knife down on the table. Lewis sighed. Cole remained steady and Cassandra was silent.

"We know what you were working on." Cole said. "The secret experiments."

"Experiments?"

"Yeah." Lewis said. "Some shit called hybridization."

Grint grinned.

"What's funny?" Cole asked.

"I guess it would've came out sooner or later."

"What came out?" Lewis questioned. "The hell you talking about?"

"My work. It has never ceased."

"And I assume that's what you've been doing here ever since?" Cole said. "Trying to complete your work?"

"Of course."

"So, you're the cause of the murders?" Lewis questioned.

"They were only failed subjects to the cause."

"You admit you killed them?" Cole asked. "And the animals too?"

"All subjects which failed to endure the trials of perfection."

"You're sick." Lewis said. "A sick man."

"Sick is just a term used by the illiterate to describe brilliance."

Grint backed up against the table, putting his hand atop a control panel. Lewis jerked his gun forward.

"Step away from the table!"

"Sure. Sure."

As Grint moved, his finger pressed the black button on the panel and the lights flickered. Distracting the detectives, Grint made a run for it deeper into the lab. Lewis noticed and ran after him. Cole went to follow, telling Cassandra to remain at the door just in case. Cole ran and reached Lewis, who had stopped in his steps, seeing Grint standing at the vertical table with the cocoon.

"What is that?" Cole said.

"My ultimate creation. I believe it's time to be awakened."

"Do not make a move." Lewis said. "One more move and I will shoot you."

"Go ahead and do your work. I will do mine."

Grint took a step toward the table and Lewis fired a shot, Grint ducked as he pressed a green button on the table, in which separated the tubes from the cocoon and from there, the cocoon began to shiver, moving with intensity as Grint stepped back against the wall. Lewis and Cole were uncertain of what to do, so they aimed their guns toward the cocoon. After a minute, the cocoon busted open and from it arose a towering figure. Its figure appeared humanoid, but its hands, feet, face, and eyes appeared very much like an animal. A mixture of a human, a bear, and a wolf. The creature screeched and it was loud to the point it reached Cassandra.

"What was that?" She questioned.

Grint applauded the creature, standing beside it. The creature glared over toward Grint, who nodded with a smile.

"You are reborn!" Grint said. "No more are you Timothy Fegan!"

"Fegan?" Cole said.

"Yeah." Lewis replied. "The man from the file."

"You are now known as The Hybrid!"

Lewis and Cole began firing at the Hybrid as Grint moved out of the way. The bullets did no harm to the Hybrid's body as the hair was dense enough to preserve the body from gunfire. The Hybrid humped down from the table, swiping the detectives out of its path and bolted into the wall, crashing through as it ran to the outside. Cassandra looked around, hearing the explosion and when she walked over to the side of the lab, she saw the Hybrid, running on all fours into the wilderness.

"He's done it."

While the Hybrid ran through the wilderness, seemly making its way toward Winnipeg, the Mutant-Thing arose from the dirt in a far region, sensing the Hybrid's essence and hearing the screeching. From there, the Mutant-Thing melted into the dirt and moved with speed, following the path of the Hybrid.

IX

<u>THE WAYS OF SCIENCE AND MYSTERY</u>

The Hybrid made its entrance in the downtown region of Winnipeg, frightening the civilians as it began hurling vehicles into the air, slamming its arms into the pavement, shaking the ground. The police had arrived and exited their vehicles. Their firearms aimed and ready. The Hybrid saw them and showed a grim smile before charging toward them. The rounds went off, firing at all ranges toward the Hybrid. The bullets did nothing as they bounced off the fur. The Hybrid moved with a much greater speed, tackling the officers against their own vehicles, crashing them into one another. The Hybrid screeched and went further into the city.

Back at the lab, Lewis and Cole followed Grint as he made his escape into the basement of the laboratory. Cassandra entered the operating room, seeing the vertical table and the massive hole in the wall.

"Where did they go?"

She looked around and turned her attention forward. She moved and glanced over to her left, seeing a portion of the brick wall was moved to the side, revealing a set of stairs going down. She didn't hesitate. Figuring Lewis and Cole went down, she was going as well. Pacing herself down the stairs, she could hear faint echoes of Lewis shouting Grint's name followed by gunfire. Stepping foot on the ground, leading into a narrow hallway with water flowing on the ground, she noticed Cole standing in the distance. Moving faster, she caught up to him and he was not pleased.

"Why are you down here?"

"I saw something outside. It was massive."

"Yeah. That was Grint's experiment completed."

"The project he was working on? That was the subject?"

"Yes. That subject you saw rushing into the woods was once Timothy Fegan."

"Ok. Where's Lewis?"

"Catching up on Grint's trail. I'm here just in case the doctor makes a u-turn."

"I can help out, you know. Find a way to lure Grint out and-"

"You're better off back at the car."

"And what if Grint gets out of your sights? What then?"

"Lewis and I have it covered. Just wait back at the car. Please."

Cassandra let out a short sigh and turned back. Once she did, Lewis ran toward Cole, grabbing her focus.

"Did you find him?" Cole asked.

"This place's a maze. However, he somewhere down here."

"Then, let's find him."

Lewis looked over Cole's shoulder, seeing Cassandra. He shook his head.

"Why are you down here?"

"Trying to find you two."

"Did you see the big thing bolt out of the wall?"

"I did. It went into the forest. My guess it's going somewhere crowded."

"The city." Lewis said. "Every damn time."

"Look, we need to find Grint now. Sun's going down soon and we don't need to be out here at night."

"The hell we don't" Lewis agreed. "Let's get this over with."

While they searched for Grint in the sewer-life tunnels, they were ambushed by several dwarfish entities. They attacked with slashes to the legs before vanishing in the air. Only leaving a small echo of laughter following their attacks. Lewis looked around as the light in the tunnels were growing dim. Cole held his gun steady, and Cassandra remained at the entrance to the tunnels. In her right hand however was a glock.

"You see those things by any chance?" Lewis asked.

"Just a quick glance."

"And what did they look like? Besides elves?"

"Hobbits."

"Great. So, Grint's down here making fantasy characters come to life."

"They've always existed, Lewis. It's just they remain in hiding."

"And how do you know this?"

"History speaks of it."

Lewis nodded.

"That's good. Didn't know you were a historian as well. Must work well in your other endeavors."

"Comes and goes in favors."

"That's great. Now will any of that history shit help us find Grint or not?"

Cole stared and before he could answer, Grint jumped in front of them, holding a knife in one hand and a gun in the other. Cole and Lewis held their firearms aimed at Grint. Neither of them hesitated in their steps. Their boldness intrigued Grint to continue stepping further.

"One more fucking step and I will put your ass down!" Lewis yelled.

"This has to end one way." Grint said. "Only one of us must survive."

"Make your move." Cole said.

Grint nodded, tapping the knife on his forehead. He lunged with such speed at Lewis with the knife. Lewis fired a shot, knocking the knife from Grint's hand and Lewis snatched Grint by his lab coat and tossed him against eh brick wall, pummeling him in the face and stomach with his fists.

"Don't kill him." Cole said as he watched. "We need to bring him in."

Lewis delivered one more punch to the face before exhaling and raising himself up off Grint's body. Grint laid on the floor, giggling with blood pouring down his face. Lewis and Cole shook hands.

"We done our duty." Lewis said. "Let's bring this bastard in."

"NEVER!" Grint screamed, raising up from the floor.

Grint reached into his lab pocket and took out a taser, quickly holding it against Lewis' ribs. Shocking him as he stumbled and fell to the floor. Cole looked on, firing his gun at Grint, who moved out of its path before throwing the taser into Cole's face. Cole stumbled in his steps and Grint kicked him to the floor.

"Such fools! A scientist is always prepared!"

Grint looked down, seeing Cole's gun. He grabbed it.

"A pity I can't use my own. Seeing how it fell somewhere in this area." Grint said. "The water must've washed out elsewhere. No matter, using your own against you is a message proved just enough."

Grint aimed the gun toward Cole's forehead and a gunshot fired. Grint stared into space as he glared up toward the entrance, seeing Cassandra standing with her glock aimed. From the muzzle moved smoke and Grint had realized he was the one shot as he never had a chance to pull the trigger. Grint chucked and fell to the ground with a bullet wound in his chest. Cole snatched his gun from Grint's hand and stood up, holding his head. He went and checked on Lewis, helping him up as they exited the tunnels, returning to the car.

"What about Grint?" Cassandra asked.

"We'll tell the others and they'll pick him up. He's not going anywhere."

Lewis sat in the back seat, still shivering from the electricity as Cole drove into Winnipeg.

Once they arrived, they saw the city in distraught, civilians running in mass as gunfire sounded in the air. Lewis remained in the car as Cole and Cassandra walked out, moving through the people. They continued further before finding several officers shooting and being killed by the Hybrid.

"Oh no." Cassandra said.

"We have to do something."

"We can't face that thing."

"We have to find a way."

While they thought, the ground quaked. Shaking to the point of grabbing the Hybrid's attention. The creature stood firm as the ground in front of him arose and underneath the rising concrete and dirt was the Mutant-Thing. Its red eyes glared toward Hybrid as the Hybrid screeched, dragging its right foot into the ground.

X

THE CURSE OF THE MUTANT-THING

The Mutant-Thing ran and tackled the Hybrid into the ground, pulling the creature by its head and slamming it into the nearby trees. Cole and Cassandra moved to a further distance to avoid the flying debris. The Mutant-Thing walked over toward the downed Hybrid, covered in bark and leaves, which arose, slashing its claws into the Mutant-Thing's chest. Stumbling the Mutant-Thing in his steps, the Hybrid grabbed the Mutant-Thing by its throat and slammed it into the pavement and stomped its chest. The Hybrid lowered its head and screeched in the Mutant-Thing's face before the Mutant-Thing grabbed the Hybrid by its jaw and pulled it onto the concrete, swiping the Hybrid's foot from its chest and reversing the attack. Now, the Mutant-Thing stood over the Hybrid with its foot on the creature's chest.

"You… do… not… belong…" The Mutant-Thing said.

The Mutant-Thing used both hands, grabbing onto the Hybrid's head and began struggling against the creature. Cole and Cassandra watched on as they saw the Mutant-Thing using all its strength as he tore off the Hybrid's head with its blood pouring and spreading. The creature is dead and the Mutant-Thing tosses the head across from Cole and Cassandra. they looked down and gazed up, seeing the Mutant-Thing's eyes on them. Cassandra nodded.

"It is done." The Mutant-Thing said, as it walked into the nearby river and evaporated away.

Afterwards, Lewis was taken to the nearby hospital and the officers had arrived at Grint's lab. They confronted him as he made it to the upper floor trying t escape. The officers had their guns on him. Grint was surrounded.

"Dr. Larry Grint, drop the gun!"

"Only one of us is making it out of here alive."

"Drop the gun!"

Grint nodded with a smirk before turning the gun on himself. News had spread the next day of Grint's suicide and everyone knew he was the one responsible for the murders. Chief Thompson thanked Cole, Lewis, and Cassandra for their help. The case of Winnipeg's mysterious murder was solved. However, the Chief handed the detectives a letter. They opened the letter, which requested for their assistance in a case surrounding a growing fear in paranoia. Cole glanced at the location of the case. He nodded.

"We going to Retropolis?"

"Might as well." Lewis said.

Cassandra had returned to her home in Vancouver and as she entered, she found a visitor sitting down in her chair next to the couch. The visitor stood up and greeted Cassandra.

"How did you get into my home?" She asked. "And why are you here?"

"My name is Doctor Donald Fortune and I am here to speak to you concerning the witch, Morhana."

"Why speak to me about her? I only questioned here concerning the case in Winnipeg."

"I know of the case and the assistance of the Mutant-Thing. I understand it and I give my gratitude for the creature's help with humanity. But, I am not here to speak to you concerning the Winnipeg case. I am here to ask you some questions."

"Why? What kind of questions?"

"Important ones that could save your life. Because something is coming and its growing fast. To put it to you simply, you're in its crosshairs."

THE MYTHOLOGISTS
A DARK TITAN UNIVERSE ONE-SHOT

Jacob Wilson sat in the British Library of London, England. He sat at a table near the King's Library. Jacob is a frequent visitor of the library due to his time in school. Always near and within. Drinking a cup of coffee, sitting near him is a book on Oceania mythology. An avid reader of such histories, Jacob became well-verse in the art of understanding. His knowledge of mythologies stood superb.

While sipping his coffee and glancing through the pages of the book, a man approached the table. Well-dressed in a suit and middle-aged. Jacob looked up to him. His first thought was the man was an employee of the library, but his presence told a different story.

"I see you're into the Oceania myths."

"I am. Seeing how they compare to the others."

"Ah, you're trying to understand how they communicate with the Greeks? Or the Egyptians?"

"Maybe."

"Or you're trying to comprehend the Oceanic to the Maori or the Aboriginal Australians?"

"You know of them?"

"I do."

"It's interesting to speak with another who knows of them."

"Well, their gods aren't quite superior to those of the mainstream. Most of humanity prefer Odin or Zeus to give them a spark. Not the Oceanic ones."

"Then you know of the *Maui* and *Tawhaki* Cycles?"

"Of their tales of becoming heroes? I am deeply aware. So deep, that both Maui and Tawhaki represent the tendencies of the liberal and conservative within human beings."

Jacob nodded with a smirk.

"You know them well."

"I'm at the age where I know many things."

"How did you come into studying mythologies?"

"Myself and my crew, we're... well-versed in every mythology known to man and history."

"Your crew?"

"There are many of us. I just happen to be the one to grab the books for the study."

"I've never heard of a group of mythologists."

"It's a secret ordeal. Only a few are aware of such existence."

"Why?"

"Because, simply put, we cannot allow the base-minded of humanity to enter the doors. Otherwise, the group would tumble into the abyss."

"What if they wanted to prove themselves? To see if they could join?"

"Then, they would be where you are right now. You have the knowledge. The mindset. The skills of study. You would fit well alongside us. Our purpose is the key."

"Purpose?"

"I cannot speak of such things in the public forum. However, I will give you an invite to one of our meetings being held tonight here in London."

The man handed Jacob a card. Looked as if it was a business card, However, upon the card was an address and an insignia. Jacob stared hard at the symbol.

"I've never seen this symbol before. What is it?"

"You'll find out if you agree to come."

Jacob took another look at the card.

"It's your call." The man said.

Jacob placed the card in his pocket, he looked up and the man was gone. Nowhere in sight.

"Huh." Jacob uttered under his breath.

When nightfall had come, Jacob went to the location listed on the card. Finding himself walking on the grounds of the Middle Temple in the City of London. Unsure he would be granted entry, he noticed those around him didn't approach him. They didn't cease him nor did they try to stop him. They all nodded. Jacob felt strange by such responses. All silent in sound, but very loud in action. Jacob entered the Temple, walking into the Hall.

Inside, sat a long rectangular table and around it were twelve individuals. Seven men and five women. All ranged in different nationalities and cultures. Jacob was still, he looked out and saw the man he met in the library and walked over toward him.

"Excuse me, sir."

The man looked and saw Jacob. A smile appeared upon his face.

"You decided to come."

"Yes, I didn't know such a thing like this existed."

"Well, you're seeing another view of the world. One not many will ever have the opportunity to see."

The man gestured for Jacob to sit at the table, which everyone else was doing. Jacob sat next to the man as they were served dinner. The table was covered in dishes, each one came from another culture in the world. The diversity was clear in the group. Jacob was amazed. They ate and afterwards, the table was cleared of the food and out came the books. Thick books, very old with worn-out leather binding. Some of the books were written in Old English, Persian, Latin, and Aramaic. Jacob felt as if he was in another world. His eyes gazing at the books. Books hundreds, perhaps thousands of years old. The man leaned in over to him, sliding over a book.

"I think you'll be interested in this one."

Jacob grabbed the book. No title was on the cover, Jacob opened it and saw the words were written in *Paleo-Hebrew*. He shook his head.

"How did you come across something such as this?"

"We have our ways."

"This language? I thought it was only written on scrolls."

"Things the world has been taught are not what they seem."

"What do you mean?"

"Look around. See all of us in this hall. We come from different parts of the world, yet we share the same values and goals. To make this world better for the generations to come. This is how we start. By restoring what has been lost."

'Then, why is this a secret. How come you don't tell the public about this?"

"If we were to do such a thing, it would put a target on our heads. Not only of the natural, but of the others."

"Others? Like governments?"

"Higher than governments." The man nodded. "Come with me to the library. I'll explain everything there."

Jacob followed the man into the library of the Temple. It was only the two of them, surrounded by more of the books the others were gazing through. Jacob also saw the globes designed by Emery Molyneux.

"It's better you sit for what I am about to tell you."

Jacob sat down at the table. The man stood by the wall and reached into his jacket pocket, taking out a cigar and lit up. Inhaling and exhaling.

"You can smoke in here?"

"It's our place. We are obliged to. Cigars for the most part, of course."

The man took another puff of the cigar before sitting down in front of Jacob.

"The truth of such a group as this is simple, yet complex. It only depends on the mind of the listener."

"I'm listening."

The man nodded with a smile.

"Good. This group is no ordinary group. We're a secret society. Kept hidden from most of the world because our purpose is deemed tyrannical and cynical to most of the general public."

"Tyrannical?"

"We do not wish to enslave humanity. Only to open their eyes to the true ways of the world."

"I noticed one of the books on the table was a grimoire."

"It's good you did. I'm sure that gives you a better understanding as to what and who we are."

"You all practice magic?"

"Some do. Myself, I stick only with history and the power of the ancients. When I said governments and the public would try to shut us down. I didn't tell you the other half of the story."

"And that half would be?"

"The deities you read about. The ones in all the mythologies. They exist."

Jacob sat back in the chair, rubbing his chin and gazing around the library. He leaned in toward the table.

"I'm not understanding. How? It makes no sense."

"To the natural mind of man, it does not. However, what we have discovered over many centuries, is these mythologies we've come to know them as just stories. Tales of legends and fables. But, what we have learned is the true fact. These tales are not myths. The legends are real. The accounts are real. It all happened."

"Where's the proof?" Jacob asked. "How can I believe you if I haven't seen them myself?"

The man nodded.

"The risen heroes."

"Can't be. They're not like the gods in the myths."

"Are you sure about that? Look at them. Their feats. Their power. The things they can do and have done. They are the purest sign of the tide turning. The heroes shall come first and the gods come after. The heroes are here and the world is aware of them. We now, wait upon the gods to make themselves known."

"Now, I'm curious. Have any of you met one of these heroes or the gods?"

"No. but, our leader has met with something from the other side."

"You speak of the supernatural."

"Yes. That is what I was referring to when I spoke about opposition. The supernatural realm doesn't take our society too well. There are a particular few who desire us to disappear. For their good purpose."

"Who are they?"

"Their names I do not know. I know only what the ancients had called them. There were three. One was deemed the Hunter of the Realms. He carried wrath wherever he went. The second one was referred to as Haunting Wanderer. He would always appear when there was someone in dire need. Be it near-death or near-revelation."

"And the third?"

"He was called by many names. But, the one that has stuck with me is the Keeper of the Cosmos. He controls all the darkness in the universe. An Astral entity. He is one I dare not to come across."

"What happens if you do?"

'Then, it will be the end of the Mythologists. Period."

Jacob took in the information and kept it close. He glanced at his watch, amazed by the time which had gone by.

"I need to get home."

"Understood."

Jacob stood up and so did the man. He extended his hand toward Jacob.

"It was a pleasure to meet you, Jacob.

Jacob shook his hand in respect.

"I have to ask, you never told me your name."

"Ah. The society calls me Deimos."

"As in the Greek God?"

"It's what they've given me." The man replied. "Best be seeing you."

Jacob nodded and left the Temple.

Inside the library, Deimos sat still as another individual entered. He was cloaked in a white robe and hood. Deimos gazed upon him and bowed his head.

"I wasn't aware you would be here."

"I'm always near. What of you talks with the young lad?"

"He's very intelligent. I believe he can become one of us."

"Very well. Keep an eye on him."

"Yes sir."

While Jacob walked home, he found it strange there was no one else outside. No sign of any vehicles of any kind. Finding it weird, he began to move faster. Upon his footsteps, a peculiar mist arose from the ground. Jacob looked in fear and immediately he turned around, finding himself staring at an entity. Dressed in a dark blue cloak, suit, and hat. His eyes clear with no pupils, yet they were glowing and shined bright as the moon. His facial hair and long hair were white as snow.

"Who are you?"

"I am one of the three Deimos told. I was known as the Haunting Wanderer in the times past. Now, humanity refers to me as he Visitant Outlander."

Jacob stood still. Fear grabbed him.

"Do not fear me, Jacob Wilson. For I am not of the malevolent side of life."

Jacob calmed down. The fear which held him had evaporated.

"Why have you come to me?"

"To give you a revelation. Your life is about to change, Jacob. The life you shall live will be drastically different than the lives of the average. You will suffer loss and you will receive gain. You will come across those of a good nature like myself and others present in evil."

"Are the Mythologists evil?"

"They're neutral. But, their goals conflict with the laws of the true nature. The spiritual realms deem them cinderblocks into the hearts and minds of the faithful. That shall not happen to you."

"How do you know?"

"Because I know the end from the beginning. I've seen your life up till now. The lives of others. I've interacted with a few of the risen heroes and others such as yourself. You will receive a change soon. Best to be prepared."

The mist evaporated and the Visitant Outlander disappeared. Jacob turned around at the sound of a horn, seeing a car pass by. Around him were other vehicles and pedestrians. Jacob scratched his head, turning back and forth.

"What I have gotten myself into?"

CREED: MEDIEVAL TIMES

I

VISITATION

Creed mediated in the clouds during the night. His eyes closed, the aura of his power surging around him as his cloak bellowed with the moving air. From behind him, a loud bang sounded, getting his attention. Once Creed's eyes opened, he turned back seeing what had caused the sound and from its location appeared a very bright light. The light was brighter than the sun, yet its brightness had no effect on Creed. Within the light, Creed saw a figure approaching. He raised himself up, levitating in the air as the figure emerged from the light.

"You." Creed said.

"It's time we've met."

The figure appeared like a woman. Elderly in age. She was clothed in a long black dress, decorated with rubies, sapphires, and emeralds within the lining. She also wore a medallion made of platinum with a carbuncle gem. Her flowing white hair shined with the light as did her white eyes which glowed in similar fashion.

"Why have you come, Madam Age?"

"To give you a warning. Someone is coming."

"Let me guess. Adrambadon is crawling back up from the Cryptic Zone?"

"No. He is currently occupied with other matters."

"Then, who is coming?"

"Medieval is coming."

"Medieval?"

"You are aware of him, aren't you? The knightly figure that caused the massacres throughout the Middle Ages. He's the one responsible for the Crusades. All of them."

"Why is he coming here?"

"He's looking for you."

"For me?"

"You prove to him as a great challenge. You remind him of another."

"I guess this other one didn't get the task done."

"He did. Just that was hundreds of years in human time."

"How soon will this Medieval figure be here?"

"Very soon. I've informed Ananchel about the circumstance. She will meet with you soon and give you the other details."

"Other details? Why won't you tell me?"

"It's not my duty. It's hers."

Madam Age walked back into the light and as she did, the portal closed and the light dimmed out. Behind Creed appeared Ananchel, flying down from the heavens. The two greeted one another before Ananchel noticed the last remnants of Madam Age's portal.

"She already told you?"

"Said you have something else to add." Creed mentioned. "What is it?"

"I have some information on Medieval. He's moving with great energy and speed outside the realms of time and space from the Middle Ages. That's how he's making his way here."

"Then why don't those on the outside stop him from breaching into our time?"

"They have matters of their own."

"I'm sure someone is watching."

"Oh, they are. But, it's complicated as you are aware."

"I comprehend. What must I do to ensure this Medieval figure doesn't cause any harm?"

"Simply wait for him to make himself known."

"Why not just stop him in his tracks?"

"Because, when he does show up, he's coming for you. You're the reason for his arrival. Not Adrambadon or Demonticronto. He wants to face you."

"Madam Age said he's after me because of another in his time."

"Yes. Another Creed from the Middle Ages."

"Another Creed?"

"I know this is a lot to deal with. But, right now, just prepare yourself for Medieval's arrival."

"I can't just sit here in the air and wait for him."

"It wouldn't do any good anyway. Medieval can't fly or levitate. He's ground-based. You'll have to meet him upon the soil."

"Where must I go to ensure there are no innocents in the surroundings?"

"Head to a peculiar cemetery in the west. There, you'll meet a man called the Caretaker. He's dealt with Medieval before and I know he'll give you some advice on him."

"The Caretaker."

"Yes. You two should get along well."

Ananchel hovered higher into the air above creed. Looking up toward the heavens.

"I must know about this other Creed you've mentioned."

"In time." Ananchel said before flying off.

II

ANCIENT TALES

Creed appeared in the cemetery, which was far further west from his current location. Creed walked upon the grounds, passing by the dozens of headstones and statues. Tall figures of angels in the catholic fashion. Other statues were those of Freemasonry. Brotherhoods and Sisterhoods. Creed's cloak flowed with the incoming gusts of wind. He walked further and saw a man standing still, a shovel in his hand.

"Are you the Caretaker?" Creed asked.

"Who wants to know?"

"That's why I asked."

The man turned around, facing Creed. Creed saw his face. One of an elder. He wore a wide brim hat and a black duster. He stuck the shovel into the ground and approached Creed with a stillness in his eyes. Yet, there was life in them. A lot of life.

"You're him aren't you?" The man said. "The Unholy Knight."

"I am. I suspect you must be the Caretaker."

"Correct. Ananchel already told me everything that's going on. Right now, we need to discuss the proper planning."

"Do you know who Medieval is?"

"I am familiar with him. However, he's not human as some of the stories tell. He's a spirit. A spirit which thrived during the second and third crusades."

"He's never been a mortal."

"Although, he shares their desires and their lusts. He craves war. In the Templar texts, he was referred to as a god of war."

"I never assumed I would be up against a god. Nonetheless, a war

317

god."

"Now, since we are aware of Medieval's arrival, the strategy is to face him head-on."

"Head-on?" Creed asked. "Just the two of us?"

"I've heard of the things you've done. Facing the likes of Adrambadon and Demonticronto. My friend, you are capable of facing Medieval on your own."

"Noted. Perhaps I should do that."

"It's what Madam Age wants." Caretaker added. "She sees you as a powerful force who can combat the darker entitles at work. You're different than the other Creeds who've come before you."

"Ananchel told me you've dealt with Medieval yourself in times past."

"I did."

"What happened?"

"It was during the third Crusade. I was a member of the Knights Hospitaller. During the battle in Acre, Medieval appeared on the field and slaughtered all the Muslim forces of Saladin, giving way for us to achieve victory. But, that wasn't his desire. He attacked all of us and killed many. I fought against him with three of my brothers-in-arms. I alone survived the attack and sent Medieval on his way back into the spirit realm."

"You defeated him?"

"My skill set was enough to keep me alive. Medieval saw my integrity and grit as a badge of honor. He let me live."

"Will he do it again?"

"Probably not. It won't be the same this time."

"I have to ask. What is all of this about other Creeds?"

"You're one in many. During the Crusades, there was one. He stayed to himself and only appeared when there was a battle to be won. He was a mystery and still is."

Creed looked over near one of the headstones and saw a quickening shadow dash right before his eyes. Creed stood his guard as the Caretaker saw his stance.

"What is it?"

"We're not alone out here." Creed said. "Someone else is

watching us. Closely."

From behind Creed, the shadow bolted like lightning, striking Creed and knocking him into the Caretaker. The two fell to the ground and Creed looked up, seeing the shadow figure molding into a physical form. Upon its body was the armor of a knight. 14th Century armor in detail. Covered in a black and worn-out tunic with no insignias or shields pertaining to any kingdom or country. He wielded a sword.

"Is that him?" Creed asked.

"No. That's not Medieval. But, he's dressed like it."

Caretaker stepped forward to face the entity with Creed's cloak surrounding the area. His shovel in hand.

"What's your name, spirit?" Caretaker asked.

"My name?" The spirit said with a hallowing voice.

"Yeah. You have a name. What is it?"

"My master calls me Middle Age."

"Middle Age?" Caretaker paused. "As in one from the period?"

"It is what I am."

"You don't belong here. Take your sword and walk on out of this cemetery."

"I cannot. For I have come under commands. To send you both elsewhere."

"Where's Medieval?" Creed asked.

"You'll see him soon. Right now, you must go there."

"Go where?"

"I'll show you."

Middle Age raised up his sword, striking the air, thus creating a rift between time and space. Caretaker looked on as did Creed. Middle Age turned toward them as the dark blue hue from the rift grew.

"Where does this go?" Caretaker asked.

"It goes where my master wants you to go."

"Alright, you smartass."

Middle Age took his sword and swiped the end of it against Caretaker's back, knocking him into the rift. Creed swooped over and grabbed the sword. Middle Age laughed before pushing creed into the rift himself. After entering the rift, Creed and Caretaker find themselves falling down within a portal. They collapse onto the grounds of somewhere else. Somewhere far from the cemetery. Creed stood up and looked around.

"Where are we?"

Caretaker stood on his feet and observed the surroundings. He knew.

"Ah shit."

"What?"

"I know where we are."

"How do you know?"

Caretaker pointed ahead of them. Creed looked out and saw bodies of knights on the ground. Blood covering their armor. Some wore the crests of the Knights Templar.

"We're in the past." Caretaker said.

"The past?"

"We're in the medieval times now."

"If I may ask, what year?"

"1202."

III

1202 AD

Creed and Caretaker walked over the field of bodies while hearing the clashing echoes of swords in the distance. With the sound of swords were screams. All of which were in a rage.

"We need to reach the battle." Caretaker said.

"Let me have a look."

Creed hovered himself into the air, passing over the trees and stone walls to see the battle before his eyes. What Creed saw was a battle of the Crusades. The Knights Templar were fighting against the Muslims. A gruesome sight to see. Creed wasn't bothered by the falling limbs and bodies. Blood covered the grounds.

"What do you see?" Caretaker asked.

"Templars. Muslims. This is a Crusades' battle."

Creed looked closer into the armies of men, finding Middle Age in the midst of the battle, killing both Templars and Muslims without being seen by the human eye.

"Middle Age is there!"

"Good. We need to get to him fast."

"Allow me."

Creed grabbed Caretaker by his arm and flew over the walls and into the middle of the battle. Quickly they were caught into the attacks of the Templars and Muslims. In the fighting, Creed fell a strange disturbance in the air. Something familiar to himself. What he was sensing wasn't Middle Age nor was it Medieval himself.

"What is it?" Caretaker asked, after impaling a Templar with his own sword.

"There's another Creed here."

"Ah. I know who you're talking about."

Caretaker looked out and saw him. Riding into battle on an armored horse was a knight. This knight's features were highly similar to Creed's own appearance. Only exceptions were the helmet and the armor. The knight jumped from his mount and crashed into the battlefield, fighting against the Muslims in such a quick succession. Creed watched him fight. Using familiar tactics of his own. Creed could even sense the Cryptic Zone's power upon him.

"He's a Creed."

"One of many." Caretaker said. "There are some things you've yet to learn."

During the Knightcreed's onslaught, another mysterious entity bolted out into the battle on a flaming horse. The flames were not the color of the average fire. These flames glowed with a bright white and blue. The rider himself was dressed in royal garbs covered with armor. His face appeared as a burning skull.

"A Chaser." Caretaker uttered.

"You're aware of them."

"Oh yes. I never suspected one to have been around during this era."

While the two fought in the field, Middle Age appeared before Creed and Caretaker. His sword in hand, ready for the fight.

"Why did you send us here?" Caretaker asked.

"I have my orders."

"I will ask once again. Where's Medieval?"

"He's here." Middle Age answered, moving to the side.

Walking up behind Middle Age was a figure, dressed in beaten and burnt armor. His face covered by the appearance of a skull. His footsteps made the sound of clashing metal. He stood at the height of Creed, yet was leaner.

"I am Medieval."

"I see you're still roaming around this era." Caretaker said. "Why?"

"Because it is where I thrive. Many souls have fallen to my blade. Yours should've been one of them."

"Turned out differently as I recall."

Medieval looked over toward Creed. He scoffed with a nod.

"You're him."

"Who am I?"

"The one they've sent to eliminate me."

"You know of it?"

"I'm a spirit. Time is only a means of travel to my kind."

"Then, you know why I'm on your trail."

"I do. Now, shall we begin?"

Medieval pulled out a shotgun from behind, aimed at Creed. The shot emitted a powerful blast, knocking both Creed and Caretaker back, but Creed felt the blow, causing a major wound on his chest. Caretaker rose up, seeing Creed holding his chest as the reddish-orange blood poured from it.

"Never in my existence have I ever saw the Cryptic-blood pour from one's body. It is something to behold."

IV

THERE'S NOTHING NEW

"Why use such a weapon during this age?" Caretaker asked. "Why not just run toward us with a sword?!"

"Because it is too simple. A weapon such as this is profound in this era. A rightful choice in war."

"I've had enough listening to him speak." Creed said.

"I'm not finished yet." Medieval replied, shooting toward Creed.

Creed moved himself out of the blast range with the strength he still wielded. Medieval sighed. Caretaker circled the enemy and from behind him appeared Middle Age, tripping the Caretaker to the ground. More of the Templar knights and Muslims ran into the foreground where they stood, covering Creed and Caretaker from their sights. Medieval commanded Middle Age to find them. While doing so, Medieval blasted all those who stood in his path, walking through the battle shooting both templars and Muslims. Caretaker carried Creed from the battlefield, laying him aside near a ravaged home. Caretaker saw the wound, it's still bleeding, not as much as before.

"You need to find a way to heal fast."

"I'm doing all I can. What weapon was that?"

"A shotgun."

"That was no simple shotgun. It took me down. Made me bleed. It has to be a weapon made by Adrambadon or someone in the same vain."

The trampling of a horse is heard near the home and came to a solid stop. Creed and Caretaker were awaiting to see who the rider could be and the door of the home opened. Caretaker saw him and Creed wondered with questions.

"Caretaker?" The rider said.

"Yes. I see you remember me."

"I do. Why does he have my likeness?"

"Why do you have mine?" Creed asked, staring at the Knight Creed.

"I see now. He's from another time. How far out?"

"From the future. Approximately eight-hundred and eighteen years."

"The Cryptic Lineage continues further I see. Well, no matter for the cause. He's wounded greatly."

"He just needs a moment to heal."

"I will handle it."

Knight Creed walked over and knelt in the presence of Creed. Placing his right hand upon Creed's chest and without a moment's notice, the wound was healed. Caretaker was astonished by the quickness of the process.

"I never knew you could heal others."

"It comes and goes. Mainly a cause for the battles."

Knightcreed helped Creed to his feet and the two gave a nod of exchange.

"Why are you both here in this era?"

"We were brought here by Middle Age. He's working with Medieval."

"You're saying what we're doing right now has no effect on the events of the future concerning Medieval?"

"They have affects. Just for a moment in time."

"You can't stay here any longer. The more you linger, the quicker you cause yourself to evaporate from the timeline."

"We don't know how to get back." Caretaker said.

"I will aid you. I have an ally who's out here that can transcend time and space. He'll be your way out of here."

"Where is he at the moment?"

"Battling the Muslims. He's Lord Klarson."

"Klarson?" Caretaker questioned. "I thought he was away when the battle took place."

"No. he's here and his fighting. With power that frightens those who don't believe."

Creed walked toward the door, passing by Caretaker and Knightcreed.

"Let's find him and get going."

"He takes after our kind." Knight Creed said.

"A little too much." Caretaker added.

Walking outside, seeing the battle continuing. Caretaker looked further, finding both Medieval and Middle Age. He pointed toward them, giving the notice to Creed and Knight Creed. Medieval continued blasting knights and Middle Age wandered around the dead bodies, checking their faces under the helmets.

"I see them." Knightcreed said, mounting his horse. "Follow my path and I will lead you to Lord Klarson."

"Will do." Creed replied.

Knightcreed rode off into the battlefield with Creed and Caretaker following. Right in the battle, Knight Creed took down several Muslims and Templar knights, giving an open pathway to Creed and Caretaker. While doing so, Middle Age gazed up from the ground over the dead bodies, seeing Creed and Caretaker. He pointed and let out a loud scream, giving the signal to Medieval, who saw them ahead.

"They're mine." Medieval spoke to himself.

Medieval ran with a mighty speed, bolting through the knights and Middle Age followed. Knight Creed led them up a hill, where they stood a small and sturdy temple. Walking out of the temple was Lord Klarson.

"The Chaser I saw." Creed said.

"Lord Klarson." Knight Creed said. "These two need your assistance."

"My assistance on what causes?"

"They need to return to their own time. They come from the future."

"The future? Yes. I see. It explains your doppelganger."

Klarson led them into the temple, where at the forefront was what looked to be a mirror. Nearly thirteen-feet in height and five-feet wide. Creed and Caretaker stood in front of the mirror as Klarson circled it. Knight Creed stood at the door, waiting for Medieval and Middle Age to arrive. Klarson whipped out a strange, sharp chain and he began to twirl it in the face of the mirror. The glass started to warp, forming a wormhole. Klarson's face turned into a skull, covered with sin fire. He pulled the chain back and pointed.

"Walk through and you shall return to your time."

Knight Creed looked out and saw Medieval and Middle Age rushing toward the temple. He grabbed his battle axe, telling Creed and Caretaker he and Klarson will hold them off. Caretaker nodded in a bid of farewell.

"Young one." Knight Creed said toward Creed. "Keep the faith. Never falter in the presence of your enemies."

"I will stand." Creed replied.

They stepped into the wormhole, hearing the clashing battle between Knight Creed and Klarson against Medieval and Middle Age. Medieval caught a slight glance at Creed entering the wormhole and screamed with anger.

"This is not over!"

Entering the wormhole, Creed and Caretaker are thrown back into their time period, right in the cemetery where they previously stood. Caretaker let out a sigh of relief.

"We're back."

"I see." Creed replied. "Although, something's off."

'What do you mean?"

"I can sense the Cryptic Zone. I sense Adrambadon. He's near."

DEATH CHASER—THE DEAL

I

REPENTANCE IS NIGH

It was a late night, elsewhere in a deserted landscape. Only the moon could be present in the midst of the barren grounds. The Death Chaser moved through the land, searching for his next target. A target which may indicate Demonticronto's apparent return. The Chaser did not utter a word.

In another location, John Clarkson continued his training with Widow by his side. He began teaching her the knowledge of the supernatural and the skills to fight against the demonic forces. The Chaser told John to instruct Widow in these ways to increase her faith and the chances for her survival in this world.

Between the physical and spiritual realms of existence, an entity emerged and stepped foot upon the earth. He was tall, dressed in black with dark-blue flashes of light emitting from his face. Only his eyes were as red as blood. Behind him stood three figures, shrouded in the shadows.

"We've arrived." The figure said. "Now, we find this Chaser and put him in his place."

"What of his allies?" Another figure asked.

"What about them? If they get in our way, we take them out. Simple."

"What if they do not?" Another figure questioned. "We leave them be?"

"Yes. We're only here for the Chaser. No one else."

"As you have spoken."

"That I have. Now, the three of you will travel to separate locations. I will give out the signal to bring the Chaser to each of you. Once, he is in your sights, eliminate him. If you fail, I hope the next one succeeds. We must take him out before Demonticronto makes his return."

"We will not fail."

"For your sakes. I hope not."

The three figures turned into mists and flowed above in the air, scattering themselves from Dieheart's presence. Dieheart smirked, holding out his arms with his hands wide open. He closed his eyes and exhaled.

"Soul of Retribution. There is a need that requires your aid. These locations are in need of your acquaintance. Go there. Do your work."

The Chaser continued moving through the desert and while on the move, he looked up, catching a bright flash of light. The light exploded and went into three separate paths. The Chaser knew of the light and the paths it made. He turned his focus from Demonticronto to the three paths and quickly made a right turn, heading toward the first path.

II

THE EARTH LIVETH

The Chaser had found himself after the traveling facing the Grand Canyon. He looked upon the structure of the area and saw a silhouette standing atop the Canyon. Even through the night sky, the Chaser keened his eyes and saw the form of the figure. He knew it wasn't human and stopped himself, pointing toward the figure.

"Whatever you proclaim yourself to be," The Chaser spoke. "Come down and face me."

The figure made its way to the ground to face the Chaser. As it stepped foot on the ground, the two entities shared a stare down. The Chaser could now see what the figure is and he nodded and pointed.

"You don't belong on this plane, demon."

"As a matter of fact, I don't. however, I was brought here in an urgent matter."

"Who sent you here?"

"A friend."

"The name of your friend?"

"You'll find out soon. If you can survive this battle."

"You threaten me?"

"It is my nature."

The Chaser stretched forth his hands and from them emerged the sinfire. The demon grinned, stepping back and raising his own arms, causing the ground to tremble. The Chaser kept his stance and his gaze focused.

"By the way, Chaser. I didn't tell you my name." The demon said. "I am Mineron, the Demon of the Earth."

"Never heard of you."

"Now you have."

Mineron raised up the dirt from the ground, forming it into a boulder. The dirt fell above the Chaser as he moved from the incoming attack. The Chaser rolled over the incoming boulder, turning toward Mineron and blasting him with the sinfire. Mineron brushed of the fire and smirked.

"I am made from the earth you see around you, Chaser." He taunted. "Fire cannot harm me!"

"So you believe." The Chaser replied. "Yet, you are not aware of how the things of the earth are made. What can change them and what can shape them. Yet, I am aware of such matters. This day, you will learn what happens to the earth when it feels the touch of brimstone."

Mineron levitated in the air above the Chaser with his arms stretched out and a large grin on his graveled face.

"Do your best!"

"I shall."

The Chaser twirled his hands and arms in a circle, conjuring the sinfire once more. He kept twirling as the circle grew in size and the flames brightened. Mineron crossed his arms and scoffed at the sight of the flaming circle. The chaser continued until the flames were in between himself and Mineron. The flames were the height of thirteen feet.

"What more is this?" Mineron asked. "What good does a jester trick do to stop me?"

"This is not a trick," The Chaser answered. "but a test. One you have failed."

"I'm ending this." Mineron dove down toward the Chaser.

"Yes, this is the end." The Chaser said, blasting the flaming circle toward Mineron.

Mineron flew directly in the circle and within mere seconds, his body was consumed by the flames. Mineron fell to the ground as the flames did not ceased and the circle started to close itself with Mineron in its grasp. Mineron struggled to get free, but the flames were like a tight band. Mineron couldn't stand up due to the circle as the Chaser walked over toward him, staring him down.

"Is this it?" Mineron asked. "What more must be done?"

"This is your end." The Chaser said. "You are done."

The Chaser waved his right hand and the flames consumed Mineron to the point his body became like magma, pouring from his eyes, ears, nose, and mouth. The Chaser saw Mineron's body melt and quickly freeze. At that point, the Chaser stomped Mineron's head into ashes and left his remains to burn in the sinfire. The Chaser left the Grand Canyon. While leaving, thunder cracked from above with a strange laughter following. The chaser looked up and felt the same energy that was within Mineron coming from the clouds above.

"Another one." The Chaser said.

III

STORMS OF THE AIR

While the Chaser sought after what was roaming in the skies above, John and Widow traveled into a small town. While tracking the source, Widow spotted a place where it read "Fortune Telling" above the doors. She stopped, pointing toward it as John gave a look.

"What about it?"

"We should go in there. See what they know."

"You already know that's not a wise move."

"How come? We need to find out if Demonti is returning soon. Perhaps, the fortune teller inside knows of it."

"There's no need for it. The Chaser will tell us everything when the time is near."

"What if it's hidden from him as well? Look, let's go in there, ask about Demonti, and see what we find. Afterwards, we'll leave and give our results to the Chaser."

John shook his head, looking back and forth between the building and Widow.

"This is on you if something goes wrong."

"I already know. I'll take my judgment justly."

They entered the building. Seeing its walls covered with gems and crystals. Near them in the front was a round table, carved with magical symbols relating to the elements of the earth. Widow approached the table, seeing the markings while John walked around the place, searching for someone. Anyone.

"Is anyone in here?" John asked. "We're at this table. Letting you know."

From the back walked out a young woman. Dressed in a violet dress from her chest to feet. She brushed back her black wavy hair as she approached John and Widow.

"I see visitors this night. I wasn't aware they'll be you."

"What do you mean?" John questioned.

"I knew you were coming here. You work alongside a Chaser."

"Yes." Widow said. "Yes, we do."

"Then, you are aware of why we're here."

"I am. You desire to find answers regarding Demonticronto's imminent return."

"Well, is he returning soon." John asked.

"Please, sit and I shall explain everything to you."

John sat at the table besides Widow while the young woman sat in front of them. She giggled.

"Forgive my manners, my name is Madame LoCasta."

"How long have you done this type of work?" John wondered. "You seem a bit young to be capable of this."

"I was born into this life. Grew up in the arts. Trust me, I am capable of accomplishing what to seek."

The Chaser moved into the skies through the fiery whirlwind and ceased himself in the air. Covered within the dark clouds and seeing quick flashes of lightning surrounding him. He could hear the mumblings of a voice.

"Show yourself, spirit."

A gust of wind blew toward the Chaser, not fazing him nor stumbling him. From there a small whirlwind appeared before him and formed into the image of a man. Yet, this form had the appearance of a man with uncertain features. Reptile-like eyes, long dark wavy and sharp hair. His teeth were like a tiger's and the nails on his fingers resembled claws. His skin was a pale blue. Yet, darker than the morning sky.

"Who are you?" The Chaser asked.

"I am Shinow. The Demon of the Air. Bringer of Storms."

"Who sent you?"

"You will know in good time."

"Your ally said the same before I ended him."

"There's only three of us and yet, you've managed to take one of us out? He didn't tell us you had such strength."

"Who is he?"

"The one who sent us."

"Enough talk, I'm going to finish you off for invading this realm."

"You can try. For one cannot catch the wind."

The Chaser scoffed and from his hands emerged the sinfire and with it he tossed it into the clouds surrounding himself and Shinow. Shinow summoned the wind, seeking to remove the fire, yet the fire was no kindled by Shinow's power. The Chaser bowed his head and a lightning bolt came from behind him, traveling through the clouds and striking the sin fire. Creating a vacuum of flames, burning the air within. Therefore, suffocating Shinow. Shinow raised his hands and rain started to fall from above. The rain was not enough to take out the flames as it had no affect.

"What is this?!" Shinow yelled. "My powers cannot contain the flames!"

"Because the flames burn all that has the residue of sin." The Chaser said. "You, demon of the air are consumed by sin. Therefore, you must burn."

Shinow yelled greatly as the sinfire consumed him. Burning him into nothing more than floating ashes of light. The Chaser sighed as he heard a distant voice higher than the clouds.

"The firmament."

Madame LoCasta sat still at the table while John and Widow waited patiently for an answer. Any answer. LoCasta opened her eyes and they were red as blood. Her pupils could not be seen and it frightened Widow, yet John was not afraid.

"I know you're not LoCasta. Who are you?"

"I am the one you seek." A deep voice said out of LoCasta's mouth with a grin.

"Demonti?" Widow said.

"You believe you can trace my actions. You sought after my patterns and it's led you here. To sit at the feet of a sorceress. What would the Chaser think of you now?"

"We're here on business. Not on some wicked adventure."

"Keep telling yourselves such lies. In time, we shall meet in the flesh. But for now, I wait until the time is appointed and I am called."

"We will stop you." John said. "When the time does come."

"We shall see. But, for now, I suggest you focus on the enemy at hand."

"Enemy?"

"Right at the door."

John turned around, hearing the front door open. He turned back to LoCasta, seeing her eyes have reverted to their natural state and Demonticronto was gone. John looked and saw who was approaching.

"Well, it seems I've just missed my chance to seek some answers."

"And you are?" John asked. "One of Demonti's dogs?"

"No. I am Dieheart. One who has worked with Demonticronto ever since the days began."

"Why are you here?" LoCasta asked. "Do you seek something of value?"

"I'm here to finally see the Chaser's allies. Fitting they'll be in a place like this. Unbeknownst to the Chaser himself."

"I suggest you watch yourself. He could show up here at any moment."

"I'm afraid not. I'm too wise to fall for the tricks of man. The Chaser is currently preoccupied with several of my own forces. Which leaves the two of you alone with me."

"We can handle ourselves."

"I'm sure you can. No need to prepare for a fight. I only came to see you as a warning. Remove yourself from this path or suffer much dire consequences."

"I think not." John said, stepping up to Dieheart. "We will live and die on this path. For The Chaser has shown us what must be done in these last days."

Dieheart nodded, grinning as he crested his chin.

"I see. Very well. When the time does arrive, I hope you're prepared for a quick death."

Dieheart turned and left LoCasta's place. She turned to John and

Widow, sighing.

"Did you get all you came for?"

"That and a little more." John replied.

"Thank you." Widow said.

IV

THE SEAS OF THE FIRMAMENT

The Chaser went high into the atmosphere, reaching the second heaven. Looking out toward the sun and the moon across from one another, he listened closely once more, hearing the strange noises coming from higher above. Much higher than the stars around him.

"Is it possible?" The Chaser questioned to himself. "If it is such, this is not a matter of my own. But of the others."

From there, a voice echoed from above the Chaser, speaking in such language familiar to the demons he faced earlier. There, the Chaser knew he was dealing with another demon. However, this one was sitting above the firmament. The Chaser keened his flaming eyes, setting them clearly to focus. Upon focusing, he saw the demon in the waters above. Nearly camouflaged with the darkness.

"You do not belong up there, demon."

"This is the perfect place to settle this business. I'm sure the others won't be bothered by the battle."

"You have trespassed a place beyond your borders!"

The Chaser rushed himself into the seas above. Now covered by the waters and shrouded in the darkness. The demon was invisible to the Chaser's eyes, yet his flaming eyes did not evaporate. The Chaser swam through the waters, he couldn't even seethe second heaven beneath him, except for the piercing dim light near the top of the waters.

"Show yourself." The Chaser spoke.

Right in front of him, the demon morphed from the waters. Creating itself a body from the waters. The demon's appearance was very similar to Shinow, only for the hair to be flowing with water. The Chaser stopped himself, lifting his body upright to face the demon.

"Who are you?" The Chaser asked.

"My name is Flrange. This is my domain."

"Your domain? No demons are allowed to dwell in these parts."

"And you speak for the authority?"

"I speak for those who cannot speak. As they cannot speak such words."

"Go about your business or else I must deal with you swiftly."

"I have come to you to send you into the pit where you belong. With the others."

"You speak of Shinow and Mineron. I am aware of their defeat by your hand. The dealmaker told me of the events."

"Dealmaker?"

"We were sent here by a very powerful ally. To see if you were truly as Demonticronto and the others have said you to be."

"Who is this dealmaker of yours?"

"You'll only find out if you can defeat me."

"I was already set on doing such."

The Chaser grabbed Flrange by his watery coat, however, the water demon twirled himself around in the water, causing the Chaser to loosen his grip. Flrange speared the Chaser through the waters, deep until they impacted into the firmament itself. Not a dent. Flrange held the Chaser down with his foot on his throat and laughed.

"It appears your fire cannot conjure within the waters."

The Chaser's eyes quickly opened, only revealing the sinfire. Flrange stumbled as the Chaser shoved his foot from his throat and the Chaser grabbed Flrange by his neck and covered his face with his other hand.

"You've seemed to have forgotten where we are, demon. There are no boundaries here that you can undo."

The Chaser blasted Flrange with sinfire mixed with the waters and evaporated the demon into nothing but remnants of ash. The Chaser took a moment of refreshment before returning to the earth below. Once returning to the earth, the Chaser placed himself in the presence of John and Widow as they were already seeking his presence.

"Good you're here." John said.

"I felt your sense. I came as I could."

"We've discovered something." Widow said.

"Is it of Demonticronto?"

"It is."

Before John could tell the details, Dieheart appeared before them. Applauding with a great smile. Widow hid behind John as he stood next to the Chaser, who's eyes were piercing with fire. And embers brewing from his hands.

"You managed to do it. You took out the demons."

"I did." The Chaser added. "You must be the dealmaker the water spirit spoke of."

"I am. Allow me to introduce myself to you. I am Dieheart. From a realm not of this earth."

"I am aware. The darkness which consumes you is emitting from your very being."

"Of course. I've already introduced myself to John and Widow. When they were seeking answers from a teller."

The Chaser paused, turning to the two.

"You spoke with a fortune teller?"

"We needed a sure answer." Widow responded. "I thought it would be simple."

The Chaser turned to John, who stood quietly. The Chaser waved his hand before turning to Dieheart.

"The deal has been made, Soul of Retribution."

"What deal?"

"You will find out very soon."

Dieheart sunk into the earth with a laugh fading away. The Chaser looked back at John and Widow.

"We'll discuss this later. Right now, get yourselves some time. Mediate. Pray. Prepare yourself for what's ahead."

"What is ahead?" John asked.

"A greater fight."

I

ANOTHER LOST GIRL

Travis Vail sat at his desk, looking over the cases which have been reported ever since the conflicts with Balthazar, the Sin Phantom, and Demonticronto. Vail remembered his encounters with the other supernatural forces. He chuckled under his breath memorizing their allegiance for the moment. He looked over as his cell phone began to vibrate.

"Who's calling?" Vail answered.

Vail listened and he listened closely. He nodded, taking out a pen and writing down the information. He nodded, ending the call. He looked at what he wrote and shook his head.

"Guess it's begun again."

He grabbed his gear, put on his coat and left. Sometime later, Vail arrived in the town where the call had come.

"Back in Chesterfield." Vail sighed. "Let's see what's happening here."

While in Chesterfield, Vail searched for the caller. The caller left an address for Vail to find. Which he traced, finding the address to be in the suburbs. A quiet neighborhood. Vail saw several children playing with each other in a field across the street. Others rode their bikes down the road. Confused, he found the address and approached the home's front door. Vail knocked. The door answered and Vail was surprised.

"Cooper Lawrence?" Vail said.

"Good to see you again, Mr. Vail."

"Wait, you're the one who called?"

"I am."

"But why? What's happened?"

"Come in and we'll explain everything."

"Certainly."

Inside the home, Cooper's wife, Janice saw Vail and she went to greet him. Sitting in the living room was Carrie. Vail saw her and she saw him.

"She's gotten older over the past few years, hasn't she?" Vail said.

"I'm not a child anymore." Carrie said.

"How old are you now? Fifteen? Sixteen?"

"I'm sixteen."

"You're not getting into any trouble, are you?"

"None of a major issue."

"Ah." Vail mumbled."

He turned back to her parents with a concerned, yet unworried look.

"Why did you call me?"

"Please come with us. We'll explain in private."

Vail nodded and followed Carrie's parents into Cooper's office. Once Vail had entered, Cooper closed the door as Vail sat down in front of the desk. Janice sat next to him while Cooper sat behind the desk. Vail was still confused, looking back and forth between Cooper and Janice.

"Why did you call me? I'm not understanding what's happening here."

"We called you because it's starting again." Janice said.

"What's starting again?"

"Carrie's been speaking to someone in her room."

"You're sure it's not just a friend of hers. Perhaps a lad she met at school?"

"No." Cooper said. "That was we thought. Until we overheard her say the name, Leta."

Vail sat back in the chair. Quiet within himself. Leta had

returned? Vail was unsure of the possibility.

"Are you sure we're talking about the same Leta? The one who possessed your daughters all those years ago?"

"We're certain." Janice said. "We've never met any of Carrie's friend who have that name."

"You believe Leta is trying to continue what she started?"

"Yes. Why bother our daughter when she's done nothing wrong. She's a good kid."

"That's the thing, Cooper. Good children are often the targets for such spirits."

"So, will you do what you did before?" Janice questioned. "I'm positive it will cleanse her again."

"I will try. But I must be sure of all of this. Carrie's older now and the connection could be deeper than before. I cannot risk anything of importance. Carrie's life depends on it."

"Thank you." Janice replied.

"Please, do what you can." Cooper added.

"I will."

Vail left the home and went to the library, as per usual.

II

REMEMBERING THE ONE BEFORE

Travis Vail sat by himself in the library, reading up on the same files as before. He closed the books and pulled out his phone, dialing a number. On the other end was Raynard Brown. Vail had begun to tell him of Leta's possible return and the connection she has with Carrie Lawrence. Raynard refereed him to search the home's land once more to find anything unusual that may pertain toward the Lost Girl spirit.

"I will do that, Raynard. Just to be sure."

Vail hanged up and left the library, returning to the Lawrence home. While walking back to his car, he saw a homeless man sitting on the sidewalk beside the library. He was cloaked in a black hooded jacket from his shoulders to his knees. He walked with a hunch in his back and frail in his steps. Vail nodded toward him and the man stood up, approaching him. His hands were out and Vail grinned.

"I would give you something if I had anything. I'm sorry."

"Don't be sorry, Spirit-Seeker."

"Pardon?"

The man raised his head up, facing Vail. He stepped back, seeing the homeless man's face. He was old, very old. His long white beard was stretched outward and his eyes were near dim.

"How do you know who I am?" Vail questioned.

"I've been around for a very long time. I've seen those of your kind for many centuries do the work you're doing this day."

"Who are you?"

"I'm only a wanderer, Spirit-Seeker. I come and I go."

344

"A wanderer? From what part of the world?"

"A place far from here. Across the pond you could say."

"East lands, huh. I see. Well, I need to get going."

"As you shall. For I am aware of the task set before you. The Lost Girl has returned. Hasn't she? Attempting to bond with another host?"

"So I've been told. I'll stop her for good this time."

"I'm sure you will. But, take heed to these words. Her connection with the young girl isn't as simple as you would assume it to believed. For when a spirit goes out of one, it indeed returns much stronger and with friends of its own."

"I know the works. No need to repeat them to me."

"Of course. Now, you will see them in action. Take care, Spirit-Seeker."

Vail nodded, waving away as he turned to his car. He looked back and the man was gone.

"Every time."

III

THE STRANGE CASE OF LETA AND CARRIE

Vail returned to the Lawrence home, seeing Janice running out of the home toward him with Cooper behind.

"What's going on?" Vail asked.

"It's Carrie." Janice said. "There's something wrong with her."

'Wait here. I'll go look to her."

Vail ran into the home, seeing Carrie standing in the living room completely still. Her hair moved smoothly as if the wind was within the home. Vail couldn't feel it as he approached her.

"Carrie, whatever she has on you, you must fight it."

Carrie did not move. Her hands twitched but could not bend. Her fingers were straightened. As if there was electricity holding them in place. Vail took another step forward and Carrie's head turned toward him in a quick rush. Her eyes were solid black, and she grinned. Vail sighed.

"You're not Carrie."

"I am not."

"Leta, release her from your control. Now."

"You believe this will end as it did before? I have learned much since our last encounter."

"I'm sure you have. Still bothering this young girl with your agendas for control."

"We share a bond. A bond that you broke."

"You don't belong here, spirit."

"Your words will not save Carrie this time. I have grown in such spiritual power since the last departure."

"You will leave Carrie and you will be gone for good."

"Make your move. Spirit-Seeker."

Vail reached into his pocket, taking out his book used in many of his cases. He began to recite a page and while doing such, Leta let out a great laugh. The laugh irritated Vail to the point where his reciting had ceased, and he could not utter the words. Vail immediately felt powerless, seeing Leta had truly grown in the spiritual arts. Peculiar for a spirit in Vail's words. Vail had no other options in his place. He paused himself, seeing the black eyes on Carrie and the laughter of Leta coming from her mouth.

"I know." Vail whispered. "I know what I have to do."

Vail placed the book into his jacket pocket, pointed toward Leta while walking back to the door.

"This is far from over."

"Where are you going?!"

"I have something in mind to get rid of you."

"You believe you can cast me away? After what I've just shown you?!"

"Not me. I know a guy and I'll be back with him on my side. And hers."

"I cannot let you leave."

"You will if you let Carrie have control of her body. When I return, then you can rise up and face me. Then, we'll see who will remain."

"Are you challenging me? Using this young girl as a tool for your works?"

"Truth be told, who's the tool in this story? It's not Carrie."

Vail walked back outside, seeing Cooper and Janice waiting in a slight panic mode. Janice ran up to him with tears in her eyes.

"Is she alright?!"

"Unfortunately, Leta has possession over your daughter."

"Aren't you going to do what you did the last time?"

"I tried. Didn't work."

"Then, what are you planning on doing, Mr. Vail?" Cooper asked.

"I know a guy who can help me with this case. Leta's become far stronger than the last time. I'll need some assistance with this one."

Vail walked to his car before turning back to the Lawrences.

"By the way, your daughter should be back to her senses. Leta would have left knowing what I'm planning on doing. Keep an eye on her until I return."

Vail left the Lawrence home. Traveling nearly afar off into the outskirts, stumbling upon an old building. Vail exited his car, approaching the building. The structure was pre-Civil War, yet with a mixture of medieval architecture. Vail nodded.

"This is the spot."

Vail walked up to the large double-doors and knocked. After a second knock, the doors open. Yet, Vail saw no one. He shrugged his shoulders and entered the building with the doors shutting behind him. The closing of the doors did not faze nor concern him. Vail continued walking forward, finding himself standing in a large room near a corridor.

"Hey, I know you're here." Vail said. "So, do us a favor and come on out."

Vail turned around, seeing a large window and hovering at the window was a silhouette of a figure, levitating in the air. Vail smirked, crossing his arms.

"I know who you are." Vail said.

The figure moved forward toward Vail, as he did not move himself. the figure came into the light and revealed itself to be Doctor Donald Fortune. Vail applauded.

"I knew this was your spot all along."

"One of many." Fortune said. "Why are you here, Travis Vail, Spirit-Seeker?"

"You're aware of my work?"

"I know everything that pertains to the mystic realms which surround our world."

"That's nice. Look, I need your help. It's a major concern."

"My help? Why?"

"There's a young girl. She's possessed by a spirit. A powerful spirit. I need your help in breaking the soul tie between them.”

“Last I read, you call on the one who’s words you read from your book. Didn’t you at least try that?”

“I worked last time. Leta’s grown more powerful since then.”

“Leta.” Fortune said. “The Lost Girl spirit.”

“Yes. You’ve heard of her?”

“I’ve dealt when her kind before. Just not Leta herself.”

“She’s become stronger after I sent her away. I’m not sure how.”

“You’re telling me you were the one who sent her away those years ago?”

“I am. I was younger and much of a novice in those days. But, I did what needed to be done to save the girl.”

“Now, Leta’s retuned to the same girl and has an even stronger hold on her?”

“That’s correct.”

“I understand.”

Fortune opened the doors of the building to the outside. Vail looked back and forth to the door and to Fortune.

“Aren’t you going to tell me what to do? I need to break the soul tie between them.”

“Yes, you do.” Fortune replied. “However, I will not allow you to go alone.”

“Why can’t you just tell me what to do? I can deal with Leta myself.”

“I need to see this Leta in person. Learn her motives. That way, I can prepare myself and my apprentice in case she returns again in the future.”

“Your apprentice? There’s no one else here.”

“He’s preoccupied on a task afar off. Now, are you ready to save this girl?”

“After you.”

“I’ll meet you there.”

“Wait a second, fellow. You don’t even know where she is.”

“I’ll follow your lead. You drove out here after all. You can drive back.”

“Can’t you just teleport us there. And the car?”

“I can. But, should I?”

“It would prove much faster and speed is what we’ll need to get rid of Leta.”

“Very true. Stand still.”

“Ok. Why-”

IV

A STUBBORN SPIRIT ENTERS THE PIT

Within a sudden moment, Vail and Fortune were standing in front of the Lawrence home. Vail looked around, seeing the home and even his car. He turned to Fortune, who only nodded.

"How'd you do that?"

"The Orb of Quirinto." Fortune answered, showing the org attached to the amulet around his neck. Glowing with mystical energy.

"Where did you get it?"

"A long story not worth telling at the moment. We need to get Leta out of the girl."

"Agreed."

"I'm assuming she's inside." Fortune said.

"Let's go in then."

They approached the door of the home with Janice opening it as soon as she saw Vail. Cooper ran up behind her, confused about Fortune's appearance.

"Mr. Vail, who's the friend?"

"He's going to help me save your daughter."

"Who is he supposed to be?" Janice asked. "Some kind of magician."

"Sorcerer, madam."

"We assumed Vail could handle this on his own." Cooper mentioned. "Like the last time."

"This isn't like the last time." Vail replied. "Leta has a much stronger hold on Carrie. Doctor Fortune is here to aid me in setting your daughter free."

"Is your friend capable of this kind of work?"

"I've faced much more and far worse than a possession. I'm skilled enough."

Cooper nodded, allowing Fortune to enter the home. Upon entering, Fortune saw Carrie's body levitating above the living room floor. Vail entered, seeing the levitation.

"She's getting stronger."

"We have this under control." Fortune said. "I desire to speak with Leta."

Carrie's body moved around in the air as her head turned toward Fortune's gaze and her eyes were locked on. Still black. She grinned heavily, starting Carrie's parents.

"Vail, you've returned. And I see you didn't come alone."

"I did not."

Fortune stepped forward as a gust of wind rustled from Carrie's body, shoving him and Vail back. Fortune twirled his arms and the wind ceased. Vail noticed the tactic and shrugged his shoulders.

"That's convenient."

"Who are you?" Leta's voice asked.

"I am Doctor Donald Fortune. Supreme Enchanter of the mystical realm and I have been brought here to rid you of this young girl and of this material world."

"Supreme Enchanter? Another one?"

"She's familiar with your kind." Vail noticed. "Are you sure you can handle this, Fortune?"

"I am positive." Fortune clapped his hands together with the energy covering them. "Prepare to do your part in this, Spirit-Seeker."

"My part?"

"Do what you've done before. I will handle the rest."

Vail turned to Carrie's parents. Telling them to go outside and wait until the work is done. They agreed with tears in their eyes as the left the house. Vail turned his focus back toward Leta, while Fortune began levitating just a few feet off the ground. Leta had full control over Carrie's body, now posing it against Fortune. Vail slowly reached into his pocket, grabbing his book.

"Do you have what you need?" Fortune asked.

"I do."

"Then you're ready."

"I am."

Leta rushed toward Fortune as he stretched forth his arms, creating a barrier between himself and Leta. Vail was in the middle of the barrier with his book opened. Fortune looked toward him and nodded. Vail started to recite from the book the same words as before. Leta's focus was not on Vail, but on Fortune as she tried beating down the mystic barrier. She screamed with rage, punching the barrier. Fortune kept his demeanor. Focused and in control as Vail continued reading.

"Add one more to the speech." Fortune told Vail. "And speak it in something other than Latin."

"I got it." Vail replied. "*Tam qate alhabl alfidiya baynak wabaynaha alan!*"

Leta turned to Vail as he closed the book. Her eyes began to show the pupils as she struggled to hold herself and Carrie together. Her body was fighting between staying levitated and coming down to the floor. She glared toward Fortune as he could see Carrie's eyes starting to appear and Leta's power decreasing.

"You heard him, Lost Girl. The soul tie is broken. Leave. Now."

Fortune clapped his hands and the barrier collapsed as Leta let out a great scream. Carrie's body floated and fell to the floor, not before Vail could catch her. Fortune cleared the home of any residue of Leta's power. About thirty minutes later, Carrie's parents entered the home to find Carrie laying down in her room on the bed.

"Is she alright?" Janice asked.

"She's well." Vail said. "Leta is gone."

"Oh. Thank you. Thank you both."

Fortune nodded. Cooper approached the two and shook their hands. Thanking them for their help. Vail wanted to wait for Carrie to wake up and once she did, he spoke to her with Fortune standing by. Carrie told Vail that she was aware of everything that was happening. She stated she no longer feels the connection she shared with Leta. But, she told him that she could also see Leta's intentions. Her intentions were dire, and she was brought forth by a sorcerer who saw fit to distract Vail from some grander plan.

"Don't concern yourself with our affairs." Vail said. "We're just glad you're alright."

Afterwards, Vail said his goodbyes, hoping he doesn't have to return due to such similar events. Later, Vail spoke with Fortune about Carrie's words and he understood them greatly. Fortune warned Vail about an opposing adversary of his to which Vail stated he had no adversaries. Balthazar could be counted as one, but not a great adversary.

"I'm referring to anyone you met in your early years." Fortune said. "Someone who was very peculiar to your work. Like an opposite of the coin."

Vail thought, "There was one, however I haven't seen him since the investigation."

"I see. Meanwhile, you should keep an eye out. Just in case."

"One more thing." Vail said. "Why did you tell me not to speak the words in Latin?"

"Because you have to get outside of your box when confronting these matters. Spirits such as Leta keep memories, you know."

"Informative of you."

"Arabic was an interesting choice."

"It's the first one that came to mind."

"Good to hear. Just keep watch. All that Carrie told you, do not forget it."

"I will keep it all in mind. Thank you for the assistance, Doctor."

"It was a necessary duty."

Fortune warped the surroundings into a portal back to his true residence, the Citadel of Enchantment. Vail saw the large structure and how it was placed amongst the trees in a wilderness afar off. Vail smirked.

"That's where you reside."

"Indeed. I will be seeing you around, Travis Vail."

"Until next time."

"We'll see, Spirit-Seeker."

Fortune entered the portal and was gone. Vail took in the moment before entering his car and driving away, mediating on all that transpired. While on the road, Vail accepted the though in his heart and mind that Leta was gone. For good this time. To him, it was a great victory for the living.

THE DEVILHUNTER: BLOODLUST GROUNDS

I

ANOTHER AMBUSH?

Once he returned to Washington D.C., Gabriel Abraham went about his business. His first duty was to track down Sierra the Succubus, whom had escaped in the woods during the battle with Hastur's demons. Abraham returned to the same forest as before, except without the assistance of Evan Wyatt or Andrea Coralline. He searched the area of the last encounter with Sierra and found nothing but dried bones of her victims. Abraham shook his head.

"Where could she be?"

Behind Abraham appeared seven shrouded figures. Cloaked in dark robes. Their faces were hidden by the hoods. Abraham turned toward them, pointing at their apparel and he scoffed loudly.

"You guys again? I thought the whole incident at the church was a clear message."

"We are not with the Cult." One of the shrouded ones said.

"Then enlighten me on who's your with. If you're with anyone to be mentioned."

"We want you to know our master knows of your works. He seeks to find you and to bring you in."

"Your master? I have to guess. It can't be Hastur because we already dealt with him. Is it Demonticronto? No? How about the Sin Phantom? Not him either. Well, you're have to do some talking with me to get my mind cleared."

"No need. Once our master gets an audience with you, he will clear your mind of all things you deeply desire. You will only desire his power and his will alone."

"And you said you're not with the Cult? Yet, you're talking the same message with me right now. They said about the same."

"Our master is very powerful."

"And your master has been around for centuries. It's no different than the others. Now, I will ask you simply to leave me be while I do my work. Otherwise, prepare yourselves for a fight."

The shrouded ones lunged toward Abraham with fangs. He saw the teeth immediately and slammed his hands into the ground. The earth quaked and opened beneath them, swallowing the shrouded ones. Before the last one was taken down into the pit, it glared at Abraham.

"Our master will find out what you've done and he will find you. Sooner than the sun can touch this city on the morning!"

The shrouded one fell into the pit and the hole was sealed. Silence covered the grounds and Abraham turned back to the bones. Still no sign of Sierra. Abraham brushed off his shoulders and entered his car, leaving the area to return to the Revelation Center.

II

HUNTINGS

Abraham enter the Center, finding Evan and Andrea scrambling
in the library. Grabbing books which pertained to the recent events
with Demonticronto. Evan and Andrea were somewhat jealous of
Abraham's team-up with Travis Vail and the others. Abraham
chuckled from their words and only waved his hands as he walked
toward his office.

"There's something else going on. The reading can pause for a
moment."

They entered his office as he grabbed a book from the shelf and
opened it. On the pages were the same shrouded figures he
encountered in the wilderness. He began telling them about their
matching descriptions and how they proclaimed themselves not part
of Hastur's Cult. Evan quickly assumed they were due to the
similarities of appearance. Andrea was a little curious as to who they
worship. If not Hastur, then who?

"I'm not sure." Abraham said. "But, one of them told me their
master will find me before the sun rises. We only have about six hours
till then."

"Well, what do you want us to do?" Evan asked. "Seal up the
doors and windows?"

"This won't end up like last time. Whoever their master is, they
talked well of him. So, I'm not expecting an ambush. Besides, they
said he wishes to bring me into his group."

"Bring you in?" Andrea asked. "That would mean he's already
aware of your existence and who you are."

"All I ask is that we be ready for his arrival. With only six hours till sunrise, he'll be here much sooner than we'll be expecting."

Evan crest his chin while looking at the images of the shrouded ones. He pointed in the air and clapped his hands. Abraham and Andrea turned toward him in confusion. Abraham stared at him.

"Looking for some music to play?"

"No. I just thought of something. The words listed here, they describe these figures of having sharp fangs and using them to attack their victims. All of this sounds like they're some group of-"

"Vampires." Abraham replied. "I know. I saw the fangs myself before they went deep into the pit."

"Wait." Andrea paused. "First, we had to deal with some great demon. Then, you go off on an adventure with the Spirit-Seeker, then you have a team-up with a bunch of supernatural entities to fight against a demon stronger than Hastur. Now, you're telling us that vampires are around? Have been around?"

"You didn't know?" Abraham questioned.

"I just wasn't certain they existed."

"Much like werewolves, demons, ghosts, and superheroes, yeah. Vampires exist. In different forms as well. The movies don't usually get them correct most of the time."

"Well, Andrea." Evan said. "Now you know."

Andrea shook her head and left Abraham's office. Evan followed her out while Abraham grinned. He grabbed the book and looked at the images himself. Turning the pages, he began to learn a little of their master. An ancient entity. Their master made them into what they became. They live to worship and obey him only. Abraham was intrigued by this figure and graciously waited for the entity to show up at the Center. Abraham was not going anywhere nor was he planning on hiding.

In an abandoned ghost town. Deep underneath the town itself was the remnants of a medieval catacombs. The catacombs was damp, with tiny rivers of water flowing through and throughout. However, there was a heat coming from within the catacombs. A peculiar heat. Inside, there was a solid black coffin. Made of onyx and heated in a great temperature. The coffin's lid tilted and slid open. Out of the coffin came a hand, pale with white fingernails. The smell of sulfur irradiated from within the coffin as the figure stood up on the outside. Cloaked in all black. He raised his head up to the sky and sniffed.

"Ah." He uttered quietly. "Devilhunter."

III

MEET THE MASTER

With almost an hour till sunrise and still no sign of the shrouded ones' master. Evan waited in the lobby with a sword in hand. Abraham walked out of his office, seeing Evan with the sword and shook his head.

"Put that down. No need to hurt yourself before the enemy approaches."

Evan put down the sword, sitting it next to the wall near the bookshelf. Andrea entered the library, seeing Abraham standing with Evan. She closed the book in her hands.

"What did Evan do this time?"

"What?" Evan said.

"Nothing. He was just practicing his swordsmanship."

They laughed and the sound of the front door creaked into the library. They looked at one another and immediacy went to see who had entered. Evan stood up and before he left the library, he grabbed the sword. They entered the lobby and saw who had enter the Center. He was dressed in all black. A long robe with a cloak. Yet, no hood. His skin was pale and his beard was dark as a raven. His eyes were red as a fire.

"Well, this guy's not human." Andrea said.

"No kidding." Evan replied.

"I think I know who he is." Abraham said. "It all fits."

"Then, you know why I've come, Devilhunter."

"You're their master. They never told me your name."

"I am aware of what you have done to my followers. Sending them into such a pit where they'll have a hard time returning to the grounds of the earth. No matter. I will seek out new followers and they will worship me. With your help."

Abraham scoffed.

"I'm not helping a vampire achieve anything."

"I am not just a vampire. I am the Head of the Vampires."

"Yeah right." Andrea said. "So, you've been around before Dracula?"

"He is of another matter. I have led the vampire species throughout the eons of our time. I will continue to lead them until the end of all things is at hand."

"Well, the end isn't here yet." Abraham said. "So, here's the deal. You can leave this Center and go back to wherever you've came from. Or you can meet our end this day by my hands."

"And mine." Evan added. "I'm sorry, I just had to get involved."

"I have no desire to fight you, Devilhunter. I know of your works in this field. Your allegiance with the Spirit-Seeker and those others you've met on your quest against the great demon. Fighting you would serve no purpose in the higher affairs."

"Then, why have you come to my place? Last I was told by one of your worshippers that you seek to recruit me into your little cult."

"Only because of what you've accomplished in such a short time. You've built this Center to protect the lives of the innocents. Except for the one you lost some time ago. What if I told you she is still alive."

Abraham paused.

"What are you saying? She's still alive? Where?"

"I cannot give you more information unless you follow me."

The master extended his hand toward Abraham. Andrea and Evan yelled toward him to refuse and step back. Abraham was torn. He knew the Vampire was the enemy, but the thought of finding his lost student gave him such higher cause for his works. Abraham stepped forward and extended his hand toward the vampire. Andrea rushed and the master grabbed her by the throat. Evan raised his sword and swiped the vampire's back. It had no effect as the vampire knocked him across the lobby floor. Abraham held the vampire's hand and he laughed. Abraham smirked with his left hand behind his back, holding a silver dagger.

"I refuse." Abraham said, raising the dagger and stabbing the vampire in the chest.

The master stumbled as he pulled the dagger from his chest, burning his hand in the process. He tossed the dagger to the ground, holding his chest in burning pain. The vampire opened the front doors as he backed up, he looked up to the clouds and piercing through them was sunlight. He snarled.

"I could've given you such power, Devilhunter. Such drive. Such motivation. You could've seen your student again."

"If she is still alive, I'll find another way to save her. As for helping your kind, I refuse."

The Vampire transformed himself into a swarm of bats and left the Center. Abraham shut the doors and sighed. Evan stood up from the floor, grabbing the sword. Andrea approached him, telling him to put it down. Abraham stood quiet while Evan returned to the library.

"You're alright?" Andrea asked.

"I'll be fine."

"His words didn't sink deep, did they?"

"Not deep enough. But, I do wonder if my student is alive. In some other dimension or world. I must know if it is true. Get this burden off my chest."

"Then, what will you do?"

"I'll make a call. See what Vail knows."

"And what if he doesn't?"

"Guess I'll have to wait and see what comes next."

As they talked, a strange figure entered the library, cloaked in a mist of darkness, reached over to the shelves, stealing several books on the occult. The figure hears Evan's footsteps approaching and disappeared through a rift between the worlds.

I

LET'S HAVE A CHAT

Denise Kira stepped through the doors of the bar. The bar filled with all sorts of magical creatures. Inside, she glanced around at the trolls, satyrs, goblins, elves, and other kinds. She approached the bar as the bartender turned around to see her. Sitting her bag on the top of the bar.

"You're not one of us." The bartender said.

"I'm not. I've come to see someone."

"Someone? Like a lover or something?"

"More like an acutance."

"Ah. Why would they tell you to meet them here? Humans aren't usually visitors to such a place."

"His name is Fable. That's what I was told."

The bartender stopped what he was doing. Only to stare. Denise looked at him, waiting for a word to come out of his mouth.

"You mean to meet with him? The troublemaker?"

"Troublemaker? He helped me."

"Listen closely. Fable is a guy who comes and goes. He never stays. Unless there's a price willing to be paid."

"Must be a large sum." A voice said from around the bar.

They turned to see Fable, leaning against the bar with a smirk on his face. The bartender sighed. Denise smiled. Fable smiled back before looking at the bartender with a questionable face.

"Tell me, what have you told the woman?"

"Only that you're trouble. You'll always be trouble with the path you're on."

"Trouble can go a lot of ways. Good or bad. Best to take our chances."

"Hmm." The bartender turned and went about his business.

Fable nodded toward Denise.

"I see you came."

"Well, you told me to meet you here. Figured you would show up again."

"And I did. Although, not to drink and gamble as before. you wanted to talk, so we'll talk."

Denise agreed and the two went to a table near one of the windows at the back of the bar. Fable preferred such an area. Gives him a full view of the place and all who are inside can be seen by him. His eyes were focused just as his revolver was loaded. The bartender came to their table, setting down a mug. Fable grabbed the mug.

"Thanks."

"I'm doing it for the woman. Not for you."

"No offense taken." Fable grinned.

The bartender walked away as Fable took a drink from the mug. He sighed as Denise watched on.

"So, what did you want to talk about?"

"Um, what had happened in town. Between you and the other guy."

"Oh. You speak of Emblem. He's a troublesome lad. Never met him until that very moment."

"And what of the woman? The hooded one."

"Pandora. She's a nice girl. Although, she can be trouble at times. Drives me insane."

"Well, she visited me at my apartment."

"When?"

"Before I saw you on the streets with her and Emblem. She warned me not to be around you. Said you were trouble. Damnation would occur."

"Damnation? Ha. Pandora does have the soft spot for those

words. I wouldn't mind her sayings. She's an ancient individual."

"She told me the world has enough to deal with. Due to the risen heroes."

"Ah, those peeps. Listen, Denise, I've never encountered any of them. Do I wish to meet some? Perhaps one day. Until then, I do what I can for Manchester."

"There is something I would like to know."

"Shoot for it."

"Have you ever crossed over through the Rift?"

"I have. When I was a young lad."

"What is it like? The place?"

"Very… magical." Fable grinned.

"I'm sure it is. Are the colors brighter there than they are here?"

"Much brighter. If the general public saw what was beyond the Rift, they would believe they're in an alien's world."

"And those who live there?"

"Very magical. Trolls, elves, dwarves. All types of races."

"Do they get along?"

"It's more complicated to explain. But, they have their methods."

"I'm sorry to keep digging, but there must be a lot more."

"There is. And if I were to tell you, we would be in this bar for days. That is time we cannot toss away. Give it some time and eventually, you will come to know it all. Eventually."

"I see."

"Don't worry yourself. It will come. In time."

"I'm sure of it."

"Oh. By the way. You don't need to call me Fable. Let the blokes do that."

"Then, what shall I call you?"

"Kurt. Kurt Wesker."

"Very well. Kurt."

Denise smiled as Fable continued to drink.

In a far-off location within the Rift, Pandora stood before The Hidden Four. Surrounded by fire, crystals sticking out the walls with various gemstones. Magic filled the place. It had a presence of its own. The Four aren't pleased with the previous actions of Fable when contending with Emblem. Pandora had sought out to reason for him before the Four, as they seek to pull him from the duty of the task.

"Fable is a skilled ally. When necessary."

"Necessary is not the focus on the task." One of the Four spoke. "We see that he should take these mattes urgently and complete them."

"I will send word to him about your concerns. I cannot change his mind."

"But, you can speak with him. See what it will take to get him on these matters. Quickly. Emblem is not far away. He is healing himself as we speak and he craves revenge."

"I can feel him." Pandora said. "Although, I shall be ready for the fight."

"And you will make sure Fable is ready as well."

"That I will." Pandora sighed before vanishing in a whiff of reddish smoke.

II

NICE TO MEET YOU

After the conversation in the bar, Denise and Fable returned to their homes. When Denise had arrived and turned on the lights, Pandora was standing before her. The presence of the hooded one startled Denise as she dropped her books and bag. She knelt to pick them up, however Pandora raised her hand and the objects lifted from the floor and onto the table near the kitchen. Denise nodded.

"I appreciate that."

"I must speak with you." Pandora said. "It is of urgent matters."

"You're not going to mute me again, are you?"

"Only if you make such a loud sound."

"I won't. Why are you in my apartment? Again?"

"To speak to you, of course."

"Why me? I haven't done nothing wrong."

"You did not heed my warnings about Fable."

"He seems like a decent man."

"He is dangerous. The things that follow him only bring tragedy to those outside of the magic realm."

"He told me enough about the Rift and how it operates."

Pandora paused herself.

"What do you mean? he spoke more of the magic?"

"Yes. It was just him and I. nothing else. I asked some questions, he gave me answers."

"Where is he now?" Pandora asked.

"He said he was heading home."

"Very well. I will speak to him as soon as possible. For the meantime, anything he has told you, keep it to yourself. Do not speak of this to another human."

"And if I end up doing so?"

"Do not make me find you. Or anyone else from the magic realm."

Denise nodded with a slight pause.

"I see."

"I am positive we will meet again."

"I'm sure of it." Denise replied.

Pandora snapped her fingers and she vanished. Denise sighed.

Fable had returned to the Cheshire Plain. Sitting in his home peacefully. Until he moment a tremor occurred. He arose from his seat, his left-hand glowing with magical energy while his right hand is placed on his revolver. The shaking of the land increased, traveling toward Fable's home. He placed himself, ready to fight as the front door opened. Revealing the Hidden Four.

"Really?" Fable sighed. "Again?"

The Four entered the home as the door shut behind them. They surrounded Fable.

"What's going on here?"

"We are here to insure you of your duties."

"What duties?"

"Your duties to stopping Emblem."

"Yeah. Emblem. I remember the lad. Pandora and I faced him in town. We defeated him and he ran away."

"He did leave the area. Yes. However, he has retreated to heal himself and to grow stronger."

"So I've been told."

"When he does make his presence known, you must be there to eliminate him."

"I see. And what of Pandora? Will she be accompanying me on this quest?"

"Pandora will do what she is commanded to do."

Fable nodded with a slight scoff.

"I'm sure she will. By the way, where is she?"

"She is on matters which attend to the quest at hand."

"Ah. So, she's going about the realms. Back and forth."

"You must accompany her on this next task."

"What task? I've already said I'll help against Emblem."

"This concerns another. Another powerful force. You and Pandora will travel into the Rift. There, you will meet with Chernabog."

Fable coughed.

"Pardon. Chernabog?"

"Chernabog has some information concerning Emblem that will be valuable for you and Pandora to learn. See to it that you visit him. There is much to be done at such a short time."

"And we are supposed to trust him?"

"You will do what is necessary. That is all."

The Four turned from Fable and left his home in a collected fashion. Fable only took a sip of his drink and shook his head.

"Every time."

III

CHERNABOG

Fable had met up with Pandora at the Gate of the Rift. There, Pandora had told him of her meeting with Denise, to which Fable could only wondered of what reason. Pandora stated she told Denise to stay away from him and Fable disagreed. He understood her reasons, but he saw himself as no consequence or threat to Denise's life. Pandora shook her head hearing the words coming from Fable.

"Let's just speak to Chernabog and get this over with." Fable said.

"Finally." Pandora chuckled. "You're focus on important matters."

Fable scoffed at Pandora's words as they walked through the gate and into the Rift. Once through, they found themselves standing at the doorway to what seemed to be an abandoned shack. Pandora looked around the shack, seeing no entry points besides the front door. Fable pointed toward it as Pandora continued searching.

"We could just knock." Fable suggested.

"I'm not certain we should. Chernabog is one not to be easily missed."

"We won't miss him if we just knock."

Fable went ahead and knocked. There was no response. Fable knocked once again, still no answer. Fable sighed and knocked three times before kicking the door once.

"What was that for?" Pandora asked.

"To get a response. The knocks weren't doing good."

As they were speaking, the door creaked open with the sound of a whistling wind. The air pulled out with the door, causing Fable and Pandora to question where they stand. Within the doorway was only a long hall. Deep down into a path of darkness. Pandora took a step forward and a strange odor moved across her face. She frowned, shaking her head.

"What is it?" Fable wondered.

"The stench. Blood."

They proceeded to enter the shack. Walking down the hallway led them into a larger room. One that would seem impossible to dwell within a shack such as the one they saw on the outside. Fable realized it is all an illusion, just as many places within the Rift are. Sitting inside the room was a man, one who had the similitude of an elder. His long white and black beard flowed down to his chest. His long black hair sat over his shoulders. Above his head he wore a silver crown. His eyes were dark as the night, yet glowing as the red of fire. He was dressed in armor resembling the Middle Age.

"Is this him?" Fable asked, staring at him.

Pandora stood before him as his eyes raised up toward hers. He grinned.

"Chernabog. I am Pandora. This is Fable. We are here on urgent matters concerning Emblem."

"I know of you." Chernabog replied, standing up from the chair. "I am aware of all that has transpired."

"You do?" Fable said. "How?"

"I have my followers throughout the natural realm."

"Then, you know all there is about Emblem?"

"I do. You want him destroyed? Yes?"

"We want him stopped." Pandora stated.

"I just want him gone." Fable said. "Guy's becoming an annoyance."

"Hmm. Well, those hoods told you all there is to know. You came to me as was scheduled. Now, I must deliver to you what you've come for."

"And that is?" Pandora questioned.

"You will need me to help you defeat Emblem. But, I do not rise up and fight for a cause unless one of my own is finished."

"What are you on about?" Fable said. "What cause?"

"I will lend my power to the battle if the two of you eliminate an ally of Emblem and an enemy of mine."

"And who is this enemy?"

"He calls himself Dark Fright. A frightening figure to humanity. Appears as a human/bat hybrid. He is very skilled. Born in the Rift like many of us, but his power comes from a darker source. Shit, even darker than my own."

"Listen, we are not hear to do your errands." Pandora stated. "We are here to get your assistance."

"You will have my assistance when you take out Dark Fright." Chernabog replied calmly. "Now, do you want my help or not?"

Pandora grunted, staring at Chernabog while Fable stepped forward, with his hands clapped together.

"Panny, we need his help."

"Panny?" Chernabog noticed. "Is that what he calls you? And you allow it?"

"That is not my name and he knows it."

"He wants to agree. I agree."

"Look, we can go on out there, find this Fright fellow and take him out. That way, Chernabog here can help us defeat Emblem."

"I know, Fable. I know." Pandora shook herself. "Fine, we will confront Dark Fright. Then, you will aid us."

"I will. You have my word and my bond."

"Your word is received. Your bond is not."

Pandora turned away from Chernabog while Fable looked back at the Slavic god. Chernabog nodded and Fable walked away, following Pandora out of the shack.

Within the realm of the Rift, Emblem sat in a throne room made of gold and iron. In the throne's seat, Emblem sat still, his wounds from the fight with Fable and Pandora continue to heal as his body is made whole. Emblem let out a small breath as he heard footsteps entering the room.

"Who's here?"

"I am, my lord."

Emblem raised his head to see Dark Fright standing before him. The man/bat hybrid entity clothed in dark-clad armor with a helmet resembling medieval knights with two wings on each side. His armor appeared to look black, but in the sunlight of the Rift, it shined a violet hue. Dark Fright was on one knee before Emblem.

"Rise." Emblem said.

"I heard you needed my services."

"I do. There are two who seek to take me out. They wounded me a bit in our last encounter. I have summoned you to face them and eliminate them. By any means."

"May I ask who they are?"

"Pandora, the hooded woman and The Man Called Fable."

"Pandora is still doing the Cloaks' bidding?"

"She is and she has a human on her side. But, he's very keen of our world and the magic powers that exists. He's seen out world with his own eyes. Keep your eyes on him, he is a sneaky one. Clever in his tricks and powerful in the arts."

"I will complete this task, my lord." Fright bowed before leaving the throne room.

IV

SEAL THE TAKE

Fable and Pandora exited the Rift, returning to Manchester. Finding themselves at the front of the bar where Fable attends, they see a figure staring at them. Fable noticed the helmet and quickly pulled out his revolver and fired a shot. The figure dodged the round by disappearing in a flash of black smoke. Pandora noticed the sound, turning toward the smoke.

"What was that?" Fable asked.

"The one Chernabog told us to find."

The smoke gathered itself and formed Dark Fright in front of them. Fright groaned as he faced off with Fable and Pandora. Fable went for another shot, but Fright caught the round in his hand, crushing it into ash as it fell from his hand. Fable squinted.

"Damn."

"You know why we must take you down." Pandora said.

"You said the name Chernabog. That tells me all I must know."

"You are in our path against Emblem. I will not let that stand."

"You have no say in the matters!"

"Look." Fable gestured. "Can we just get this over with?"

"I agree with this one." Fright replied.

Pandora bolted toward Fright with energy blasts. Each one missing the mark as Fright transformed them into the black smoke. From there, Fable went ahead shooting more rounds toward Fright as he blocked the rounds from impact while fighting against Pandora's blasts. Fright speared Pandora to the ground and kicked Fable into the bar wall.

"Enough of this little play." Fright said, clapping his hands as bats emerged from the sky.

"Did he just summon bats?" Fable said. "Like real bats?"

Pandora looked up toward the swarm and rushed toward it, attacking the savage bats with her blasts. Meanwhile, Fable stood up and rushed toward Fright, trying to attack him with punches. Fright's speed was beyond average as he dodged every incoming blow. Fright ducked under the punch, grabbing Fable by the collar of his duster, slamming him into the concrete. Fright turned around, kicking Fable across the ground.

"Shit." Fable grunted. "This guy's strong."

"You are a nuisance, magician."

"I've been told."

Fright walked over to fable, snatching him up by the coat and tossing him into the nearby truck which was parked at the front of the bar. Fable struggled to get up as Pandora appeared from behind Fright, grabbing him by his head, tossing him across the street into the incoming traffic. Fright saw the scenery as an opportunity, rushing into the streets as the vehicles begin to cease and crash. Pandora ran into the street, shoving Fright out of the vehicles' path. Fright laughed.

"Knew you had a soft touch for humanity."

Fright head butted Pandora, backing her into the street as a car rammed her down the road. Fright nodded and walked through the traffic toward Fable at the bar. Fable was on his feet and he looked around for Pandora, not seeing her. He turned forward to see Fright approaching him. He continued firing more shots, but Fright walked through them as the rounds evaporated into smoke once again. Fable sighed.

"It's not enough,"

"You are right, magician. It is not enough."

Fright grabbed Fable by his throat, lifting him off his feet. Fright savored the moment, squeezing Fable's neck.

"I have something to tell you." Fable coughed.

"And that is?"

"You like fairies?"

"What?"

"Do you like fairies?"

"I will not partake in these foolish games!"

"You just have." Fable grinned, opening his hand as dozens of small fairies appeared.

The fairies swarmed al around Fright as he tried swiping them from his body. The fairies covered Fright in their dust, which shined with the sunlight. Fright yelled as the sunlight began piercing through his armor. Fable took notice and fired one more shot at Fright's helmet. The shot blew a hole through Fright's helmet and he fell to the ground. The fairies vanished into a small pocket of the Rift, which opened by Fable's hand. He sealed it as Pandora returned, holding her ribs.

"I see you came back."

"Don't. Do not joke now."

"If not now, when?"

Pandora walked over to Fright's body, seeing the round's entry spot on the helmet. However, she could sense Fright was not dead, just unconscious. Fable sighed as he approached her, looking down at Fright. Fable nodded.

"So, we've completed the task. We've defeated Dark Fright."

"Indeed you have." a voice said from behind them.

They turned to see Chernabog exiting the bar with a drink in his hand.

"You were in there the whole time?" Fable asked,

"Well, yes. I had to keep close eyes on you. Only to make sure you went through with the task. I now see you have."

Chernabog walked over toward them, gazing down at Fright's body. Chernabog grinned and waved his hand, causing fright to vanish. Pandora looked around for Fright, not seeing him. Fable was confused, extending his arms out.

"The hell just happened?"

"What did you do with him?" Pandora questioned. "Where is he?"

"He's right where I want him to be. No need for you or your

hooded friends to worry about.”

“So, you’ll help us with Emblem?”

“You have my support.” Chernabog replied, turning away. “You will see me again when the battle commences.”

“How will we contact you?” Fable asked.

“You won’t need to.” Chernabog took a last gulp of the drink and disappeared in a dark portal, returning to his shack.

“Well, what do we do now?”

“Return to your home, Fable. I will contact you when the next objective is at hand.”

“You or the Hidden Four?”

“I’ll do the talking next time.”

Sometime later, Fable returned to his home, speaking with Denise over the phone for some hours. Many hours later, a knock came from his door and he went and answered. It was Pandora, breathing heavily.

“What’s wrong?”

“The books.” Pandora said. “They’ve been stolen.”

“What books?”

“The books. The grimoires of great power.”

“Where are they now?”

“I do not know. But, you must find them. You’re the only one who can.”

“What about you?”

“I have some matters to attend to in the Rift. I will speak to you again soon.”

Pandora left his home. Fable shut the door and sighed.

“Back at it again.”

CINDERELLA: A HUNTSMAN IN LONDON

I

LONDON CALLING

The City of London have now heard the rumors of Cinderella throughout the area. Civilians arrived out of nowhere, claiming they have seen her at one time or another during the nights. Now, Stepmother Anne had sent out a notice to the city concerning Cinderella's threat to the people. She had hired a Huntsman to track down and find her before she makes a reappearance within the city.

While the city goes in a frenzy concerning the Sly Detective, a fellow woman from Germany arrived at the police headquarters in London. An officer approached her with caution.

"Ma'am." The officer said.

"I have a reason for being here."

"Your name?"

"Snow White."

Snow White later appeared to the people of London, proclaiming herself as a detective who's heard of the Cinderella sightings. Snow believed Cinderella is a product of the risen heroes throughout the world, something she distains. Now, she sees capturing Cinderella as an opportunity of stopping them one at a time.

During the scuffles of the public and the authorities, Cindy sat inside her home with her friend Charlotte, watching the news, seeing the outcry for her arrest. Charlotte shook her head.

"Can't believe they see you as a threat."

"It was bound to happen." Cindy said. "You help them and they want you dead."

"It must be a burden."

"Not exactly. I've done what I can to protect the innocent in this city. Not everyone will see my actions as beneficial."

"What you do is beneficial. To me. To all of us. The things you told me about what you had to do when fighting that demon guy, if these people heard that story, they would appreciate all you have done so far. You helped save the lives of everyone. Not just in London, but the world."

"You know these people don't believe in demons, right." Cindy scoffed.

"But, they seem to believe you exist. Without ever seeing you. Only going by the notions of some bystanders on street corners."

Cindy sighed, laying back on the couch.

"What of your stepmother and sisters?" Charlotte noted. "Have you heard from them about any of this?"

"I know they're behind it. They always are."

"Well, since you're friends with others in your field of expertise, perhaps you could call one of them to help you out with all this."

"I think they're busy enough with their own affairs."

Elsewhere, Stepmother Anne arrived at an office building not too far from Blackpool. She entered and inside the room stood a man. Tall, lean, wielding an axe. Anne paused when she saw him as the guards inside pointed her to the man.

"So, this is the guy." Anne said. "He has the appearance of a hunter."

"You sent word for my skill set." The man said. "I am here to accept your offer."

"This is good. Now, you received all the details to this task?"

"I read you wanted me to find Cinderella. Not sure why you would have me go and search for a fairy tale figure."

"She is not a fairy tale. Not in London anyway."

"Then, who is going around proclaiming themselves to be Cinderella? And why do you wish them captured?"

"Because. She is my stepdaughter. Her actions have led her down this path and I cannot tolerate it any longer. She must be stopped. By any means. She's a capable fighter."

"A fighter? A young woman called Cinderella?"

"She's taken out armies of guards with her own hands. She was trained by a skilled fighter."

"I see. Very well, I will go to London and find your stepdaughter."

"Thank you for your aid in this cause."

II

SCOUTED

Later that night, Cinderella was out, scouting on the trail of her stepmother's criminal affairs. While on the search, the Huntsman was also out searching for Cinderella. After following the path she previously had taken, she returned to the warehouse where she saw her stepmother. There, she entered the building and immediately the alarms went off. Several armed guards rushed out from the doors, aiming their firearms toward her. Cinderella stood still, exhaling slowly.

"Nowhere to run, thief!"

"I'm not running anywhere." Cinderella replied.

"Don't shoot unless she moves first." Another armed man said.

"If I move first? Sure thing."

Cinderella slowly reached in her outer coat pocket as an armed one spotted her arms. He raised his weapon and she tossed out smoke bombs and quickly moved out of their sights as they began firing. She stood over them in the warehouse as the smoke cleared. The men moved with haste searching for her. Some spoke of her stepmother, saying she won't be happy with her reappearance.

Over at the main offices, Hale Prince spoke with Snow White concerning her disapproval of Cinderella's methods. Hale tried to reason with Snow about Cinderella's benefits to the city. Snow would not hear them. She stated Cinderella is a vigilante and must be

382

removed from London in order to provide a safe and secure city for the people. Hale told Snow he can find a way to get her to meet Cinderella and understand why she is good for the city. Snow disagreed once more and left the office. As she exited the building the Stepsisters, Angelica and Alexis entered the office, seeking to meet with Hale once more.

Cinderella sat still, watching the armed men search for her throughout the warehouse. They finished their third attempt at searching and she was nowhere in their sights. One of the armed men entered the room, telling the others Anne asked for them to stand down, as the Huntsman she called is on his way. Cinderella was confused. A Huntsman? Looking for her, she asked herself. She sighed and jumped down on the floor in front of the men, attacking them from all open corners. Taking them out as she had done before, she fled from the warehouse, running outside and when she stopped, she saw a figure staring at her, wielding an axe.

"Who are you supposed to be?" She asked.

"You must be this Cinderella I've been informed about." The figure said, walking into the lights of the streets.

"Ah." Cinderella replied. "You're the Huntsman I heard about."

"I've been brought here to eliminate you. It is my duty."

Cinderella stepped into a pose. Moving her coat back from her legs. Her fists out and her feet placed. The Huntsman scoffed, holding out the axe.

"You get the first hit." Cinderella said.

III

DO YOU BELIEVE IN FAIRY TALES?

Cinderella dodged the incoming attack by the Huntsman's axe, which slammed into the concrete of the road. Cindy ran behind him, jumping on his back and pummeling him in the kidneys and ribs. The Huntsman, grunting in pain, grabbed her by her leg and tossed her off.

"You're skilled." The Huntsman said. "Who taught you?"

"A good friend."

Cinderella kicked the Huntsman in the face, he stumbled as she grabbed for his axe. He pulled it away and tackled Cinderella into a nearby wall with his shoulder and swung the axe, colliding into the wall as Cindy ducked out of its path. The Huntsman pulled the axe, discovering it was stuck in between the wall. Cinderella noticed and tossed small daggers into the Huntsman's legs. He yelled, dropping down to his knees.

"Now, just hear me out."

"Why should I?" The Huntsman asked. "I know all there is to know."

"And what is that?"

"You're a criminal in this city. The people want you gone. The authorities are searching for you. That is why I was brought here. To find you and I have. The only thing left is to eliminate you or take you in."

"Well, I'm not being taken to the authorities. They don't know what's truly happening in this city."

"And you do?"

"Yes. The woman who hired you, my stepmother. She is the cause of the crimes in this city. Her men tried to kill me before. Didn't go as planned."

"Nonsense. She appeared to me as a kind woman. Only seeking to get you the help you need."

"No. she's the one who planned all of this. The only way this all stops is if she's eliminated. Her and my stepsisters. They are the cause."

Cinderella looked over to her left, hearing police sirens. The Huntsman sighed, holding onto his axe in the wall. He shook his head.

"If what you're saying is true, I will discover it for myself."

"How? You have two daggers in your legs. You can't walk."

"You are mistaken."

The Huntsman pulled the daggers from his legs and the wounds healed immediately. Cinderella startled as the Huntsman pulled his axe from the wall and stood up facing her.

"I have my ways as well."

The Huntsman looked at the daggers. Smelling the metal. He nodded.

"I will hold on to these. I'm intrigued as to what they're made of."

The sirens increased in volume, getting the Huntsman's attention. He looked over and Cinderella was gone. He scoffed, placing the daggers in his pocket as he walked away from the area just as the police cars drove by.

In a nearby area, Snow White followed the police to the warehouse. While making her way there on the sidewalk, Cinderella appeared before her from the shadows. White paused, aiming a taser toward her.

"You!" She yelled.

"I don't know you." Cinderella said.

"You're her. The Sly Detective they call you."

"Put down the taser."

"No. I've come to London to find you. Here you are. Now, I can take you in. justice will be served."

"Not today."

Cinderella kicked the taser from Snow's hand and punched her. Snow fell to the ground, holding her nose as she gazed the surroundings. Seeing Cinderella had disappeared.

IV

ONE TO REMEMBER

Anne arrived at the warehouse just as the police were going in and out speaking with the armed men. She passed them by as she saw the Huntsman standing guard with several of the men.

"What happened here?" She asked.

"Cinderella was here." The Huntsman replied.

"And where is she now? Did she escape?"

"She walked away.'

"Walked away! How could she have walked away?! You were supposed to take care of her!"

"I did what I could. But, you're wrong about her."

"Oh am I?"

"After our scuffle, we spoke. She told me all I needed to know."

"Did she? She told you about her criminal activities."

"No. I could sense it within her. Her true motives. They aren't set to cause chaos in this city. No. She wants to make London better than it was before she decided to put on the hat and coat. Cinderella is a true hero to this place. I understand she's your stepdaughter and you wish her dead."

"More than anything."

"And that is why I cannot help you. You're consumed with envy, covetousness, greed, and anger. Such impulses I cannot aid in my works."

The Huntsman turned and walked away, hearing Anne screaming words toward him concerning his work and Cinderella. The following day, Snow White had told Hale about her encounter with Cinderella, seeing the bruise on her face. Hale could not reason with Snow any longer. She desired to find Cinderella and to bring her in. The Huntsman had left London, after he was paid by Hale in the full price Anne had set for him. For Anne, she had traveled far from London to a small island near the Netherlands. There, she had a meeting with a woman, cloaked in all black, wearing a crystalline-gold crown. The meeting was simple, Anne wanted Cindy dead and the woman agreed to take the mission upon her own hands.

"You will do as the Huntsman should've done?" Anne asked. "Are you sure of it?"

"I'm a woman of my word. I take my missions seriously and I complete them at any cost."

Anne nodded with a dark grin.

"This is better. Much better."

"A Queen does as she desires."

HEAVEN HAS CALLED: THE BOOKS OF THE HORRORS

I

BEWARE MANY BOOKS

Travis Vail, the Spirit-Seeker cracked open the door to an abandoned home during a late evening. A quiet one. The home was far from the standard suburbs of a city or town. Vail entered the home, seeing nothing but damaged furniture and torn walls. The floors creaked with every footstep he took. He walked through the rooms, going down the hallway toward what appeared to be the office area.

"There it is."

Vail entered the office and went straightforward to the portrait on the wall. The portrait was of a large field with two figures standing in the midst of follies. Vail pulled the portrait off the wall, finding a safe. Vail used his wits to find the code, unlocking the safe. Once he opened it, he saw the safe was empty.

"The hell?"

Vail searched through the office, not finding what he was truly searching for. He sighed.

"They're gone." Vail uttered to himself. "The books are gone."

Vail exited the home, while on the phone speaking with Dr. Galen Donovan concerning the books. Donovan told Vail the books should've been in the house for centuries after being left there by a powerful psychic. Vail suggested the books might've been taken and sold. However, Donovan had an alternative.

"Have you felt the strangeness in the air recently?"

"I have?" Vail replied. "You believe the books are responsible?"

"If they are, it would only imply they were stolen and are being used by some powerful forces."

"You think Balthazar may have them?"

"Not likely. To use the books properly, it would take more than one man to get them operating. It would need a team of many."

"I'll pay Abraham a visit. See what he knows. He has some of the books in his center."

Vail entered his car and drove from the premises. As he went further down the road, a silhouette of a figure stood at the window of the home. Watching the Spirit-Seeker drive away.

II

THE HORROR, THE HORROR

Gabriel Abraham walked through the Revelation Center while Andrea Coralline and Evan Wyatt sat at the desk, researching files pertaining to vampires. The front doors bolted open, snatching their attention and focus. Abraham turned around to see Vail entering the Center. Vail waved with a nod.

"I know you weren't expecting me, lads. But, this is of most importance."

"What's happened now?" Abraham asked.

"Some grimoires have been taken from a secret stash. That stash being an abandoned home that belonged to a long-time past psychic."

"Grimoires?" Evan said. "Are you sure they were such books?"

"I would know for certain. Anyway, we need to find these books and fast."

"Well, it's strange you've come and spoke of a similar action."

"What are you speaking of, Gabriel?"

"Grimoires here have been taken as well. After we dealt with the Vampire Lord, it appeared someone or something infiltrated the Center and took the books. Currently, we're not sure where they are or who has them."

Vail nodded.

"You know this isn't a coincidence. Someone has stolen the books from certain locations. Gathering them together. With those books together, they could cause a dire stray across the world. Everything could very well end as we know it."

"Maybe it was just a thief looking to get rich." Andrea noted. "I mean, that's what one of them would do."

"By any chance have you checked the library here in D.C.?" Vail asked Gabriel.

"No. perhaps, we can head there and see what we find."

"Noted. Then let's get going."

Vail and Abraham headed out to the library in downtown D.C. Once inside, they made way toward the New Age section of the library, Vail realized the people would place grimoires in such a spot. They found the section and began searching. Skimming through the books on the shelves from top to bottom, they found nothing. Vail sighed.

"This is not good."

"I know."

They stood talking about alternatives and behind approached a man. Well-dressed in suit and slacks. He was middle-aged and clean-shaven. Vail could smell the scent of cologne on him. Abraham was unsure who the man was, yet he was keenly aware of their reasons for being in the aisle.

"I see you are searching for something and yet have not found it."

"It happens at time." Vail said. "Good day to you."

"I wouldn't leave just yet Travis Vail." The man said.

Vail turned around slowly.

"How do you know my name?"

"We know you very well. As do you, Gabriel Abraham. My. My. I never thought the day would come where I would meet the infamous Spirit-Seeker and the renown Devilhunter at the same time. Let alone in a public place."

"Who are you?" Abraham asked.

"My name is not important. But who I am associated with is."

"What group are you with? The Cult? The Doctors? One of Demonticronto's followers?"

"I am with the *Mythologists*."

"The Mythologists?" Abraham replied. "Never heard of them."

"I have." Vail said. "Only heard of their name. never seen them or encountered them. But, today has ruled that out. This man claims to be with the Mythologists. So, why are you here?"

"I am here to tell the two of you there's no need in searching for the books. They're in good hands."

Vail stepped forward toward the Mythologist. Abraham prepared himself for the possible altercation. The Mythologist himself was very calm. No fear in his eyes.

"Where are the books?" Vail questioned.

"My master has them."

"Your master?"

"He has plans to use them to shape a better world."

"One man cannot harness the power of those books."

"He knows. That's why he has brought in an associate."

"Associate?" Abraham said. "Who else could manage that kind of power?"

"A greater kind. But, you'll know eventually."

The Mythologist walked away, he turned back toward them with a grin on his face.

"Best to prepare yourselves for what's ahead. The world is about to have a drastic turn of events."

The Mythologist had walked away, leaving Vail and Abraham mediating on plans and theories. Vail clapped his hands, getting the attention of the others in the library by accident. He waved them off.

"What's next?" Abraham said.

"We gather everyone." Vail replied. "We gather the team."

III

A GREATER KIND

Without haste, Vail and Abraham sent out word to gather the team together. With the aid of the Visitant Outlander and Dark Manhunter, they were able to teleport several of the members to the Revelation Center for the meeting. Vail and Abraham waited for the team to arrive and two bright flashes of light emitted within the lobby of the Center and out of the first flash came Outlander with Cinderella and the Ghost of England. The second flash walked out Manhunter with Creed, Death Chaser, and Papa Afterlife. Vail looked around as the light dimmed out.

"Where's the other lad?"

"Who?" Cinderella asked.

"The one with the white mark on his chest?"

"He has other matters to attend to." Afterlife said. "You have heard about the '*Steeler Incident*' haven't you?"

"Not to my knowledge. No."

"Terror will be fine. We're enough for this task."

"Depends on who we're facing." Abraham noted. "Anyone have any clues?"

"Signs of the books have been felt throughout the universe. Both naturally and spiritually." Outlander stated. "Those who have them are gaining knowledge and power from them. Shaking the fabric of reality in total."

"I did hear about a stash somewhere in Manchester. "Cinderella said. "It was taken from some place."

"Then, you can lead us there." Vail said.

"I don't operate in Manchester, Trav. That's the other guy."

"What other guy?" Abraham asked.

"She's talking about the Fable bloke."

"Never heard of him."

"Few have." Cinderella replied. "Anyhow, that's where one stash was located."

"Ok. Anyone know of any other places?"

"Well, we only know two." Vail said. "Manchester and somewhere here in D.C."

"True."

"There is another place surging with energy." Manhunter spoke. "It's in a deep cemetery. Guarded by a restless spirit."

"Where is this cemetery?" Creed asked.

"Deep in Ireland."

"I see." Vail said. "Looks like we'll all be doing some traveling."

"How are we going to get to these places as quickly as possible?" Abraham wondered. "How will it be done. Not all of us can teleport."

Vail clapped his hands together with a smirk.

"I have the idea. We split up into teams. I'll led one over to the UK, find out about the books in Manchester while you, Gabriel, take a team and head on out to find out more about these Mythologists."

"It'll work. But, it still doesn't conclude the travel."

"I will aid Vail." Manhunter said.

"Then, I shall accompany Abraham's unit."

Vail nodded. "Then, it's settled."

"Now, who's going with who?" Abraham asked.

"Shaw and I will go with Vail." Cinderella said.

"I will accompany you as well." Death Chaser added.

"Fair point." Vail nodded.

"Creed and I will join Abraham and Outlander." Afterlife said.

"Everyone knows what they must do?" Vail said. "Good."

"I met a young man in London who had an encounter with the Mythologists." Outlander said.

"So, myself, Cindy, and Shaw will speak with him once we leave Manchester."

"I cannot allow that. the young man must see me. That way he will not be in fear."

Vail nodded.

"I understand."

Vail went and walked toward the door, stopping as everyone began heading out. Cinderella approached him, seeing something was on his mind.

"Those words." Vail uttered. "How could I have let them slip."

"What is it?"

"Me and Abraham met a fellow from the Mythologists. He told us they were working with someone outside of their group."

"Any chance you may know who it is?"

"I do now. The Mythologist said their helper was of a greater kind."

"A greater kind? I'm not getting what that means."

"It means Vernon Lance is working with them and that is trouble for all of us."

"The Satanist?"

"Yes. We need to find the books now."

IV

THE CON MAGE OF MANCHESTER

A portal opened in an alleyway in the city of Manchester with Vail, Cinderella, Shaw, Chaser, and Manhunter walking out. As the portal closed, they each looked at the location in which they stood.

"Recognize this spot?" Vail asked Cinderella.

"No. Should I?"

"Might as well see what's on the end of this alleyway." Vail replied.

They followed him through the alley, reaching the outer parts, seeing a bar just up ahead. Vail looked around, seeing the vehicles driving on the street, yet on one side of the road, construction was being done. Vail pointed toward it.

"What happened there?"

"Maybe a wreck." Cinderella replied.

"A wreck would not have caused that much damage." Shaw added. Something happened here and not long ago."

Death Chaser turned his focus toward the bar behind them. Sensing an energy coming from within. He pointed as Manhunter also was sensing the energy.

"The bar." Chaser said. "Something's inside."

Vail and Cinderella walked forward, facing the bar. Hey keened their senses. Cinderella knew there was something strange with the bar, while Vail shrugged his shoulders and walked.

"Let's go have ourselves a look-see."

Vail went ahead and entered the bar. Once inside, he saw the bar was filled with magical creatures. Vail spotted an orc near the back of the bar while there was a satyr sitting at the bar drinking whiskey. Cinderella looked around and was amazed. The Chaser entered with Manhunter following and the entire bar went from lively to dead silent. Vail raised his hands.

"Hello lads. Now, we're not from these parts. However, we have come for a purpose. Do any of you know of the Man Called Fable, the bloke who operates in this town?"

Everyone in the bar turned and gave each other looks. Quiet looks. But knowledgeable. The bartender stepped forward as Vail turned toward him.

"Yeah. We know of him."

"Mind you tell us where he might be? We need to speak with him."

The bartender pointed to the further section of the bar near the back. They looked and saw Fable himself sitting at a table, having a drink. Fable looked up toward them, grinned and held up his drink. Vail shook his head, thanking the bartender before approaching Fable's table. Vail and Cinderella stood in front facing Fable. Fable extended his hand at the chairs.

"You guys can sit."

Vail and Cinderella sat at the table while Shaw, Chaser, and Manhunter stood guard as there were several trolls who were glaring toward Fable.

"Listen, we've never met before." Vail said. "But something has happened which brings us to this moment."

"First off, my guy. Who are you people supposed to be?"

"I'm Travis Vail, Spirit-Seeker. She is Cinderella. While the others are-"

"Cinderella? Bullshit." Fable grinned. "She's not Cinderella. Can't be. Fairy tales don't exist."

"And yet you interact with a realm where such creatures are relative in fairy tales." Cinderella smiled.

"So, you're the one they've been searching for in London."

"I am and I would like it to remain quiet. Until this is all over."

"And what is all this?"

"Some powerful grimoires have been taken. Gathered to cause

some major damage to the world. All of creation could suffer if those who have them succeed."

Fable took a drink and shook his head.

"She said something was gone."

"Who said what?" Cinderella asked.

"Oh. Pandora. She told me some books had been taken. I couldn't' find out where but she panicked over it slightly."

"So, what has this Pandora woman found out?"

"Nothing so far. But, the fact the two of you came here asking about grimoires leads me to believe this isn't just a Manchester-only situation."

"It's not."

"Fable, may I ask if you knew where the books were kept?"

"I have no clue. Never saw the books. Only heard of them being stored up in a place by Pandora and those Four fellas."

"What four fellows?" Vail asked.

"Doesn't matter. Look here, I will do what I can to help you guys out with this. By doing this, I'll be helping Pandora and she can stay off my back when it comes to matters like this. I can't take the stress."

Manhunter's cloak began flowing, getting the attention of everyone in the bar. Vail looked up toward him with concerned face.

"What is it?"

"Someone's coming." Manhunter said. "Someone powerful."

A flash of light emitted from the middle of the bar, startling the creatures inside and as the light faded, Vernon Lance stood in its place. Vail jumped from the table, ready for a fight. Cinderella followed and Fable stood up, his hand on the revolver. The Chaser's hands emitted with sinfire, and Shaw was prepared as his body was slowly glowing.

"Who's this guy?" Fable asked.

"Vernon Lance." Vail said. "A thorn in the sides of many."

"It is good to see you again once more, Spirit-Seeker."

"Why are you here?"

"To tell you and your friends something you should know."

"And what is that?"

"The grimoires you are searching for? They belong to me now.

Their power already flows within me and soon all of the world will bow before me.”

“Is he always like this?” Fable asked.

“Every day.” Vail replied.

“What are we going to do?” Cinderella asked.

“You will do nothing.” Lance told Cinderella. “Stay away from my work or suffer.”

“Suffer what?” Chaser said.

“A greater fate worse than death.”

“Meh.” Fable said, raising up the revolver and firing a shot.

The round went straight through Lance’s body, hitting the shelf at the bar. Vail knew it then. Fable stood confused. Cinderella stepped forward.

“He’s not really here.” Vail said.

“I know how to operate, Spirit-Seeker. You should’ve known by now.”

Lance faded away from their sight. Vail grunted, pacing in anger.

“We have to find out where he is,” Cinderella said. “It’s the only way.”

“And how are we going to track him down?” Vail asked. “His magic is too powerful now. I can’t track him myself. Manhunter, Chaser. Can either of you track him?”

“He’s shielded.” Manhunter said. “Even from my own eyes and might.”

“I cannot trace him.” Chaser replied. “Something dark is over him. Hindering my power.”

Vail walked toward the door as the others spoke of possible solutions. Fable was well involved. Fable told Cinderella he was no sorcerer and Vail clapped his hands together, returning to the team.

“That’s it.”

“What is?” Cinderella asked.

“A sorcerer.”

“What about one?” Fable asked. “I’m not one.”

“Not talking about you. I know one. He may help us.”

“When did you meet a sorcerer?” Cinderella questioned.

“Very recently. He helped me with a favor to a family.”

Cinderella nodded. "Then, where is this sorcerer?"

"We'll have to check the last place I met him."

"Then let's get going." Fable said. "I'm tagging along for this."

Elsewhere, Abraham's team walked through London during the night, standing outside of the library. Abraham looked around, seeing only civilians walking and going about their night.

"Where is he?" Abraham asked.

"Give me a moment." Outlander replied, extending his arms.

The ground became covered in mists. The civilians had vanished and the vehicles which were passing through were gone. Abraham looked around as did Afterlife and they were astonished by Outlander's feat of power. Creed stood quiet, looking past the mist and he saw someone approaching.

"There." Creed said.

Abraham looked out and saw someone coming toward them. Outlander stepped forward as he saw Jacob Wilson coming through the mist.

"You heard my call." Outlander said.

"I did. Why did you contact me?"

"Because my allies here need to know more about the Mythologists. They have taken something which does not belong to them. In turn, they could very well destroy all of creation if they are not stopped."

Jacob looked behind Outlander, seeing Abraham, Afterlife, and Creed.

"Who are they?"

"Those who you can trust."

"Jacob," Abraham said walking forward. "We just need to know what you know about them. Like the kind of places they meet up. Where do they operate out of? You know anything of them?"

"Primarily, they meet at all kinds of places. Restaurants, city halls, schools, stores. But, they mostly operate out of museums or libraries. That's where they keep their collections."

"Museums. Libraries. Ah, I should've known." Abraham replied.

'They've been sitting under our noses the whole time."

"At least you have your answer." Outlander said. "You did well, Jacob Wilson."

"We need to return to D.C." Abraham said.

"We cannot." Afterlife replied. "We have to reach the cemetery first. Find the books hidden there."

Abraham nodded. "You are correct. Let's get going. See you around, Mr. Wilson."

Jacob nodded as Outlander opened the portal for them to exit the area. As the portal closed, the surroundings returned to normal. Jacob looked around, seeing familiar events as before. He chuckled under his breath before walking away.

V

A SUPREME ENCHANTER AND A RESTORATION MAN

Vail led his team to the source of his information, following a path of peculiar magic within the air. Unseen by the natural eyes. With Manhunter and Chaser's assistance, Vail led them toward the Citadel of enchantment. Fable looked on at the structure.

"Where did this place come from?"

"It's been here." Vail said. "For a very long time."

"Do we knock or wait?" Cinderella asked.

"He'll know we're here." Vail replied.

"Who's he?" Fable wondered.

The doors of the Citadel opened and out of them came down Doctor Fortune, levitating down the stairs toward them as his cloak flowed with the wind. He saw Vail and nodded with a smile. Vail nodded back as Fortune measured the others. He looked at Chaser with a keen eye.

"A Soul of Retribution. Nice to meet one of you."

"You know of us?"

"I know of all of you. Robert Shaw, I am familiar with the events that made you what you are this day. Make no mistake, you will have your vengeance soon."

"I am honored of your words."

"I've heard of the stories across London of a sneaky individual. Famed by the fairy tales that proclaim your existence. Now, I stand before you, Cinderella."

"I'm not as detailed as the stories suggest." Cinderella grinned.

403

"I can very well see that." Fortune replied. "Manhunter, I know of your purpose and I know of your hatred to those of magic."

"Then, you know what I aspire to do."

"I do. However, we are not here to fight one another. Regardless of our paths. It seems Travis Vail has brought you all here for a reason. Vail, I would like the know that reason."

"I must guess you've felt a strangeness in the air. Reeking of some dark power?"

"I have. Me and my apprentice have been studying its paths. It's bouncing across the sky like I've never seen before."

"Because it's energy from powerful grimoires."

"What do these grimoires suggest?"

"Vernon Lance, a powerful priest in the Satanic field has them in his possession with the group calling themselves the Mythologists. I don't know what they're after, but I know why Lance is involved. He's seeking to become powerful. Much more powerful."

"What is your plan currently?" Fortune wondered.

"We don't have one exactly. The others are already heading to the cemetery to find the third stash of grimoires."

"So, Lance and the Mythologists have the first two stashes in their hands?"

"Correct." Vail said. "We need to know how to weaken the power that comes from them. By doing so, we'll weaken Lance and the Mythologists will cower in fear of what's to come."

"Books such as those should not be in the same place at the same time. Explains the darkness above the earth. The solution is simple. Separate them from each other."

"Wait." Cinderella said. "That's all? Just separate them?"

"Yes. How many grimoires are there?"

"Five from each stash." Vail replied. "Lance and company currently have ten."

"While the remaining five are in some cemetery." Fortune nodded. "Understood. I will help you find Lance and these Mythologists. You face them and scatter the books across the four corners of the earth. You do that, the task is done."

"Lance is too powerful for us to face head-on." Vail said. "we need some assistance."

"You're asking for my help in this endeavor?"

"You helped me with Carrie. I'm just asking, help with this. If Lance succeeds, all of creation could very well end. I know you cannot allow something as powerful as that to happen."

Fortune nodded, turning back toward the citadel.

"When the time comes, you will have me on your side." Fortune replied. "Right now, do what you must do."

Fortune entered the Citadel as the doors closed behind him. Fable threw his arms up, looking around the forest area behind them.

"So, that's it?" Fable asked. "He's not going to help out?"

"Fortune's a trustworthy guy." Vail said. "He'll help out. He already said it."

"We need to return to the others." Manhunter said. "Gather ourselves together and confront Vernon Lance and the Mythologists."

"Then let's return to D.C." Vail said.

Over in Ireland, Abraham's team arrived at the cemetery. A foggy and damp night. The cemetery had a presence of its own. A crawling sense tingled down their backs aside from Outlander and Creed. Abraham searched for the sight, but was unable to track it down. Outlander extended his right hand across the cemetery and one peculiar grave with an unnamed headstone shined like the sun.

"There it is." Outlander said.

They reached the grave, seeing it had appeared to have been dug up recently. Abraham sighed.

"No sign of the books."

"No." Creed said. "The books are here."

"How do you know?" Afterlife wondered.

"Because he has them." Creed pointed in front of them.

They looked out and a decomposed hand arose from the ground. The trembling feeling underneath them shook the cemetery and from the hand arose a head and a body. The figure stood above the ground, standing at the same height as Abraham and Afterlife. Dressed in rags of clothing, ripped pants, torn shoes. Its hair long and white. White as snow. Its eyes soulless, yet there is some form of life within them. Piercing through the veil. Creed's cloak spread widely, flowing with caution, Afterlife's hands became covered in smoke while Abraham steadied himself. Outlander stepped forward toward the figure.

"I know what they call you." Outlander said. "The Restoration Man."

"I cannot be killed." The Restoration Man said.

"True. we are not here to fight you. We seek the books. Where are they?"

"Why should I give them to you?"

"Because you do want to know what the second death feels like." Outlander replied. "Not yet anyway."

The Restoration Man paused himself. Stepping back behind the unnamed headstone. Creed noticed and rushed over, knocking the stone over to reveal the books.

"There." Creed said.

Abraham went over and grabbed the books. He nodded to the others. The Restoration Man stepped back as Outlander kept his eyes on him.

"You do well with those." Restoration Man said.

"We know what must be done." Outlander said. "Return to your service, fleshly spirit."

Outlander opened the portal and they returned to the Revelation Center where Vail and the others waited.

VI

A PRIEST IN THE BOOK

Vail stood inside the Center with the others just as Abraham returned with the books. Vail smirked.

"You found them."

"Yeah. What did you guys come up with and who's that?"

"I'm known as Fable. Some call me The Man Called Fable."

"Why is a stranger in this place?"

"He's here to help. Seriously. He's been tracking down the books himself."

"We have all that we need." Chaser said. "Now, let's find Vernon Lance and end this."

"That's a good idea." Vail said. "Only where do we find them?"

"At the library." Abraham said. "That's where they are."

"How are you certain of that?" Shaw questioned.

"Because it's what the young Wilson had given us." Outlander said. "He's familiar with their movements. He would know where they operate."

"And you rust the young one?" Manhunter asked. "So blindly?"

"It is not blindness, Manhunter. It is justice."

"Only when you're betrayed for a just cause."

"Now, there's no need to stir each other up." Vail said. "Save it for the fight ahead."

"We need to get the library now." Creed spoke. "End all of this."

"I agree with the darkly gruesome one." Fable said. "Let's find these guys, finish all of this so we can all return to our lives."

"He's right." Cinderella said. "I'm sure someone in London needs my help right now.:

"Eh, alright." Vail mumbled. "Let's get going. Teleporting again?"

"No other choice." Manhunter said.

The group teleported themselves into the library late in the night.

Upon their arrival, they found themselves facing off against strange shadow figures. Vail knew Lance has summoned them to keep the library guarded. Immediately the library became a place of war. Creed, Chaser, and Shaw took the fight to the shadow figures while Vail, Cinderella, Abraham, Afterlife, Fable went ahead as Outlander and Manhunter used their power to shroud the library from the public eyes. For when a civilian passed by the library, they only saw the emptiness within. The lights appeared off and the library seemed closed to their natural eyes.

"Where could they be?" Vail questioned.

"Downstairs." Abraham said. "I'm sure of it."

They went forward, finding themselves in what appeared to be an exceptionally large room. Large enough to be kept hidden from the public. Within the room were the Mythologists who were sitting in a circle, their heads were down with Lance standing before them.

"Your games end here, Lance." Vail yelled. "Give us the books."

"And why should I do such a thing when the plan is fully coming into motion?"

"Enough of your words." Fable said. "We're here for the books. Hand them over."

"Or what?" Lance grinned.

"You know what to do." Vail told the team.

They all rushed toward Lance without haste. Lance turned toward them as the Mythologists themselves did not move as Lance raised his hand toward them, stopping them in their tracks. He laughed as eh tossed them back to where they entered. Lance scoffed, returning to the books as they were opened.

"I'm not stopping here." Vail said, raising himself up.

"Keep coming, Spirit-Seeker. I will always knock you down. It is our fate."

"It is. But, it could use an extra hand." Vail said, stepping back.

Within the room streaked a bolt of lightning and from the lightning appeared Pandora alongside Doctor Fortune. Fable looked on, seeing Pandora. She turned toward him and nodded. Fable nodded back in respect as Fortune stared down Lance, seeing the Mythologists on the ground and the books ahead.

"This has come to an end, Priest." Fortune said.

"A Supreme Enchanter." Lance scoffed. "More power must I receive this night."

"Not likely."

Pandora whipped her hands around forming a magical bind, causing the Mythologists to rise from the ground and attack Lance. While she held her power upon them, Fortune quickly pulled the books toward him as Lance let out a loud yell. Vail saw what was happening and ran toward Lance, but Cinderella grabbed his arm.

"What are you doing, Cindy?"

"Now is not the time for your anger to get the better of you. Fortune has the books. We can go now."

"No. I cannot let Lance escape. Not this time."

Vail went to move ahead, and Cinderella kept her hold on him. Fortune appeared to him with the books in hand.

"We must go, Travis Vail. Pandora can only hold them for so long."

Vail looked out, string at Lance. Vernon saw him and smirked while fighting off the Mythologists. Vail sighed as they left the room through Fortune's wormhole. The Mythologists ceased their attack and fell to the floor. Lance looked around, seeing the books were gone as were his adversaries. He screamed as the floor beneath him opened and he went down into the darkness, only with his laughter to echo out into the open.

Afterwards, they gathered at the Center where Fortune spoke to Vail and Abraham, telling them the books must be scattered by only five of them across the earth. To keep them hidden from humanity and other forces which seek to do harm. Vail took three, Abraham took three, Fable took three, Outlander took three, and Manhunter took the remaining three. They all went and scattered the books to various locations which will not be named. Only the ones who scattered the books will know the locations of the earth.

Returning to their own lives and operations a day later, Vail kept his ears and eyes open for Lance's return. Fable and Pandora returned to the Rift to meet with Chernabog concerning Emblem, Abraham went ahead with his studies with Andrea and Evan, Afterlife returned to educate the Yonderers, Creed kept his spiritual senses keened for Adrambadon's return as did Chaser with Demonticronto. Cinderella returned to London, finding a search warrant out for her arrest, Shaw had wandered throughout London and the spiritual plane alongside Outlander and Manhunter. The two figures hovered above the earth, looking down.

"Do you believe they'll manage to take on what's to come?" Outlander asked.

"In time, we will see what makes of them." Manhunter replied. "For I know we both are certain they will be ready when the war begins."

"As will we."

DOCTOR DARK: DARKNESS AND LIGHT

I

THE FOOTSTEPS OF ONE MANY FEARS

Standing in the realm of the Astral Dimension, Darkous looks upon Michael The Archangel. The two discuss with one another about the previous victory over Mazakala and how much they have to repair in order to avoid another event with his release in the near future.

"There is another command that has presented itself to you, Darkous." Michael said.

"What has been commanded of me?"

"After the events of your battle with Mazakala, there have been incidents occurring throughout the realms of the darkness and the light. We know that only you should be given this task to discover what is truly happening across the cosmos."

Darkous nodded.

"I will begin on this task as soon as possible."

Michael nodded and flew up in the air, exiting the Astral Dimensional realm of existence. Darkous prepared himself mentally for the task at his hand and exited the Astral Dimension, heading first to Earth.

On Earth, Carol Hunters, the supernatural reporter continues her studies of the occult, diving into more knowledge that she was aware of in her early beginnings of research. She later came upon a series of old documents from the museum that contained information that she recognized from the men within the museum who call themselves the Mythologists.

"I am curious as to what they are talking about." Carol said.

Carol continued studying and was tempted to contact Malach HaMavet for more details concerning the Mythologists, but decided on waiting to find more information before telling Malach about the circumstances in order to have herself prepared for what could possibly happen.

Darkous moved across the earth. Day and night. Going from country to country. He searches the ancient lands of old, finding nothing that would be tampering with the darkness and light powers. While going through the lands during nightfall, Darkous could feel a uncertain energy coming from the homes of people. Darkous stopped by at one person's home and entered in through the door, walking through it like a living vapor of mist.

"The energy here." Darkous said. "It is of another realm."

Darkous walked upstairs in the home, seeing the bedrooms of two children, a girl and a boy. Down the hall was the bedroom of their parents. Darkous could feel the energy surrounding them all, but the energy was strong on the little girl. He entered her room and walked toward her, seeing her fully asleep.

"What is happening amongst you, young one."

Darkous placed his right hand onto the little girl's head and instantly, he entered her dream. Within her dream was the little girl playing with friends in a yard. Her brother was seen walking amongst them. Darkous looked around, feeling the energy growing in strength.

He looked toward a tree and spotted a being staring at the young girl with piercing eyes.

"What are you?" Darkous said walking toward the being.

The entity glared at Darkous and vanished into the air with a swift blow of wind. Darkous looked around, not able to find the being and turned back to the young girl, still playing amongst her friends and brother. Darkous exited her dream and entered her brother's dream. The dream of the brother was different, involving a room covered in video games and action figures. The boy played with the figures along with the being from the girl's dream. Darkous approached the being.

"Tell me what you are."

The being turned to Darkous and smiled before vanishing. Darkous turned to the little boy and he stared at him.

"Where did my friend go?" The little boy asked.

"I don't think he was your friend, young one."

Darkous left the boy's dream and proceed to enter the parents' dream. Within their dream was a crowded interstate. They were in their car with their son and daughter in the back. Darkous walked through the street of the crowed roadway.

"So many stopped." Darkous said. "So many trapped."

Darkous could see the being once again standing in front of the road, causing the traffic jam. Darkous hovered up and flew toward the being. In great speed, Darkous tacked the being and rushed him into one of the cars.

"Tell me what you are now!" Darkous said.

"I'm what the little ones fear." The entity said. "I'm what their parents teach them of the night. I am what keeps them in line during the night."

"Your name." Darkous said. "Tell me your name, entity?"

"I'm the Bogeyman." He said with a smile on his face. Showing his decaying teeth.

Darkous released the Bogeyman as he vanished once again. Darkous exited the dream of the parents and left the home. After several hours going through the earth, Darkous discovered the Bogeyman had been traveling through the dreams of many. Tormenting them to the point of even killing in his running spree.

Darkous returned to the Astral Dimension and Beatrice is waiting on him. She sees the purpose in his eyes and can feel that something is taking place throughout the realms of the cosmos.

"I can sense some power going through the cosmos, Darkous."

"It's a power of torment and fear." Darkous said. "The Bogeyman is freely roaming the earth."

"The Bogeyman?" Beatrice said. "I thought he was killed during the early purge."

"Apparently not. He survived the purge and has made himself known once again. Now, I have to deal with him and the events taking place within the darkness and light."

"What do you have in mind concerning The Bogeyman?"

"I have to visit an old associate of ours."

"Who would that be exactly?"

"I'm going to the Patchlands."

Beatrice looked at Darkous as if he said something that made her feel ignorant of her place.

"You're not considering working with him again are you?" Beatrice said. "You know how cunning he can be toward us and those above."

"True. But, he knows the Bogeyman more than most would assume him to know. He could be of useful assistance."

Darkous prepared himself to head out for the Patchlands.

"Make sure you keep your awareness keen."

"I will. Surely."

Darkous hovered into the air, leaving the Astral Dimension as if he was a gust of wind during a thunderstorm.

II

PUMPKIN LANGUAGE

Entering the Patchlands during the brink of day, Darkous comes down from the sky, seen from the ground like a horde of bats or crows. Walking through the trails of the Patchlands was a figure that resembled a man but possessed a pumpkin for a head. Darkous stood on the ground walking towards the man.

"Mr. Pumpkinhead." Darkous said.

He turned and faced Darkous. His face showing a smile as he laid down his rake and approached the Keeper of the Cosmos.

"The Shrouded One makes himself known unto me in my own realm."

"I do and I come with a purpose of intent."

"Such as?"

"How much do you know of The Bogeyman?"

"I know much about him. His power, his hobbies, his lusts. I know much about him to tell dozens of stories with."

"I need to know all that you know."

"Why would you want to know all about The Bogeyman?"

"Because he's out there causing torment amongst the sleeping ones during the nightfall."

Mr. Pumpkinhead nodded.

"Ah. So, he has been released you're saying. I thought he was dead and gone."

"That is what we all assumed. But, we were wrong."

"I will help you, but it will involve you going in several directions to find your answers.”

“You’re sending me on a puzzle quest?”

“In a matter of yes or no, I am.”

“What will be in possession of these quests?”

“The answers you seek concerning The Bogeyman. Don’t worry, you might have some fun in this. I know I would.”

“Go back to your harvesting, Pumpkinhead. I will find what I need in your trails.”

Darkous took his first step toward the first trail in searching for the knowledge of The Bogeyman. Mr. Pumpkinhead watched him walk forward and smirked.

“Wait till he sees what’s in store for him. Ha!”

Back on Earth, Carol meets with Malach HaMavet inside of his cabin as she brought along her detailed and studies concerning the Mythologists. Malach looked at her findings, within the books she carried along the way and the papers of notes that she written.

“How long did it take you to study all of this?” Malach said.

“It took some time.” Carol said. “I had nothing to do other than put my time into learning who those men are and what they’re planning in the shadows.”

“How are you feeling, exactly?”

“What do you mean?”

“I mean, how do you feel after seeing that horde in the streets a while back.”

“Oh. It laid an effect on me that I probably will never have removed. But, it showed me there’s more to this world than what we see with our own eyes.”

“Trust me when I say this to you, what you seen is only a small drop in the sea to what is really out there.”

Carol smiled as she laid her eyes back onto her findings.

On the Patchlands trail, Darkous walked through, looking around at the fields of plentiful harvest. He could see what appeared to be portals into parts of the earth. Within those portals were images of people sleeping and The Bogeyman circling them around their bed, tormenting them in their sleep.

"He circles them. Why?"

As Darkous walked, a bolt of light flash in front of him. Halting his steps. Darkous walked through the light and swiftly wiped it away with his hand. He looked forward seeing two figures that appeared to be made of light.

"Who are you?" Darkous said.

"We were sent here to halt your findings on The Bogeyman." One figure said. "You cannot learn more about him."

"I will."

Darkous raised his hand and from it was released a small wave of energy that knocked the two figures on their back. They looked at Darkous with fear in their eyes.

"But, you cannot learn more. We promised him we would keep you away."

"Who is him?" Darkous said. "Tell me his name and I will deal with him."

"We will not speak his name." The other figure said. "He might destroy us from existence."

"His name. Now."

"We… we will not speak it."

Darkous stared at the two figures. No emotion on his face as his eyes are locked onto them and his pupils turning a dim blue.

"Very well."

Darkous raised his arms up toward the sky and above the two figures emerged a thick cloud of darkness. The two figures started firing blasts of light bolts toward the cloud. Having no effect except causing the cloud to grow in size, covering more ground.

"Please stop the cloud!"

"I will not." Darkous said. "You two have made your decision."

The cloud came down upon the two figures and swallowed them up. The faint sounds of their screams could be heard before silken came in. Darkous walked past the cloud and continued on forward down the trail.

"This is no matter of games."

Further down the trail way, Darkous finds himself surrounded by a group of shadow creatures. Darkous shook his head and released a small sigh. He looked at the shadow creatures.

"Do you know who you're surrounding?" Darkous said. "From the very realm you were birthed from, I rule."

"It doesn't matter now." One shadow creature said. "You're on our turf now."

"I see what I must do in order to make you understand."

Darkous released several shadow creatures of his own and they combated against the shadow creatures of the trail. Darkous stood by and watched the fighting commencing before him.

"Finish them off." Darkous said to his shadow creatures. "Send them on their way back home."

The shadow creatures of Darkous instantly killed the shadow creatures of the trail and they vanished into the air with a gust of wind. Darkous continued walking down the trail and spoke to himself.

"Something is not right. What has Pumpkinhead sent me on?"

After finishing the trail, Darkous returned to the Astral Dimension to take further looks across the cosmos in search of The Bogeyman. From behind him walked Beatrice. She looked at him as if he made some mistake. He glanced at her.

"I know what I did, Beatrice."

"You were taken for a fool by Pumpkinhead."

"I am aware of that. Though, the portal that showed the humans sleeping was no folly play. It was real and it confirms to me that The Bogeyman is still on earth. He hasn't left the earth because he cannot at this particular time."

"You think Pumpkinhead may know what Bogeyman needs to escape from being earthbound?"

"I think I do. You mind coming along with me?"

"With pleasure."

Mr. Pumpkinhead sat inside of his home on the Patchlands and the front door opened with a gust of wind. Pumpkinhead looked over toward the door and stood up, walking towards it to close it.

"Damn wind."

Pumpkinhead placed his hand on the door and closed it. He turned around and was stopped to see both Darkous and Beatrice standing inside of his home. He pointed at them while laughing.

"So, the wind that blew my door open. That was the both of you?"

"It was." Beatrice said.

"My, my. Don't you Astrals have amazing feats."

"We're not here to discuss feats, Pumpkinhead." Darkous said.

"Why are you both here? You again mostly."

"Don't take me for a fool." Darkous said. "You sent me on some folly trail surrounded with small diversions to keep me ignorant of the knowledge of The Bogeyman."

"Oh. You discovered what I was doing all along, huh. Funny."

"It is not something to laugh at." Beatrice said. "We need to know all there is about Bogeyman."

"Wouldn't it be best if you only left him alone. He's stuck on earth for holy's sake."

Darkous walked toward Pumpkinhead and snatched him by his throat, shoving him against the wall of his home.

"Give us what we came for or suffer a fate that is worse than a blinding light."

"Ok." Pumpkinhead said. "Alright, I'll give you what you want. Just let me back on the ground."

"Sure." Darkous said as he dropped Pumpkinhead onto his feet.

Pumpkinhead was crouched on the ground, catching his breath and gazing up at Darkous and Beatrice.

"Fair play." Pumpkinhead said. "Fair indeed."

"The knowledge!" Darkous said. "Speak it now."

"Sure. The reason why The Bogeyman is out and tormenting the humans is to find a way back to his plane of existence called the Dreamscape."

"The Dreamscape?" Beatrice said. "I thought that place was destroyed during the Purge."

"Apparently, my darling, it was not." Pumpkinhead said. "It was locked down to keep The Bogeyman from entering back into the realm. He derives his power and strength from that place."

"The Bogeyman is only trying to find his way back home?" Darkous said. "That is what you're telling me, Pumpkinhead?"

"That is what I'm telling you, Shrouded One. For right now, he is weak. Too weak to fight against those against him. But, if he finds his way back into the Dreamscape, he will be more powerful than he ever could be."

"We thank you for this information, Pumpkinhead." Darkous said. "We will meet again."

"Anytime, Astrals."

Darkous and Beatrice vanished into the thin air. Pumpkinhead sighed as he sat back down into his chair and continued to smoke his pipe.

III

MYTHOS TO EXPLORE

In her apartment, Carol read a newspaper that contain some information regarding a secret meeting between the men whom she knows as the Mythologists. The city is calling them the Bankers. They are scheduled to have a bank meeting amongst themselves and a few selected others during the day. Carol knows that there is more to the story and contacts Malach to aid her in discovering what is truly taking place at City Hall.

Carol traveled to the City Hall and saw the Mythologists sitting amongst each other. She proceeded to approach them, but one spotted her. Smoking his cigar, he looked at Carol and remembered her from their previous meeting before.

"I remember you, lady." He said.

"You… you do?"

"I do. Come over here and sit with us for a brief moment."

"Ok."

Carol sat down with the Mythologists. Shaken up a bit and hesitant to speak a word that might get her in trouble. She looked at what they were reading and it was an ancient grimoire. She pointed at it and the Mythologist looked and turned toward her.

"Do you know what that is?"

"I do not."

The Mythologist chuckled. He grabbed the grimoire and handed it to her. She grabbed the book and opened it, seeing it covered in spells and invocations. She looked at the Mythologist with uncertain ease.

"Is this a spell book?"

"It is. We found it amongst this old place. Makes you think how the politicians win their elections, huh."

"It does in a way. What do you guys intend on doing with it?"

"Ma'am, what we do with this book is none of your concern. But, I'll give you a little insight into what we have planned with it."

The Mythologist leaned toward her, his breath the smell of ash and smoke, covering the scent of his cologne.

"There's a certain figure that lurks in the dreams of Man. His power is beyond what average humans are aware of. We intend on bringing him here to aid us in our mission. To grant us entrance into his realm."

"Your mission?"

"Creating a new order of the world. Cleaning it up from its foul and awful stench of human selfishness and emotions. We have to do it because we're the only ones who can."

"How can you do it?"

"With this book, we will conjure up our figure. He will tell us of his realm and will aid us in entering the Third Heaven."

"The Third Heaven?"

"Yes. The highest of all the realms. The domain of the Eternal One."

"But, how could you do that? You do understand that you said the Eternal One."

"I did. There are powers that are at work that can do marvelous things for those who use it properly."

"So, that bank meeting that was in the newspaper, that was for show?"

"Of course, we had to come up with a diversion to keep the commoners away from knowing our real intent."

"Maybe they could help in some way."

"No ma'am, they cannot help us. They cannot help you and they certainly cannot help themselves. They are lost and they need order in guidance."

Carol looked at her watch, seeing the time. She stood up from the chair and the Mythologist grabbed her arm. Frightening her, he looked into her eyes.

"I will grant you an invite to our little get tighter this evening. If you desire to learn more."

Carol nodded with a faint smile.

"I would love to."

"Splendid."

"Will I have to ask for your name?"

"My name." The Mythologist said with a laugh. "We have no names. Only purpose."

Carol nodded.

"We will see you tonight, ma'am."

"Yes you will."

Carol left City Hall and contacted Malach on her phone.

"Malach, I have to speak with you and its very important that we do it immediately."

"Come by the cabin and we can discuss it all there." Malach said.

"Sure."

Carol hung up the phone and left in her car, going to Malach's cabin. Carol later made it to Malach's cabin. Malach, already sitting outside, sees her approach. He stood up and opened the front door as she walked toward him.

"How bad is it, Carol?" Malach said.

"I would pick worse over bad."

Both of them walk into the cabin and Malach closes the door. Inside, Carol sits down at his table and Malach sits alongside her.

"Tell me what you came here to speak."

"I met with the Mythologists."

"Again?"

"One spotted me and allowed me to sit with them for a moment. He told me of their meeting tonight."

"What of their meeting?"

"They had a book. It contained spells and invocations. He told me they're going to use it tonight to conjure up some being that inhabits the dreams of people. Said that he would grant them entrance into his realm and would help them enter the Third

Heaven.”

“Wait, wait, wait.” Malach said standing up. “The Third Heaven?”

“That’s what he told me.”

“This isn’t good. Even if they can’t breach The Third Heaven, they’ll still cause harm to the cosmos. We need more help.”

“But, who’s this being that inhabits dreams? I’m unaware right now.”

“The Bogeyman.” Malach said. “They’re going to conjure him up.”

“The Bogeyman’s real?”

“Yes, he is and funny enough, my Master has been searching for him.”

“You think he’ll want to help us out with this?”

“If it concerns The Bogeyman, his realm, and The Third Heaven. I believe so.”

Malach walked outside to the front. Carol watched him go as he closed the door. Outside, Malach stood still, his eyes closed. Though in his mind, he is contacting Darkous. Telling him of the recent news. From the sky comes down Darkous like a lightning bolt. His eyes intense. Malach opened his eyes and seen his Master before him.

“Master, You’ve come.”

“I have. Let us enter inside and tell me more of this news you’ve spoken of.”

Darkous and Malach enter the cabin and Carol sees Darkous for the first time. Frightened and excited at the same time, she stood up and faced him.

“Master, this woman is Carol Hunters. She’s a supernatural reporter and has been aiding me on some information and I her.”

“I recognize your features, Ms. Hunters.” Darkous said.

“You do?”

“I know of you and how you wish to interview me.”

“I… I didn’t know.”

“The interview can wait. I am here about what you said of The Bogeyman, his realm, and The Third Heaven. What of all this, Malach?”

"Carol knows of a secret society that calls themselves The Mythologists. They have in their possession a grimoire and are intending on using it to conjure Bogeyman and receive information as to enter his realm and The Third Heaven."

"This I will not allow." Darkous said. "Where is this group of theologians?"

"They're at the City Hall." Carol said. "They'll most likely be underneath the building for their meeting."

Darkous nodded.

"We will head there tonight. Confront these men and show them what true power is."

"Yes, Master."

Darkous walked out of the door and turned back to Malach and Carol.

"I will meet the two of you there."

"Yes, Master." Malach said. "We will be there."

Darkous flew up into the air and was gone.

The night fell upon the land and the moon glinted across the ground. Beneath the City Hall sat the Mythologists around a circular table and in the middle of the table laid the spell book. The lead Mythologist walked into the room and sat at the table.

"Gentlemen, we know why we're here this night and it is truly of great importance."

Outside of the City Hall walked Malach and Carol around the building toward the front doors. Malach had his sword prepared for battle as Carol noticed the door was being blocked by two men. She stopped Malach.

"What are you doing?"

"They granted me entrance into the meeting. Let me go in and when your Master arrives, you can enter then."

"I understand you. Be careful."

"I will."

Carol approached the two men. They stopped her from entering the doors.

"I was granted entrance to come to the meeting tonight."

"Let me check." The security guard said.

He contacted the Mythologists on the phone. He listened and put the phone away. He took several steps back and opened the door for Carol.

"You may enter."

"Thank you."

Carol entered City Hall and instantly could feel an energy going through the place. The energy was luring her downstairs to the meeting. She found the stairway and walked down to the floor. While walking down the stairs she could see the Mythologists at the circular table with the book in the middle. She walked toward the table and the Mythologists looked at her.

"Appears you've decided to come." The Mythologist said. "Wonderful."

"I couldn't miss something such as this."

"I can't agree with you more, ma'am."

She sat down at the table next to the Mythologist as he started to talk and go over the information that was given to them through the book.

"This book, lady and gentlemen, will grant us power beyond all belief of human reasoning. With this, we will possess true power."

Carol looked around for Malach, yet she didn't' see him. Outside, Malach killed the two security guards and entered City Hall. As he approached the stairwell, Darkous communicated with him through his mind.

"Wait." Darkous said. "Just wait."

"Yes, Master." Malach said. "I will wait on you."

The Mythologists opened the book and stopped on a page that referred to The Bogeyman. The Mythologist pointed at the spell and smiled to the others.

"This will give us power. I am thrilled for this."

He picked up the book and began to recite the spell. He spoke the spell in Latin. As he spoke, the lights began to flicker, he smiled.

"It is working!"

The lights flashed and the bulbs bursts above them. The

Mythologists and Carol covered themselves from the falling glass. They looked around and could not see a thing. The room was in complete and thick darkness.

"What is going on in here?" The Mythologist said. "This isn't part of the ritual."

"No. It is not." said a voice within the darkness.

"Who is there?!" The Mythologist said. "Who is speaking to us all?!"

"You seem to be afraid."

"We fear what we do not understand because we know the power it possesses."

"Do you seek wisdom of the arts?"

"YES! WE SEEK WISDOM OF THE ARTS!." The Mythologists said altogether.

"Listen and listen good." said the voice.

"We are listening."

Within the thick darkness, they could feel an energy that was unknown to them, strange and uncomfortable, but their internal fear was becoming external.

"We're getting a little uneasy in this darkness."

"Do you fear it?"

"We do fear it. Because we do not fully understand its power."

"Why do you fear it?"

"We don't know who you are and why you've answered our request of appearance."

"The shadows are my domain. The darkness is where I dwell. Those who fear the darkness. Fear me."

The darkness faded away as the lights returned to its former state and atop the table in the middle of the Mythologists stood Darkous, staring at the lead Mythologist. Carol sat in awe of Darkous' feat as Malach entered the room with sword in hand. Darkous leaned in toward the lead Mythologist, seeing his fear.

"That is the wisdom you have received this night."

"Who the hell are you?!"

"I am Darkous, Keeper of the Cosmos and I am here to question you concerning your plots to conjure The Bogeyman, to enter the

Dreamscape, and to make an attempt at entering The Third Heaven."

"Because we have to do so."

"Why would you even dare a feat that is impossible for humanity to partake?"

"Because humanity is lost to themselves. They have no guidance. No direction. They need it now or they will die amongst themselves in foolishness and ignorance."

Darkous stared at the lead Mythologist and kept his gaze toward him. Searching the innermost parts of his heart and mind.

"You are not the true leader of this clan." Darkous said. "Where is your Master?"

"Our master?"

"You heard my words. Where is your Master?"

"Right there at the door."

Darkous turned and seen a man approaching them. Wearing a white cloak and his face hidden. He removed the hood and faced Darkous.

"Speak of your name, mortal."

"I am Dr. Geoff Hoff and this is my clan of Mythologists."

"Do you even understand what you are bargaining with, human. The feats that you have not even bared in your flesh?"

"That is why I sought out power and have discovered it."

"What do you mean?"

"I met a man, who possesses the powers of the dark arts. He aided me and gave me that spell book."

"Who is this man?"

"They call him Vernon Lance."

"Where is he?"

"He travels from church to church. Satanic churches and abandoned churches."

Darkous stepped down from the table and approached Hoff. He stood in front of him, towering over him in height. Hoff showed no fear in facing Darkous.

"What of this ritual to summon The Bogeyman, to enter the Dreamscape, and to break into The Third Heaven?"

"For you to know where The Bogeyman truly is located, you'll need to find a man they call the Spirit-Seeker. He will aid you in finding the answers you are seeking."

Darkous stared at Hoff and nodded before walking past him toward the door. Carol proceeds to follow him. Before exiting the room, Darkous turned back and looked at Hoff.

"Hoff. I give you this warning. If you ever make a breach into the cosmos, I will find you and show you what true power really is."

"I will look forward to it, Cosmos Keeper."

Darkous, Malach, and Carol left the room of the Mythologists, whom were frightened out of their seats. Hoff looked at them and shook his head.

"It seems there is more work to be done upon you gentlemen."

IV

DARKNESS SEEKS THE SPIRIT THAT SOUGHT IT

Leaving a small coffee shop is the Spirit-Seeker, Travis Vail. Returning to his base of operations, covered in books containing knowledge of the supernatural and mystic arts. Vail sat down at his desk and started reading through a grimoire, which contained information of conjuring deities from their dominions. The book was taken in an earlier event.

"I've never dealt with this before."

While he took sips of his coffee and read through the book, he hears a knocking at the door. Vail looked over toward the door and stood up from his desk. He walked to the door believing it to be someone who's stopped at the wrong location and is preparing himself mentally to tell them to go somewhere else.

"Who could this be?" Vail said. "I hope you've found the right place and not wasting time."

Vail opened the door and was immediately stunned. For Vail was staring into the eyes of Darkous himself. Darkous stood still and quiet. His eyes were locked on Vail's own.

"Travis Vail, I presume."

"Yes." Vail said. "You've come to the right place."

"Appears I have."

Vail let Darkous enter his place and closed the door afterwards. Vail returned to his desk while Darkous took a small look at the place. Seeing the relics that Vail has collected during his occult cases. From an ancient Indian burial relic to a photo with the name *Leta* attached to it.

"You have been out there much haven't you."

"I go where I'm needed."

"Very well, Mr. Vail." Darkous said turning toward Vail. "I need something of you at this appointed time."

"What do you need from me?" Vail said. "Cast out some demons, remove some spirits from a location? What will my assistance require?"

"I need you to help me find Vernon Lance."

Vail paused for a moment.

"Vernon Lance? As in the satanic priest Lance?"

"Yes."

"So, he's popped back up again."

"He has something that I require. It is of great importance to my mission and cause."

"Do tell me of your mission and cause, Mr.?"

"Darkous, Keeper of the Cosmos. But, you can call me Doctor Dark if you would prefer."

"Fair enough." Vail said. "I can tell from your aura that you're not human."

"I am not. I am an Astral entity."

"An Astral entity? So, you're basically from the outer realms."

"I am. Will you aid me in finding Vernon Lance?"

"I will. But, it might take a while to find him."

"We don't have a while to take, Mr. Vail." Darkous said. "We must confront him and take what he has in his possession."

"I can see you're in a rush to find him."

Vail grabbed his black coat and walked toward the front door. He looked at Darkous.

"I might know a few places to look."

They walked outside toward Vail's 1970 black Impala. Vail entered the car and he looked at Darkous, who was only standing there, staring at Vail and looking at his car.

"You're not going to get in the car?"

"No."

"Thought you need me to locate Lance."

"I do. Go to the place and I will meet you there."

"How will you do that exactly?"

"Because I can."

Darkous vanished into the air. Vail shook his head as he started the Impala.

"I guess this comes with the revelations."

Vail drove from his base down the streets. After a while, Vail stops by an old abandoned home. The home was once used by Lance and some of his satanic followers as a small base of operations to keep their rituals a secret from the outside world. Vail exited the car and walked toward the home. A small gust of wind blew across Vail. He nodded and turned around, seeing Darkous standing behind him.

"You found me." Vail said. "I am impressed."

"He's not here." Darkous said.

"How can you tell?"

"I searched the home while you parked your vehicle."

"That fast, you say?"

"Indeed. The energy within the home has eroded away."

Vail shook his head, walking back to his car. Darkous looked at him after glancing at the abandoned home.

"The next two locations you know of, what are they?"

"Well, one is an old storage facility and the other is an abandoned church."

Darkous nodded. "Let me do a search on the two and I will come back with the information needed in finding Vernon Lance."

"Sure thing." Vail said. "Search away."

Darkous flew up into the night sky, disappearing in the darkness above. Vail sat by his car, looking at his watch and counting the time.

"Thought he would be faster than that."

Darkous came down from the sky, landing in front of Vail. Vail chuckled a bit and started applauding Darkous' entrance.

"My, my." Vail said. "That was only a couple of seconds."

"Vernon Lance is located at the abandoned church. His aura surrounds the place. Let us stop him."

"Sure thing. I take it you will meet me there."

"I will." Darkous said before flying in the darkness again.

Vail entered the Impala and drove away. Making the rounds to reach the abandoned church, he finds himself being surrounded by individuals wearing black and scarlet robes with purple attachments standing outside in the street near the church.

"His lads are out here." Vail said. "Walking about in the damn street."

Vail honked his horn and the hooded figures turned toward him. He looked and noticed their eyes were glowing a bright red as they slowly made their way toward him. Vail prepared himself for the possible fight to come.

"First one to make a move gets sent to the Lake!"

As the hooded figures made their way toward Vail, a large gust of wind blows them across the street into a yard. Vail looked forward and could see Darkous standing in the street. The hoods stood up and surrounded Darkous in the street. Vail exited his car and reached into his pocket, pulling out his book of rituals.

"I can take these guys, Dark." Vail said.

"I know you can." Darkous said. "But, your energy is required in use against Lance. I will deal with these reprobates immediately."

"I would like to see this." Vail said. "Show them your power."

Darkous raised up both his arms toward the night sky as the moon shined above them. Thunder began to crack from the sky and lightning started to flash. From the sky came down a small tornado, blowing only through the street, picking up the hooded figures and tossing them around the yards. Clearing the street of the hoods, Darkous turned to Vail.

"May we finish what we've come to do."

"Sure. After you, Dark."

Darkous and Vail walked toward the church's front doors and Darkous blew them open with a gust of wind. Inside the abandoned church sat Vernon Lance and around him were four of his followers, dressed in black and scarlet. Lance looked at Vail and Darkous, smiling. His long wavy hair glowing with the moonlight, wearing his black clothing and black trench coat.

"How are you still around?" Vail wondered.

"Travis Vail makes his presence known to me once again." Lance said. "I am deeply flattered."

"Don't take it as a friendly visit, Lance." Vail said. "We're here on some important causes."

"I can tell by the way your friend blew the doors open."

"Vernon Lance, give to me what you have taken from a realm you do not understand."

Lance laughed as he stood up from his seat and started walking toward Darkous and Vail. He pointed at Darkous, looking at his dark violet and black apparel.

"I recognize you from somewhere." Lance said. "Have we encountered one another before in time past?"

"This is our first meeting, Vernon Lance." Darkous said. "I can sense the aura of evil around you. You have consumed its power and believe you cannot be stopped."

"I can't be stopped, Dark One. No one can stop me with the power that I possess from the ha-Satan."

"You believe he cares for you, don't you?" Darkous said. "I will tell you, he cares for no one but himself and enjoys seeing others suffer to his own mischievous acts."

"How would you know what he thinks and does?"

"Because, unlike you, who speaks to a statue with a goat's head and a woman's body, I have spoken to the ha-Satan face to face. Angel to Astral. You have no idea as to what exists and transpires throughout the cosmos of this universe. Your little worship here and there will continue to go forward until you are stopped permanently."

"Is that why Vail has brought you here? To kill me?

"No. I have come to take from you what doesn't belong to you."

"Which is what?" Lance said, pulling a small pouch from his coat pocket.

"What is that?" Vail said.

"Sand." Darkous said. "Dream sand. It belongs to The Sandman in order to enter the dreams of those who sleep."

"Sandman, you say. This is getting more and more open by the minute."

"This was given to me in a sale." Lance said. "I don't intend on returning it to Sandman."

"You won't have to because I will."

Lance raised up his hand, shoving Vail against the wall. Darkous looked at the worshippers as they tried to attack him. One by one he grabbed them with a cloud of darkness and snapped their necks without the use of his hands. Lance noticed Darkous' power and giggled.

"When you said Astral, you were talking about yourself, huh?"

"I am." Darkous said. "What kind of spirit do you possess to wield such power?"

Lance showed a sinister grin.

"A greater kind."

Lance began reciting a spell, opening up a portal that released several demonic spirits to come out and they attacked Darkous. He fought back with the powers that he possesses while Vail got back to his feet. He glared at Lance.

"This is the kind of mess that you cause for the fun of it."

"I am a human with demonic intellect, Vail." Lance said. "Will you never understand that. I have true power in the palm of my hand. To do with as I please."

Vail looked around the church and noticed dozens of symbols that referred to portals across the world in different languages.

"You're using this place to conjure demons all across the world?"

"You're just now figuring that out. How slow has time made you, Spirit-Seeker."

Darkous defeated the demons and turned his attention toward Lance. He walked toward him. Lance tried to use his supernatural power against Darkous, but it has no effect on him.

"I know I can stop you, Dark One." Lance said. "I have the true power of darkness!"

"What do you know of darkness, mortal?" Darkous said. "You believe it to be of evil, yet, darkness was present before the light. I know all of this because I control the darkness and was commanded to keep it bound in its rightful place."

Darkous swooped over toward Lance and snatched away the pouch of sand from him. Lance looked and could see Darkous placing the pouch into his pocket.

"How dare you take something of such power away from one such as I." Lance said. "I possess demonic intellect! I am the kind of human that can change this world! A greater kind!"

"No." Darkous said. "You are not."

Darkous looked at Vail and nodded. "Send him to a prison somewhere. Do it quickly."

"I would love to." Vail said. "With great pleasure."

Vail opened up his book of rituals and turned the pages. While doing so, Lance began to recite a spell that started to suck the church up from the ground. A miniature earthquake was created as the wind started to blow like a hurricane and fires began to grow from the wooden floor.

"I got something for him." Vail said.

"Do it." Darkous said.

"Abba Pater, ex toto corde tuo et in virtute Spiritus Sancti , ut hoc mando tibi per gyrum dentium eius a daemonio in prisona ibi usque ad tempus statutum. Exite!"

Lance looked around and found himself being pulled into the ground by the spirits of Sheol. Lance screamed at Vail and Darkous with angry passion.

"This isn't the last of me, Vail! You hear me! I shall return!"

Lance was pulled and had vanished. The church and its location became silent as the wilderness. Vail looked around seeing no one inside but him and Darkous. He turned to Darkous and smiled.

"Looks like our work is done."

"It is." Darkous said. "I thank you for your support, Travis Vail."

"Anytime, Dark."

Darkous was preparing to leave, until Vail stopped him.

"I need to ask you of something."

"What do you want to ask?"

"All of this, Astrals, demons, gods, what more out there don't I know yet?"

"Travis Vail, I know you're new to all of this and I know the beginnings of your journey within the walls of paranormal investigation. It wasn't until you were visited by Kamagrauto that your whole world opened up. In time, you will see it was done for a much greater purpose. The team you've formed from the heavens. A purpose that will not only benefit those of the Spirit, but the future Kingdom to come as well."

"So, there's more of your kind out there? Astrals?"

"Yes."

"Any on the malevolent side of things?"

"There are. Some work for the forces of good. Others, the forces of evil. It's all for the balance of the universe."

They walked outside and Darkous looked up to the moon.

"I have to go, Travis Vail." Darkous said. "It was an honor to work alongside someone of your caliber."

"Whenever you require of my assistance, you know where to find me."

Darkous nodded as he disappeared. Vail returned to his Impala and drove away from the church that began to crumble apart.

Back in the Astral Dimension, Darkous looks at the pouch of sand. Analyzing it for the purpose of learning its power.

"With this, I shall find you, Bogeyman. I shall."

V

OUTER SLEEP

Searching for The Bogeyman's location, Darkous went through various attempts at finding him across the earth. He was nowhere to be found. Darkous later circled the earth's atmosphere to find him and he did not.

"He wouldn't take a break in the First Heaven. I know that to be true."

Darkous returned to his place in the Astral Dimension and studied the sand pouch. Beatrice appeared to him, seeing Darkous studying the pouch of sand.

"Is that dream sand?" Beatrice asked.

"It is." Darkous said. "It was earthbound."

"Last I knew, the Sandman wasn't walking about on the earth at this time."

"Because he's trapped inside the Dreamscape. The Bogeyman trapped him there to get out. This sand was in the possession of a Satan follower."

"Where's The ha-Satan now?"

"Going to and fro in the earth and walking upright in it as always."

"Can the sand give you a signal to finding Bogeyman?"

"No, it cannot. But, It can show me the entrance into the Dreamscape."

Darkous poured a tiny inch of the dream sand into the palm of his right hand and tossed it in the air above himself and Beatrice. The

438

sand began to fall, but caught its own balance within the air. Flowing across the air by a cosmic current, the sand directed Darkous toward the entrance to the Dreamscape. Darkous looked and recognized the location the sand has chosen.

"The doorway is set within the Second Heaven."

"Are you sure about that?" Beatrice said. "I've never known there to be a door within the Second Heaven."

"I entered the doorway to Sheol through in the Second Heaven. Why not the doorway into the Dreamscape."

"Didn't seem to be a likely location is all I'm saying."

"I better be on my way to finding him. Contact me if something else comes up concerning the darkness and light issues."

Darkous left the Astral Dimension, traveling into the Second Heaven. Upon arriving in the Second Heaven, an archangel appears before him and stopped him in his tracks.

"Uriel." Darkous said. "What brings you to me?"

"Details concerning the matters of the darkness and the light."

"I was told about the issue by Michael. He gave me and advance notice."

"True. Though, you have been so concerned with the matters of The Bogeyman and he had diverted you from the real cause of concern."

"You mean to tell me that The Bogeyman is nothing more than a diversion set upon me? By who?"

"Who do you think, Darkous."

Darkous nodded.

"Should I let The Bogeyman be and Heaven will take care of him?"

"No. You have already made this your mission currently. After you have dealt with Bogeyman, you will receive a call and you will answer the call."

"Who will contact me afterwards?"

"You will know his voice."

Uriel disappeared before Darkous' eyes. He looked around for him and couldn't find Uriel. He set his attention toward the Dreamscape entrance and took some more of the dream sand and scattered it through the vacuum of outer space. The sand took some rounds and revealed the doorway to Darkous.

"There it is." Darkous said.

The doorway to the Dreamscape opened and Darkous could see the brightening colors pouring out as if it was a place of peace. Darkous made his way toward the door and could feel and aura surrounding him.

He entered the doorway and stepped on the grounds of the Dreamscape. Standing in front of him was The Bogeyman. Holding a set of blades ranging from a sword to a scythe. His eyes held a sense of torment within them as his stare could send a human into utter shock.

"You decided to appear to me without making a move?" Darkous said.

"You're in my realm now." The Bogeyman said. "Are you afraid of me, Shrouded One?"

"No. The thing is, after we have our battle, you will fear me."

"We will see about that."

VI

IN THE DREAM, WE SEE OUR CALLING

Darkous and Bogeyman engage in a battle of the powers of the realms. Darkous using various attacks against Bogeyman, whom used his sword and scythe to slash away at the darkness that Darkous would conjure up against him. Bogeyman laughed at Darkous.

"Your power isn't as strong within this realm. You're in my domain now!"

"You underestimate the power of an Astral entity." Darkous said. "We have more than what was given to us."

Darkous waved his hand to his side. Bogeyman was confused at the matter. Back on earth, Malach looked around his cabin and could feel and energy calling to him. He grabbed his sword and stepped outside and looked up, suddenly he disappeared from his home and appeared standing next to Darkous in the Dreamscape. Malach looked at Darkous, who turned to him and nodded.

"I need a little bit of your assistance on this one, Malach."

"Whatever you say, Master." Malach said. "So, this is The Bogeyman?"

"It is. In the flesh."

"Rather in the dream." Bogeyman said. "This will be fun for me, but tormenting for the two of you."

Darkous and Malach attacked Bogeyman at once. Ranging from side attacks to attacks from behind and front. Darkous fired a sphere of dark matter toward Bogeyman, knocking him back into the Dreamscape gates.

"What kind of place is this?" Malach said.

"They call it the Dreamscape." Darkous said. "This is Bogeyman's domain and the Sandman's."

"The Sandman is here?"

"I believe him to be. We'll have to release him from his prison."

The Bogeyman began conjuring illusions of himself and demons of the dreams to attack Darkous and Malach. Both using their abilities against the illusions to find Bogeyman within them. Darkous blew the illusions away with a gust of wind from his hands and grabbed Bogeyman by the head, slamming him into the ground of the Dreamscape, creating a sound resembled to a bell being rung.

Malach ,take this!" Darkous said giving Malach the pouch of sand.

"What am I supposed to do with this?"

"Use it to find the Sandman. He will help us trap Bogeyman back into his prison."

Malach looked around at the tall buildings within the Dreamscape and could see a castle ahead.

"Toss the sand into the air, Malach!" Darkous said. "The sand will lead you directly to the Sandman!"

"Yes, Master." Malach said throwing the sand into the air above the battle.

The sand rotated in the air, circling itself twice before moving across the sky, heading toward the castle. Malach ran after the sand, following its trail. Darkous and Bogeyman continued their battle with Darkous taking Bogeyman's sword and snapping it within his hands.

"Face me with your hands, dream demon."

Malach arrived at the castle, which the sand made a turn toward its lower doors connected to an underground area. Malach followed as the sand slid through the crack of the door. Malach used his sword to open the door. He continued to follow the sand until it stopped at a dark cell. Malach looked inside and seen a man sitting on the floor.

"Seems my sand has returned to me." The man said inside the cell.

"Are you the Sandman?" Malach said.

"I am. Thank you for bringing it to me."

"Me and my Master need your help right now."

"I am aware of the current circumstance. Lead the way, young one."

The cell doors busted open as the Sandman walked through. Malach stood quietly and stared at the Sandman.

"Lead, young one."

Malach led the Sandman to the outside where they could see Darkous and Bogeyman continuing their battle. Malach held his sword tightly, preparing to run into the battle, but Sandman placed his hand across Malach's chest.

"I need to assist my Master." Malach said.

"Do not run into the battle." Sandman said. "Let us deal with The Bogeyman."

Darkous slammed Bogeyman, but was kicked in the chest. He looked across the open area, seeing Sandman walking towards him and Bogeyman. Darkous released a wind of darkness, slamming Bogeyman back onto the ground.

"Keeper of the Cosmos." Sandman said. "I will finish this battle."

"By all means."

Darkous moved out of the way as the Sandman approached Bogeyman. Bogeyman, who stood up from the ground faced Sandman in the eyes. He released a small gesture of laughter.

"They set you free?!"

"They did and not I will place you in your eternal chamber."

Sandman tossed his sand toward Boegeyman, entering his eyes as he fell to the ground. The ground beneath his feet opened up, revealing a horde of shadow men as they grabbed Bogeyman by his limbs and dragged him into the ground. Bogeyman yelled for repentance.

"You will not be given repentance this day, dream demon." Darkous said. "Now, go into your prison in peace."

The ground closed itself with Bogeyman inside. The area was calm, Sandman turned toward Darkous and Malach.

"I thank you once more for releasing me from my prison."

"It was our duty to restore the balance of the Dreamscape." Darkous said.

As the Sandman spoke to them, Darkous glared up into the air. He could hear a voice calling to him. A voice only few can hear. Darkous listened and he recognized the voice he could hear. Malach looked at him and could feel there was a communication taking place.

"Master, what is it?" Malach said.

"I am needed." Darkous said. "My Master demands my presence."

Darkous returned Malach back onto earth at his home. Meanwhile, Darkous made his way toward the voice that called to him. The voice came from the Third Heaven.

THE RISE OF THE MUMMY'S TOMB

1863
EGYPT EYALET

It is the beginning of summer as the Monster Hunter and Ufologist, Gabriel Kane travels to Cairo, Egypt by ship to investigate the Pyramids of Giza and the ancient tombs of the old leaders. He also seeks on discovering if extraterrestrials had any part in the construction of the pyramids and had any influence on the pharaohs of old. Even though it is at risk from the ruling Ottoman Empire.

Upon arriving in Cairo, Kane, wearing a brown hat and trench coat, he searches for a camel to use in order to gain access toward the location of the pyramids. He ends up finding a man who is selling camels and he approaches him.

"Camel will cost you." The Camel seller said.

"I know. How much for the camel?"

"I personally accept gold or silver."

Kane smiled as he pulled out five shekels of gold and three shekels of silver from his coat pocket. The facial expression of the Camel Seller changed in an instant, showing excitement and shock.

"That will do, my good sir. That will do."

The Camel Seller accepted the shekels of gold and silver from Kane and gave him the camel. Kane mounted onto the camel and set his sights toward the pyramids that were in his eyesight within a distance.

"Move it." Kane said to the camel.

The camel began to move as Kane kept his eyes of the pyramids.

Kane continued his movement toward the pyramids as night immediately approached and covered him along with the landscape. Kane decides to stop and allow the camel and himself some rest before arriving at the pyramids, which are within a three to six-mile radius of his location.

Waking up along with the sunrise, Kane mounted back onto the camel and moved along closer to the pyramids. Kane raises his head upon entering El Giza, seeing the Great Sphinx in the horizon as he approaches the Pyramids of Giza themselves. Astonishing in some form by their height and size, he began to wonder how the structures were built and how much strength was needed to complete a task of that size.

Kane mounts off the camel and begins his investigation on searching and studying each of the three pyramids. He begins with the smallest one, known as the Pyramid of Menkaure. Already with the knowledge of the pyramids as tombs for the pharaohs, Kane searched the smallest one for any details concerning extraterrestrials either involved with the building or with the pharaohs themselves.

"I understand and know of the legend of Herodotus." Kane said. "Believing how Menkaure was more of a benevolent Pharaoh than the ones that came before. So, it may be."

Kane entered the mortuary temple of the pyramid and discovered how the foundations of the inside were made of limestone. Kane glanced down at the floor and realized they were made from granite and had granite facing surrounding him by way of the walls.

"Judging by the minerals it took to build this thing, this must have taken a long time to complete and this is just the interior."

Kane looked and seen what appeared to be an inscription in the temple. Kane stared at it while deciphering the language. After deciphering, Kane understood the inscription stated that the temple was made as a monument for the Pharaoh's father, who was the king of upper and lower Egypt. While inside, Kane also discovered carved images of the old kingdom and understood it due to its high presence of evident details it held.

Kane continued his search of the Menkaure pyramid, before deciding that he should search the other two before the next nightfall. Kane continued his search with only a little water to drink and hardly ate anything before his investigation of the pyramids. Kane finished his search of the Menkaure pyramid. He set his sight on the second pyramid, known as the Pyramid of Khafre or Pyramid of Chephren. The second tallest of the three pyramids. Khafre is the tomb of the fourth dynasty pharaoh Khafre, who had ruled from the time of 2558 till 2532 BC.

The Khafre pyramid has the length of two hundred and fifteen point five meters leading to seven hundred and six feet. The rising height of the pyramid went from one hundred and thirty-four point four meters, equaling four hundred and forty-eight feet in height.

"Amazing are these structures."

Kane had understood that the pyramid may have been robbed ages ago and decided to head straight toward the burial chamber of the pyramid. Kane had questioned if the pyramid possessed two locations of entry, but he never figured it out to be exact. He continued walking until he had entered the subsidiary chamber. Which had opened from the west of the lower passage. Kane believes the chamber was used to store precious items that belonged to the pharaoh or anyone close to him. The passage above appeared to be made in a clad of granite, which descended into a horizontal passage that lead Kane straight toward the burial chamber. Kane followed the passage directly.

Kane found himself standing inside the burial chamber. Kane looked at the size of the chamber and noticed it was carved from the bedrock through a pit. The roof of the chamber was constructed of limestone beams that appeared to have been gabled. Kane saw how the chamber had a rectangular shape and stared at the sarcophagus of Khafre. Seeing how his coffin was carved out of complete block of solid granite and how it had sunk into the floor. Kane looked down closer to the sarcophagus and seen what appeared to be small animal bones laying close to the coffin.

"Animal bones. Hmm."

Kane looked around and decided to leave the Khafre pyramid and to finally search the third pyramid, the largest of the three and the most known one of the three pyramids. Kane exited the Khafre pyramid as he stared at the Great Pyramid of Giza, also known as the Pyramid of Khufu or the Pyramid of Cheops. The Great Pyramid is the oldest of the pyramids in the Necropolis Giza area.

Kane searched the three known chambers of the pyramid. Going through the three of them in the amount of time he had left until sundown. The lowest chamber appeared to be cut from bedrock and laid where the pyramid was built, however left unfinished. The second and third chamber were the King's and Queen's chamber. Kane noticed that the pyramid was the only one to possess ascending and descending passages. The three smaller pyramids near the Pyramid of Khufu appeared to have belonged to his wives.

While searching, a loud bang had sounded from the outside, gaining Kane's attention, he rushed out of the pyramid to the outside to see what caused the loud noise. Kane had exited the pyramid and found himself standing in the presence of an ancient Egyptian army with a living mummy in front of them.

"What is this?" Kane said.

Kane continued to stare at the Egyptian army and the living mummy that apparently led them. Kane slowly reached for his pistols on his side until the mummy took a step forward in front of him.

"Who are you and how are you even alive?" Kane said.

The mummy spoke in Egyptian and Kane could understand the ancient language the mummy had spoken. Kane gripped his pistols tightly, waiting for the mummy to strike with his army.

"You are Akhenaten." Kane said. "If that is the case, then why are you over here?"

"I am here to tell you to leave this land before the curse falls upon you and those that will follow you in the future."

"What curse will follow me into the future?"

"It appears as if you lack spirit and do not seek to understand the curses that dwell in this land. The curses that those before you in times past felt, the plagues that ran their course on this land and the curses of the ancestors that lived here in times past."

"You won't be able to fool me, Akhenaten. The curses will not affect me in any way because I know what is going on around here."

"Be that as it may, stranger. But I warn you to leave this land at once."

"So, I take it that this curse of a mummy's tomb is your doing. You're the mummy that folks say has risen several times and placed curses on those who entered this land in search of knowledge."

"I warn you to leave. This is your final warning, stranger."

"I won't leave." Kane said as he fired his pistols toward Akhenaten and his army.

Akhenaten didn't make a flinch as the bullet flew past him without any harm. Kane continued to fire before placing the pistols back in their holsters as he pulled out his sword and ran toward Akhenaten. Akhenaten placed his left hand in front of Kane, shoving him back a few feet as lights shined down from the sky. Kane partially covered his eyes to see where the lights were coming from and seen three unidentified flying objects in disk shapes, hovering over the three pyramids of Giza.

"What is this?" Kane said. "The flying disks."

The sun had set, and the moonlight shined down upon the area. Kane looked above the disk and noticed the pyramids were in the exact alignment with Orion's belt in space.

"Interesting placement they did."

Kane turned to see Akhenaten, but he and his army had vanished without any noise being sounded. Kane turned back to the three flying disks as they began to levitate higher in the air and leave at warp speed. The sky was clear of the disks and silence filled the area. Kane nodded with his hat and turned away, seeing his camel still sitting in the same location as he left it. Kane makes the decision to leave the area as his theory had presented itself before him in the form of Akhenaten and the three flying disks.

THE UFO CRASH OF 1863

NOVEMBER 28 1863
AMERICAN CIVIL WAR

During the night, something mysterious in the sky is falling towards the ground. As it falls, it glows a reddish-green color and coming down faster and faster. It slams into the ground and is stuck there. The next day, Confederate soldiers discover the crash and take the object to one of their bases. Their leader, Robert E. Lee confirms that it was only a bombing accident but didn't tell them the description of the object. He commands his soldiers to take the object in their possession and to keep it highly secret.

On a ship, heading towards the United States, is Gabriel Kane. A monster hunter and ufologist. Kane is a man in his early twenties. Twenty-Three exactly. He's lean and gloomy, somewhat somber-looking at times for his age. His skin appears pale with his cold eyes. His face is shadowed by his hat. He is dressed entirely in black and is equipped with a weaponry that features a rapier, a dagger, a cutlass, a saber, and a pair of flintlock pistols.

He arrives in the United States to discover the crash site. As he travels across the northern lands, he runs into a group of confederate soldiers, who are weary of his presence.

"Identify yourself, sir." One soldier said.

"I am Gabriel Kane. Monster hunter and ufologist from Europe." Kane said. "I am here to visit the area of which an object crashed."

"There was no crashed object." The soldier said. "I believe you've been given wrong information. Now, return to your home."

"I don't live here." Kane said. "I came across the Ethiopic Ocean on ship. I heard directly that something fell from the sky around this area. So, that's why I'm here and my information is never wrong."

"This time it is." Another soldier said. "Now, leave this area at once, boy."

"Just tell me where the location is." Kane said.

One of the soldiers smacked Kane in the face with the butt of his rifle. Kane's head turned quickly before he wipes the blood off his mouth and turns to the soldiers, smirking.

"If that's how you want to play it." Kane said.

Kane kicked the soldier and knocked him to the ground. He looked toward the other two soldiers standing by, who ran toward him, Kane fired at them with his flintlock pistols.

Kane defeated the soldiers and continued looking for the crash site. As he continues searching the woods, he sees tracks on the ground in front of him. Kane walks over to the site and kneels, tracking the snow around the area. He looked up and spots something buried in the snow. He walks over and wipes the snow from it. It's a metallic object, a small, but heavy piece. Kane picks the object up and examines it. With his confused expression he says that this object appears not to be man-made. He puts the object in a small bag and continues walking toward the nearest town, just a few miles north.

Kane sees the town in front of him, surrounded with a few wooden buildings. He enters the town and sees the Union soldiers. Kane walks up to one of the soldiers and get his attention.

"Excuse me, but do you have any idea about the crashed object?" Kane asked.

"I'm sorry, sir. Who exactly are you?" The soldier asked.

"I am Gabriel Kane. I am a visitor from Europe."

"From Europe." The soldier said. "Why would you be in a place like this, especially during these times."

"I don't understand what you're talking about." Kane said.

"As of right now, we're in a civil war. North versus South." The soldier said. "See, me and the others you see around here are Union soldiers, the north. While the men in red are the Confederate, the south."

Another soldier in the distance calls out to the soldier speaking with Kane. He looks and tells Kane that he should look out for himself and that he might have to choose a side if he decides to stay a little longer. Kane looks on as the soldiers leave the town, heading into the forest. Kane walks through the town, looking at the buildings and certain areas. He sees both soldiers and civilians throughout the town. He decides to buy a map of the area and he looks through it. Going through the forest and heading to Adams County. Kane leaves the town and heads back into the forest, following the map.

Kane arrives west of the woods and discovers a frontier, surrounded and occupied by Confederate soldiers. Kane smiles at the sight of them, as if they're just targets to be taken down. Kane hides in the bushes to avoid any contact with the soldiers. He looks to his right and sees a group of them carrying an object of a large size, the object is covered with a blanket of sorts. The soldiers take the object into the large building in the middle of the frontier. Kane decides to sneak into the frontier, passing by soldiers swiftly. As he moves faster, he runs into a soldier.

"Who are you?" The soldier said.

The soldier took Kane's hat off and slammed it. Kane raised up and looked at the soldier. From behind Kane, more soldiers appear and eventually surround him. Kane notices that the soldiers are seriously hiding something due to their level of secrecy of hiding in the forest. The soldiers grab Kane and take him to the head center of the frontier. Inside the center building, sits Jefferson Davis. Davis sees the soldiers bringing in Kane.

"What are you doing?" Davis asked.

"We found him sneaking into the frontier, sir." The soldier said. "We caught him just in time."

The soldiers hold Kane in the center, facing Davis. Kane looks at Davis.

"What is your name?" Davis asked.

"My name is Gabriel Kane." Kane said. "I'm only here to investigate the crash that occurred in the woods."

"There was no crash." Davis said. "It was only an accident that happened out there. What could possibly crash?"

"There had to be a crash." Kane said. "I saw tracks and I found debris."

Davis stared deeply toward Kane. Staring him in his eyes with a slight confusion in his face."

"Debris? Of what?"

The soldiers let Kane go as he reached into his pocket, showing Davis the metallic piece that he found. Davis' face expression changes drastically, showing a sign of nervousness, along with an expression of anger.

"I found this piece in the woods, right around the crash site." Kane said. "The object was here in this spot."

"Ah! This doesn't prove anything!" Davis yelled. "Take him away."

The soldiers grabbed Kane by his coat and dragged him out. Once they reached the outside, Kane head butted the soldier and kicked the other one in the gut. Kane ran off into the forest as the soldiers began firing at him. Kane entered the forest and the soldiers run after him. Kane continues to run deeper into the forest as the soldiers track him by his footprints in the snow. As the soldiers follow the tracks, Kane turned left of the forest, his footprints disappear since there's little snow in the area. Kane continues moving and the soldiers lose tracks of the footprints.

"He couldn't have gone far." One soldier said.

The soldiers turn back and return to the frontier. Kane has now entered a complete grassy area, with only little snow. The sun shined down on him, as his hat have given him shade. As Kane continues walking, he looks at his map for the surrounding areas.

"Where am I?" Kane said, looking at the map. "What is this location?"

He looks at the grassy locations, not seeing nor hearing a single sign of life anywhere close. As he continues to walk forward, he spots a group of soldiers, wearing blue uniforms on horsebacks. Some are walking behind them. Kane stops and stands still as the leader of the Union soldiers comes toward him on his horse.

"Who are you, sir?" Kane asked.

"I am Abraham Lincoln." he said. "The President of The United States."

Kane is taken along with Abraham Lincoln and a group of Union soldiers to their frontier. Upon arriving at the frontier, Kane looked around the location, scouting the area for any sign of Confederate soldiers. Lincoln signaled to Kane to follow him inside the frontier. Kane followed him into the frontier.

While entering the frontier, Lincoln sat at a table and waved his arm toward the other seat which faced him. Kane looked and wondered.

"Please sit." Lincoln said. "We can talk right here."

Kane sat down at the table, facing Lincoln. Other Union soldiers walked in and out of the frontier. Many of them stayed outside guarding the location. Lincoln signaled the nearby soldiers in the frontier to stand guard outside, leaving him and Kane alone inside to discuss what's taken place. The soldiers exited the frontier leaving Kane and Lincoln inside at the table. Lincoln offered Kane some water and he took the cup. Both drank the water before speaking to each other.

"If I may ask, Mr. Kane. What were you doing out there?"

"I was running from some Confederate soldiers, sir. They were chasing me until I ran into you and your soldiers."

"When we found you out there, we didn't see any Confederate colors wandering about. So, why were they chasing you if I may ask?"

"I'm a resident from Europe. I came over here to investigate a crashed object that fell near this location. When I was searching for the object, the Confederate soldiers took me in and claimed that no object crashed, but I found evidence that goes against their words."

"Where is this evidence that you speak of? Do you possess it on you at this very moment?"

"I do."

Kane reached into his coat pocket and pulled out the metallic-like object. He handed over to Lincoln, who looked at it and rubbed his chin, questioning himself about the object. He handed back over to Kane, who placed it back into his pocket.

"I've never seen a texture like that in my lifetime. You believe the crashed object was made of that material?"

"Yes sir. I found this little fragment at the crash site. I didn't find the whole object. Someone took it and has hidden it from the eyes of many."

"I take it you believe the Confederate took the object and has hidden it from the people and mainly the Union. Might they believe the object could give them some form of extra help in this war that's taking place?"

"Whatever the case may be, sir. The object is not something to be toyed with. It possesses power of unspeakable energy. Energy that this world has yet to study and figure out."

Lincoln nodded while lying back in the chair. He took another sip of water from his cup and looked over at the door, seeing the soldiers walking about and keeping guard. He raised himself up from the chair closer to the table. He lies his arms across the table.

"I figure that you align with us and we can find this object you're speaking of. That way we will know for sure if the Confederates have taken it and are planning to use it for their own personal gain against us and the North. What do you say to that, Mr. Kane?"

Kane sat quietly, thinking to himself. He looked toward Lincoln and extended his hand. Lincoln extended his and both shook on the agreement.

"So, where do we head toward to find this object?" Lincoln said.

"We'll have to enter their domains. The only way to be sure about the whole situation."

"It's a fair start."

At a Confederate frontier, Jefferson Davis speaks with other Confederate soldiers about Kane's whereabouts. He questioned them on where he could have run off to and if he was a spy sent by the Union and Lincoln. The soldiers declined the statement and said he was only a man looking for the object. Davis walked out of the frontier and looked around the location. Giving himself some air from the inside.

"For goodness sake. We must find that man. By any cost."

Kane stood outside the frontier along with Abraham Lincoln discussing way of entering the Confederate frontiers. Lincoln gathered some soldiers to accompany them on their investigation. Gathering the soldiers, Lincoln considered the possible cost of having his men die because of a alien craft being hidden.

"I truly hope there's a craft." Lincoln said.

"There is a craft and you'll see it for yourself when we get to the destination."

"I believe your word, Mr. Kane."

Kane and Lincoln gather their supplies and head out for the Confederate base where the spacecraft is hidden. The Union soldiers follow them with their rifles in hand.

Upon leaving the base early on, Davis and a group of Confederate soldiers find a Union army base and immediately attack. Davis yells out orders to destroy anything and anyone they find within the base. The Confederate soldiers ransacked the base, destroying all that sits in the base. After the search, no Union soldiers are found by Davis and his Confederates.

"You cannot tell me that we've been made fools of." Davis said. "Where are they? Where could Lincoln be?"

Traveling a few miles from their base, Kane and Lincoln see a Confederate base in front. Kane sights no sign of Confederate soldiers nearby. He points out toward the base as Lincoln looks ahead.

"I see no bodies around the area." Kane said. "Shall we enter in?"

"Be cautious I warn." Lincoln said. "We don't know if this is a trap played by Davis and the Confederates."

They approach the Confederate base slowly, hiding behind the snow-covered trees and bushes to avoid possible sight. Kane looks around and sees no one, the area is as quiet to the point where only bird could be heard or the falling snow from the trees.

"This place is abandoned." Kane said. "We have our opportunity here, Mr. Lincoln."

"Where would they keep this craft, you speak of?"

Kane sees a large settlement ahead that sits near the back of the base. He points toward it.

"That's where it would be."

Kane mounts off the horse and runs toward the large settlement as Lincoln follows him and commands the Union soldiers to keep watch of the area in case Confederates appear to enter. Kane reaches the settlement and enters it and Lincoln looks around at the base before entering the settlement himself. Once they both entered, their eyes were locked on the craft, which sat on the ground in the middle of the settlement.

"This is it." Kane said. "This is the craft that fell from the sky."

"You were speaking the truth, Mr. Kane." Lincoln said. "Now I can see you're a man of your word and a loyal one."

"Don't give too much credit ahead of the victory."

Kane walks over to the craft and examines the encryptions and designs that are carved on the craft's surface and understands that it is an alien spacecraft. He pulls out his notes from his coat pocket and compares the drawings to the carved images on the craft. He sees that they are one in the same.

"This is an alien spacecraft indeed." Kane said. "There's more to the universe than what we know."

Kane and Lincoln immediately hear shots fired from the outside. They rush to see what's taking place and discover the Union soldiers firing at the Confederates that have appeared to the base. Lincoln looks ahead toward the entrance of the base and sees Davis with them.

"Men, we must leave at once!" Lincoln said. "We'll take this battle out into an open field!"

"You're planning on ending this now." Kane said.

"You don't have to stay with us any longer, Mr. Kane. You'll already found what you've been looking for and now you can continue on with your journey into the mysterious."

"No. You helped me and now I must aid you in your war against Davis and the Confederates."

Lincoln nods.

"Let's leave now!" Lincoln said.

The Union soldiers begin to leave the Confederate base. Davis shoves soldiers aside and sees Kane with Lincoln. He points toward them with anger in his eyes.

"There's that adventurer! He's traveling alongside Lincoln! I knew he was a Union soldier to begin with!"

The Union soldiers leave the base. Davis moves quickly to see where they're heading, and he spots an open field in front of them. He looks to his Confederate soldiers and hands them more rifles.

"We head toward that open field and we eliminate these Union soldiers for good and we take down Lincoln and this adventurer!"

The Confederate soldiers cheer as Davis leads them toward the open field. Kane looks back and sees Davis and the Confederates coming behind them near the field. He gets Lincoln's attention and points. Lincoln looks back and sees Davis coming. He smiles.

"Let them come and let them die."

Kane stands with Lincoln and the Union soldiers in the snow-covered field awaiting Davis and his Confederate soldiers to appear before them. The Union soldiers are ready for combat just as Kane and Lincoln are. In front they see Davis approaching and the Confederates at his back. Lincoln points out at Davis.

"This is the moment where this civil war will end." Lincoln said. "No more bloodshed upon this land amongst Americans battling Americans."

"Let's go ahead and finish this, Mr. Lincoln." Kane said.

The Union soldiers are ready as Davis and the Confederates face them. Both the Union and Confederate are opposing each other in the open field as it snows down above them. Davis smirks at Lincoln and Kane.

"I see you have the adventurer at your side, Abraham."

"I do and he is keen to do his work and move on from this."

"This is not his war. Its ours. The North versus The South. Nothing More. Union or Confederate and he made his decision to become a Union fool."

"We didn't want this war between us, yet you've asked for it and now you have it. For right here, it ends for good and there's no reason to continue this bloodshed on this land amongst Americans."

"Enough of your words, Lincoln. Let's get to the bloodshed."

"Suit yourself, Jefferson Davis of the Confederate."

The Confederate soldiers quickly run toward the Union, which do the same as Lincoln and Davis stand behind and watch the two armies run to each other in battle. Kane stares at Davis and glances at the armies battling it out amongst each other.

Shots are being fired and some are stabbed to death with blades. Davis looks at Kane and points at him. Kane spots Davis pointing and decides to approach him. Lincoln stops Kane as he walks toward Davis.

"What is it?" Kane said.

"Do not kill Davis. He's lost within his mind."

Davis looks ahead at Kane and Lincoln and laughs.

"Why are you holding the man back, Abraham? Afraid that he'll fail before you and give the Union a bad name on your expense?"

Lincoln looks at Kane. Concerned, yet trustworthy.

"Be careful."

Kane begins to approach Davis until the sky lights up above them and the battling armies. Kane looks up, holding his arm up to avoid the blinding light from above. What Kane sees is an alien spacecraft above the battlefield. Lincoln and Davis also spot the craft above them. Both are afraid, fear settling in their hearts at the sight of the large object.

"Oh my." Davis said. "It is real."

"What is it doing, Kane?" Lincoln said. "Why is it just sitting above us?"

"I do not know."

The craft begins to charge up as the sound of its engine begins to roar. Kane decides to get away from the battlefield. He pulls Lincoln alongside him.

"What are you doing, Kane?!"

"We have to get away from this area immediately! The craft is about to shoot down at us!"

Davis continues to stare at the craft, seeing its energy forming from beneath it. He is astonished at what he sees.

"Oh, how you can aid us in this war. The possibilities are

endless."

The craft shoots down a beam of energy on the battlefield, separating the remaining Union and Confederate soldiers. Kane and Lincoln are behind a set of trees to avoid the blast. Davis is knocked to the ground at the impact of the beam. Kane looks up and sees the craft take off into the sky and it vanishes. The area is now quiet with a large burnt circle in the battlefield with melted and burned snow.

A few days later, Lincoln announces the civil war is still ongoing and the Union soldiers are preparing for more battles against Davis and the Confederates. Kane has taken the crashed craft with him on a ship as he returns to Europe to study the craft even more so than he could within the woods of a civil war going country.

THE UNDEAD AND THE EXTRATERRESTRIALS

1866
FEUDAL JAPAN

Three years after The UFO Crash of 1863, Monster Hunter and Ufologist, Gabriel Kane has now taken a trip to Japan to study of the ancient Japanese history and its culture. Now, during the final years of Feudal Japan. Kane is highly aware of its history and looks to discover more about it.

Kane, now twenty-six, three years after his involvement with the American Civil War, has learned a lot more about his occupation as a monster hunter and ufologist. Kane, wearing what appears to be a grayish-white trench coat and hat, with red Japanese markings on the coat, arrives at a small museum in downtown Edo. Inside the museum are dozens of artifacts containing amounts of history about Japan and the early years of Feudal Japan. Kane looks at one book and reads about its history.

"A very interesting history here." Kane said as he looked through the book.

Kane continues to look through the book and the museums, loud screams are heard from the outside of the museum. Kane, quickly turns and runs outside. Once outside, Kane sees a swarm of zombies. The zombies appear to be wearing ancient Japanese armor and gear. The zombies turn to Kane and run after him. Kane pulls out a sword and runs through the zombies, slicing them apart. As he slices through them, they spew out a liquid which is glowing green. One of the last zombies runs toward Kane, Kane moves toward the right and slices the head off the zombie's body.

After fighting off the zombies that surrounded the area, Kane kneels and examines the green liquid. As he gathers some in a small container for experimentation. Once, he stands up the Shogun military arrive. They stare at Kane, knowing that he's a foreigner. They walk over to him, speaking in Japanese.

"You are to come with us, sir." One soldier said.

"Very well." Kane said. "If you suggest it."

Kane holds his hands out as the soldiers handcuff him and take him onto their carriage back to their base.

Once they arrive at their base, they bring Kane, who's blindfolded, into a sort of interrogation room. They sit him down in a wooden chair and leave the room. Kane listens to see if anyone is inside the room. Hearing no sounds, he finds a way to take off the blindfold and looks around at the room. The room is completely covered with Japanese art from each wall. The room resembles a samurai dojo room to an extent. Kane looks behind him and sees the brown wooden double doors.

"Would like to speak with someone, please." Kane said, speaking in Japanese. "Anybody around here who I can speak with?"

Kane hears the double doors open, a Japanese man, wearing a white robe walks into the room with two Shogun soldiers. They stand on both sides of Kane as he looks in front of him, seeing the Japanese man.

"Do you really believe your staring will frighten me?" Kane said to the man. "I've come across worse."

The Japanese man stands silently while staring at Kane.

"For starters, where am I?" Kane said.

The Japanese man walks closer to Kane. Kane looks up at the man, seeing hardly any emotion in the man's face.

"You, sir, are in Edo Castle.' The man said.

Kane pauses as he begins to think. He looks at the man, startled.

"If we're in the Edo Castle, that makes you the Shogun." Kane said. "You're the military dictator of Japan."

"I am Shogun Yoshinobu." The man said, "The seventh son of

Tokugawa Nariaki, daimyo of Mito."

"So, you're the current Shogun." Kane said. "But you said you'll never step foot in this castle nor Edo if you were Shogun. Why are you here?"

"I had to break my vow because of your troubles." Yoshinobu said. "For that reason, you must pay gravely and by gravely, I mean dreadfully."

Kane tries to break free of the ropes tied to his hands. Yoshinobu walks around him, quietly.

"You destroyed our test drill and that is why you must pay with your life.' Yoshinobu said. 'You've come into my country and disturb my governance.'

Kane continues to sit in the chair with his hands tied together behind his back as Shogun Yoshinobu walks around him in circles and later sits in front of Kane. Yoshinobu stares in the eyes of Kane, who does the exact same.

"Why don't you just kill me while I'm here." Kane said. "Because you know, I'll be out of here immediately within seconds."

"Your courage doesn't frighten me." Yoshinobu said. "Though my creations will certainly frighten you."

"Don't even bother trying to have your inventions to frighten me." Kane said. "Like I said, I've seen much worse."

Yoshinobu stood up.

"We know who you are, boy." Yoshinobu said. "You're Gabriel Kane, that monster hunter, ufologist man."

Kane stares at Yoshinobu.

"How would you have known?" Kane said.

"We've heard about your tale of being abducted by higher beings." Yoshinobu said. "We even heard about your tale in the Americas."

"So, I'm sure you know how that ended." Kane said.

"It doesn't matter how it ended." Yoshinobu said. "What matters is why are you in Japan to begin with."

"I was only here to study to country's history, nothing more." Kane said. "Why else would I be in Japan."

"Why did you destroy our Shogun undead?' Yoshinobu said.

"Excuse me?" Kane said. "What do you mean by your Shogun undead? You created those things?"

"We have such objects that can do a lot of things." Yoshinobu said. "We created them for a future military run. Today's event was only a test run, which your actions came along and destroyed them."

"You have no reason for creating zombies." Kane said. "What more could they do for you or your military."

"We can do so much more for our military." Yoshinobu said. "We've been doing very much so."

"I hope you and your country are enjoying your time in the sun. Because as soon as I get out of here, I'm exposing your plot and your reign will fall."

Yoshinobu smirked and began walking towards the door.

"We'll see about that, Mr. Kane. If you can escape this room anyway."

Yoshinobu leaves the room and locked the door. Kane turned his head towards the door behind him. He begins to move his arms around to let them loose. After moving left and right, he releases his left arm and lowers it towards his left leg. Reaching into his boot, he pulled out a blade and cut the rope from his arms and legs. Kane stands up and walked to the door. He tried to open it, though the door wouldn't bulge. Kane shoves his shoulder into the door three times. The door does not even move. Kane decides to pull out a small sharp knife from his coat pocket and jams it into the crack of the door. After shoving it through, the door opened as Kane jumped out of the room. He sees he's in a hallway covered with red, green, and white Japanese art and paintings.

"Which way should I go?" Kane said.

Kane chooses to head left in the hallway, passing by closed doors that could be a room like the interrogation room he was previously locked into. He turned down the hallway and quickly stopped as he seen two soldiers guarding a gate that leads into the other side of the castle. Kane slowly slips through the guards and finds himself entering the Shogun army base. He scans the interior of the base, noticing all the army's weapons and armor. Passing by one of the tables of weapons, he discovers two circular blades that look like two shrunken. He sees they have handles on the back as he pulled them, the blades quickly turn with a loud buzzing sound. Kane releases the handles and smiles.

"What a great invention."

Kane takes the blades and looked forward, seeing another door. He opened the door and sees numerous dead Shogun soldiers laying on beds and laboratory tables. Kane scans the bodies and notice their veins are glowing a greenish color. Kane's eyes squint as if he's seen the liquid before. He looks on the right side of the room, seeing a blanket covering a large object. Kane yanked the cover sheet off the object, revealing it.

"It makes sense now." Kane said. "Perfect sense."

Kane paused as he stared at a destroyed and somewhat damaged alien spacecraft. He walked over to touch the object but notices the green liquid that surrounds it. He backed up and looked at the bodies again, doing the math in his head, he realizes that the spacecraft liquid was used on dead soldiers to resurrect them as zombies. Kane searches the room to find a way to release the ship from its connection to the wall as its pumping the liquid into the dozen bodies of soldiers.

"How do I release this object from this wall?"

Kane reached to his right side and pulled out his sword and tries to swipe the long cable that its connected to the spacecraft to the wall. The sword doesn't leave any sort of mark on the cable. Kane pulled out two knives and tries to stab the cable from the wall. Not making any improvement as he tried jamming the knives in between the cable and the wall, Kane finally decided to use the Edo Blades. As he swiped the cable with left and right attacks, the cable suddenly gives loose, snatching itself from the wall as the spacecraft leaned and fell to the ground, causing a great disturbance to the soldiers standing outside the base.

Kane heard the footsteps of the soldiers entering the base and heading closer to the door. He searched the room for a way out and finds a small door to the right of the room hidden by a dirty brown curtain. He leaves out through the door just as the soldiers enter. Seeing the spacecraft on the ground and the cable cut from the wall, they sound the alarm. Kane tries to escape the castle's premises as he ran faster than he could possibly think. Though, he found himself surrounded by more Shogun soldiers, with Yoshinobu behind them.

"You thought you could easily escape my grips."

"It was worth a shot. Just wanted to see what you would do."

Yoshinobu looked at his soldiers. He nodded towards them and turned back toward Kane.

"Men, bring Mr. Kane to the dojo."

The soldiers snatch Kane by his arms and pull him into the dojo arena. They toss Kane in the middle of the room, facing Yoshinobu. Kane gets to his feet and sees he's surrounded by over a dozen soldiers, standing guard with their swords in hand. He looked at Yoshinbou, who's getting out of his robe, wearing a somewhat form of militaristic-martial-arts uniform. He grabbed his sword from the wall and approached Kane.

"I'll give you a chance. If you can defeat me in battle, I will let you leave the castle grounds and you can be on your way out of Japan."

"Very well. If that's what you want."

Kane stands face to face with Shogun Yoshinobu. Both have their swords drawn, facing each other. They began to circle each other as the Shogun soldiers stood still. Yoshinobu started to smirk at Kane, causing him to question the uncertainty of the battle.

"Well, are you ready to fall?"

"Only if you make the first move."

Yoshinobu swiped a rough swing toward Kane with his sword. Kane jumped back and slowly paused while he stared into Yoshinobu's deadly eyes. Kane moved slowly as he circled Yoshinobu, who did the same. The soldiers continued to surround them without making any moves or sounds. Kane turned to one soldier, who's holding a French rifle and swiped his arm, cutting it off.

"They won't even move." Kane said.

Yoshinobu jumped toward Kane with the sword in front. Kane swiped the sword with his own. Knocking it to the ground, Yoshinobu picked it up and raised the sword in the air, coming down like a strike of lightning. Kane held his sword up, blocking the impact of Yoshinobu. Kane struggled to hold back Yoshinobu's impressive physical strength. Kane noticed he was going down toward his knees as he couldn't fight off Yoshinbou's strength. He pushed back, slowly rising above Yoshinobu. As he faced Yoshinobu in the face, he kicked him in the abdomen, knocking him back.

"You decide to use your own body?" Yoshinobu said.

"In a fight, you use all that you have."

Yoshinobu dropped his sword and kicked it toward the wall. He began to set up in a pose as Kane stared. Yoshinobu moved swiftly as he kicked Kane in the face, knocking him into the soldiers. Which the soldiers shoved Kane back towards Yoshinobu, who proceeded to pummel Kane with various martial arts techniques of punches and kicks. Yoshinobu raised his elbow up above Kane's back and slammed it down. Kane fell to the ground in massive pain. Spitting out blood, he laid on the cold and hard wooden floor as he looked at Yoshinobu standing above him with his sword.

"It would seem you're not a great fighter, Mr. Kane. To which you appear to be much weaker than what the stories have told."

Yoshinobu raised the sword above Kane's throat. As he drove the sword toward Kane, he moved and kicked Yoshinobu from behind, knocking him through the window and outside. The soldiers began to move towards the window. Jumping through it and going to the outside, Kane proceeded to follow them. While outside, Yoshinobu noticed that most of Edo's civilians were standing by, staring at their Shogun. He yelled at them in Japanese to return to their homes. Kane jumped out of the window behind Yoshinobu. The civilians were covered with fear as they stared at Kane.

"So, you want to continue this battle?" Yoshinobu said.

"I plan on defeating you in front of your own people. To show them that even a leader of a country falls."

Yoshinobu ran toward Kane. Making a variety of attacks toward him. Kane dodged the attacks and backhanded Yoshinobu, who turned around as he held the right side of his face. He rubbed his lips, seeing blood on his hand. He turned to Kane with a fire in his eyes and he ran back toward him. He continued the attacks toward Kane. Getting a few jabs and haymakers in on Kane, Kane kicked

Yoshinobu in the stomach and punched him in the face, knocking
him to the pavement. Kane looked up at the civilians and turned to
the soldiers.

"This is your Emperor."

As the civilians stared, an abrupt sound of distant groans began to
approach their location. Civilians began to run as a horde of zombies
approached the location. The Shogun soldiers ran over and began
fighting off the horde. Swiping their heads and arms off with their
swords and firing at them from a distance with their rifles. Other
soldiers were ambushed by the zombies. Two zombies spot Kane and
Yoshinobu. As they approach, Kane went back into the dojo, picked
up his sword and ran back through the shattered window and began
cutting off the heads of the zombies. Yoshinobu looked up and seen
the horde of zombies against his soldiers, as well as Kane fighting a
few of them off. He got back to his feet as Kane turned toward him.

"What are you staring at, Yoshinobu? Aren't you going to fight?"

Yoshinobu didn't say a word and walked back into the dojo. Kane
shook his head as he continued to fight off the rest of the zombies.
Many of the soldiers were killed by the zombies or by the green liquid
that dripped from their decayed bodies. After the fight, Kane
returned into Edo Castle and grabbed whatever was left of his gear
and decided to leave Japan.

Upon leaving Japan, the following year, Kane discovered that
Yoshinobu had retired from being the Shogun of Japan and wasn't
seen by anyone of the public eye again. He also found out that it was
the last and final Shogun, thus making it the end of Feudal Japan.

THE DEVILS AND THE DEMONS

1870

VICTORIAN ERA

In the middle of the year 1870, Monster Hunter and Ufologist Gabriel Kane walked into the lair to have a meeting with the Knights of the *Symbolum Venatores*, the Order of Hunters. Once inside the large conference room, covered in memorabilia of hunters throughout the ages, they sat. Kane sat with the Order as they discussed their new plan to him. The Order requested for Kane to end a group that is called The Cult. Kane asked them more about the group, figuring out how they worked and what they've done to others that have crossed their path. The Order told Kane The Cult are a group of Satan worshippers who have committed various murders across Europe and have been involved in Satanic rituals of both human and animal sacrifices.

Kane agreed to find the group and annihilate them off the earth. As he walked out of the room, they warn him to be very careful of apparent demons that follow them in the shadows as well as their strength, a gift due to their high worshipping. Kane stated he'll take his chances and headed off onto his quest.

Kane traveled to the eastern side of England, searching for The Cult. Showing no signs of the satanic group, Kane decided to travel to the northern area of England. Kane traveled almost nonstop searching for The Cult.

Nightfall caught up to Kane and the sun's light dimmed away. Kane pulled out a lamp to see where he's walking. His coat and hat stood out as his silhouette shown through the shadows and the wind was slightly blowing.

"There has to be some way of finding this group before complete darkness covers the lands."

While moving, he heard sudden sounds of footsteps are heard around Kane. He slowly reaches for his pistol and aims it around him. The footsteps are getting closer.

"Whoever you are, I suggest you reveal yourself." Kane said.

Kane continued to hear the footsteps around him as the sound appears to come closer. Kane reached to his other pistols and holds it up along with the other pistol. He circles himself around the location as he begins to see cloaked figures circling him. Dressed in all black robes with hoods covering their faces. They're not making and noises of any kind, except for their creepy footsteps. Kane glanced back at the entire crowd before one of the cloaked figures approached him directly. Kane holds the pistol towards the cloaked figure's forehead.

"State your names immediately!" Kane said. "Before I have to just rid you off before me and continue on my journey."

"We are The Cult."

"Cult of what? Wizards? Demons?"

"We are The Cult of Hastur, our Fallen Angel and Savior."

"Hastur? The Fallen demon."

"He is our Angel and our Savior! You will speak of him not. Until you become a member of his Cult."

"That will never cease to happen."

"Be that as it may. For we and Hastur know who you are. Gabriel Kane, the monster hunter and ufologist."

Kane smirked and cocked his head slightly while holding his pistols toward the Cult around him.

"So, you know who I am. I take it that Hastur sent you here to stop me from finding you and killing you all."

"Hastur warned us or a coming force that rides in the night to stop his works as well as ours. We will not stand by and let you destroy what our savior has created and built for us. For he has spoken and has declared that we vanquish you off the face of earth, so that he can continue his work for his coming rule."

"If what you're saying is true and your boss wants me dead. Why don't you and your guys take care of me now while I'm still here by myself."

"Don't worry. We're about to."

The cloaked figure turned around facing the Cult. He raised up his hand and lowered it in the direction of Kane. He turned toward Kane and revealed his eyes. A piercing red glow emits from them as Kane pointed both pistols toward him.

"What the hell are you people."

"We're worshippers of Hastur. He's given us power that many humans cease to believe in our time and later in the future generation. Until our savior returns and turns this world into his own kingdom of chaos and death."

"Not while I'm still around."

Kane fired a shot to the cloaked figure's head. The bullet goes through his head as he fell to the ground. The Cult looked down at his body and raised their heads toward Kane in complete silence.

"Anyone up for the next round?" Kane said.

The Cult ran toward Kane as he fired shots continuously around him. Blowing off heads and shooting through abdomens. The Cult reached closer as Kane placed his pistols back into their holsters and took out a sword. Kane began slicing through the Cult as they came closer toward him. One member of the Cult slapped Kane in the face. Kane smiled and cut the head off the member. Kane continued fighting off the Cult and discovered their seemly increasing in numbers.

"How are they doing this."

Kane found himself being smothered by The Cult, until a blast of light appears from behind him. The Cult look up toward the light and immediately covered their faces as the light burned them. The Cult ran off into the darkness of the nearby forests as Kane was crouched on the ground, covering his head. After a brief of silence, Kane stood up and looked around, not seeing any of the Cult in sight. He looked behind him and seen a man standing, facing him.

The man wore a suit and had a moustache and short black hair. Kane took a greater look at the man as he closed a book he was holding before placing it into his pocket.

"I suggest you say something. That way I know you're not possessed and in control of your own self." The man said. "So, I won't have to kill you."

"I recognize you from somewhere. I may ask who you are?"

"We might have cross paths once, for starters. But, allow me to introduce or reintroduce myself. My name is Thomas Carnacki."

"The Thomas Carnacki. The Ghost-Finder."

"Correct, Mr. Gabriel Kane."

Kane and Carnacki stare down each other as they meet for the very first time. Kane placed his sword back into his holder as Carnacki stood still.

"How do you know my name?"

"There are so many tales that concern you, Mr. Kane. Many describe who you are and what you've done throughout your illustrious history."

"So, I take that I can ask what you are doing out here?"

"I'm looking for a being that's known as Hastur. A fallen demon of sorts. I had understood that a group called The Cult were his army or worshippers that gave him the power to do the things that he wished."

"You just ran them off with your light sorcery."

Carnacki waived his hand toward Kane while he shook his head.

"I possess no sorcery of any kind. I've trained in many ways that I've learn how to use the energy that lives around us in our everyday lives."

"Be that as you say, I'll rather use my weapons to get the job done. That way it's a clean kill."

"Seems that you do not have much faith in using the energies of this world."

"I have faith. Only not in those who decide to use other means to fight their battles for them."

"If you believe your words so. Why are you out here exactly? If I may ask. For investigation purposes."

"I'm also on the hunt for Hastur and I found The Cult. Had them in my grasp before you arrived and ran them off.

"They nearly had you on the ground to rip your body apart for the worshipping. I came along and saved your life here. So, I suggest you show someone like me a little respect and say thank you."

Kane walked up toward Carnacki and looked him in the eyes.

"You'll get your respect when I receive my respect."

Carnacki nodded with a smile.

"We'll see how you'll get your respect, Mr. Kane. Until then, we'll travel together to find Hastur. Remember, two hands are better than one."

"We'll see how your work will pay off. This isn't some ordinary ghost that you're dealing with. This is a demonic force that preys on fear and hopes on gaining control of the world as we know it."

"I know what we're dealing with and I will handle it accordingly to how I do my work. As for you, just do what you know how to do and don't get in my way when we come across Hastur and his Cult."

Carnacki walked off into the forest as Kane looked on. He reached down and picked his hat up from off the ground and placed it back onto his head.

"The suggestion is the same here, Carnacki."

Kane walked into the forest behind Carnacki. Holding his pistols in hand as Carnacki continued to carry his book throughout their walk in the forest. Carnacki looked back and nodded his head.

"So, how many things have you come across in your lifetime of being a hunter?"

"I've come across things that the world disbelieves. Many of those things include the undead, extraterrestrials, mummies, spirits, and so on."

"So, you've never come across a werewolves or vampires?"

"I have yet to encounter such creatures. I know I will in the future, but for now, my focus is on finding Hastur and stopping him and his cult of crazed mortals."

While walking through the forest, they find a spot in the middle of the forest where no trees stood tall and hardly any bushes or high grass was settled. Carnacki walked over toward the cleared spot and kneeled. He reached and rubbed the ground and sniffed his hand.

"Smells like this area was burned by something."

Kane walked over and sniffed the ground. Taking a second to think, he slowly reached for his pistols.

"It's sulfur."

Kane looked up and in front of him and spotted a horde of demons. All with sharp teeth and claws that smelled like brimstone on their darkened scaled bodies. Kane shoved Carnacki as he glanced up toward the demons.

"Oh dear." Carnacki said. "What shall we do about them?"

"What do you think. We'll fight them all off and clear this area."

Kane ran toward them as he fired shots from his pistols. Killing a few of the demons as Carnacki took out his book and began reciting rituals against the demons that threw them off of what they sought out to do. Kane took out his sword and sliced through the demons. He glanced back as Carnacki who was reading out of his book.

"Carnacki! What the hell are you doing over there!"

"Patience, Mr. Kane. For I am about to save our lives at this moment in an instant."

"We'll see who saved who."

Carnacki began reading from the book and immediately the demos started to vanish completely. Kane looked around as the demons disappeared through a thick black smoke. As they vanished by numbers, Kane looked over toward Carnacki, who held his book in the air and continued reciting the ritual. Once he completed the ritual, the demons were vanished completely from the entire area. Kane walked over toward Carnacki and took one glance at the book.

"What the hell is in that book of yours?"

"Words that will save our lives for this purpose of saving this world."

"If you say."

"Let's continue on searching for our leading quests."

Carnacki and Kane continued walking through the forest. While walking, Kane could hear something rustling around in the trees above them. The sound was intense enough to the point that Kane began firing shots into the trees. Carnacki turned and looked back at Kane.

"What are you doing?"

"Whatever is in the trees is too big for an animal."

"For God's sake, its only animals running around in those trees. Nothing more could it be."

Carnacki took one step further, a member of the Cult jumped down from the trees in front of Carnacki and smacked him through the trees and into another large tree trunk. Kane looked and reached for his pistol before being snatched and thrown across the trees.

"You individuals will never cease to understand the power of our savior, Hastur. For he is great to us as we are to him."

"I'm tired of hearing what you believe about your demon."

Kane lunged toward the member and punched her, knocking her on the ground. Carnacki gets to his feet and approached Kane. Wiping the dirt and moss of his coat, Carnacki looked down at the member and recognized it was a woman. He looked at Kane.

"Tell me you didn't hit a woman."

"She attacked me first. She deserved it for being a worshipper of a demon."

They began to hear footsteps coming from behind them. Crushing fallen branches with each step. Kane and Carnacki turned around facing the entire Cult. All of which had glowing red eyes. Kane pulled out his pistols as Carnacki reached for his book.

"You've come too far to ruin our savior's work. Now, we have choice but to kill the two of you and sacrifice your bodies and your blood to Hastur, our savior."

"Not today." Kane said.

Kane fired shots, though the bullets went through the Cult completely. Not even leaving a mark of any kind. Kane paused as he looked over to Carnacki, who began turning pages in his book as the Cult ran toward them.

"Carnacki, they're approaching us."

"One moment, Gabriel Kane. I'm searching for something here."

"We don't have time to do this, Carnacki."

"Just have patience this once, young one."

The Cult inched closer toward them as Kane held his sword in front. He glanced at Carnacki who continued turning pages. Kane began to become enraged at Carnacki's actions.

"CARNACKI!!! DO YOUR WORK!!!"

"If you insist so greatly."

Carnacki opened the book to the point of which the book could nearly be ripped in half if it opened more. He began reading what he called the Sigsand Manuscript. The Cult had suddenly stopped and looked at their bodies. Carnacki glanced over toward Kane.

"Fire your shots, Mr. Kane. Before this ritual runs off."

"If you say."

Kane fired shots from his pistols and immediately began killing the members of the Cult. He continued firing as he thought to himself what exactly is Carnacki dealing with within that book of his. Nearly running out of ammo, Kane decided to use his sword and began cutting through the Cult completely from every angle he could possibly picture in his mind. It finally came down to the last three members of the Cult in which they ran toward Kane and Carnacki. Carnacki dodged a punch and slammed the member to the ground before stomping on his chest. Kane ducked the shots from the other two and sliced them both in half. He looked down at the other one and stabbed it in its hearts as Carnacki looked on.

"I didn't suspect you had any physical fight within you."

"I prefer to use my book to get the jobs done rather than my fists and feet."

Kane turned around and noticed a building nearby. He pointed in the direction as he and Carnacki walked over toward the area. Once they reached the area, Kane realizes it's a church. He also spots significant symbols and lettering around the church's walls and notices that a cross that sits atop the church is upside down.

"Appears we've found their worshipping site."

"Seems you are correct on that statement, Mr. Kane."

They approached the door and Kane kicked in the doors. As both walk inside the church, they discover a large amount of animal skins laying around the walls of the church and they also noticed a strong odor of blood within the church's walls.

"I take it you smell the blood." Kane said.

"I surely smell it."

"Now, we need to see what's in here to stop Hastur."

They walk near the altar before hearing a sudden rumbling sound coming from underneath them, near the altar.

"What is going on?" Carnacki said.

"It's him."

The floor blows open, knocking Kane and Carnacki to the ground in the aisle. They can only see dirt flying in the air. Kane fans his arms, moving the dirt from his sight. As the dirt and dust cleared from the air, they found themselves staring at Hastur himself. A large demon with rough burned skin, ram-like horns, and bones on his back that resembled wings.

"I've finally come to terms of seeing my Cult couldn't rid you off this decadent wasteland."

"So, you're Hastur. The fallen demon that's come to rule over the lands." Kane said.

"I am that and much more. More of which you couldn't possibly understand with your human minds."

Kane and Carnacki continued to stare at Hastur. Staring at his large physique and his towering height of which nears the height of a grizzly bear on its hind legs. Kane pulled out his sword and pointed toward Hastur, who smiled.

"I do not know what you're smiling about, demon. Your end has finally come and has come to your own doorstep."

"The two of you combined don't have the strength or willpower to defeat me all on your own."

"You have no idea what kind of power we possess, Hastur. Many will remember this night greatly as the night the fallen demon Hastur met his death."

"We shall see whose death will culminate on this very night. One thing is highly sure, it won't be my death."

Hastur rammed at great force with impressive speed into both Kane and Carnacki, shoving them into the concrete walls of the church. Both struggled to let themselves free from Hastur's rough horns.

Kane began stabbing Hastur in both his abdomen and back with his sword. Hastur roared in pain as he backed away from Kane and Carnacki. Carnacki tried to regain his breath as Kane ran over toward Hastur and continued stabbing the large demon in his abdomen. Hastur swiped his arm across Kane, who ducked and went behind him, stabbing him in his back. Hastur raised his foot up and back kicked Kane into the wall.

"Weak mortal. You believe giving me mild pain from a metal blade will end my existence."

"I'm trying what I believe has a chance to work against a being such as yourself."

"Just accept your death as a favor of my gratitude."

While Hastur started walking toward Kane as he reached onto his side, pulling out from his coat a double-barred shotgun. Hastur stopped and stared at the weapon. Preferably into the barrels.

"Guess I'll give this a try." Kane said.

Kane fired the shotgun, blasting Hastur on his chest, blowing him back a few steps. Hastur was appalled by the force of the shotgun and looked at his chest. Rubbing it before looking down at Kane. Only black and reddish ash fell from Hastur's chest. It even smelled of a greater sulfur mixed with the gunpowder. Carnacki looked on as he turned pages through his book.

"That weapon you possess has great power. Yet it fails to have the power to finish me off."

"I haven't used it to its full potential."

Kane fired another shot that blew off one of Hastur's horns. He roared in massive pain to where Kane and Carnacki covered their ears to protect them from any damage due to the loud road. Hastur shook his head and his eyes began to glow a dark red emitting smoke from them.

"I've toiled with you humans enough! Now I finish you completely."

Hastur reached down as Kane took another shot, shooting a small hole through Hastur's right hand. He smirked as he jerked Kane by his coat and held him up to the equal height of himself. Hastur stared into Kane's eyes as he began talking in an unusual way. Carnacki looked on and stopped on one page.

"He's trying to possess Kane."

Carnacki ran over toward Hastur, who spotted Carnacki and swiped him back against the wall. Hastur looked back toward Kane and smiled.

"If you shall not perish, I shall make you one of my own. Someone with your skill set will be very useful for my ruling army in the days to come."

"Your days won't be coming, Hastur." Carnacki said. "For your days are done away with as I read this ritual to send you back into your prison."

Hastur threw Kane to the wall as he ran over toward Carnacki, who read the ritual aloud. Hastur noticed that his body was degrading in front of him. He looked down at Carnacki as he continued to yell out the ritual.

"No! Stop what you're doing, mortal. Stop!"

"I now send you back into your prison for all eternity."

Hastur's body completely falls apart as he turned to black smoke before a bright light appeared out of the book and approached the smoke as it inhaled it completely as it disappeared. The church is silent as Kane gets to his feet and nodded at Carnacki.

"Great job." Kane said.

"Same goes to you, Mr. Kane."

The church began to rumble as it started to fall apart. Kane and Carnacki ran out of the church as it fell to the ground and became nothing but dust and debris. They took one last look at the demolished church before facing each other.

"Seems the job is done." Carnacki said.

"For now."

"Until we meet again in this matter."

"That's what I was thinking."

They shook hands. Ending their recent partnership as they walked their separate ways, leaving the church completely abandoned in the middle of the forest.

Several days later, Kane returned to the Order, where they thanked him for stopping Hastur. Kane replied to them how he had assistance in his quest to which the Order stopped him from continuing and mentioned that Carnacki was given their blessings for helping. Kane stood silent as he stared at the Order.

"How did you know Carnacki was aligned with me?"

"Because we sent him. We know you're still a young man who's learning his steps in this new life, so we thought we should send someone who's well-trained in this field of the supernatural."

"You could've at least said something to the extent of him investigating the same incidents."

As they spoke with each other, Carnacki had walked through the doors as he handed the Order a scroll. They nodded to him as he glanced at Kane and nodded. Kane nodded back as Carnacki left the room. The Order placed the scroll on the table before speaking to Kane.

"Still, you've done your job and it has done us greatly."

"If there's anything out there that might need my hand involved, you know how to contact me."

Kane left the Order's lair and stood outside, watching the sun arose from behind the clouds.

THE HOWL OF THE WOLFMAN

1877
LONDON

England has been on the rough end of murders throughout the past few weeks. Witnesses have reported over a dozen killings that were apparently caused by a "Wolfman". The police have been on the series of murders for weeks and haven't found a trace. Now, they have decided to contact Gabriel Kane to investigate these Wolfman murders. After three days, Kane arrived in London, starting his search for the Wolfman.

Kane headed into the London City Police Headquarters. When he entered the building, the people turned to him, automatically knowing he's the Monster Hunter and Ufologist known across the world. Kane walked toward an officer standing by the lobby counter.

"The commissioner of your city wanted to see me." Kane said to a officer.

"Yes, Mr. Kane." The officer said. "His office is right down that hall."

Kane looked down the hall, gazing at the newspaper clippings on the walls, all focused on the Wolfman sightings and murders. Kane saw a door in front of him and entered the room. Inside is the commissioner of the police sitting at his desk. Kane knocked on the door.

"Who's there?" The commissioner asked.

"Gabriel Kane." Kane said. "The man you've contacted."

The commissioner raised his head up from the desk, covered with paper, staring at Kane. He welcomed him into the office. Kane sat in the chair facing the commissioner.

"I'm truly glad you could make it." The commissioner said.

"I go where I'm needed." Kane said.

"We needed you here because of your certain background with these types of investigations." The commissioner said. "We've received reports that the series of murders that have been caused over the past few weeks were done by a werewolf or Wolfman as the witnesses call it."

"I've heard of such a beast, but never encountered one. What location have these murders occurred?"

The commissioner revealed a map of the city from his desk drawer. He laid it out on the desk, Kane glanced over it as the commissioner pointed to the location.

"Right here, in the City Park." The commissioner said. "Most of the murders have occurred at this site. Others were in the woods and two in an alleyway just across town."

"Any traces of a suspect?" Kane asked. "Just to be sure?"

"There haven't been any signs of a suspect. Nor any traces."

"Here, I will help you on this investigation." Kane said. "Get to the bottom of it."

"I thank you for that, Mr. Kane." The commissioner said.

While Kane prepared to leave, another man entered the office. The man has curly black hair and he's wearing a black frock coat with an upturned collar shirt, a brown silk waistcoat, and black slacks with brown dress shoes. The commissioner stood up to approach the man, shaking his hand. The man later turned his attention toward Kane, who walked toward him.

"Kane, I like you to meet Mr. Sherlock Holmes." The commissioner said. "He'll also be on this investigation as well."

"The well-known Sherlock Holmes." Kane said. "An honor to meet you."

The two detectives shook hands.

"You're the great Gabriel Kane." Holmes said. "The Monster Hunter/Ufologist. Let me ask a question. What's a Ufologist, really?"

"This isn't the time for questions. We're on a serious investigation and I'll like to get to it."

Kane leaves the office as Holmes and the commissioner look back at him.

"He's got quite the temper." Holmes gestured.

"He takes his job very serious, Mr. Holmes. I hope you do the same on this case."

"Don't worry about it, Commissioner. I'm highly excited for this case. Its about a Wolfman."

Outside, Kane gets onto his horse and rode off, looking at a map of the city. He begins the investigation by heading towards London City Park. Holmes walked outside of the police headquarters, taking note of Kane riding off in the distance.

"Impatient one I'm guessing." Holmes said as he gets onto his horse and follows Kane.

Kane rode through the city of London toward the City Park, Holmes came over on the side of him. Kane took a quick glance over at him with uncertainty.

"How would someone like you be a part of this particular case?" Kane asked.

"Because, I can solve any case. Ordinary or supernatural. I can get the job done."

"I hope so." Kane remarked.

"By the way, my partner, Dr. Watson will be joining us. He should meet us at the City Park."

"I'm not a fan of being in the crowd. Much less a fan of anything."

They reached the City Park and began their search. Kane took to the eastern portion of the park while Holmes searched the western portion. Civilians stared at Kane, due to his well-known background. He approached one male civilian.

"Excuse me, sir, have you seen anything unusual in this park?"

"No. Nothing." The civilian answered.

"Thanks."

On the other side of the park, Holmes continued his search for clues as he flirted with a pair of women walking through the park. As he flirted, Dr. John H. Watson, wearing his casual slacks and vest coat with a brown coachman's hat, approached from behind.

"What exactly are you doing, Holmes?"

"What does it look like?" Holmes said. "I'm speaking with these beautiful women here. But I'm glad you've arrived to help."

"Help with what? You're flirting techniques or this Werewolf case?"

The women look at Holmes, questioning him about the Wolfman case. He grinned, enjoying and savoring the women' attention. Holmes continued speaking with the women as Kane walked up behind the women.

"This isn't the time for messing around." Kane declared with certainty.

"Just relax. Here, meet Dr. Watson."

Kane glanced at Watson and shook his hand.

"It's good to meet you."

"Indeed." Watson said. "What have you discovered so far?"

"Nothing. Haven't found a clue."

Holmes looked to Kane and Watson. Smiling.

"I think it's best we return later tonight and investigate." said Holmes. "Since the murders only occurred during the night."

"Agreed." Watson said.

"Good thinking." Kane remarked. "At least you're using your mind this once."

Kane leaves the park as Holmes looks back at Watson.

"He doesn't like me very much, does he." Holmes said.

"You can't tell, Holmes." Watson said.

Kane, Holmes, and Watson return to the City Park later that night and its completely dark and quiet. The only thing they can hear is the sound of crickets and their horses as the snow falls from the sky. They walk together, not splitting up, though that's what Kane wants to do. Holmes look at the sky, towards the moon. He sees the clouds covering it.

"They say that this 'Wolfman' always appeared when there was a full moon." Holmes said.

"That is correct." Kane said. "Why do you ask?"

Holmes pointed towards the sky, as Kane and Watson look right above them. The clouds are covering a partly of the moon. They can't tell if it's a full moon or a crescent moon.

"Can't tell.' Holmes said. 'What do you guys think? I'm just observing it right now.'

"Judging by my view, it seems to be a crescent moon.' Watson said. 'If you look just towards the right, you can see the top point of the moon.'

"Really?' Holmes said. 'I don't see it.'

Kane looked towards the direction of Watson's. He turns back to Holmes.

"Just wait for the clouds to move over.' Kane said. 'Once that happens, we'll get a good view of the moon.'

"So, Kane, what types of cases have you been on before this one?' Holmes asked.

"I've done a few exorcisms, I also encountered a living mummy controlled by aliens nine years ago.' Kane said. 'When I was twenty-three, I was involved, well rather pulled along into the American Civil War while investigating an extraterrestrial crash site. I've encountered zombies, gargoyles, warlocks, and among other things.'

"You've basically been through hell and back over your lifetime.' Watson said.

"Pretty much.' Kane replied. 'It's what keeps me going.'

Holmes and Watson discuss the moon to each other, Kane notices something in the bushes towards the left of them. He slowly walks over to the bushes, with his right hand to his side, slowly grabbing hold of his pistol. Watson notices Kane moving slowly and so does Holmes.

"He's found something.' Watson said.

"I wonder what exactly?' said Holmes. 'There has to be something around here with a clue.'

Kane reached closer to the bushes and pulls out the pistol, aiming it into the bushes. He looks around it and sees a brown cat jump from the bushes, running into the darkness. Kane looks on as Holmes and Watson come from behind him.

"It was only a cat it seems.' said Holmes.

"At least he debunked it.' Watson replied.

Kane moved toward them, looking up and noticed the clouds have moved, unveiling a full moon. He then sees something huge, standing a few feet behind Holmes and Watson. He sees it has a long snout, long high ears, the claws on its hands and feet, and its body covered completely in brown fur. Kane has finally seen the Wolfman.

"Move!" Kane yelled. "It's behind you!"

Turning around, facing the Wolfman. Howling and pouncing toward them on all fours. Holmes and Watson raised up their revolvers and begin firing at the Wolfman. Kane reached into his left side, pulling out silver bullets, reloading his pistols.

"Why aren't our shots working?" Holmes asked.

"You need silver bullets?!" Kane yelled.

Holmes turns to Watson, no sign of expression on his face. Watson looks at Holmes, while still firing at the Wolfman.

"We don't have silver bullets, do we?" Holmes wondered with confusion.

This is not the time!' Watson said.

Kane finished reloading and fires at the Wolfman. It swiftly moves side to side, avoiding the shots. It looks down and notices the silver bullets. It looks up at the three and roars, before running into the darkness of the park.

"Damn it! Where did it go?!"

Holmes takes out a flashlight and points it towards the darker area of the park. He notices something moving around. He starts running toward the darker area.

"There it is!" Holmes said. "Right down here!"

"Be careful, Holmes!" Kane yelled. "It can be a trap!"

"Don't worry yourself, Mr. Kane. I know what I'm doing."

Holmes, walked through the dark area, hearing rumbling throughout the bushes around him. He looked around, not seeing anything. Holmes turned back toward Kane and Watson. They glanced at him, questioning.

"There's nothing here." Holmes said. "It must've run off."

"You sure?" Watson asked.

"I'm positive There's nothing here."

Kane ran over to Holmes, looking both left and right for the Wolfman. He gets to Holmes and searches the area himself. Holmes only stares at Kane.

"You really had to look for yourself, I see.' Holmes said. 'I just said there's nothing over here.'

"Over here, yes. But, what about over there."

Kane points to the left of the area, facing the exit to the park. Standing by the exit is a man, whose only wearing torn pants. Kane runs over to the man, as Holmes and Watson follow. Once they reach the man, they notice that he's out of breath.

"What's his problem?"

"Have to find out."

Kane attempted to grab the man's attention, but nothing worked. Holmes knelt in front of the man, staring into his shocked eyes.

"Excuse me, sir." said Holmes. "Have you seen a Wolfman anywhere?"

The man slowly turns his head toward Holmes, facing him. The man starts to sob as if he's both sad and afraid.

"Wolfman?" The man uttered loudly. "There's no Wolfman here."

Kane's temper starts to get the better of him as he gets into the man's face, aiming his pistol towards the man's forehead, staring a hole deeply through him. Holmes looks at Kane and backs off, standing next to Watson.

"Now tell me, have you seen this creature?" Kane asked the man. "Have you seen it?"

"No!" The man yelled. "I haven't seen a Wolfman!"

Holmes looked at the moon, the clouds have shaded its light. He tapped Kane on his left shoulder, pointing up.

"If the moon's cover, does it stay a werewolf, or does it change back into a human?" Holmes questioned.

Kane gazed above him at the shrouded moon, turning back towards the man.

"Him." Kane said. "He's the Wolfman."

"Really?" Holmes asked. "Because he's looks a little slim to be a gruesome beast."

"It's him!' Kane yelled. "Watch the clouds, for when they move, he'll turn back into the werewolf."

Kane pulled out both pistols, aiming them towards the man, Holmes does the same and Watson looked up at the moon, the clouds started to fade away, revealing the full moon once again.

"The clouds are gone." Watson said.

"Cover me." Kane yelled.

They backed up, watching the man. Within seconds, they noticed him starting to twitch. He cramped up into a cradle on the ground, holding himself in his arms. As he screamed in pain, the tone in his voice decreased in pitch. Growing deeper, beast-like. He glared toward them.

"Run for your lives, gentlemen. RUN!"

The man's skin starts to peel off his body like dead shreds of hair. Beneath the shredding skin, thick brown hair starts to grow in its place. The man's head transforms painfully into a snout as he ears heighten. His eyes change from green to yellow. His nails transform into sharp razor claws as his hands and feet turn completely hairy. The man turns toward them and reveals himself to be the Wolfman. He roared at them and lunged.

"Watson!' Kane yelled. "Watch out!"

Kane fired a shot toward the Wolfman's chest, straight into the heart. The Wolfman and Watson both fell to the ground after the fire.

"John!" Holmes yelled. "Are you alright?!"

They helped Watson to his feet, dusting the dirt off his shoulders. He looks at them, holding his right side.

"I'm ok. Just a bruise will remain. Nothing dire."

"That's a good thing you didn't get bit." Kane said. "Otherwise, that could've been you later."

Placing the pistols back onto his sides, Kane approached the Wolfman's body, realizing he's transformed back into human form and dead.

"Looks like we're done here." Holmes said. "Who wants a drink?

I know I do.”

“Indeed. This was something I never studied for.”

“Not many in your fields have study such truths.” Kane said. “*Requiescat in Pace.*”

The next morning, Kane returned to the police headquarters as the entire city of London thanked him, Holmes, and Watson for finding and killing the Wolfman. They thanked the city and Kane’s work was finished. His focus was set to leave London, heading off into the western side of Europe. Outside, Holmes came towards him.

“I only wanted to say that I appreciated the time we worked together.”

“I have to say it’s an honor to have worked with a famous detective.” said Kane. “You take care and tell Watson that I said get well.”

“I will.” Holmes said. “Surely.”

Kane rode off out of London, not even looking back to the city. Holmes prepared to leave when spotted Watson nowhere to be found. Inside a public bathroom, Watson is staring at himself in the mirror. As he removed a part of his clothing from his right side, he saw blood. When he fully removed his shirt, he knew he wasn’t bumped or scratched by the Wolfman. He was bitten.

“No.” This cannot be happening.”

JOURNEY TO TRANSYLVANIA

1887
TRANSYLVANIA

Transylvania is a highly known location to the world. A place where people fear due to its known history of vampire tales. Now, in the mid-1800s, Gabriel Kane, a monster hunter and ufologist, highly known for his encounters with legendary beasts across the world. Kane is a man in his late forties, lean and gloomy, somewhat somber looking. His skin appeared pale with cold eyes. His face is shadowed by his hat. He is dressed entirely in black and is equipped with a weaponry that features a rapier, a dagger, a cutlass, a cross made of steel, and a pair of flintlock pistols.

The reason for Kane becoming a monster hunter and ufologist is the fact that he believes that he was abducted in his early days by extraterrestrials. Now, with that knowledge, Kane's main goal in life is to rid the world of all evil in both legendary and extraterrestrials.

Kane, who's now on the road, heading towards London. As he is heading there, he makes a stop upon Hertfordshire. Kane enters the small country town, seeing its residents and how they look at him with fear. Kane sees a small bar and enters it, leaving his bold black horse standing in front of the bar, tied to a pole. Kane walks into the bar, which is filled with mostly men and a few women. The people in the bar notice Kane and stare at him. Kane walks towards the bar and sits on a stool as the people continue to stare. Kane looks at the female bartender.

"May I have a glass of whiskey?' Kane asked the bartender.

The bartender pulls out the whiskey bottle and pours it into a glass and hands the glass to Kane. Kane takes the glass and begins drinking the whiskey. As the bartender turns to put the glass away, Kane grunts, getting her attention.

"Leave the bottle here.' Kane said. 'If you please.'

"Yes sir.' said the bartender as she leaves the bottle in front of Kane.

She leaves the bottle and from behind Kane comes two men, wearing Victorian clothing, with one wearing a hat. They each stand on both sides of Kane and they stare at him.

"So, you must be Gabriel Kane.' the Man with the hat said.' 'The monster hunter.'

"The ufologist, too.' the other man said. 'So, tell me, Kane. What actually is an ufologist?'

"Do I really need to speak with you.' Kane said.

"You do if your life depended on it.' the man in the hat said.

"Hmm.' Kane said. 'If my life depended on it.

The man in the hat taps Kane on his hat. Kane feels the vibration and quickly turns around and punches the man in the hat. Kane stands up, staring deeply at the other man. He runs outside the bar. Kane looks down at the man on the ground.

"You dropped your hat.' Kane said smiling.

Kane finishes his last glass of whisky and leaves the bar. Outside, he gets onto his horse and rides off into the forest, continuing his journey.

Kane arrives in London and heads for the church. Inside the church is the Priest, who knows Kane on a professional and personal manner. He hears a horse outside and from the door comes Kane.

"Didn't expect you so soon." The Priest said.

"When I'm on a journey, I arrive faster than expected.' Kane said. 'So, what do you have for me?"

The priest walks over into the office and leans toward the desk.

On the desk is a scroll. He hands the scroll to Kane, who opens it and reads it.

"From the look of this scroll, it seems Dr. Jekyll is on the loose again.' Kane said.

"It appears so.' The priest said. 'He was last spotted here in London. Which is why I contacted you."

"You want me to catch Dr. Jekyll and bring him to justice.' Kane said. 'I can do that, no problem."

"But, there is a catch, Gabriel.' The priest said. 'Jekyll has been seen as his alter-ego, Mr. Hyde."

"That should make it more exciting for me." Kane said.

"According to the local reports, Jekyll has been using his other persona to terrorize homes." The priest said. 'He has also even killed local civilians as well as their animals, if they owned farms, of course."

"Don't worry, old friend.' Kane said. 'I can take care of Jekyll and his big ego."

Kane thanked the priest. Leaving the church.

Outside Kane looks at the scroll and heads for the first location, East London. The sun is now setting as Kane travels to East London, during that period, Kane ran into a large pack of wolves. He passes them quickly them, though they chase him and his horse. Kane pulls out his pistols and begins firing at the wolves. He only kills two as the other three run off into the nearby woods.

The sun set and the moon arose, Kane arrived in East London. As he enters the location, the streets and surrounding are all but noisy. Usually around nighttime, the location would be crowded with individuals who would go out and have a good time with one another. But, Kane believes that everyone is in their homes only to avoid Dr. Jekyll's other half. Kane continues going through the location. He then notices a poster on a brick wall.

He gets off his horse and walks to the wall. He looks at the poster and sees an illustration of Jekyll's other half, Mr. Hyde. it's a Wanted, Dead or Alive poster.

"So, that's what he looks like." Kane said.

As he read the description of Hyde and as he reads it, he hears a loud scream. He runs over to his horse to track down the scream.

Kane's horse runs quickly toward the screaming. When Kane arrives he sees a man and a woman, laying on the ground, dead. Kane looks at their bodies, searching for any bite marks or animal wounds. Instead he only finds what appears to be saliva, from an unknown creature. Kane takes a sample of it and heads off, saying a prayer to the deceased man and woman. As Kane goes around the area, he sees a man on the side of the road. Wearing what appears to be a robe, his head covered with a hood.

"Excuse me.' Kane said. 'Do you know where I can find Dr. Jekyll?"

The man continues to stand still and silent, only throwing rocks into the nearby bay.

Kane gets off his horse and walks toward the man.

"I asked you a question, sir." Kane said.

Kane grabs the man and he turns around. Kane backs up, noticing that the man has no face.

"What the hell are you?" Kane said.

The man runs to Kane and knocks him down. The man pounces on top of Kane, trying to bite his face it seems. Kane struggles to get the man off and pulls out his dagger and stabs the man in the neck. The man falls to Kane's side as Kane gets to his feet and pulls the dagger out. Kane kneels and looks at the man, checking his features. Kane's very confused.

"What are you?" Kane said.

Kane leaves the body there and continued. In front of him, he sees an old abandoned church. He leaves the horse in front of the church as he enters. Inside the church, which is very, very old. From the look of the church, it hasn't been used in decades, maybe centuries, depending on how old the building is. Kane walks slowly on the wooden floor. His footsteps can be heard throughout the entire church. He reaches the upper floor and sees a man, sitting in the corner. He's not wearing a shirt, so Kane can only see him from behind. Kane stops and looks.

"Excuse me." Kane said. "Who are you and why are you here?"

"Leave me alone." The individual said. "I have peace here."

"Doesn't seem so." Kane said. "Tell me your name."

The man stands up and turns around, facing Kane.

"I am Dr. Jekyll." The individual said. "I know who you are, Gabriel Kane."

Kane pauses.

"Well, you know why I'm here." Kane said.

"You've come to take me out." Jekyll said. "Or should I say, you've come to take my other half out."

Kane walks slowly toward Jekyll, hands above him.

"Dr. Jekyll, let's not bring your big friend in here with us." Kane said. "He would cause a lot of trouble and damage."

"Well, it's too bad, Gabriel Kane." Jekyll said smiling. "Because he's already here."

Kane grabs Jekyll's arm and Jekyll hits Kane, knocking him across the room. Kane looks up and sees Jekyll transforming into Mr. Hyde. Now, Kane is staring in the eyes of Hyde.

"It's about time that wretched doctor let me out." Hyde said.

Kane stands up, facing Hyde. Hyde looks at Kane, smiling.

"Gabriel Kane!" Hyde said. "I'm a big fan of your work. Especially that time when you were in America. Great story."

"Hyde, we don't need any trouble here." Kane said. "Just let Jekyll out and we'll call it a night."

Hyde holds his chin, thinking. He looks down at Kane, who's only staring at him.

"Well?" Kane said.

"Nope!" Hyde mocked.

Hyde backhands Kane into the wall. Kane pulls out his pistols and begins firing at Hyde. He jumps around the room, avoiding the pistol shots. Kane stops firing as he sees Hyde in front of him, standing still.

"Ran out of ammo, Kane?" Hyde said smiling.

Kane runs toward Hyde and punches him. Hyde staggers, but catches Kane's next punch and slams him on the ground. Kane looks and sees Hyde's foot above him. Kane rolls out of the way as Hyde's foot goes into the floor, breaking the wood. Hyde sees that his foot is stuck in the broken wood. He desperately tries to pull it out as Kane attacks him with his rapier and cutlass. While Kane was attacking Hyde, he noticed that his saliva was similar to that of the deceased man and woman he previously saw. Hyde smacks Kane back and pulls his foot out of the wood. Hyde turns and sees Kane on the ground. He runs and jumps, Kane pulls out one pistol and aims it at Hyde. He fires and Hyde falls to the ground.

Kane looks and sees Hyde reverting to Jekyll. Kane turns him over on his back and sees that he shot him in the chest.

"Jekyll, I'm truly sorry." Kane said. "But, it was your doing."

"I shall thank you, Gabriel Kane." Jekyll said. "For now, I'm free."

"Yet, you are." Kane said.

"Though, I was meant to send you a message, if we ever came into contact." Jekyll said.

"Which is?"

"I've been under the control of Count Dracula. He's the reason why my alter ego has been causing havoc."

Dracula? Why tell me now?!"

"Because, if you were to kill me, he would like to see you. In fact, he's been wanting to meet you for a while now."

Kane watches as Jekyll gave up the ghost. He leaves him in the church and exits the building. He gets onto his horse, returning to the priest.

Kane returns to the priest and tells him that Dr. Jekyll is dead. The Priest looks at Kane with a little uncertainty. Kane walks toward a table, covered with a map of certain locations across Europe. Kane looks up and places his finger on one particular location. The Priest walks over and looks at the location.

"That's Transylvania, Gabriel." The Priest said.

"I am aware. Dr. Jekyll said Dracula desires to meet me. I intend on traveling to Transylvania to encounter him. Just to see what he wants."

"I do not know why Dracula would want to see you, Gabriel.

Unless, he requires you to do a bidding of his."

"I do a lot of biddings, you know that for sure." Kane said with a smirk.

Kane gathers more equipment and ammo before leaving the church. As Kane walks toward the door, he turns and faces the Priest. The Priest nods as Kane smiles, leaving the church. Outside, Kane rides the horse into the clear, quiet streets, that lead to the mountains.

Kane travels through the deserted streets, he reaches the mountains. According to the map, Transylvania lies just above the mountains. Kane looks up at the dark and foggy mountains, not seeing any source of a trail or lead to Transylvania or Dracula. Kane, instead makes a left turn, entering a small forest. Kane travels through the forest. It's quiet, and foggy. As Kane travels through, he stumbles upon a cemetery. Kane looks at the cemetery, as he looked he spots what appears to be a white dress running through the cemetery. Kane stops his horse and goes to look. He pulls out his pistols, walking slowly into the foggy cemetery.

"Mmm." Kane uttered. "Anybody here? I saw you."

A white mist passes from behind Kane as quick as a light. Kane turns, not seeing anything behind him. He continues walking deeper into the cemetery. He now spots something that looks like the dress he saw, standing behind the tree, covered in shadow. Kane walks to the tree.

"Excuse me." Kane said.

Kane looks and sees a woman, who appears as mist. Her face appears reminiscent of a skull. She looks at him and shrieks loudly. Kane covers his ears, trying to block out the loud and painful scream. She flies by Kane and knocks him down. Kane rolls over and starts firing at the mist, knowing that the pistol has no effect on the apparent ghost. Kane gets back on his feet and notices that there's two more mists flying around the cemetery. He spots one and pulls out his rapier sword.

"Who's first?" Kane said.

One mist flew toward him, screaming in pain. Kane ducks and

slices through the mist with his rapier. The mist screams and flies into the air. Kane spots the other two approaching him. He stands still, holding the rapier, preparing to slash them. As he raises the rapier, a bright light appears from behind him, causing the mists to fly off into the distant. The light dims and Kane turns, seeing a woman with long black hair and wearing Victorian attire. Kane looks and places his rapier by his side.

"What are you doing here?" The woman asked.

"I thought I saw someone out here.' Kane said. 'So, I went to look. Who are you?'

"My name is Victoria Gretchen. Descendant of the Gretchen Liege."

"I've heard of that name before. I'm Gabriel Kane. What are you doing out here?"

"I was traveling through the forest, until I heard that shriek. So, I came to see what the problem and the problem was just you."

"I'm not the problem, miss. I'm looking for a way to Transylvania and to Dracula."

"You're looking for Dracula?" Victoria said.

"Do you have any clue where I can reach Transylvania?" Kane asked. "I heard that it's behind these mountains. Is that the case?"

"Transylvania is indeed behind those mountains.' Victoria said. 'But, if that's where you're going, you'll need my assistance."

"I'm sorry, miss. But, I work alone. It's what I do best."

Victoria smiles as Kane looks at her weary.

"Well, now you'll have to deal with a traveling teammate. First, we need to reach the lower town. To the east."

"Why the lower town? What's there that we could use?"

"The villagers know the exact trail to Transylvania. Besides, it's where I live."

Kane and Victoria head off into the darkness toward the lower town.

It is now daylight, cloudy morning as Kane and Victoria arrive at the lower town. Villagers roam the main town area, buying food and supplies. Kane looks around the area.

"I don't see how you could live here." Kane said.

"Why is that?" Victoria said.

"Because you don't seem to fit here. By your appearance, it doesn't seem that you could be living here."

"For one, I grew up here as a child. I was born in London, but my family decided that the city wasn't their type of standards. What about yourself, Kane?"

"Never really knew my blood family. Such is a very long story."

Victoria walks toward an old building, that appears to be housed of elderly villagers. Kane walks behind her, as the villagers look and stare at him. Some appear as if they are afraid of him. Kane follows Victoria through the building.

"These people seem to fear me. I do not know why."

"The people across this land know who you are and what you've done. You might not know this, but, you're famous to them."

"I don't see how. I'm only a monster hunter and ufologist. I don't see how that's being called famous. I would suspect ridicule or distain. Some form of persecution would do nicely."

"Trust me, it's around."

Victoria finds a wooden box in the corner of the building. She walks over and pulls out a key, opening the box. Kane walks toward her and looks into the box. He sees a large amount of ammo and weapons.

"Where did these come from?" Kane said.

"They were my father's. Like yourself, my father was on a quest to find Dracula some time ago. Unfortunately, he didn't succeed in finding him."

"Sorry about that. Well, for now, we can accomplish your father's goal. You and I."

Victoria turned, staring at Kane.

"At first, you wanted to do this alone. Now, you want to do this with me. Someone had a change of heart or something?"

"No." Kane said. "It's just that since your father was on the same journey as I, it would be suiting that you can be involved as well.

Achieving your father's goal."

"I see."

They look throughout the box, sounds of screams are heard from the outside. Victoria and Kane run to the front door, leading to the outside. They reach the outside and see villagers running in panic as a swarm of vampires chase them. Killing the ones that can't run as fast.

"Vampires!" Kane said. "They belong to Dracula."

"Who else could own an army of vampires." Victoria said. "Come on!"

Victoria and Kane attack the vampires. Kane fires at them with his pistol, shooting one in its wing, causing it to crash into a house. Victoria pulls out a pistol from her back and shoots one vampire in the head. She fires at the others surrounding both her and Kane. Kane reloads one pistol and a vampire lands in front of him. Kane goes for a punch, the vampire catches his fist and kicks him in the stomach, knocking him into a wall. Victoria looks and fires at the vampire, hitting it in the shoulder. Kane stands up and runs toward the vampire. Kane punches the vampire and pulls out his rapier sword, slicing the vampire in two.

"Good one." Victoria said.

They continue fighting off the remaining vampires. Kane reaches into his trench coat pocket, pulling out a small bottle of water. One vampire spot it and screeches toward the other vampires. They turn and fly off into the sky. Victoria, confused, turns to Kane. Spotting the Holy Water in his hand.

"They fled." Victoria said.

"I noticed. Probably the water.'

"One of their primary weaknesses." Victoria said. "Along with the cross."

"Not exactly. The cross is a dud. Takes a stronger force to eliminate them. Believe me, I've seen it."

Kane looks around, seeing the villagers surrounding both him and Victoria.

"It was them!" A villager yelled. 'They brought that plaque upon us!"

"No!" Victoria yelled. "We did not. You all know for a fact that vampires have always entered this location to feed. This was only one of their outings."

Kane walks toward Victoria. Looking around the area for any signs of the vampires. He also looks at the number of villagers that surround him and Victoria.

"Do you have any idea where those vampires fled?" Kane asked.

"They went east." Victoria said. "If we follow them, they should lead us to Dracula."

"Good."

After gathering the gear out of the box, Victoria and Kane left the lower town, following the trail of blood left from a few fleeing vampires. After hours of tracking, the trail leads them to a small cave. They enter the cave, its dark, damp, and cold. The only sound throughout the cave is the sound of water flowing in the darkness.

"What could possibly live in here?" Victoria said.

"Anything from rodents to dragons." Kane said.

"Dragons?" Victoria said with a stare.

"Yeah, I've ran into a few one time." Kane said.

Kane takes one step forward, he feels something rough under his boot. He stops and looks down as Victoria stops behind him.

"Kane, what is it?" Victoria said.

"This isn't rock I'm standing on. Something else."

Kane looks down and sees a scaly tail. He jumps off and the tail slithers deeper into the cave. Victoria goes to turn back to the entrance. Kane grabs her by the arm, not letting her leave the cave.

"What are you doing?!" Victoria said. "You've seen the size of that tail?!"

"I've faced worse throughout my lifetime. Come on, we need to find out what's at the end of this cave."

They walk further down into the cave. They reach an apparent dead-end, Victoria turns to Kane. He looks around not finding another way around the dead end. He looks behind Victoria and sees the scaly tail. He points to that direction and follows it. Victoria turns and runs behind Kane. Kane runs as he follows to keep track of the tail. He turns from corner to corner, following the tail. Victoria tries to keep up with him.

"Slow down, Kane."

"This tail is leading us somewhere! 'We have to find out where!"

Kane turns one final corner before facing the creature that the tail belonged to. Victoria runs behind him and stops as she sees the huge scaly creature staring at her and Kane. Kane pulls out his rapier, staring at the scaled beast. The creature roars at them with its wings flapping. Kane holds his hat as the wind is so intense.

"What is this beast?!" Victoria screamed.

"It appears to be a Basilisk with wings. Dragon wings at most." Kane said. "I've never believed in these things."

Kane raises his pistol and fires at the beast. The shot had grazed the beast's head, just above the right eye. It shakes its head and rams over into Kane, knocking him down. Victoria raises her sword and starts to stab the creature. It roars in pain as she continues diving the sword into its side. The beast swipes Victoria across the small area of the cave. Kane jumps onto the beast, trying to reach for its head. The beast shakes Kane off and tries to bite his leg, only for Victoria to run over and cut the tongue of the beast.

"Great work." Kane said.

The beast staggers as blood dripped from its mouth. It rams toward Victoria, exiting the small area of the cave. Kane walks over to her, helping her up. As she gets to her feet, she looks behind Kane, noticing a locked wooden door.

"There's a door." Victoria said.

She runs over to the door. As she notices a chained lock on the handle. Kane pulls out his pistol and shoots the lock off of the door handle. Victoria looks at him as he opens the wooden door. Behind the door is a small tunnel with light at the end. They walk towards the light and as they get closer, they can hear a man talking. They decide to run towards the light. Once they reached the end, they noticed that they were in a castle corridor. Kane looks to his left and turns to his right, he spots a male, wearing nothing but black turn the corner.

"This way." Kane said.

They follow the man in black to his location. Once they found the location, the man was standing in the middle of the room, covered in marble, with a huge window at the front, overlooking the front of the entire castle as the moon shined down upon it.

"It appears you have been looking for me, Gabriel Kane." The man said.

Kane pauses and looks at Victoria, who is speechless.

"Who are you?" Kane said.

The man turns around and stares at Kane with a smile. Victoria's facial expression shows that she knows exactly who the man in black really is.

"It's him.' Victoria said softly.

"Dracula." Kane said with a determined voice.

Kane stares directly toward Dracula. Their eyes locked on one another. Kane's hand slowly reaching for his pistol. Dracula stares deeply through Kane, smirking.

"Reaching for your pistol, Gabriel Kane." Dracula said.

"How do you know me? We've never met."

"I know everything that's needed to know. Besides, I've heard a lot about you. Your days over in the States during their Civil War, you're time against the Shogun's undead and their captive extraterrestrials."

"How do you know this?"

"I also remember you facing those demons with the Finder and taking on the Wolfman. You've been through a lot of trials at such a young age."

"All you need to know is that I've come here to kill you."

Dracula walks toward Kane, slowly. Kane raises up his pistol and aims it directly at Dracula's heart.

"Go on. Shoot me. Shoot me and you would've accomplished what you came for."

Kane holds the pistol, still aiming at Dracula's heart. Victoria looks at Dracula walking toward Kane as she turns to Kane, forcing him to shoot Dracula. Kane is caught in a daze as he doesn't understand how Dracula knows his history.

"GABRIEL!" Dracula yelled. "SHOOT ME! END MY LIFE AS YOU WISHED!"

Kane fires, shooting Dracula in the heart. Dracula stumbles as

Kane and Victoria watch. Dracula stands still and rubs the wound. He turns to Kane, laughing. Kane and Victoria start to worry as Dracula was not wounded from the shot.

"What is this? I shot you in the chest!"

"I'm not like your past adversaries, Gabriel. I am beyond what you fully understand!"

Kane pulls out his rapier and starts to slash at Dracula. He dodges every move from Kane. Dracula moves toward the left of Kane, he grabs him by his coat and slams him into the brick wall.

"Highly determined to kill me." Dracula said. "But, you don't fully understand."

Victoria pulls out her sword and stabs Dracula from behind. He stands still, laughing at Victoria. He reaches toward his back, pulling out the sword. Victoria backs up slowly as Dracula turns toward her and tosses her back the sword. She catches it and stares. Dracula bows before her.

"Impressive, my lady. Impressive indeed."

She runs toward Dracula. Delivering kicks and punches at him. He's quickly dodging them. He moves to the right and kicks her in the abdomen, knocking her into the wall behind her. As he walks toward her, behind him, Kane is staggering to get to his feet. Kane reaches into his pocket and pulls out the water. As Dracula walks slowly toward a downed Victoria, Kane lunges at Dracula. Kane opens the bottle and pours all of the water onto Dracula's face. Dracula shakes and twitches on the ground, clawing at his face and body. Victoria gets to her feet and stands on the side of Kane, watching Dracula on the ground. After a quick second, Dracula stops moving and turns his head, looking at Kane and Victoria. He smiles at them and laughs.

"Blessed Water." Dracula said. "Good choice. Too bad it doesn't work."

Kane slowly backs up, looking at Victoria.

"I thought the water would have an effect on him." Victoria uttered.

"It appears that it doesn't. We need to figure out something else."

"Agreed."

Kane runs toward Dracula and slams him into the ground. Kane gets over him and starts to pummel Dracula with punches. Victoria watches on as Kane continues beating Dracula to a pulp. Dracula doesn't even attempt to counter an attack as he only laughs as Kane pummels him.

"Why won't you die?!" Kane yelled.

"I am already dead! I would expect you to have known that before you've come to see me."

Dracula shoves Kane and kicks him into the air and watches as he falls to the ground, grunting. Dracula gets to his feet, walking slowly toward Kane on the ground. Kane reaches for his pistol, but Dracula speeds over and snatches it.

"Your guns won't do you any good. For you have already attempted its use upon me."

Dracula walks toward the windows and looks outside at the full moon rising above the clouds. He turns toward Kane as Victoria runs over to him, helping him up slowly, as he appears to be bleeding from the mouth.

"I believe that we should save this for another time, yes." Dracula said as he opens up the windows.

He looks back again at Kane and Victoria. They notice that he's transforming. Giant leathery wings span out from behind him. His head starts to change shape, as his teeth sharper and his eyes turn red as blood. Dracula has now fully transformed into a giant humanoid bat. He screeches at them and flies out the windows. Kane runs over to the windows, seeing Dracula in the sky, flying off into the distant, trailing the moonlight.

"This isn't over." Kane declared with intention. "This is definitely not over."

WEREWOLVES AND VAMPIRES

1890
EUROPE

Late October of 1890, sightings of Dracula have risen to an extreme, so extreme that the Venatores have sent Gabriel Kane to follow these sightings to track Dracula down. Kane's ultimate goal is to kill Dracula and vanquish him from the earth, now he has that opportunity in searching for him and his supposedly new castle in the mountains of Europe.

Kane decided to travel through the valleys, where the first sightings surfaced. He spotted old homes and carts but saw nor heard anyone. As his horse slowly walked through the small pairs of homes. The surroundings were silent. Only the whistling of the cold. Kane knew this was uncommon, especially in the location which he moves through. Without notice, a small gang of vampires, dressed in villager clothing bolt out from the bushes around Kane and move to attack him. Kane revealed his rapier and started to slash the vampires with the silver blade. The vampires scurried away from the scene, in fear of the blade. Kane placed the blade into its sheath and continued. Moving further out of the valleys, he hears a sound in the tress nearby.

"More of them." He said, believing them to be the vampires again.

Upon moving closer, his vision went black as he was attacked from behind and dragged away.

Kane awoke from the fall from the trap. He saw Victoria and Tom to his left, all of them tied to chairs with their hands behind their backs. Kane scouted the surroundings, knowing they're inside a cabin. He saw his weapons and gear sitting on a wooden table not too far from himself. Kane pulled himself over toward the table. As he moved, he caught the sound of the cabin door opening and closing. He moved himself back, seeing a young man and woman. They walked in and stared at Kane, the young woman stared at Kane, running to him with a knife in her hand.

"What were you doing over here?!" The young woman yelled.

"Relax." The young man said. "He's not going anywhere. He's tied up."

"Why am I tied up?" Kane asked. "Who are you two?"

"We're what people like you should fear." The young woman said.

"We're called the Night Watchers." The young man said. "We scout the night to stop any monsters or creatures from causing harm to the living."

Kane nodded.

"So, you're telling me you have no idea who I am?" Kane said. "Not an ounce of a clue?"

"It doesn't matter who you or your people are." The young woman said. "What matters is why were the three of you out at this time of night."

Victoria slowly moved as she began to regain consciousness. When she began to have a clear view of the area, she saw the young man and woman and realized she's tied to the chair by her wrists.

"Where am I? Who are you people?"

"Like we told your friend over there, we're the Night Watchers." The young woman said.

"What do you want from us?" Victoria said.

"We want answers, damn it!" The young woman said. "Nothing less than that!"

Tom woke up from the young woman's yelling. She looked to

him. He attempted to move as well, but couldn't because of the tied ropes.

"What the devil is this?" Tom asked. "Where am I? Kane? Victoria?"

"I'm going to ask this question again." The young woman said. "Who are you people and what were you doing out this late?"

They heard the front door open and in walked an middle-aged man, wearing a gray hat and coat. The young man and woman turn and move to the side of the cabin as the man walks over to the three. He looked at them and stopped at Kane. Squinting his eyes to get a better look.

"I know you." The man said. "You're Gabriel Kane, the monster hunter and ufologist. Word travels abroad about your achievements and adventures."

"Wait, he is?" The young woman said.

"Indeed." The man said. "Riley, please untie them."

The young man and woman untie Kane, Victoria, and Tom. Kane stands up and goes for his weapons and gear as the man walks over to him.

"It's an honor to meet a legend in our field." The man said.

"Legend?" Kane said. "I'm just doing what needs to be done."

"Sorry about them tying you and your people up." The man said. "They're very strict when it comes to trespassers."

"So, what your name?" Kane said.

"I'm Raymond Rogers." The man said. "The young girl is Riley Hazelwood and the young man is Connor Hartley."

"Sorry about yelling at you." Riley said.

"Don't bother. You were just doing what needed to be done."

Raymond watched Kane set up his gear.

"If you don't mind, Kane, where were you three headed off to?" Raymond asked.

"Looking for Dracula's new castle. Sightings have surfaced and we intend on ending them and Dracula permanently."

"Funny you say such a thing." Raymond said.

"Why is that?" Kane said.

"Because that's who we're hunting down as well." Connor said.

"The big baddie himself."

"That so?" Victoria said. "You know of Dracula and his intentions?"

"Of course, ma'am." Raymond said. "We do what must be done. That's the reason why we're out here."

"So, I take it you do it your way and I do this my way." Kane said. "That way, neither of us will get in each other's way."

"The guy is smart for a change." Riley said.

"Why don't we all travel together." Connor said. "The more of us there is, the easier it will be to track down Dracula and get past his army."

"Dracula now has a pack of werewolves at his disposal." Kane said. "By that count lots of people will be easily tracked down by them."

"Not if we're skilled." Riley said. "I'm good with a sword. Some slicing would do us a service out there against his forces."

"I have the bow and arrow to back it up." Connor said. "Quick and quiet is my asset."

Kane looks at them and turns to Raymond.

"What about yourself?' Kane said. "What field are you useful in terms of weapons?"

"I'm one of the greatest gunslingers and occultist that ever lived in Europe." Raymond said. 'I can hold my own and then some. You'll see when we head out there."

Kane nodded.

"Fair enough." Kane said. "Let's all go hunting."

They grab their weapons and gear and leave the cabin. As they walk outside of the cabin, a gray werewolf lurks at them from atop a small hill and runs off into the woods.

The werewolf climbed up massive amounts of hills and reached a castle. One of old construction. Gothic in nature, yet ancient. As it climbed the castle, it reached the top floor and on top stood Dracula. The werewolf paused and stood still in front of Dracula and was intimidated by his presence.

"What do you have for me on this day." Dracula said. "Anything useful to decipher."

He walked over to the werewolf, glaring into its eyes. By doing such, he saw Kane, Victoria, and Tom speaking with the Night Watchers and leaving the cabin.

"It seems Gabriel has more company. It won't matter very long."

Dracula turned to one of his assistants. Staring toward them with his glaring eyes.

"Command the herd to track them down. Make sure they kill them."

He turned back toward the werewolf. Petting it on its head.'

"You're doing a very good service for your lord. Now, go back out there to help the herd track them and bring some backup with you."

The werewolf climbed onto the wall, jumping from the roof as Dracula grinned, over viewing the valley.

Kane and the Watchers walked throughout the woods, not spotting anything that seems to be vampire or werewolf relatable. Keeping their eyes closely to their surroundings. Which were dark and only to be seen with the glimpses of moonlight.

"Haven't ran into anything yet." Connor said.

"Keep your eyes open, young one." Raymond said. "Be at your guard at all times."

From the woods, bolted out a small army of vampires. Snarling with their teeth toward them. They stood together, forming a circle in front of the vampires. Kane held his gun out in front as did the others.

"When they come for us, fire." Kane said. "Make sure to aim for their heads."

"We've done this before." Riley said. "This isn't some new thing for us."

"Show some decency, Riley." Raymond said. "Do as the man said."

The vampires lunged at them, they fired their guns toward the vampires with Riley slicing them with her sword and Connor shooting arrows into their heads and mouths.

"Take this." Connor said, firing an arrow into a vampire's mouth.

Using the techniques they know, they eliminate the vampires and nod toward each other in their small victory. Upon walking away, Kane turned seen three werewolves staring them down from atop a hill in the distance.

"We're not finished yet." Kane said to the group as they gazed toward the three werewolves atop the hill.

"What should we do?" Victoria said.

"If they start running down and lunge, we kill them. But they seem to be of a different mission."

"What do you mean a different mission?" Riley said. "You mean they're not here to kill us?"

"They could if they wanted to. But it appears they're up to something else."

The werewolves continue to stare down at Kane, Victoria, Tom, and the Watchers. As they slowly crawl down the hill toward them, snarling with saliva dripping from their mouths and their fowl stench inching closer, Raymond turned to Kane.

"So, what do we do now?!" Raymond said.

"We fight if they run down." Kane said. "Kill them just as we did with those vampires."

The werewolves seem to prepare themselves for the attack, but immediately pause and run away, whining, as if they were startled. Catching Kane and the group off their guard, they look around for the werewolves and cannot find them anywhere.

"Where did they go?" Riley said.

"They ran off." Kane said. "But, why?"

Stomping sounds are heard coming from behind Kane and the group. To which they turn around to see and find themselves face to face with hybrid creatures. Drooling and snarling at them.

"The hell are those?!" Connor said.

"I know what they are." Kane said. "They're called the Beast Folk. Human and animal hybrid creations."

"Created by whom?" Victoria said.

"I know a guy."

The Beast Folk roar as they run toward Kane and the group, who are already prepared for the fight ahead.

Meanwhile, at the castle, Carmilla sits with Dracula inside of his main room, gazing out through the windows, overseeing the mountains with the moon above them. She slowly places her arm across Dracula's shoulders and kisses him on his cheek. He chuckled and shook his head.

"No need to try and seduce me, Carmilla. You know that I am already dead and not alive. Also, I am aware that you have no interest in the pleasures of men."

"With time, many things can change."

"Not things such as we have spoken. It appears you want to say something to me."

"I have a proposition for you, if you would like to hear it."

"I am listening."

"I thought since you're planning on ruling this world and I am here to witness it take full circle. How about we both rule the world? A dual ruler-ship?"

"Dual ruler-ship?" Dracula said. "You must be joking with me."

"I am not joking with you, Lord Dracula. I am being completely honest with you on this one."

"Very well, Carmilla. I will be completely honest with you when I say no."

"No?"

"That's right. No. This world is only meant to be ruled by one individual and that individual will be me."

Dracula turned and walked away from the windows. Tossing Carmilla's arm from his shoulders. She gazed at him with anger, but pressed it down as she wanted to see the outcome of the long-term planning.

"Carmilla, focus on your part and everything will go as planned."

In the woods near the mountains and hills, Kane and the group battle it out with the Beast Folk. Many have already been killed by the group and only two of them stand remaining. Kane tackles one and shoots it in the head, while Victoria and Raymond deal with the other Beast.

"Just kill the thing!" Kane said.

Victoria raised up her sword and chopped the head of the Beast completely off its body. Its head rolled across the dirt and the surroundings were silent.

"What person would create such abominations?" Raymond said.

"Doctor Moreau." Kane said. "He's working with Dracula."

They continued to walk through the woods, nearing the mountains in the horizon. Upon coming close to the mountains, they find themselves near a large body of water and atop the water laid an island. With a large structure upon it. Kane looked up and pointed toward the island.

"What is that up there?" Kane said.

The group looked up toward the island. Uncertain of what to make if it. Victoria looked and could recognize the structure. She turned to Kane, while looking at the large and tall structure.

"Kane, it's a castle."

"A castle?" Thomas said. "Who's castle?"

"I may have an idea as to who resides on in that castle."

"What do you mean by that?"

"That would explain why those Beast Folk came at us so easily. We were near their place of creation. That island is the Island of Moreau.

Kane and his crew reach the island. An island that's known for Doctor Moreau's creations. They walk toward the large building.

"Is this where Moreau's Beast-Folk were created?" Riley said.

"Some." Kane said. "This island appears to be the place for the other work he's had a hand in occupying."

Kane bolted through the front entrance, entering the main laboratory. Only finding old remains of surgeon tables and doctoral tools, Kane gazed the area continually, spotting two doors, both lead deeper into the building.

"He's not here?" Victoria asked.

"Doesn't appear to be." Kane replied. "However, those two doors could give us the answers we need."

"So, we'll have to split up." Riley said. "Easy tracking."

"As it may be." Raymond said.

"Very well." Kane replied. "Myself, Raymond, and Tom will check the left door. Victoria, you, Riley, and Connor will search the right door."

"And what if we don't find anything?" Conner asked.

"We all return to this spot. We'll give out details if we find any then."

The groups split and went there separate ways. Behind the left door waited a long hallway. Kane nodded as they entered. On the right, waited another hallway, yet, with doors on both sides. Unsure if they were entrances to other labs, restrooms, bedrooms, or anything else of such nature. Victoria shook her head as they entered. Riley kept his right hand on the handle of her sword. Connor had his bow ready with an arrow already in place.

Kane, Raymond, and Tom continued moving stealthy down the left hallway. Not seeing any doors or any exit points in their reach. Tom was frightened of what could happen. Raymond had his revolvers in hand, Kane was prepared for a fight. Whether it were against a vampire, werewolf, or another beast folk.

"I must ask." Tom said, gazing around. "What happens if we don't find Doctor Moreau?"

"What do you mean?" Kane asked.

"Well, if he's not here, then, where will he be?"

"He could be somewhere roaming the area for all we know." Raymond said. "I'm positive he wouldn't go too far from this place."

"Maybe he would." Kane said.

"Why is that?" Tom asked.

"He's working with Dracula. If he needed a quick place to hide or to continue his work in secrecy, Dracula's castle is the perfect hiding spot. The perfect place to create monsters of his own making."

"Yes." Raymond added. "And, if he were to create monsters under Dracula's rule, those beasts could very well form Dracula's new army."

"An army of vampires, werewolves, and beast folk?" Tom said. "This isn't going very well is it."

"It's certainly not."

Meanwhile, on the right side, Victoria, Riley, and Connor search the rooms within the hallway. Only finding them to be closet spaces for surgery tools, some restrooms, and one storage room.

"I must ask, why are the two of you with the older man?"

"Because he saved us." Riley said.

"Saved you? From what?"

"A werewolf attack." Connor said. "Our parents were ambushed by werewolves. Raymond appeared and saved us.'

"You're brother and sister?"

"No." Riley said. "We lived in the same village. The werewolf had appeared and slaughtered most of the villagers. My family was killed first before Connor's. Raymond saved us and believed we needed to be watched over. So, he took us in as one of his own."

"And the monster hunting?"

"Once we were older, Raymond told us of his profession. Hunting monsters. That explained why he appeared in the village during the attack. We've never seen him before that. So, in order to protect us, he trained us. I learned how to wield a sword. Connor grew in the skill of archery."

"I see."

"After our training, we went out with Raymond on hunts." Connor said. "Saving lives and killing monsters. We were given the name 'The Night Watchers' because of our efforts."

Victoria nodded.

"Do either of you miss the childhood days or do you wish you didn't have to live this life?"

"I've grown into this." Riley said. "I'm better off protecting others from what I suffered."

"And I loved the thrill of the hunt." Connor smirked. "Vampires, werewolves, gargoyles, anything that's a challenge makes this all worthwhile."

While walking on the checkered floors, Connor spotted another door in front of them. Directly in place, a two-door entrance to another room.

"Maybe, something's in there." Connor said.

"As always." Riley added. "We'll have to check it out."

"Agreed." Victoria replied.

Opening the double-doors, they find themselves in a large room. Not as large as the front laboratory. But, within they see tables. Long tables lined up parallel to each other. Victoria looked around and knew what the room was.

"This place is a dining hall."

"A dining hall?" Connor said. "In a dump like this."

"I'm guessing this was a place for scientists before they left it." Riley said.

"It seems so."

Checking out the beaten-down hall, a stumbling sound of glass shattered behind them. They turned with quick pace as the double-doors shut. Connor raised up the bow, Riley twirled the sword, Victoria held his blade. Each was ready for the fight. Connor looked around, not seeing anything in the darkness. Only the moon was the light source.

"Do you hear that?" Riley asked.

They listened and what they could hear were footsteps. Each step inching closer. They manage to look and standing before them was one of the beast folk, standing approximately seven-feet in height, and its skin torn and hairy, upper body was of a man. The lower was of a goat... A Satyr-Man. Victoria jolted with the blade in place, Riley held the sword still, Connor fired an arrow. The arrow pierced the Satyr-Man in the arm. It pulled the arrow from its body and shrieked. Lunging toward them. Connor moved from its path and fired another arrow while Riley ran up toward the creature, slashing it with her sword. Victoria wielded her blade and attacked the creature from behind, Riley took the front, and Connor circled the Satyr-Man. Each one delivering attacks on the creature. The Satyr-Man swiped its arm toward Riley, who ducked down and slashed the ankles of the creature. The beast folk fell to one knee, where Victoria jumped on its back, stabbing it in many places. Connor ran up and fired two arrows into the eyes of the creature. The Satyr-Man knocked Victoria from its back and ran forward, impaling itself into Riley's sword. The creature still attempted to grab Riley and eventually died due to the sword impaled through its heart and the amount of blood that had fallen.

"See." Connor said. "That was a challenge."

"What kind of creature was that?" Riley asked.

"One of Moreau's experiments." Victoria replied. "Come on, we need to tell the others."

Upon them returning to the lab, they found them already waiting on them. Now regrouped, they each told one another of their findings. Kane, Raymond, and Tom found nothing. No sign of Moreau. Victoria told Kane of their encounter with the Satyr-Man and their lack of finding Moreau. Kane took all the information in and quickly knew where the doctor was located.

"We need to go to Dracula's castle. They're all there."

"I must ask." Connor said. "What if they're waiting on us to come?"

"Then, it makes this task very easy."

The following day, word had spread to the neighboring lands of strange activities of a sudden arrival of a strange and dark castle atop Mount Elbrus.

Within the castle, Dracula waited patiently, staring out of the large open window. Carmilla approached him from behind, gazing out toward the small village and snowy range of the mountain.

"Have you done what you've offered to do?" Dracula asked.

"I have. The armies are prepared and ready for your command." Dracula nodded.

"Excellent. Because we have guests in a matter of time."

"Guests?" Carmilla questioned. "You speak of the hunter and his allies?"

"Who else do I speak of. I'm positive they visited the Doctor's island and found not him. Therefore, Gabriel Kane knows he's here with us and they're coming."

"Perhaps I can make a distraction. A diversion of sorts. Weaken them for you."

Dracula turned to Carmilla and agreed. She exited the room and right after came Moreau. Hesitant to speak with Dracula. But, it would be necessary if he did.

"You've heard the news haven't you?" Dracula asked.

"I am aware the hunters invaded my island and entered my laboratory. The signals have went off."

"And you are aware hey are headed here. To find us all and eliminate us."

"I figured such a thing would happen. It explains the vampire and werewolf armies outside at the gates.

"What of your beast folk?"

"What of them, my lord?"

"Are they ready for the fight to come?"

"Oh, yes." Moreau grinned. "They are ready."

"Then, make way."

Moreau bowed and left Dracula to himself, who continued to look outside. Patiently awaiting the arrival of Kane.

After some mere hours of travel, Kane and the group stood at the entrance to the small town. There, the townspeople rushed toward him, telling him of the strange castle that stood on Mount Elbrus. Victoria turned to Kane, while gazing up at the mountain in the distance, they could see the castle for themselves.

"He's there." Kane said. "He's in there right now. Looking down at us."

"How can you be sure he's looking at us?" Riley asked.

"I just know."

Just as Kane said, Dracula was indeed looking down toward them. Still in the same place as he was hours before. Only, this time, he felt a jolt go through his body. Dracula shrugged the pain away.

"He's here. He's down there."

Kane and the group prepared to make way toward the mountain. Knowing that the possibility of reaching it during sunup is a slight chance. More so, they estimate their arrival at the gate of the castle directly at nightfall, which will cause more trouble for them in the form of vampires and werewolves. Not to mention Moreau's beast folk.

"How do we proceed?" Tom wondered. "Do we just walk in or do we move quietly?"

"We'll manage." Kane said. "It's going to take all of us to enter the castle. Just leave Dracula to me."

"Understood." Tom replied.

"And what of the vampires, werewolves, and those other things?" Connor asked. "We'll handle them I suppose."

"We must." Raymond said. "For we can only wonder what else dwells in such a dark place."

"Very well." Kane said. "Let's get moving."

After some travel, they arrived at the base of Elbrus, looking up at the dark and gothic structure that was the castle. Kane was ready. He blood was pumping, ready to face Dracula. Victoria could sense Kane's anger searing.

"I would keep that inside until you have the opportune moment."

"I agree."

Tom looked up toward the sky and noticed something strange to himself. He pointed, giving signal to the others.

"What is that?" He asked.

Coming down from the sky above hem was Carmilla and six other vampires. Screeching loudly as they made landfall. Carmilla stood in front of them, facing the group. Her smile was beautiful and sinister. Kane pulled out his rapier as did the others.

"Who is she?" Riley asked.

"I am Carmilla, my dear. And you look so beautiful."

"I'm not taking that compliment."

"No bother. Soon, I'll be taking all of you."

"Enough." Kane said. "Where's your boss?"

"My boss?! Gabriel, if you only knew. This is the both of us combined. Our union will shake the foundations of this world and build a new one. One of monsters."

"There's too many humans to make that a possibility." Victoria said.

"Try it when they refuse to fight for themselves."

"We'll fight for them." Connor said.

Carmilla chuckled.

"How kind of you. Take them!"

The vampires went in for the attack. Swiping their clawed hands and talons across the air above them. Kane raised his rapier and slash one's leg. Victoria and Riley managed to bring down two more. Leaving the other three to Tom, Raymond, and Connor. Connor fired several arrows into one, leading it to crash into the snow. Raymond took out his revolvers and shot one in the head.

"This is a trick." Raymond said.

Tom threw a knife toward the last one, but missed.

"Oh dear." Tom uttered.

The vampire rushed toward him and as it inched closer, Kane jumped in between them, stabbing the creature before it could slash Tom's neck. The vampires were defeated. Carmilla applauded them and flew away.

"After her!" Kane yelled.

They chased Carmilla toward the castle. Moving closer and closer. As they were almost near the entrance. Several of Moreau's beast folk appeared. Halting their progress. Raymond, Riley, and Connor stood against them. Their weapons ready.

"Go!" Raymond yelled to Kane. "We'll hold them off!"

Kane nodded with respect as he, Victoria, and Tom went off to the castle gate. Behind them, they could hear the gunfire, arrows flying, and a sword slashing.

"I hope they make it." Tom said.

"They can take care of themselves." Kane added. "They'll be fine."

Right when they entered the castle, Carmilla flew up and standing before them was Moreau, twirling his hands.

"I am delighted you've come."

"Where's Dracula?" Kane asked.

"He's here. But, you'll only get to him if you can kill my most prized creation."

Walking into the open room was a tall figure. It appeared humanoid, yet, it was hairy and with it came the smell of blood and water.

"The hell is that?" Tom said.

"It is what I call a Vamp-Wolf!" Moreau yelled. "And, it is not alone."

Behind the creature came three werewolves. One grey, another black, and the last one brown. Moreau ran out of the room in a hurry. Kane was agitated to the point where it was everything or nothing. He went for the Vamp-Wolf with his rapier, swiping its chest and legs. The creature backhanded Kane and Victoria went in for the attack herself. Tom was chased around by the werewolves, leading to Kane killing one and standing before the other two. Victoria kicked the beast and the creature grabbed her, throwing her against Kane. During the fight, Dracula entered the room, hoping to gain a closer look and Kane turned to see him.

"Gabriel Kane." Dracula said. "We meet again."

"For the last time." Kane replied.

"Then come. Come and end my life as you desire."

Kane went for Dracula and was snatched by Carmilla from the air and tossed into the wall. Tom saw Dracula walking in the midst of the battles, he reached into his pocket, revealing a small dagger made of silver. Kane stood up, shaking himself. Victoria managed to kill a werewolf while dodging the claws of the Vamp-Wolf. Tom moved quietly behind Dracula, raising the dagger and as it came down, Carmilla grabbed his arm.

"No, my dear. That is not going to happen."

Tom dropped the dagger, Kane saw it fall and it gave him a opening. Possibly. Carmilla held Tom up off the ground, ripping his cloak to reveal his neck. She could feel the blood pulsing through him and it moisturized her. She opened her mouth, unveiling the sharp fangs.

"I need some help over here!" Tom yelled in panic.

Kane grabbed the dagger and Carmilla went for the bite.

However, Tom had another blade and pierced it in the heart of Carmilla. She paused with a shocking jolt. Her eyes turned from black to white. The fangs reverted. She dropped Tom and fell to the ground. Dracula watched on. He nodded.

"Impressive from a friar of such low nature."

Kane rushed toward the Vamp-Wolf, stabbing it with the dagger. Victoria jumped up and beheaded the creature. Its body fell as the one werewolf remained. Lunging toward Victoria, only to be shot by Kane's revolver. The room was paused. Dracula clapped his hands in their victory.

"You three are very skilled in the art of the kill. How can you manage such a foe as myself? I can only reveal in battle and in your deaths."

Raymond, Riley, and Connor entered the room, seeing Kane and Dracula facing off. Connor fired an arrow toward the vampire lord. Dracula caught the arrow with ease, breaking it into small shards of wood.

"You're not fit for this kind of challenge, boy."

"This is between you and me." Kane said. "Just us."

"Indeed. But, by the way you look, you're tired. Beaten. I don't want to kill you at your lowest. I want you at your best."

"What are you saying?"

"I will come to you when you are in your best shape. Then, we will battle."

"NO!" Kane went for a shot and Dracula was gone. "Dammit!"

After a bit of calming down, they returned to the small town. Connor looked up at the mountain and noticed the castle was gone. As if it had never been there. Kane knew Dracula moved it. He and Raymond shook hands.

"Are you sure you don't need us to help you in this endeavor?" Raymond asked.

"I'll find him." Kane replied. "It's fate."

Raymond nodded.

"May you kill him for the best."

The Night Watchers left. Tom approached Kane as did Victoria.
"I have to ask, besides finding Dracula, what is next?"
"Finding Dracula." Kane said. "That is all that's next."

THE SEARCH FOR DR. FRANKENSTEIN

1891
BISMARCK GERMANY

Gabriel Kane heads toward Germany after being contacted by The Knights of The Holy Order to investigate the missing Dr. Victor Frankenstein. Currently, the year is 1891 and Kane has had many encounters that would appear strange to the normal society. As Kane enters Germany on his black horse, he notices the location's areas are covered with pictures of Dr. Frankenstein, all have the word "missing" above his headshot photo.

Kane's first location to investigate is the University of Ingolstadt, the museum that Dr. Frankenstein attended during his early years of studying. Kane always heard rumors that Frankenstein was high on creating life, though it seems that he never succeeded in accomplishing it. Kane enters the university, noticing many physicists walking throughout the campus. He heads toward the front office.

"Excuse me." Kane said to the lady at the front desk. "I'm here to discuss the missing doctor. Dr. Victor Frankenstein."

"Oh, sir.' The lady said. 'We haven't seen or spoken to him in months.'

"Is there a trail that I can follow.' Kane asked. 'Did he mention anywhere he was headed?"

"Last we heard; he was living in the mountains."

"Thank you." Kane said as he left the university.

Kane now travels to the mountains, searching for the missing doctor. As he travels through the crowded forest, heading down the trail, he spots a cabin above him, towards the front of the mountains. Kane commands his black horse to run faster, moving quicker to get a closer look at the cabin. Once, he has a better view, he sees that it's a large cabin, with smoke coming from a pipe in the roof, meaning something's inside. Kane gets off his horse and walks up the pathway heading into the mountains, right at the cabin.

By nightfall, Kane reaches the top of the mountains. He walks slowly toward the large cabin. He stands by the wall, taking a look into the window. He sees nothing inside, but a lab table and some equipment. As he looks deeper into the window, he notices someone walking around. He quickly moves from the window and heads toward the front door. Kane stands by the door, with one hand on the doorknob, the other hand at his side, holding his revolver.

He quickly opens the door to the cabin and walks in. As he enters quietly, the door squeaks as it closes itself. He turns and sees no one behind him. He walks around the cabin, seeing dozens of jars containing human remains and surgeon equipment and tools.

"What was he doing in here?"

Kane continued searching the cabin and its surroundings. As he walks toward the operating table, he hears footsteps from behind. Kane quickly turns and aims his revolver at Dr. Frankenstein.

"Dr. Frankenstein." Kane said. "Where have you been? You've been declared missing by the country of Germany."

"My good sir, I've been here the entire time.' Victor said. 'You look familiar. You're Gabriel Kane, the monster hunter and ufologist.'

"I am. I've been sent by the Symbolum Venatores to find you."

"The Knights?" Victor asked. 'What would they want with me."

"They believe that your grave robberies and goal to create life is turning a little chaotic. They want to stop what you're doing."

Victor stared at Kane as he walked over to his wooden desk, surrounded with jars and paper.

"I cannot stop Mr. Kane." Victor said. "This is my life's work. I do not have anything else to live for."

"You can start a new life. A new journey."

"No. There's no possible way I'm leaving this life and moving on like the rest of you. Besides, my work has already been completed."

Kane pauses.

"What work?"

"The ability to prove that God is not the only one who can create life." Victor said. 'I've accomplished it."

"How do you know you're telling the truth and not some false lie?' Kane asked.

Victor walked over into another room and opened the doors. Kane walked behind Victor as he saw someone sitting down in a chair in the distance.

"Who is that man, Victor?"

Victor commands the man in the chair to stand up and face him as well as Kane. The man stood on his feet; his height was around eight to nine feet in length. He had long black hair that reached his shoulders, he was wearing nothing but torn cloth and what appeared to be a ripped cloak. The man looked up at Victor and pointed at Kane.

"He is my creation." Victor said. "The Adam of my labors."

"A modern Prometheus."

The man walked over to Kane, looking down at him. Kane nods with his hat as the man only growls. Victor pushes the man back away from Kane. Kane only stares at the man, looking at his greenish-grey skin, with knots and bolts in his body.

"You created a creature, Victor." Kane said. "You must get rid of it, immediately."

"Never, Mr. Kane."

Victor turned to the man, whispering something in his ear. Kane only looks on as the man turns his focus on Kane. The man runs over to Kane, knocking him through the cabin wall. Kane rolls onto the ground, reaching for his revolver, seeing the man walk out of the cabin and into the dawning sunlight. The man roars as Kane only stares.

"This is going to be very difficult."

Kane gets to his feet and fires a shot at the creature's leg. The creature stumbles and looks at its leg. It turns to Victor, who commands him to get rid of Kane. The creature runs over to Kane, knocking him into the mountain walls. Victor walks outside and stares at his creation. As it pummels onto Kane. Kane takes out a knife from his coat and swipes at the monster's arm. The monster backs up, holding its arm in pain. Groaning at its arm, it looks at Kane and rams him into the mountain wall. As Kane tries to get to his feet, Victor walks outside as he holds his hands behind his back, watching his monster attack Kane.

"What are you doing, Victor?!"

"Just standing by while my creation destroys you for trespassing." Victor said.

"Trespassing? I was sent here to look for you."

"You see that I'm doing just fine here. Now, just lay there and die."

The monster grabs Kane by his coat and throws him toward the cabin, laying right in front of Victor. Kane looks up and lunges at Victor. Now holding a pistol at Victor's head, the monster stops moving and stares at Victor.

"Tell your monster to step back." Kane said to Victor.

"Stand down, my creation."

The monster steps back as Kane shoves Victor toward it. Kane continues to hold the pistol at Victor and watches closely at the monster.

Now, you will come with me, Victor." Kane said. "That isn't a question."

"I've already said, I'm not going with you."

Kane points and shoots at the monster's leg with his pistol. The monster groans and falls to one knee while holding the injured leg. Victor screams at Kane not to kill his creation. Kane turns to Victor, demanding that he come along with him. As Victor continues to decline, Kane fires another shot at the monster, hitting him in the other leg. Victor goes down to his knees and surrenders to Kane.

"Enough!" Victor yelled. "I'll go along with you. Just please don't kill my creation."

"Fair enough."

Kane placed the pistol back into its holster and takes Victor back to his horse. Kane walks back and grabs his hat off the ground, which fell off during the fight. As Kane prepares to leave, Victor notices his monster staring at him. Victor tells the monster to go back into the cabin and that he'll be safe. The monster nods and enters the cabin. Kane looks ahead and rides off on his horse with Victor in tow.

Back at the Venatores base, Kane brings in Victor to the Order. The Order stare at Victor intensely. One knight walks up to Victor and places his hand on Victor's shoulder.

"It is a proud privilege to see you in our presence, Dr. Frankenstein." the hunter said.

"Why am I here to start with?" Victor said. "What do you want with me?"

"Your unparalleled talent, of course." A hunter said. "We know about your creation, the monster."

Why bring up my precious creation?' Victor said.

Because you have proven that God isn't the only one who can create life." The hunter said. "Which is why we would like you to join us in protecting this plane."

"Protect it from what?"

"I wouldn't expect you to know all the information, doctor. But, you live in a world where evil presents itself in pure form. No hiding, no disguises."

Kane stands up from against the wall, presenting himself in front of the Order.

"What they want is you to work for them and your monster. I'm sure they would like to use him on quests."

Victor looks dazed.

"My creation is not a weapon to be used upon. It is a living being with emotions."

"A living abomination of deceased people, doctor. Sure, it can be used as a weapon."

Victor shakes his hand in disagreement.

"I will never let my creation be used for such purposes.' Victor said.

"It seems that you do not have a choice."

The hunter waves his hand towards the door and as it opens, Victor sees his creation in a cage being rolled into the room. Kane looks and begins to reach for his pistol. The Knight notices him and raises his hand toward him.

"That won't be necessary, Gabriel. We have it under control."

"Are you sure about that?' Kane asked.

The cage is shaking as the monster roars at the Order. Victor walks over towards it, trying to calm it down. He does very little as Kane walks across to the other side of the room, hand still on his pistol.

"If I may ask, what's the main purpose of this monster being here?"

"The same purpose we just told Dr. Frankenstein here. His great creation can be used to protect the world from the evil that lurks."

"Thought that's what I was for." Kane said.

"You are. We just feel it's more suitable to have others to do the work for us as well.'

"Don't hurt my creation!" Victor yelled.

"We're not going to, doctor.' The Knight said. 'You have nothing to worry about here.'

Victor looks around and turns his attention towards the Order.

"I'll help you on your quests.' Victor said. 'As long as my creation isn't harmed in any means.'

"Fair enough." The Knight said. "Welcome, Dr. Victor Frankenstein to the Order.'

The Knight walks over and shakes Victor's hand.

"You're doing a great service for your world and its people."

Kane walks around as the Order turns to him. He realizes it and looks back.

"Kane, you've always done what was right and you have succeeded once again." The hunter said. "We thank you for helping us."

"No problem. It's what I'm here for. So, what's the next quest?"

The hunter smiles and hands Kane a piece of paper, covered with an encryption. Kane reads it and looks at the Knight, smiling.

"I'm on it."

Once outside, Kane gets onto his horse and rides off, heading on his next journey.

THE INVISIBLE MAN

1898
THE LATE ENLIGHTENMENT

In the mid-winter season of 1898, Dr. Kemp, a fellow British scientist has met with the Symbolum Venatores. He travels all the way to enter their headquarters. As he walks through their temple, seeing many artifacts and paintings from centuries past, he enters their main conference room. As he sits down inside the room, he tells them of many cases being sought out in England by a man who cannot be seen with the naked eye. Once he finishes speaking, the Order declares they will investigate the case, thus contacting Kane.

Kane arrived, entering the conference room, Kemp is nowhere in sight, since he left and returned home.

"You know why you're here, Gabriel." The lead hunter said.

"Another case I suppose. What is it this time?"

"We need you to go to an English village in West Sussex, England to find a man who cannot be seen with the naked eye."

Kane pauses.

"Wait, you're speaking of the cases that have been raising across England." Kane said.

"Of course. We need you to head over there to stop them. Only God knows what more could happen if its not stopped."

"Where's the doctor? Doctor Kemp?"

"He has returned home. You shouldn't have to speak with him. We've already done that part."

"I would like to speak with him myself. Just for my own sake at least."

"If that's what you would like to do, go ahead. You may leave."

Kane nods as he walks out of the room.

Kane leaves the headquarters and heads for Port Burdock. Within a week, Kane enters Port Burdock and looks through the town for Dr. Kemp's location. Traveling through, he spots a house with the name "Kemp" on the side of the door. Kane mounts off his horse and walks toward the front door. He knocks as he hears someone walking towards.

"Who's there?" Kemp asked.

"I am Gabriel Kane. I was sent by the Venatores to speak with you about the man who can't be seen."

Kemp opens the door, smiling.

"Oh, please come on inside, sir."

Kane enters the home as Kemp closes the door. Inside the house is warm, due to the fireplace being set. Kemp allows Kane to sit in the chair facing the fireplace, Kemp sits beside him.

"I was wondering what you knew about this man?"

"His name is Griffin." Kemp said. "I worked with him on finding a way out of his troubles."

"What kind of troubles, if I may ask?"

"He discovered a way to turn objects or life forms invisible. He Didn't have much to do tests on, so he did it onto himself. Thus, becoming the man who cannot be seen."

"How are you sure that its him who's doing these attacks?"

"The reports suggest that the culprit of this cases cannot be seen. The witnesses who were at the site speak of the victims dying in the hands of an invisible force."

"Do you know where I could find him?"

"I have no idea where he could be. He burned his house and all that could lead to him."

"No evidence." Kane said. "Smart of him."

"I'm sure you'll find him, sir. He'll turn up soon enough."

While Kane and Kemp drink their coffee, they hear screams coming from outside the home. Kane gets up and opens the door, seeing a man on a horse ride through. Kane walks over and stops the man.

"What's the problem?" Kane asked.

"There's a incident in Iping." The man said. "The police are shooting at something we can't see."

"It has to be him." Kemp proclaimed.

"An Invisible Man it must be."

Kane gets onto his horse and looks back at Kemp.

"Where are you going, Mr. Kane?"

"I'm going to do what I was sent for."

Kane nods his hat at Kemp and rides off, heading for Iping.

In the streets of Iping, police are shooting at a force they cannot see. One officer walked over to the leading officer.

"What are we shooting at, sir?" The officer asked.

"The man who cannot be seen." The leading officer said.

"How do you know he's still there?"

"Enough with the questions and keep firing at that spot!"

As the officers continue to fire at the spot, the citizens run throughout the town in horror, most of them are leaving through the town as Kane enters. He mounts his horse and runs over to the officers.

"It's him." Kane said.

Kane pulls out his pistol and fires at the location. After he fires, the officers turn to him and he continues to look ahead, spotting the dirt on the ground to bounce up as he someone is running through. Kane shoves the officers out of the way as he chases the Invisible Man.

He follows the trail of dirt that's been shoved around and later finds footprints. He tracks the prints down a few streets and finally into an alleyway. Kane slowly reaches for his pistol as he follows the track, through the other end of the alley, he sees civilians running all over the place, but Kane spots a man leaning against the wall, wearing a brown trench coat and a hat.

Kane looks again and notices that the man has no legs nor a head. The man turned toward him and Kane fired his pistol. The Invisible Man runs down the other street as Kane follows him. When Kane reaches closer to him, The Invisible Man stops and turns toward Kane.

"I suggest you leave me alone."

"I will not." Kane said. "You're coming back to the Venatores with me."

"I think not."

Kane jerks the Man's left arm. The Invisible Man turns.

"If that's the way you want this to go."

The Invisible Man punches Kane, knocking him back as he continues to run off. Kane shakes his head and looks around, spotting the tail end of the trench coat turning right. Kane runs and continues to chase him. As Kane catches up to him, he pulls out his pistol and fires, hitting the Invisible Man in the right leg. The Invisible Man is now limping at he tries to outrun Kane.

As Kane gets closer, The Invisible Man enters a large crowd of people trying to find their way through other areas of the city. Kane rams through the crowd, looking for The Invisible Man. Once through the crowd, Kane looks down and sees the hat and coat that the Invisible Man was wearing with smears of blood on them. Kane uses his blade to cut a cloth off the coat and places it inside his coat pocket. He looks around the snowy areas of the town for other footprints, he spots none.

"Damn it."

Kane returns to Port Burdock to speak with Kemp. As He arrives at Kemp's home and enters, he sits down.

"What happened in Iping?" Kemp wondered.

"I found him. Though, I lost him.'"

"Oh dear."

Kane reaches into his coat pocket and pulls out the cloth from the Invisible Man's coat and hands it over to Kemp.

"It's his blood on the cloth."

Kemp grabs his glasses and observes the cloth. Smiling.

"How did you get this?"

"I shot him in his right leg."

"Excellent work you've done here. I will examine this as soon as possible."

"I thank you for that. I should be leaving now. Most High only knows what I have next on my list."

"Good to see you again, Mr. Kane."

"Always a pleasure."

Kane leaves Port Burdock, returning to the Venatores. The next week, sightings in western Europe have been on the rise of a mysterious Invisible Man causing harm to the villages.

THE PHANTOM OF THE OPERA
1910
BELLE EPOQUE

In the late winter of January 1910, Gabriel Kane travels to Paris, France to uncover the mystery behind the apparent Opera-Ghost. It is said that the Opera-Ghost appears as a man, wearing opera clothing and a white mask. The Secret Society have told Kane that the Opera-Ghost is always sighted inside the famous Paris Opera House known as *Palais Garnier*. When Kane arrived in Paris, he notices everyone around the downtown area and throughout are wearing the similar white mask that the Opera-Ghost wears. According to the citizens, the mask is known as the Phantom Mask, referring to its appearance and color.

Kane enters a church that's not far away from the Opera House. Inside the church, he is greeted by a young man, short, with brown hair. He's a friar known only as Tom.

"You must be the Gabriel Kane? The Gabriel Kane known across the lands."

"Indeed, I am." Kane said. "You're Tom. The Knights speak heavily of you."

"The Symbolum Venatores?" "They don't even know I exist, yet I work for them."

"They know you exist." Kane said. "You're just not in their high rankings is all."

"Maybe if I could team with you and others, I could be in their sights."

"Me entering this church and meeting you means the Knights have an eye on you. They wouldn't send me here otherwise. Definitely not for a friar of any sort of the imagination."

Kane pulled out a note and handed it to Tom. He put on his glasses and read the note before glancing up at Kane with a blank stare. He held the note above his shoulders.

"You're telling me that the Knights want me to assist you in investigating the Opera-Ghost?"

"Yes. Didn't you just mention that if you could align yourself with me or any of the others, you would be in their sights."

"But that was just me talking out of my ass. I didn't think that it would happen. Not until I became a monk."

Kane takes the note back from Tom and placed it inside his leather coat pocket. Tom only stared as Kane looked at him and glanced toward the church doors.

"We need to go immediately."

"Why immediately? Why not tomorrow?"

"Because tomorrow, the Opera-Ghost could be gone and lost in my sights."

Kane and Tom head toward the opera house, they notice posters and banners covering the exterior of the house as well as other buildings throughout Paris, which represent the Opera-Ghost himself. Tom is terrified by the number of banners that are surrounding Paris for the Opera-Ghost. As more people are seen wearing the ghost masks, they finally arrive at the opera house, where they meet, Viscount Raoul, Vicomte de Chagny.

"Ah! The legendary Gabriel Kane has arrived in Paris." Raoul said. "What a pleasure it is to see you here in Paris."

"The pleasure is all mine." Kane said. "It's been a while since I've stepped foot in Italy."

"It's good to have you here in our presence. I'm sure you're not in the mindset to take a small break so we could have a conversation."

"I'm set for a conversation."

Raoul walks Kane and Tom through the house, seeing many banners and posters that speak of the Opera-Ghost. To the people walking around inside the house, it's just an ordinary trick played by well performed actors. Raoul enters an office room where Kane and Tom follow. They sit in the chairs as Raoul closed the door. He sits by the wooden desk facing Kane.

"So, what was this conversation that you wanted to speak to me about?"

"It concerns the Opera-Ghost as well as this opera house."

"Is this place cursed because of the ghost?" Tom said.

"No. I hope not. It only seems that he's bringing people into a trance. Whenever they see a poster, a banner, or even when they wear those masks. It's like they have no control over themselves."

"You want us to look into that mystery."

"If you can. I don't want a bunch of zombies entering this opera house."

"Believe me when I say, you haven't seen what a zombie exactly is."

Raoul smirked and extended his hand toward Kane.

"Just please help the City of Paris out on this one."

Kane shook Raoul's hand and nodded.

"We'll do what we can about the trance state while we search for the Opera-Ghost."

Kane and Tom leave the office as Raoul sits behind the desk, rubbing his hands together as he looked outside the window, seeing many citizens wearing the ghost mask and staring at banners and posters.

"Please help us."

Kane and Tom walk around the downtown area of Paris. They examine the streets and the people. Kane also studies the banners and posters. He stares at the Opera-Ghost on the posters. Scratching his chin, Kane turned to Tom, who was glancing around at the Paris citizens.

"Tom, come over here and look at this."

"What have you found this time?"

Kane pointed toward the Opera-Ghost's face on the poster. Pointing toward the eyes.

"Do you see what I'm seeing?"

Tom squints his eyes and shook his head.

"I'm not seeing anything, Gabriel Kane. What are you talking about exactly?"

"These posters and banners. They're all laced with something."

Kane reached up and snatched the poster off the brick wall and onto the ground. Citizens looked on and stared at Kane and Tom. Tom looked back toward them and held his hands up.

"There's nothing to see here ladies and gentlemen. So please continue on with your sight-seeing."

"He ripped down the Opera-Ghost's poster!" A gentleman said.

"He tore it off the wall like it was hardly anything!" A lady said.

Tom backed up near Kane as the citizens slowly approached the two of them.

"Gabriel, The citizens are approaching us and they're not looking so nice."

Kane turned around, facing the crowd. He raised up his pistols toward them. The crowd stopped moving and slowly took steps back from Kane and Tom.

"If any of you want to live after this day, I suggest you back away and return to your previous occupations. Do it now I say."

The crowd raised up their hands and turned away, returning to their sight-seeing and other activities. Kane placed the pistols back into his pouches. Tom looked at him with a worried eye.

"Were you really going to shoot them if they stepped closer?"

"Would've shot at their arms and legs. Nothing more."

Kane returns to looking at the poster and grabs Tom.

"The eyes. Do you see the glow coming from them?"

Tom looked and noticed a glare coming from the Opera-Ghost's eyes. He looked at Kane and took another glance at the poster.

"What is that supposed to be exactly. Is that what's causing the trace state in these people?"

"Its magic. Someone is using magic to bring people here to see the Opera-Ghost. Once the trance is in place, the people will never leave Paris under their own power."

Kane takes out a match and burned the poster in front of the citizens. Many of them ran off from the area as Kane and Tom watched the poster burn.

"So, what's next on our agenda?"

"We'll return to the opera house tonight and find the Opera-Ghost ourselves. Once we achieve that goal, we'll end all of this."

A full moon shines bright over Paris as Kane and Tom travel toward the opera house for the investigation. Upon arriving at the house, Raoul stood outside by the front entrance as Kane and Tom approached him.

"I see the two of you are for this."

"Its why we're here."

Raoul opened the front doors and allowed Kane and Tom to enter. Raoul turned toward Kane, calling him out. Kane turned, facing Raoul.

"I wish you two the very best of luck on this."

"You won't have to worry."

Raoul leaves the opera house and only Kane and Tom are inside the house.

They walk through the house, completely silent to where they can only here their own footsteps while walking or even hearing their own heart beats while standing still. Tom carried a lamp while Kane had a pistol in hand.

"So, what area shall we search first, Gabriel?"

"I believe its best that we search the auditorium. It is where the Opera-Ghost does his work."

Once they reached the auditorium, Kane begins to feel uneasy as they enter. Tom looked around and feels as if something flew past him to where he couldn't see it.

"Something just went by, Gabriel. I don't know what it was."

"I'm having an uneasy feeling standing in here."

Kane stared at the stage and clenching his pistol. Tom looked around with the lamp. A black cloth passed by Tom, knocking the fire out of the lamp out. Tom screamed as Kane stood quiet, facing the stage.

"It just knocked the lamp out."

"It's him."

"What do you mean its him?"

"Up on the stage!"

Kane moved as he grabbed Tom from the chandelier, which fell over their heads. Slamming on the floor where they were standing. Tom looked back at the chandelier and turned to the stage, where he sees Kane aiming his pistol toward the Opera-Ghost.

"He's here, Tom. The Ghost is in our sights."

The Opera-Ghost stood still as it stared into the eyes of Kane. He pointed toward him as Kane took a shot. The Ghost jumped out of the bullet's frame and lunged over to Kane, punching him across the auditorium. Kane falls against the wall as he stared at the Ghost, which slowly approached him with no sound coming from him.

The Opera-Ghost approached Kane slowly as Tom looked around the auditorium for anything to use as a weapon. Kane got to his feet as the Ghost inched closer toward him.

"You've caused enough trouble here. Using magic to bring innocent people into your opera house to watch you perform mysticism."

"They come because they have nowhere else to go to achieve greatness or to feel greatness within them. I give them the illusion of greatness and they love it most."

"Not by my sights do they love it. They can't even leave Paris under their own willpower."

"Who would want to leave this beautiful city. There's not other place on Earth that could equal the amount of beauty and love than Paris herself. Who are you to say otherwise."

"I'm the man that come to end your reign of magic and to bring forth justice into the lands of Paris and all places throughout France. I am Gabriel Kane and I am what you fear most."

Kane lunged at the Opera-Ghost, tackling him onto the ground. Kane begins pummeling The Ghost in the face, cracking its phantom mask. The Ghost backhanded Kane and kicked him in the gun, later ramming him into the walls. Kane slides off the walls and onto the floor. The Ghost rubbed his mask, noticing the crack, his eyes begin to fill with rage as he reached over and grabbed Kane by his black leather coat and started slamming him against the wall. Tom, meanwhile, continued searching for a weapon and finds a metal rod.

"There we go."

Tom grabbed the rod and ran over toward Kane and the Ghost. Tom jumped up and hit the Ghost in his back with the rod. The Ghost stumbled before turning around, facing Tom and staring into his eyes. Tom slowly backed away with his hands in the air.

"No worries. I was just trying to help my friend out. That's all."

"You would use other means to try and fight me off. When will foreigners ever learn that Paris and this opera house are powerful in nature. They fuel me, just as I fuel the citizens."

Kane looked up at the Ghost, through his blurry vision, seeing him reaching for Tom. Kane gets up and rams into the Ghost's back and reached out toward the Ghost's face and snatched off the mask. The Ghost backed up, covering his face. He mumbled to himself as Kane and Tom watched. The Ghost stopped moving and removed his hands from his face. Holding his head down, he slowly raised it up, revealing his disfigured face.

"Oh, dear lord." Tom said.

The Ghost yelled in fury as he ran and shoved Kane into Tom, knocking them back on the floor and he began to choke them both.

"It's always those who do not fully understand. Leave me be at this moment or else suffer your sudden death."

The Ghost released his hands from Kane and Tom's throats. Tom backed away as Kane stood up. The Ghost raised up his cloak and disappeared through sudden smoke that appeared from his feet. As the Ghost vanished, Tom looked around the damaged auditorium.

"Where did he go, Gabriel Kane?"

"He vanished to another hiding spot."

"He might try and sneak up on us."

"He won't. We've just agreed on equal terms. We leave this place and he refuses to use magic in his performances."

The following day, Kane speaks to Raoul about the Opera-Ghost and gives him the great detail of their encounter and what took place inside the auditorium. Upon leaving Palais Garnier, Kane and Tom run into a woman, who suddenly stopped them.

"Please stop. I need to have a small word with you." the woman said.

"By all means, miss. Speak."

"You shouldn't worry about the Opera-Ghost anymore. He's in good hands and will do all that he can to bring good into this city."

"Excuse me, miss. Who are you exactly?" Tom said.

"My name is Christine Daae. I'm very close to the Opera-Ghost. As I said, you won't have to worry anymore about his activities. I'll take good care of him to make sure of it."

Kane stared at Christine and nodded toward her. She smiled and walked away. Tom looked back at her before turning to Kane.

"That was surreal. She's close with the Opera-Ghost."

"We'll leave the Phantom of the Opera alone. For now."

Kane and Tom ride off on their horses, returning to Rome where they'll speak once again with the Knights.

HOD

PROLOGUE - THE MURDER

The forest was cold, snowed in, and completely iced over. The atmosphere would cause a person to shiver in their footsteps to even taken the daring chance of walking through the forest covered in snow. Especially during nightfall where the forest would become silent as the outer depths of space. No sign of any animals either. Complete quietness.

Though, there was that one time during the night, when a man decided to take the daring opportunity to enter the snowy forest during a full moon. The man seemed to make an impression on his friends and possible lover. He took pleasure in taking those daring actions that many seem to do today. His dare was to enter the forest during nightfall and overcome the cold and shivering atmosphere.

Not even wearing a coat, he went out with only a short sleeve shirt and shorts. He might've had wore sandals, but we couldn't tell due to the fact that when we found him, he was halfway eaten and his feet were bare, his clothes ripped with claw marks and bite marks. His friends didn't know what to make of their friend's death and were too afraid to tell anyone of his daring feats.

We spoke to his friends concerning him and they hardly spoke a word besides the fact of him running into the forest with a smile on his face. The detectives however believed it to be a bear that attacked and killed him. But a hunter who discovered the remains believed it to be something more than a bear. Funny enough, one detective joked that it might have been an elk that killed him and used its antlers to create the claw marks.

"No elk could've done this." said the Hunter. "I can tell you exactly what killed this man. But, you'll end up locking me behind a steel door."

"Tell us what could've killed this man."

"A full moon was out on the night he entered these woods and we know the legends of this land."

"We are not buying this folklore tale of a werewolf being responsible, sir."

"Just hear me out, detectives. I know this sounds crazy, but you have to believe me and take this in."

"We prefer not to."

The detectives would laugh in the hunter's face and walk away to their vehicles, preparing to leave the forest and head back into town. The friends had already left the scene with little tears in their eyes and softness in their hearts. Without any ideas as to who or what might have killed the man in the snowy forest, the detectives were out of options. Until that Sunday, where the freezing rain had begun to come down and when he entered through the doors of the detective building that they knew something was happening in those woods.

I - THE INVESTIGATION

After a series of days had passed away, the detectives took slight heed to the warning of the hunter concerning the possibility of a werewolf as the culprit of the forest murder. Everyone within the small town kept the information of the murder to themselves, most were afraid to speak to someone about it. The hunter stayed in his cabin outside of the small town to avoid certain mockery and scrutiny. He was already the laughingstock of the town months back dealing with his hunting of deer to the point where deer figured out the shooting grounds of the hunter, thus never making a return to the field.

The hunter sat alone in his cabin, covered in snow. Placing wood into his wood stove to heat up the cabin, he sighs while sitting down in an old beaten chair. The hunter's cabin is covered with trophies he acquired in hunting games. The cabin is even packed with stuffing of his kills, ranging from deer to bears to an mountain lion. He reached over to a table nearby and grabbed a book, began to read it until a knock comes from the door. Reluctant to answer the door, believing it to be a towns person coming over to mock him or throw snowballs at him.

"Go away." said the hunter.

They knock again with the hunter's patience being tested. He refused to stand up and answer the door. Going back to reading his book, he ignored the door and the knocking.

"I am not in the mood to be playing with snowballs. Thank you."

The knocks continue and increase. Nearly out of patience, the hunter stands up and walked to the door. He took a peep outside through the peek hole, seeing a man standing there. The hunter gently sighs before placing his hand on the doorknob. He opened the door and standing there is a man dressed in amalgam of modern and Victorian era clothing. The man is wearing a black duster coat, a gray buttoned-down shirt with black slacks, black and gray leather boots, and a black hat. The man's black and gray hair strands down to his shoulders, covering his ears. The man stands still while the hunter thinks to himself as to who the man could be.

"Hello, sir" The hunter said. "How can I possibly help you?"

"I heard about the murder in these woods. I understand that it was you whom discovered the remains of the victim."

"Yes. Yes, I did. Is there something wrong?"

"I would like to talk to you about it."

"I'm not in the mood to speak on the subject, sir. If you want more information on it, go to the detectives' office and they can give you all the information that you'll need."

The hunter proceeded to close the door, but the man placed his foot in between. Frightening the hunter immediately, he opened the door wildly.

"Sir, whatever you want, just take it."

"I don't want anything of yours. I only want to speak with you."

"About what? I told you where to go about the murder."

"I'm not here about the murder. I'm here about the werewolf."

The hunter paused and slowly took the time to regain himself back to normal, he calmed down and allowed the man to enter his cabin. The man entered and looked around the interior of the cabin, sighting the stuffed animals and trophy mounts.

"You are a hunter I can see."

"I am. Do you want anything hot to drink?"

"Do you have any coffee available?"

"I do."

"I'll take some of that. Thank you."

The hunter pours a cup of coffee for the man and brought it

over to him. Giving him the coffee, he sits in his chair as the man sat in the opposite chair. The man took a sip of the coffee as he looked at the hunter.

"What can you tell me of the werewolf?"

"I didn't see the creature. I only brought it up as a possible suspect in the murder. The victim had marks on his body that were made by an animal and it couldn't have been made by a bear. The marks were too detailed."

"The bite marks and claw marks were very distinctive is what you're saying?"

"They were. I tried to tell the detectives, but they tossed the idea away. Blaming it on a bear in these woods."

The man nodded as he took another sip of the coffee.

"By the way you've spoken, you know a lot about werewolves I presume."

"I've heard about the legends. The transformation of man into beast. I've had family that have told me they've seen werewolves around this forest and in town. A legend that lives this long cannot be made of folklore tales."

"No. They cannot."

The man finished his cup of coffee and stood up, walking to the door. The hunter stood up and followed him. The man opened the door, taking his steps outside.

"Thank you for the coffee. You've shown me compassion."

"Where are you headed? If I may know."

"I'm going to speak with those detectives you've said. I want more information on the victim."

The man stepped outside of the door, walking in the snowy grounds. The hunter watched and he wanted to say something, it sat on the tip of his tongue.

"Pardon me, sir. But I would like to know your name. You didn't tell me your name."

The man turned and faced the hunter. He stared at him for quite a moment.

"Hod." The man said. "You can call me Mr. Hod."

The hunter looked on as Mr. Hod walked away from the

cabin and into the forest. The hunter closed the cabin door and sat back in his chair and continued the reading the book he had placed on the table.

In the small town, the residents walked around the area, buying from local shops and selling from local shops. Many of whom only spoke about business ventures and homesteading as they refused to bring up a conversation about the murder and the mentioning of the werewolf. While the residents were doing their daily business, they spotted Mr. Hod walking into the town.

All the residents stopped what they were doing and only stared at him. Hod kept to himself, avoiding eye contact with the residents. He walked through the streets. Residents began to talk amongst themselves as to who Mr. Hod could be.

"Why's he wearing those clothes?" said a man.

"He looks dirty." 'a female said speaking with a friend.

"He scares me." a child said.

Mr. Hod looked around the small town and found the detectives' office and proceeded to approach it. The residents would move out of his way. Avoiding contact with him period. They continued to stare at him and make comments pertaining to the way he dressed and look as far as he appearance was concerned. Hod found himself standing in front of the detectives' office. The building was entirely made up of wood and stone. He walked up the steps of the office and entered through the door as the residents walked closer to the building.

Inside the detectives turned and stared at Hod, who stood by the door looking at them. One detective approached him, shaking his shoulders with a thrust walk, trying to intimidate Hod, but he was unshakable.

"What can we do for you sir?"

"I came here to speak on the matter of the forest murder."

"Why is that? You know the animal that did it? Or did you do it?"

The detectives laughed slightly at the detective's remark.

"I know the animal that killed the person."

The detective chuckled as he walked toward his office. Hod

followed him. The detectives look on at Hod, confused about his choosing of apparel, stating it looked too ancient for their time.

"So, you found the bear that did it?"

"Wasn't a bear, detective."

"A mountain lion is what you're telling me? I thought were rid of those damn things around here."

"Neither was it a mountain lion?"

"Well, what the hell could it be?"

"The victim was killed by a werewolf."

The detective slowly turns to Hod and stared.

"You haven't been around that lone hunter, have you? Because if you have, maybe his fanatics and kookiness have rubbed off on you."

"I did speak with him and no. His fanatics have not rubbed onto me. But, they have given me insight onto this town of yours."

"Listen, sir. We aren't listening nor buying into some children's horror tales. We have our own fictitious troubles to deal with around here."

"The werewolf is no fabled tale. Of course, it has its place in ancient folklore, but those folklores are based on actual events that have taken place ages before our time."

"How would you know any of this to be true? You're part of the government's secret agency or something?"

"What I know, the government would kill, rape, and slaughter anyone to find it out for themselves."

"I'm sorry. But we're not listening to any werewolf stories here."

"I have a proposition for you, detective. You and this entire town of yours."

"Which is?"

"I will find the werewolf and I will kill the creature. After which, I will leave this town and never bother to return."

The detective looked at his colleagues, who were also silent and were unable to come up with anything to say to Hod.

"So, when you kill this werewolf you're talking about, you want some reward before you leave?"

"I want and ask for nothing in return for the werewolf's kill. As of right now, I ask to see the victim's remains."

"The remains are nothing but bone and torn muscle."

"The remains have clues that contain where the werewolf has headed and will strike next. Show me where the body is."

"The body is kept at the morgue across the street. You can go there and ask for the remains. They should let you see them."

"Thank you for the talk." Hod said as he nodded with the tip of his hat.

Hod walked to the office door and exited, leaving the entire building of detectives silent. Outside of the office, Hod walked down the steps and through the crowds of residents that surrounded him and watched him approach the morgue. Before he entered through the morgue doors, a young girl approached him. He looked down at her, noticing her smiling, but could sense her fear of him from within.

"What do you want, little girl?"

"Why are you wearing those kinds of clothes?"

"Because, the clothes present what I am and where I come from."

"So, you're old?"

"You could say that."

"How old?"

"Older than you can possibly count."

"Oh...." The little girl said.

Hod showed a faint smile before entering the morgue while the residents continue their frightening stares. Hod opened the door and entered the morgue building. He glanced around the room, searching for someone inside to speak with concerning the body of the victim. He spotted no one inside the room until he took a few steps toward a door and it opened. Out of the door walked out the morgue attendant, who was frightened for a bit at the sight and presence of Mr. Hod. Slowly shivering.

"What can I help you with, sir?"

"I'm here to see the remains of the victim that was found in the forest."

"Why would you want to see that?"

"Because my purpose here requires me to take a small study of the remains to understand what committed the murder."

"So, you work with the detectives?"

"I work alone. I am not from around here."

"But, how would you get the right to come here and solve a murder that doesn't concern you. You're not even from here and you want to solve this. Why?"

"The murderer is known throughout the lands. I came to this dead house to see the remains to uncover more of what I need. I know what killed the individual in those woods."

"We all know it was a bear that killed him."

Hod stared at the morgue attendant. Silent and showing no emotion on his face.

"A bear was not responsible for the murder."

"Then what could possibly have the strength to do such a thing?"

"It was a werewolf and apparently the people here seem to keep quiet about the lore of werewolves. As if you're all trying to hide something that cannot be hidden no longer."

"We refuse to speak of such folktales around here. We don't want to frighten the children and spread fairy tales across the town."

"By lying to yourselves, you already have."

The attendant leans her head down, facing the floor as if she's in shame of Hod's words. Hod approached her and raised up her head and stared, slightly encouraging her to spread the truth about the werewolf lore.

"Show me where the remains are, and I will be out of your sight."

The attendant nodded slowly. "This way."

Hod followed the attendant through the door and walked down a quiet and cold hallway heading toward the chamber. While walking, the attendant was hesitant to bring Hod into the chamber, fearing he could kill her and run off with the remains. Hod didn't say a word. Hod continued to follow the attendant down the hall and kept to himself.

The attendant reached the chamber doors and opened them as a cold breeze swiftly went out through the opening. The breeze touched Hod, gently touching him on his face. The cold had no chilling effect on him as he kept to himself and walked into the chamber. He looked around and seen the amount of bodies that were laying on the tables. Many of them appeared to have animal-like marks on their bodies.

"The remains are over here, sir."

"What happened to these people?"

"I fear they suffered from the same animal that killed the man in the forest."

"How long has this been going on for?"

"Almost three months now."

"The detectives don't do anything about this. Who's in charge around here?"

"The detectives don't like it when we bring it up. They're owned by the upper-class elite. They control most of what goes on here. The finances, the news we receive, and so on."

"Where can I find your elite class?"

"I, I do not know, sir. They keep to themselves and appear as they please. We only answer to them. Most of us here don't even question them out of the fear of death."

"Seems to me that there's been enough death going on around here to worry about your own selves."

The attendant walked over to one of the walls and pulled out the table, where the remains laid. Hod walked over and looked at them. Pulling out tools like a forensic scientist. He glanced at the remains and took deep looks at the bones, the muscles, and the skin fragments that remained. The attendant stood by and watched Hod study the remains in every detail that he possibly could. Using a magnifying glass to look closer at the bite marks within the bones. Hod looked around and didn't see the skull.

"Where's the skull?"

"This is all that remained."

"They didn't find the skull?"

"It is possible it's still out in the forest. They won't go back and check. They told us this is all they needed to start their search for the killer."

Hod pushed the table back into its closing and closed the chamber door. He walked out of the room and back down the hallway. The attendant tried to keep up by following him because of him power walking.

"Wait. Where are you going?"

"I am going into the forest to find the skull. When I do, I shall return here and deliver it to you to compete the remains. Without the skull, I won't have all the information I need."

Hod walked out of the morgue with the attendant looking nervous as to what could come up between Hod and the skull. Outside, Hod noticed the number of residents that stood outside of the morgue had increased. They stood around him, making way for him to walk by. The residents stared at him as he kept to himself.

"Who do you think you are." A man said. "Why are you here trespassing our town. We don't need foreigners like you around here."

Hod stopped and turned toward the man. The residents took a few steps back to avoid being in Hod's eyesight. He kept his attention focused on the man who appeared to be a farmer as he wore a farmer's garment.

"Trespassing your town. How could I do such a thing when I am here on duty."

"We don't know who you are. Hell, we've never even seen you before. You must be some guy from the outer borders of the forest."

"I am from the outer borders and once again, I am here on a duty. Not a vacation. As I told the attendant inside the morgue, you, townspeople live in an area of lies. You all know the truth and refuse to believe it and accept it. You'll rather live in a world of make believe than live in a world where the truth reigns. The truth of the matter is that it wasn't a bear that committed those acts of slaughter in the forest. It was a werewolf and the beast is still out there."

"You can't talk to us like that! You're not even a resident of this town. You have no right to speak to us in such a manner!"

"I have spoken. When I return from the forest, if I am to see you or any of these people again. I will speak once more. Your detectives won't solve your problems for you and now I will solve this one problem as it affects more than this measly little town."

Hod walked away, heading toward the exit of the town into the forest. The residents stood watch and looked at the farmer. The farmer looked around and glanced at his fellow towns people.

"Don't you even dare look at me like that! I was standing up for you people and what do I get? No respect, no aid, not even another voice to stand up with mine own."

Hod continued walking through the snow-covered ground as he entered the forest. The sounds of people form the town began to fade away as he went deeper into the forest. Hearing nothing but silence and a few specks of bird in the sky flying over the trees. He looked around in the snow, searching for the spot where the victim was killed.

"By the look of the snow, the victim's final place of living isn't far from this particular spot. Its closer than it appears to be."

Hod walked past the pair of trees and spotted claw marks in the wood. The claw marks were dug deep into the wood. He rubbed the wood, searching for something that could be remaining inside. Hardly finding anything, he pulled out a knife from his coat and started to slice the tree in the areas of where the claw marks were stamped. Slicing and even cutting through the wood, a small object fell out of the hole and into the snow. Hod stopped what he was doing and placed the knife back into his coat. He kneeled and searched in the snow to find what had dropped from the tree. He picked up the small object and looked closer at it with his magnifying glass.

"The object is a piece of a nail. The werewolf must've broken it off when it dug into the tree. Possibly at the moment of pouncing the victim. By the look of it, the beast is very strong and could've possibly killed the man with just the force of its lunging toward him."

Hod turned around and looked in front of him about a few feet away and seen dried blood in the snow. He walked over to it and rubbed the blood.

"This is the spot of the victim's fall. Now, where is his skull?"

Hod began digging in the snow with a pair of branches that were laying in the snow nearby a tree. He dug until he could see the dead grass underneath the snow. He continued digging in the surrounding areas and couldn't find the skull. After several minutes of digging, Hod stopped and looked around to see anything sticking up in the snow.

"Where is it?"

Hod started to walk and noticed something in the snow that laid in front of his left foot. He dug into the snow at the exact spot and instantly seen the eye socket of the skull. He reached down and pulled the skull up from the snow and wiped away the snow. He placed the skull into his bag and proceeded back into town.

II - THE BLUE MOON

While the sun was preparing itself to set away from the town and night was slowly approaching, Hod entered the town with the skull in tow. The residents returned and followed him back to the morgue. He didn't look back at the residents as they slowly followed him and were almost on his back. They noticed the bag and tried to take peeks to find out what was inside. Hod grabbed the bag and held it tightly to his chest and maintained his focus.

"I ask of you all to leave the bag alone and let me be."

"We only want to know what you have inside."

"An important object in finding the werewolf."

The residents stopped walking and stood still as they watched Hod enter the doors of the morgue. The residence kept to themselves and not even one of them spoke a word as they went back to their regular business. Hod entered back into the morgue and the attendant seen him come through the door and approached him.

"I take it you've found the skull?"

"I have."

Hod placed the bag onto the table and pulled out the skull. He handed the skull carefully to the attendant who placed it next to the remaining parts of the victim's body. She scanned the remains in full, trying to sort out the possibilities of the victim's body. Mr. Hod carefully examined the body himself. From the skull to the feet.

"What do you perceive now?" The attendant said.

"I perceive a full evaluation of the victim. There could be some werewolf venom in the bones."

"We can do a search through the bone marrow."

"Let's give it a test."

Hod and the attendant did their part of the test runs. Operating as best as they could.

"I'm sure you heard about the other cases besides the one in the woods."

"What other cases?" Hod wondered.

"There was a couple that was attacked, and a pair of bankers ambushed in the streets."

"I was not aware of such events. Were these before this recent one?"

"Yes. All the bodies had similar marks to this one here. I'm not sure what kind of animal would do such a thing so discreetly. But I'm hearing a lot about werewolves. So, I'll take what I can get."

"Believe my words, werewolves exist, and they come in all shapes, sizes, and forms. Some are just wild beasts, others intelligent creatures."

Upon the work, they discovered the venom of the werewolf indeed remained inside the bone marrow. Yet, when removed, the venom glowed a bright blue. Its hue was brighter than the lights in the room. The attendant stepped back from the table as Hod kept his gaze upon it. Before quickly covering the glow with his hand.

"What was that?"

"Spirituality." Hod said. "A powerful one."

While the attendant gathered the venom, Hod glanced toward the window and saw nightfall had arrived and the moon's light glistened upon the clear barrier between Hod and the outside.

"How are we going to tell the detectives about this?"

"Tell them." Hod said, his eyes locked on the outside.

"What will you do?"

"Find the creature. Night has come and it's out there. Lurking. Waiting."

"You said the light from the venom was spiritual."

"Which means we're dealing with a spiritual werewolf."

"I don't understand. I've never heard of such a thing."

"Spiritual werewolves are rare. Very rare."

"As in treasure rare?"

"Rare as in Eden rare." Hod proclaimed. "Either the creature came through another dimension or from worship. Doesn't matter. I will find it."

Hod left from the morgue and went outside. Walking towards the woods. A loud screech echoes through the surroundings. Hod stopped in his tracks, circling the area, listening to the scream. Tracking its whereabouts and without notice, Hod ran toward the sound and found himself running deeper into the town and as he reached the source of the scream, he stopped and could only stare.

"What is this?" Hod uttered.

Standing in front of Hod was a deceased woman and on top of her, gnawing at her throat was the werewolf. Tall, grey-haired, and brute size. The werewolf stood up, facing Hod. The werewolf let out a howl and the color of the moon transformed into a blue moon. Hod looked up, seeing the change in color.

"What are you?"

The Werewolf roared at Hod. Moving his hand to the side, pulling out a revolver and firing toward the wolf, which runs from the shots. Hod went and chased the beast into the woods. Hod stopped near the entrance and mediated. Looking at his revolver, he nodded and reloaded.

"I have to stop this."

III - THE LIGHT OF THE MOON

Hod entered the forest in search of the spiritual werewolf. Following its tracks in the snow at every turn, except for the moment where the tracks are nowhere to be found. Not even a scratch mark in the snow. Hod continued moving through the woods, hearing the faint sound of howling in the distance. Covered in the trees.

"I know you're here." Hod said.

From the distance, the werewolf lunged out at Hod. Its fangs sharp and pointed. The hair of the wolf glistened in the moonlight. Hod moved quickly and took a shot, missing as the werewolf returned to the trees in the distance. Hod breathed quietly while continuing to aim the gun.

"Just one time."

The werewolf lunged once more toward Hod, the gun rose up as it fires, hitting the wolf in the left shoulder. The werewolf slips in his steps and tumbles down to the snowy ground. Hod runs toward the beast, which swipes toward him with his right arm, Hod fires another shot as the wolf lets out a screeching howl. Hod sighs, lowering the gun slowly.

"That's it."

The moonlight looms over the wolf's body and from it rises a spirit. The spirit startles Hod without question, yet with curiosity in his cold eyes.

"What is this?"

The spirit flows higher into the air, passing over the trees and vanishing into the night sky. Later, Hod returns to the town to tell them of the news. The werewolf is dead, but the spirit still wanders.

"What must we do now?" A civilian asked.

"Take care of yourselves." Hod replied. "My work has just begun."

Hod left the small town of Rosebane. Returning to the lair of the *Symbolum Venatores*, the monster hunters within the shadows of the world.

Hod will return…

ACCOUNTS OF THE DEAD DAYS

TOGETHER AS ONE

Running for their lives in the darkness of the night, Erica and Grady lead their group of eight into the woods near the suburbs of Denver, Colorado. They run through the woods, terrified by what they just encountered. As they continue to run, Grady looked back and noticed whatever they were running from has stopped following them. He turned to Erica and glanced at the group.

"They're not following us anymore."

"That doesn't mean they'll leave us alone. We have to keep moving."

"Erica, look around you, it's night and we have nowhere else to go. We'll stay here for the night and head off at the brink of dawn."

Erica nodded and walked toward the other members of the group, checking them for injuries or cuts. Grady looked around the area, not hearing or seeing anything that's approaching them. He sighed and walked toward the group.

At the brink of dawn, Grady leads Erica and the other members of the group out of the woods and towards a set of streets. Grady is a Caucasian male with dirty blond hair coming down to his neck as Erica is of Hispanic descent with a little Italian. Grady tells them that they must keep moving straight. As they move straight, following the street paths, they find themselves inside a suburb area. The streets abandoned by cars being left with their doors open and trash surrounding the homes. Grady spots a few homes and sees the windows broken in and doors kicked down. He walked ahead and saw five homes that looked undamaged.

"Erica, check this out."

Erica approached Grady as he pointed out the five homes, comparing them to the other seven that surrounded them. Erica looked at Grady and turned toward the group, signaling them over to their location.

"Five houses and ten of us." Grady said.

"You're thinking of searching those homes?" Erica said.

"Two to a house. We'll search for supplies and gear."

Grady began telling the other members of the group to search the homes. He pairs Danny, a scrawny Caucasian boy with Chase, his current girlfriend. Jesse, an African American male with Clyde, a close friend of Erica's. Lucy, the young girl of the group with Chloe, the spoiled girl. Tyson, the fighter of the group with Ross, the expert hunter of the group.

Sending them towards the homes, he and Erica search the house in front of them. A two-story home with a Yukon parked in the driveway. They find a spare key under the mat in front of the door. Grady used the key to open the door and enter the house. The house is quiet to the point where they could hear a pen drop on the wooden floors. They walk through the living room and enter the kitchen.

"I'll check the rooms upstairs. You'll check up here." Grady said.

Erica checked through the first floor for any supplies, weapons, or food. Grady walked up the stairs toward the second floor. He moved quietly to avoid making any kind of noises. As he stepped up on the second floor, he sees the bathroom to his right and two bedrooms, one in front of him and another to his left. He entered the bedroom on his left, seeing an array of posters and books in the room, not finding anything useful. He entered the other bedroom. He looked around the room, noticing it was a young girl's room. Not finding anything in the bedroom. He checked the bathroom and found only two boxes of bandages and a bottle of alcohol. He grabbed the bandage boxes and alcohol bottle and placed them inside his backpack.

Downstairs, Erica searched through the living room, the kitchen, and the den. While inside the den, she finds a stash of ammo rounds for a shotgun, though no shotgun is in her sights.

"Damn it." Erica said. "Where could the shotgun be."

She left the den and walked into the backyard. Seeing the patio and swimming pool in the yard with floats and pool equipment along with barbeque pits and lounge chairs. She smiles as she thinks of what the world once was. She glanced around the backyard, seeing the downtown city of Denver in front of her in the distance, with smoke in the air with a mist of fire in it. She returned inside the home, going upstairs to check on Grady.

Grady walked down the hall towards another door. As he inched closer to the door, he moved very slowly. Reaching for the doorknob, he tried not to yank or push the door open. As he slowly opened the door, he sees its a master bedroom and the floor, Grady spots two decayed bodies of a man and a woman. Flies buzzing around the bodies with maggots coming out.

"Jesus Christ."

As Grady sighed and Erica approached him.

"Anything up here?" Erica said.

"Only two boxes of bandages and a bottle of alcohol."

"Not the one you can drink, huh."

"Not even close to that one."

They laughed at the comment before they both heard a loud pitched scream come from outside in the streets. Their laughing immediately stopped as they looked at one another. The first thing coming to their minds is the other members of the group.

"The group!" Grady yelled.

"Holy shit!" Erica said.

They run down the stairs at a very quick pace and run to the outside where they see the other group members running out of the homes in panic as they're being chased by hordes of The Dead.

Grady and Erica run out of the house and see their group being chased by The Dead. As they run toward their group, Grady spotted Lucy being cornered by three of The Dead. Grady pulled out his 9mm Glock and fired three shots into the heads of The Dead. Saving Lucy, he ran over toward her, helped her up as they began to run down the streets from The Dead.

The other members of the group run out of the homes with supplies in their grasps. Danny ran out of the home with a bag of beef jerky and eating some at the same time. He ran over towards Grady.

"What are you doing eating that?"

"I'm hungry, Grady."

"Put that up and help us get out of here!"

Danny placed the beef jerky in his backpack as he helped the other group members exit the homes safety. Grady looked around and seen the entire group with him. As he prepared the runoff, he sees Erica looking inside the Yukon back at the house. He ran over towards her as one of The Dead slowly approached her from behind.

"Erica! Behind you!"

Erica bust through the window of the car door. As Grady ran closer toward her. She turned around, facing The Dead, with a shotgun in her hands. She fired the shot, blowing The Dead's head completely off its body. Its corpse fell to the ground as Grady approached her.

"The shotgun was somewhere."

Grady smirked as they ran off along with the group down the deserted streets of the suburb. They ran as fast as they possibly could with The Dead following them at the same speed, some slower. They continued to run down the streets, before making a right turn.

"Where could we go?!" Erica said.

"There has to be someplace we can go!"

While they ran, Grady looked ahead and seen a bus. He gets an idea in his head and starts running at full speed toward the bus. Yelling at the group to follow him at his own pace. He ran toward the door of the bus. Opening it by shoving his shoulder through the middle of the door. He looked inside, checking for any bodies. Not seeing anyone inside the bus, he looked around for the keys. Erica signals to the group to get into the bus.

They rammed themselves into the bus. Erica looked behind

her and saw Grady staring at the corpse of the bus driver with the keys sticking out of his pocket. Erica raised her head, seeing the Dead inching closer. Grady also saw the Dead approaching as he goes for the keys. Not seeing a head wound on the driver, he moved slowly to grab the keys. He moved slowly to grab the keys. The driver sat up, groaning at Grady. He moved back and the driver's head is shot off. Grady looked behind him, seeing Erica with the shotgun.

"Get the keys, Grady."

Grady snatched the keys and jumped into the bus. He sat in the front seat of the bus and started the engine. He backed the bus up, running over the horde behind him. He puts the bus in gear and looked ahead of him, seeing downtown Denver in the distance.

"Let's get out of here."

Grady drives the bus down the streets, escaping the horde behind him. He glanced back at the group, all sitting in the seats of the bus with Erica sitting behind him.

"Is everyone alright?!" Grady said.

The group responds in saying they're all alright. Erica looked at Grady and glanced to where he was driving.

"Where are you heading?"

"I'm heading through Denver so we can get out of this city."

Grady drives the bus down the streets, passing by a sign that reads, *"DOWNTOWN DENVER, DO NOT ENTER!!!"*

Grady continued to drive the bus at forty-five to fifty miles per hour. Passing by signs that suggest not the enter the downtown area or even get close. Ignoring the signs, he continued to inch closer to downtown. Erica stood behind Grady, looking outside the windows and seeing the abandoned, deserted streets and suburbs.

"So, how do we get pass downtown?" Erica said.

"I know a few ways through the area to get us out of the area faster. We'll have to avoid those things at all cost. We can't be risking the lives of our group, let alone our own lives."

He drove past a few streets, knowing he's about to enter the downtown area. He slowed the bus down to get past a few vehicles that were in the street. Not able to continue driving straight, he turned to his left and drove down the street.

"Looks like I'll have to find another way into the city." Grady said.

Driving straight, he noticed a large truck blocking the street. Slowly losing his patience, he turned down the street on his right. Getting closer to the city as the building became taller. He spotted what looked to be a boulder in the middle of the street. Erica looked through the window, confused.

"What is that?"

"I don't have a clue, but we're about to find out."

Getting closer to the object in the road, Grady quickly stopped the bus. The other group member stood up and looked to see what was in front of them. Erica also looked. Grady was uncomfortable with what he saw. What they saw in front of them was a massive horde of The Dead. From an estimate amount, it had to be over forty to fifty corpses standing in front of them and slowly approaching the bus. Grady is lost deciding as Erica turned to him.

"Ram through them."

"What are you talking about?"

"Just ram through them, Grady! You backed up on the others, just ram through."

The Dead was closer to the bus that previously. With the group members beginning to panic, Erica turned to Grady and kicked him on his right leg. He jumped from the impact of her kick.

"Ram through them, dammit!"

Grady looked at Erica and glanced at the group before turning back toward the front. He stared at the horde and smiled.

"Fuck this."

Grady stomped his foot on the pedal and the bus began to move at a quick speed. The bus moved faster and faster as it reached the horde. Grady yelled as the bus rammed through the horde. Body parts flew in the air and against the bus windows. Covering them with dark blood. The group members held their heads down as Erica watched Grady ram through the horde. He even honked the horn for more excitement at ramming them.

"Now, this is what I call fun!" Grady yelled.

While ramming through the horde, a tire spike strip laid in

front of the bus. Not able to see the strip on the ground due to the amount of blood that's covering the windshield and windows. The bus rammed through the strip, blowing out the tires. Grady grabbed the steering wheel as he tried to gain back the control of the bus. Hearing the tires screeching and scratching across the concrete road. The bus rammed into another vehicle that was sitting in front of them. The impact of the bus hitting the vehicle caused the bus to turn over on its left side.

Getting up slowly from the impact of the fall, Grady looked at the group and seen that most of them died on the fall's impact with only a few that are still alive, although have serious injuries. He looked at Erica, who's getting up with a few cuts on her arms, face, and chest.

"You alright?" Grady asked.

"Good as I'll ever be. Yourself?"

"I'll manage it."

Grady looked through the bus's back window and seen more of The Dead approaching the bus. He grabbed whatever supplies he could get from the other group members that had died and helped Erica get to her feet. Grady kicked the bus door opened and crawled out. Helping Erica crawl out of the bus, he sees there in the city park. He looked over to his right and spotted the Denver Zoo.

"Over here, quickly!"

Erica moved as fast as she could alongside Grady as they approached the entrance to the zoo. They look back at the bus and see its surrounded by The Dead as they tear through the bodies of the group members and hearing a few of them scream in pain as they're being ripped apart from almost every limb.

They approach the front entrance of the zoo and began knocking on the doors for anyone's assistance. They scream as The Dead turn toward them and slowly approach their location. They continue to knock on the door and the door opened. They looked and seen a zookeeper standing in the doorway with a rifle in his hands.

"What are y'all just standing there for! Get in here!" The zookeeper said.

Grady and Erica ran into the zoo entrance as the zookeeper fired shots toward The Dead that were approaching the zoo. He fired a few more shots before turning around and closing the door, blocking The Dead from entering the zoo at any cost.

They entered the zoo as the zookeeper closed the door and blocked it from The Dead entering. He turned toward Grady and Erica and gave them the direction to follow him. They followed him into what appeared to be his own office space. Grady and Erica looked around the office, seeing photos of visitors and animals.

"So, I see I'm not the only survivor out here." The zookeeper said.

"True. Where are the other zookeepers?" Grady said.

They left the zoo right at the start of the outbreak. Many of them died in the front, some took their own lives. They couldn't live in a world where the dead reigned supreme."

"I'm sorry about that."

"I wouldn't be. They made their own choices during this cause."

Grady and Erica looked at each other before turning back toward the zookeeper, who stood up.

"Just follow me to my apartment complex."

They looked at each other confused as they followed the zookeeper through the zoo toward his apartment. Leaving the office, they walked through the zoo, seeing many of the animals still inside the spaces. They passed by the monkeys, the lions and tigers, the fish, and even the alligators. They arrived at the zookeeper's apartment complex, which sat towards the left end of the zoo.

Upon entering it, they noticed that it was covered with food, supplies, and weapons. Ranging from handguns to rifles. The zookeeper sat behind a table and started eating an apple. Grady approached him while looking around the apartment.

"I see you've been staying here for quite a while."

"It's the only place I can be. So, what's your names?"

"I'm Grady and she is Erica."

"Well, you can just call me Kirby. I'm the lead zookeeper here."

"Nice to meet you, Kirby."

Kirby allowed Grady and Erica to sit at the table with him as he allowed them to eat some of the fruit that was sitting on the table. As they ate the fruit, Kirby looked at Grady.

"So, could you two tell me what the hell is going on?"

"That's what we're trying to find out. Last I heard this was all over the east coast. The south and west coast I'm not too sure about. London was the last place that was talked about. The whole city is said to be a quarantine zone."

"Never thought that I would live to see the day that London would be closed down as a quarantine zone. Though, I'll probably never get the chance to visit now."

Erica glanced around at the weapons that laid on the couch and the floor of the apartment. She turned to Kirby.

"I see you have yourself an array of weapons to fight off those things."

"They were kept in the armory in case one of our fierce animals became highly aggressive to control or escaped its space."

"About those animals?" Grady said. "You're feeding them while you're here?"

"Someone has to. You can't just leave these animals here defenseless. The only way to let them loose is to open their spaces, though, I just can't let these animals go. I've grown an attraction to them."

"I see."

"So, where were you two heading? If I may ask."

"We're planning on heading north. Maybe south if the decision comes up again."

"So, I take it you'll need a vehicle to get on your way."

"We'll like one if you have a spare." Erica said.

Kirby nodded. He stood up and walked toward a closet door. He opened the door and pulled out a key. He handed the key to Grady.

"This is the key to the suburban out in the parking lot. You shouldn't have to worry, its gated up."

"Thank you."

Kirby walked over to the weapons and gave them two rifles and two handguns. He also gave them a bag of food and water with a few medicine boxes.

"I'm sure you'll need that as well for your journey."

"We don't know how to thank you." Erica said.

"Don't worry about that."

"Why don't you come with us." Grady said. "Try to find a way out of this hell."

Kirby shook his head. Disagreeing to Grady's offer.

"I belong here with the animals I love and care for. Nothing else out there matters to me anymore."

Kirby walked to the door.

"Follow me to the parking lot."

They followed Kirby to the parking lot. He pointed at the blue suburban in front of them.

"That's the suburban right there."

Grady and Erica place the weapons and gear in the back of the suburban. They get into the suburban and Grady started the engine. He drove towards the closed gate, seeing only a few of The Dead in front of them. Kirby ran over and unlocked the gate. Grady turned to him.

"You're sure about staying here?"

"I have no other option, but to stay here. I still thank you for your proposal. Now, please go."

Grady nodded as he drove through the parking lot and out of the zoo. He turned to his left and drove down the street. Kirby watched them leave and showed a slight smirk before closing the gate and returning inside the apartment.

LOST CAUSES

Running through the deserted streets, avoiding the Dead that roam throughout the entire area, breathing heavily and slowly losing his pace, Lyle finds his way toward the Denver Convention Center. Running near the building, he glanced behind himself and sees The Dead surrounding him. Moaning and screeching at him, trying to catch him.

Lyle ran to the entrance of the center and started banging on the glass and metal doors.

"Help! Anyone home, please!"

Lyle turned around seeing The Dead inching closer to him and the center. He continued banging on the door and yelling for help. As he yelled, he noticed something moving inside the center, approaching the doors. The Dead were closer and only a couple of inches away from grabbing Lyle. As their moans grew louder, the doors burst open and three men are standing in the doorway, with shotguns and handguns in their hands. The man in the middle glances at Lyle.

"Well, aren't you coming in?!"

Lyle nodded and ran inside the center. The three men began firing shots at the horde as it approached them. Firing shots to eliminate as many as possible from the entrance. Blowing the heads and upper bodies off the decayed corpses. Lyle watched the shots fire in front of him. The three men began backing up toward the doors. Once they were back inside, they closed the doors and blocked them with table counters, chairs, and trash cans.

"That was worth a shot." One man said.

They turned around and stared at Lyle, who was still standing behind them, worried about his life. One man signals to the other man to check Lyle for any bite marks or scratches. The man snatched Lyle by his left arm and pushed him against the wall.

"Just take it easy." Lyle said. "I haven't been bitten or scratched."

"We are taking you easy." The man said. "If not, you would be laying on the ground outside dead right now."

Checking Lyle for any marks or scratches. Not finding any, he turned toward the other man and nodded. He nodded back and approached Lyle.

"Looks like you're clean, pal." The man said.

"No kidding."

The three man stand in front of Lyle. They extend their hands as Lyle looked at them, uncertain about their behavior or motive.

"You don't have to be afraid of us, son." The man said. "What's your name?"

"My name's Lyle. Lyle Macken."

"Nice to meet you, Lyle."

The man turned toward the other two. Lyle looked at them and shook their hands as well as shaking the other one's hand.

"These two are Wilbur and Jett."

"Good to meet you two."

"My name is Truman. Hope you will be safe in here with us."

"Better to be safe than sorry."

Truman appears as a man who is a hunter, Wilbur seemed like a construction worker and a potential alcoholic, and Jett was a young kid who could barely survive on his own. Lyle.

"Let us walk you through." Truman said. "Show you around this merry place."

They walk through the Exhibit Hall of the convention center. Lyle looked around at its stellar structure and architect.

"This is a nice place."

"You can say that again." Truman said. "When we came into

this place, there was no one else here. No employees or managers. Just us and only us.”

“Do you have any exact idea as to what happened here in Denver?”

“I don’t have a clue. Heard some things from the radio and the news. Hardly any information I’ve heard has yet to be true.”

“So, those things out there, you’ve been around them?”

“Before the three of us found each other, we were all out there basically on our own. Jett, though lost his friend by a horde when they attacked his camp site.”

“I ran as fast as I could to survive.” Jett said. “When I came closer to finding a place, I ran into Truman and we were teammates ever since.”

Lyle looked at Wilbur and approached him.

“If I may ask, what about yourself?”

“I was drunk before the outbreak took place. When I awoke from my nap, I seen a bunch of those motherfuckers on my yard, so I decided to blow their heads off their shoulders. I left my home and seen the entire streets covered with those things. After a while, I ran into Truman and Jett and that brings you to this place.”

Lyle nodded as he continued to follow Truman through the hall and toward the Mile-High Ballroom. Truman unlocked the door and opened it, entering the ballroom. Seeing a stage in the front with over dozens of chairs standing and knocked down on the floors. The ceiling had its circular and square design structure. Lyle was in awe of the ballroom and what it had presented itself to look like.

“This is a nice-looking room.”

“It is. Too bad we won’t be able to see anymore performances inside this place.”

Lyle looked around toward the stage and seen it covered with guns and ammo. Also, some clothes were sitting in the chairs at the front. He turned toward Truman who was walking near the stage.

“So, you guys sleep in this room?”

“We certainly do. Its big enough for the three of us. If you want to stay in a room to yourself, there’s a meeting room down this hall through that door.”

"Thank you."

Lyle walked through the door and down the hall before entering one of the meeting rooms. Seeing how it was heavily designed and presented, he showed a slight smile and Truman entered the room, handing him a pillow and some bedcovers.

"I'm sure you'll need these for your rest."

"I highly appreciate it, Truman."

"Don't mention it. I'm only trying to help. Good night."

Truman closed the door as Lyle set up the covers and the pillow and went straight to sleep. Shutting his eyes and thinking about how the world once was.

Lyle suddenly jumped up out of the covers with sweat pouring down his head. What woke him up was the sounds of several shots being fired inside the ballroom. Lyle places his clothes back on and runs out of the room and down the hall toward the ballroom. Upon entering the ballroom, he sees Truman, Wilbur, and Jett firing shots at a horde of The Dead that have entered into the building somehow and have burst down the ballroom doors completely.

"Holy shit." Lyle said.

Wilbur turned and seen Lyle looking at the horde. He ran over toward the stage and grabbed one of the handguns. He approached Lyle and tossed the gun at him. Lyle caught the gun in his hands and stared at Wilbur.

"Help us that these bastards out!" Wilbur said.

Lyle started firing shots at the horde as they continued to enter. Each of the men fired as many shots as they could to take out The Dead. Reaching closer to reload their weapons as the horde is getting larger. Truman turned around and ran toward Lyle. Wilbur and Jett follow him.

"We'll have to move out of this location!" Truman said.

While running out of the ballroom, one of The Dead caught Wilbur by his left leg and bites into his calf. Wilbur grunted in massive agony and shot the Dead in its head. He ran behind Lyle in pain and slammed the door. They later regrouped inside the Four Seasons Ballroom. One of the newly set rooms inside the convention center. As they got back together. Truman started checking each of them for any marks or scratches.

"Everyone alright?" Truman said.

"I'm ok." Lyle said.

"Same here, Truman." Jett said.

"What about you, Wilbur?"

Truman turned toward Wilbur, who was standing still, with his face looking as if he's in tremendous pain. Truman looked down at Wilbur's leg and noticed blood pouring out of his pants.

"What the hell is that, Wilbur?!"

"What do you think, dumbass. I was bit."

"What the fuck!" Jett said. "What are we going to do?!"

Truman silenced Jett as he turned toward Wilbur. Cautiously looking at him and slowly reaching for his pistol on his right side.

"I'm sorry it has to come down to this, Wilbur."

"Whoa! What the fuck are you doing, Truman?! You're not going to shoot me!"

"What other option do I have?"

Wilbur looked at Jett and Lyle before reaching into his back and pulling out his gun. He aimed the gun toward Truman's head as Truman held his pistol toward Wilbur's head.

"Killing me won't save you the harm of turning into one of those things, Wilbur."

"I'm not ready to die! Not yet."

Truman started quietly at Wilbur, who did the same. Lyle and Jett stood silently against the walls of the ballroom. The room is completely silent. Truman and Wilbur continued to hold their firearms up aiming at each other.

"Sorry it has to end like this." Truman said.

"So am I." Wilbur said.

Wilbur fired a shot at Truman's chest He yelled in pain as he began to hold his chest. Wilbur began to approach him, but Truman looked up and fired the shot at Wilbur. Shooting him straight through the forehead, killing him. Wilbur's body fell to the ground with a thump to follow the impact. Truman fell to the ground and had died from the bullet, which had gone directly through his heart.

Lyle and Jett looked at the dead bodies of Truman and

Wilbur. The blood draining from the body of Truman and the head and leg of Wilbur.

"Why did this have to happen?!" Jett said. "Why did this happen."

"Just calm down." Lyle said. "We're going to be alright."

"So many lost causes. How many more must I endure in this new world. How many!"

Jett panicked and ran toward the ballroom doors. Lyle yelled at Jett not to open the doors. As Jett opened the door, he was mauled by the horde that was waiting on the other side. Lyle ran out of the room through the side door as he heard Jett screaming as his body was being ripped.

Lyle found himself on the outside of the center in the parking lot. Not seeing as many of The Dead as before, due to them mainly being inside the convention center itself. Lyle searched the cars to see if they were unlocked. He finds one red Mazda and sees that the door is unlocked.

"Oh, thank God."

He gets into the car and realizes he doesn't have a key. He checks the glove box for the key and doesn't find it. He later searched the upper mirror and only a few pieces of paper fell out.

"Where the hell could a key possibly be?"

He later looked in the back of the car, not finding them key. He decided to look under the seats and found a key under the driver's seat. He looked at the key and smiled. Putting the key in, he started the car. He yelled in excitement as he drove the car out of the parking lot. Passing by The Dead.

13 DAYS

DAY 1

The sun shines down on Denver, Colorado. The streets are quiet and covered with abandoned cars and streets of trash. In other streets are covered with walking corpses that appear to be chasing a group of five out of the city and into the woods.

"Run and keep running!" Yelled Lucas toward his group as they ran out of the city of Denver, Colorado and into the woods toward the outskirts of the city. They are running from the out slew of undead corpses that have risen from the graves and morgues that are seeking to devour them completely. They are called the Dead.

"Where are we supposed to go?! You think there's such a place for us anymore?!" said Bret.

"We have to find a safe place to keep quiet and to cover us from being discovered by these things!"

"Where could we find a place like that, Lucas?" Marylyn said.

"We'll find a place soon. We just need to worry about getting out of our current circumstance with these things on our trail."

The group is a pack between Lucas, their leader. A slim guy with light skin, Marylyn, a young woman with dark hair who is paired with Lucas before the outbreak. Bret, a young guy that is a close friend to Lucas before the outbreak, Jeanette, Bret's on and off girlfriend, and Curtis, a friend of Bret's and Lucas that joined them when he escaped the Dead.

Curtis reached into his side and pulled out his gun and began firing at the Dead that surrounded them from outside the city. Lucas screamed toward Curtis to stop shooting them and continue running deep into the woods.

"I have to keep firing at them!" Curtis said. "If not, we'll be their food out here and I'm not interested in being their serving."

The group continues running further into the woods to the point where they are surrounded by the trees and bushes. They find a nice spot and they remain quiet for a few minutes. In those minutes, they could hear the Dead walking in the distance, their feet sliding across the dirt and grass, breaking downed tree branches, and their moaning that sends fear into one's body without touch.

The sun begins to set as Lucas decided that they will set a small camp in the space they currently stand in. Once nightfall approached, there was no noise or sign of the Dead. Lucas was thrilled as was the rest of the group. They each found a place to settle in the small space to where all of them were comfortable in their own space. Lucas started a fire to give them some light and heat as the night brought a cold temperature upon them. The night had settled, and the group was calm and quiet.

DAY 2

Dawn has reached the wilderness as the sunlight shined down on Lucas and Marylyn, who were already awake and sitting down near the worn-out wood from the fire. Bret and Jeanette had some time to themselves while Curtis decided to take a small walk into the woods.

"So, where do you think we could find some place that will keep us safe from those things?" Marylyn said.

"Out of all the places that have been built on this earth and in this country. I would expect there to be some place of any kind to be a safe haven for an amount of people. No matter how many."

"What about weapons? I mean we can't just keep going around with little to no ammo in our guns and we barely have any machetes and staffs to use."

"We can always search for that, but we could use some of these larger tree branches as weapons. If we can find one that is already on the ground."

"That's right, you don't want to become a disturbance and send those things near us."

"That's the reality."

They laugh at each other. Hearing the sound of kissing and look over and they see Bret and Jeanette kissing each other to the point where they were almost getting ready to have sex with each other. Lucas looked around and didn't see Curtis.

"Where did Curtis go?"

"He went out for a walk. That's what he said." Bret said.

"Out there?" Marylyn said.

"That's right. He shouldn't be too far from us. He didn't walk out that far from where we are."

Lucas stood up and knocked the dirt off his clothing. Marylyn stood up, concerned about Lucas' current train of thought.

"What are about to do?"

"I'm going out there to find him. I just need to be sure he's all right and has a weapon on him."

"I'm sure he has a weapon on him, Lucas. There's no need to go running out there like some sort of hero. Curtis will be back, and we'll continue on to our safe haven."

Lucas looked into Marylyn's eyes and released a slight sigh.

"Sorry, but I'm going out there to find him."

Lucas grabbed his handgun and a medium sized tree branch from the ground and headed out into the woods to find Curtis. Marylyn only watched on and wiped the sweat off of her forehead. Bret and Jeanette continue kissing and cuddling underneath their covers.

Curtis walked around the forest, not too far from the group's camp site. He walked around, thinking to himself how the outbreak started and could there be a possible way in finding a cure to bring back society as it previously were.

"It can't be the whole country can it?" Curtis said to himself. "I mean, it just can't be possible that the whole country was wiped out. What about the world itself?! Could the entire globe be populated by those walking corpses?! I'm starting to freak out talking about this to myself."

While walking, Curtis stepped on a downed branch. Its cracking sound traveled through the quiet wilderness and he began to hear moaning coming from deep within the woods. Curtis begins to hear steps not too far from his location. He slowly walked to see what else was walking in the woods. He moved a bush from his viewpoint and saw several of the Dead walking around and near his current spot.

"Oh shit! Oh shit!"

Curtis took a few steps back and tripped over another larger branch. The sound of his fall was heard by the Dead. All of whom began to moan louder and approach his location. Curtis began to panic quietly as he reached for his gun and placed it to his head. He hears some footsteps coming closer and a hand comes down on is shoulder.

"Dude, get up!" Lucas said.

"Oh shit! You're here. They're on their way to this spot. We have to move!"

"No kidding, Curtis."

Lucas and Curtis walk back toward the camp site as the Dead slowly enter the woods where they previously were standing.

DAY 3

The group continued walking through the wilderness in search of a haven to keep themselves protected from the Dead that walked constantly around the woods and some even in the woods. While walking in the wilderness, they see an opening and taking that opening had brought them onto a highway where they could see both ends of the streets. The streets were empty, no vehicles were laying on the streets. Lucas decided that taking the highway trail would probably help them in finding signs for a location to keep occupied.

While taking the highway trial, they come across a lone hitchhiker. The hitchhiker sees them and immediately runs toward them. Lucas tells the group to be on edge when the hitchhiker approaches them. The hitchhiker confronted them and stood in their pathway.

"Please, I need some help." The hitchhiker said. "I could help you and your people. Please?!"

"I'm sorry. We don't know who you are, and you do not know who we are." Lucas said. "There's nothing we can do for you."

"Are you sure?" Jeanette said. "He can't join us?"

"Please?! I will do anything for you and your people, and I mean absolutely anything."

Lucas took a few steps back from the hitchhiker as he reached out toward him in a lustful manner. Lucas looked over the hitchhiker's left shoulder and saw what was behind him. The group also saw what was approaching the hitchhiker from behind. Lucas and the group ran as the hitchhiker seemed confused. He hears moaning behind him and is backed by the Dead, three of them. They began to rip him apart from his abdomen and bite his neck and arms, eating the flesh thereof.

Lucas looked toward them and see the Dead eating the hitchhiker. Lucas quietly lead the group pass the Dead as they continued looking and following the highway trail. Upon finding themselves entering a small patch that lead them back into the woods, Lucas spotted something ahead, something big and tall. He ran toward the object.

"Lucas, wait!" Marylyn said.

Lucas continued running as the group tried to catch up. The group finds him standing still looking a building in front of him. They walked toward him and set their eyes on the building. Lucas and the group were appalled.

"You see what I'm seeing." Marylyn said.

"I am, Marylyn." Lucas said. "This looks like our spot."

The group were staring at an abandoned warehouse that stood at least three stories tall and was wide enough to have clear space to do anything inside of it. The warehouse didn't appear to be rusty or old in any sort of way. The warehouse appeared to be recently built and planned to be used for construction before the outbreak began. Lucas smiled as they walked toward the warehouse.

Lucas noticed the sun going down and the moon slowly rising up, indicating that nightfall was approaching. He decided that he group would set camp in the small garage area of the warehouse for the night and that they would find a way into the warehouse in the morning.

DAY 4

Lucas and Bret try to find any tools to use in order to get into the warehouse. Curtis, Marylyn, and Jeanette also searched around the outside and around the warehouse for any tools. Curtis decided to check the garage itself for any tools. He searched the desk's drawers and found a key that was laying underneath a drawer. He walked outside toward Lucas and Bret as they were trying to break the lock on the front doors.

"Guys, I found a key."

"Where did you find it?" Lucas said.

"It was underneath a drawer in the desk back in the garage. I figured it would be worth a try."

Lucas grabbed the key and placed it in the lock. He turned the key and it unlocked the lock pad on the door. Bret pulled the chain and padlock off the door. Lucas turned around and smiled at Curtis. They opened the warehouse doors and they entered the warehouse. Seeing its interior space, the area they stood in appeared to be a lobby of a sort. The warehouse was clean and filled with tools that would be used for building construction and had car parts such as engines, tires, and used doors and seats.

"This is our new dwelling place, guys." Lucas said. "As of right now, this is our new home."

"Look at the size of this place." Bret said. "We can each have our separate spots in here."

"Yeah we could." Curtis said. "I wonder what else they have in here that could be useful."

"I would worry about that tomorrow. For right now, its best

that we bring in our gear and get settled. We'll do some more searching tomorrow and that way we can search this entire place."

"Fair enough, Lucas." Curtis said. "I'm taking that spot over in the corner over there."

Marylyn walked over to Lucas as the rest of the group grabbed the gear and placed it inside of the warehouse. She patted Lucas on the back and smiled at him. He turned toward her.

"Seems like a good place to start." Marylyn said.

"This is our place until the time is necessary for us to leave. As of right now, we're staying in this place."

DAY 5

The next day, Curtis is the first one to awaken and he sets out on searching the other parts of the warehouse. After a couple of minutes pass, Lucas also awakens and sees Curtis walking up on the first set of stairs that head toward the second level of the warehouse.

"You're going to wait for me or are you in some hurry?" Lucas said.

Curtis turned around and seen Lucas looking at him from below. Curtis laughed as Lucas smiled. Lucas began walking up the stairs, following Curtis up onto the second floor of the warehouse. They reach the second floor of the warehouse and see that its nearly empty except for the wooden planks that sit at the opposite end of the floor.

"What do you think of this level?" Lucas said.

"I think it's a good start at least to have something going. I mean, we could build stuff ourselves in here. We have the tools necessary to get the jobs done."

While looking around the second floor, they began hearing slight footsteps coming from the third floor of the warehouse. Lucas grabbed his gun and slowly walked toward the staircase that lead up to the third floor. Curtis followed Lucas quietly as he held a 2x4 in his hand. They get near the staircase, until they see two men walk down the staircase and stand in front of them. The men appeared to be rugged and seemed like they've been drinking.

"Whoa. What do we have here?" One man said.

"Looks to me like there's more people living in this place with us." The other man said.

"Nah. These guys had to break the lock on the door in order to get in. Tell me who are you and what are you doing here in this warehouse?"

"My name is Lucas, and this is Curtis. We entered this warehouse yesterday with our group and we don't intend on leaving."

"Well, my name is Dreyfus and my friend over here is Kurt. We're not telling you to leave. This warehouse is big enough for us all to live in."

"Is that right?"

"Yeah. That's right. I need to see you and the rest of group in full before we can come to terms on how this kind of living will suit with us all. Remember, we were in this warehouse first. We placed the lock on that door."

Lucas nodded as he and Curtis began walking back down to the first floor with Dreyfus and Kurt behind them coming down the staircase. Marylyn, Bret, and Jeanette are all awake as they see Lucas and Curtis coming down the staircase.

"Lucas, what's going on?" Marylyn said.

"That sounded like a woman and I mean a woman!" Dreyfus said.

The group stood together as Dreyfus and Kurt stepped off the staircase and approached them. Marylyn began to have a small sense of fear, so did Jeanette. Lucas, Curtis, and Bret stood in front of them and faced Dreyfus and Kurt.

"You brought women into this place. Two of them at that." Dreyfus said. "Seems our deal has just changed a bit, Lucas."

"You're not touching them by any means." Lucas said. "We won't let you do such a thing."

"Damn straight, boys." Bret said. "Make one more toward our girls and you'll regret having made the move."

Dreyfus and Kurt laughed as Lucas and the group stood still and kept themselves in a serious fashion. Dreyfus placed his gun back in his belt and held his hand up.

"Our deal is simple. This is our warehouse, we got here first. So, that gives me and Kurt here total leadership of you and this usage of this warehouse."

"Is that all you're asking for?" Lucas said.

"Our second add-on to this deal is full control of your two women."

"I don't think so, boy!" Bret said.

"We already said you're not getting near them by any means." Lucas said. "We made that statement perfectly clear."

Dreyfus nodded as he stared into Lucas' blue eyes. He took a step back and gave a smirk.

"You have till tomorrow to make the decision." Dreyfus said. "We'll be up on the third floor while you think it over with your group and by tomorrow morning, we will be back down here and if no decision is made between all for you, we'll go ahead and make the decision for you. Very simple."

"Oh, it's simple all right." Lucas said. "It's very simple. We'll talk with you two in the morning."

"You surely will, Lucas. Good day and night, ladies."

"I can't wait to touch your skin tomorrow, ladies." Kurt said. "It will be a pleasure worthwhile."

Dreyfus and Kurt walk back up the staircase toward the third floor. Lucas sat with the group about their circumstance. The group believe they should leave the warehouse and go searching for another place to dwell in. Lucas believes otherwise.

"We're not leaving this place." Lucas said. "Not by any chance we are leaving from this place."

"What do expect us to do when those guys come back down here in the morning?" Curtis said.

"When they come back down here and if they make any sudden movements, we kill them. Very simple."

DAY 6

The following morning arrives as Lucas didn't sleep at all. He sat down near the staircase waiting for Dreyfus and Kurt to come down. Bret and Curtis wake up along with Marylyn and Jeanette. After a few hours near noon, Dreyfus and Kurt come down the stairs and face the group. Lucas stood firm as he stared Dreyfus in the eyes. Dreyfus laughed.

"So, we would like to hear your answer now concerning our arrangement from yesterday."

"There is no answer." Lucas said. "We're not handing over our girls and we're not leaving this place."

"Let me get this straight. You're not giving us your women and you're not leaving our warehouse? Is that what I heard come out of your mouth?"

"That's exactly what you heard."

Dreyfus nodded and swiped Lucas in the face with a punch. Lucas dropped to the ground on one knee. Dreyfus laughed as Bret rammed him into the wall and began pummeling him. Kurt grabbed Bret and punched him in the abdomen and threw him toward the ground. Dreyfus rubbed his face and walked over to Curtis and punched him.

"Your women are ours and you're under our ruler ship, boys!" Dreyfus said.

Dreyfus walked over toward Marylyn and began rubbing her from her forehead down to her breasts. He exhaled as he looked at her face.

"We are going to have so much fun, honey. Believe that."

Dreyfus stood in front of Marylyn, Kurt approached Jeanette and immediately tossed her down and tried to unzip her pants. She began kicking to shove him off her, but he kept coming.

"I'm going to show you how to use that mouth of yours, baby." Kurt said. "Now, open yourself up for me to make my entrance."

Jeanette began screaming as Bret stood up and ran over toward Kurt. Bret snatched Kurt off her and started beating him in the head with both his fists.

"I told you ass not to place your hands on her!" Bret said. "Told you, bitch!"

Curtis got back to his feet and attempted to get Dreyfus away from Marylyn, but Dreyfus punched Curtis again and shoved Marylyn against the wall and completely closed her in.

"It's time we have some fun, honey." Dreyfus said. "Trust me, you'll love it."

Lucas stood up and seen Bret pummeling Kurt on the floor. He turned and seen Dreyfus having Marylyn against the wall. He ran over toward them and grabbed Dreyfus by his scraggy hair and threw him down on the ground. Lucas started punching Dreyfus, But Dreyfus counted and smacked Lucas in the face with an open slap.

"You're one tough boy!" Dreyfus said. "Too bad you have to go now and without your women."

Dreyfus walked over toward the downed Lucas and kicked him in the gut. Dreyfus laughed as he walked over toward Marylyn. Lucas pulled out his gun from his side and shot Dreyfus in his right leg. The sound of the gun caused the entire place to echo and suddenly became silent. Kurt looked over and seen Dreyfus holding his leg. He punched Bret and shoved him off and looked toward Lucas, where he seen the gun in his hand. Kurt stood up and ran toward Lucas.

"You shot him!"

Lucas turned and shot Kurt in the chest. Kurt stopped in place as he reached over to his chest and placed both hands above the bullet wound. Lucas walked over toward him and kicked him in the chest, knocking him to the ground. Dreyfus looked and seen Kurt dead on the ground with his hands on his chest. Lucas turned toward Dreyfus.

"Remember now, it's very simple." Lucas said. "We're not leaving this place."

Lucas fired another shot at Dreyfus, going through his head with his blood splattering the wall behind him near Marylyn. Dreyfus' body collapses to the ground. The group looked on and they looked at Lucas who only stared at the two bodies of Dreyfus and Kurt. Curtis rubbed the blood from his lip onto his hand and walked around the bodies.

"We don't have to worry. This place is ours."

DAY 7

The group settled themselves to be calm. Lucas and Bret had taken the bodies of Dreyfus and Kurt to the other side of the warehouse to rot. Marylyn began to worry about how Lucas would behave after killing Dreyfus and Kurt in front of them without any means of hesitation. Bret comforted Jeanette and Curtis continued to bandage the scars on his body from the fight.

"Are you ok, Lucas." Marylyn said. "You haven't said much since you killed those two men."

"There's nothing wrong with me for you to start concerning yourself with my well-being. I did what I had to do to keep all of us safe. Those men made their choices clearly and they were given the warning not to do so."

"So, you're just going to leave their bodies to rot out there in front of this warehouse? Their stench could draw in those corpses out there and they could be on us like hounds."

"No need to worry about that. We took those bodies deep into the woods so those things out there wouldn't get near this place. I will say this again, Marylyn. We're not leaving this place. This is our home now."

"I understand you clearly."

"Thank you for doing that and I appreciate it with much gratitude."

Lucas turned away and began walking up the staircase to the second floor of the building. Marylyn grabbed some of her gear and decided to place it on the second floor where she decided she would dwell in. Bret and Jeanette made the decision to stay on the first floor to keep an extra eye out on anything that might come near the front and back doors.

Curtis had joked around that he would take the third floor and so he had done. He grabbed his backpack and went up to the third floor where he was surrounded by mechanic and engineering tools and some food and supplies left from Dreyfus and Kurt.

"Hey, Lucas. They're some very useful stuff on this floor." Curtis said. "I think you should come up here and see this for yourself.

"I'm coming on up." Lucas said.

Curtis hears the footsteps of Lucas approaching him on the floor. Lucas walked up behind him and looked around the floor, seeing the tools and the supplies of some to little food and a bunch of ammo and three handguns laying down that once belonged to Dreyfus and Kurt.

"First thing is we take those bastards' weapons and food." Lucas said.

"I figured you'll do that from the start."

"Someone has to, and we'll find some sort of way to use these tools for killing those things out there."

Curtis laughed at Lucas' words of choosing. Lucas didn't understand why Curtis was laughing.

"What's funny? What did I say?"

"You said we're going to kill those corpses out there and you didn't realize you said corpses and kill in the exact same sentence."

"They're undead corpses. So, we would have to kill, kill them. If that makes any kind of sense."

"It works for me, Lucas."

"You're taking this floor from what I heard, correct?"

"Yeah. I got this floor. No problems at all."

"I just wanted to make sure everyone knows what floor they are on so there won't be any kind of problems between us."

"No issues coming from me. I got the top floor and I'll do pretty well."

Lucas walked back down to the second floor and noticed the sun setting. He and Marylyn settled on the second floor for the night as Bret and Jeanette took the first floor. Curtis laid on the third floor by himself and fell asleep after eating the chocolate pudding that was left behind by Dreyfus and Kurt.

Later that night, Curtis walked down to the first floor, knowing he had to take a leak, he decided to use the back door to avoid waking up Bret and Jeanette. Curtis went toward the back door and pushed it open. The doors open and Curtis is staring in the eyes of the Dead. About seven of them stare at Curtis and he looked toward them in a solid manner. His body not moving an inch.

"Oh shit." Curtis said.

The Dead lunged at Curtis, taking him down on the ground. Curtis yelled loud enough for the rest of the group to hear. Bret was up and had his gun in hand. He ran toward the yelling and seen Curtis on the group, being eaten alive by the Dead.

"Shit! Shit!" Bret said.

Bret began firing the gun at the Dead, killing them with shots to their heads. Lucas ran in from behind Bret and locked his eyes on Curtis, who was continually being ripped apart by the Dead. Lucas shook his head and pulled out his handgun and walked over toward the Dead and began shooting them one by one.

"This isn't happening to us right now!" Lucas said. "This cannot be happening to us right now!"

Marylyn and Jeanette stood back as they watched the shooting take place. They also noticed Curtis' body on the ground and the large amounts of blood that poured out from his body. After they killed the Dead, Lucas kneeled at Curtis' body. Seeing Curtis is dead, Lucas took his handgun and shot Curtis in the forehead, to avoid him turning into one of the Dead.

"So long, friend."

The group remained quiet for a few minutes before more of the Dead began to approach the warehouse. The group ran and realized that the warehouse would be surrounded within a few more minutes. Lucas had wrestled with the thought of staying at the warehouse, but he knew it would potentially cause more deaths in their group. Lucas told Bret to pack their gear quickly and that they were leaving. Bret and Jeanette had their gear packed up and ready.

"Do we really have to go?!" Marylyn asked.

"I'm sorry, but we have no other option to do. We have to leave this place before we end up like Curtis."

Marylyn had her gear packed. Lucas began packing his and decided to run up the third floor and take some of Curtis' gear along as well. He also grabbed the remaining food, a crowbar, and a wrench. Lucas ran down the stairs and seen more of the Dead coming from the back, appeared to be over a dozen of them in that short time.

"You guys have all of your stuff?!"

"Yeah! We're good to go!" Bret said.

The Dead began to inch closer toward them as they stood in the front and grabbed whatever else was left that they could take along with them. Their moans and footsteps began to send a chill down their spines and fear began to consume the entire group, including Lucas in the situation.

"We have to go now!" Lucas said.

"We're on it!" Bret said.

The group ran out of the warehouse through the front door as over a dozen of the Dead had fully taken over the warehouse in hordes. Lucas decided to take one look back at the warehouse and continued running back into the wilderness where they came before.

"Damn it!" Lucas said.

DAY 8

The group walked constantly through the woods, trying to find any sort of shelter possible while also avoiding the large amounts of Dead that surrounded them from all angles of the wilderness. They're all exhausted from the running they've had to do in order to avoid the Dead from seeing them. Jeanette begins to slow down as she leans against a tree to catch her breath.

"We have to keep moving." Lucas said. "It's necessary that we do so."

"Just let me get a little breather, please." Jeanette said. "That's all I ask."

"Five minutes and we continue on moving."

Bret decided to stay with Jeanette at the tree. Lucas decided to take a small walk to see what was ahead of them. Marylyn stayed behind him as he walked through the bushes.

"Keep yourself ready for any sign of those corpses." Lucas said.

"I'm aware of my surroundings, Lucas."

Lucas moved the bushes from his viewpoint and saw what appeared to be an open field straight ahead of him. He rubbed his eyes and took another look. Lucas sees a schoolyard that is clear of any Dead nearby. He glanced over toward the right and saw the school itself sitting still with no Dead around it.

"There's our place." Lucas said.

Bret and Jeanette catch up with Lucas and Marylyn and they also see the school and the schoolyard in front of them. Lucas turned toward them and pointed at the school.

"We can take that place and make it ours."

"I don't see any of those things around the school." Bret said. "Let's check it out to see for ourselves if its secure."

"What if some of those things found a way to get inside the school like they did back at the warehouse." Jeanette said. "We should be careful on this one."

"She has a point, Lucas." Marylyn said. "Overall, it's your decision to make."

"We're going in."

They run out of the bushes to avoid the Dead from catching up to them and they begin to jump over the gate to get into the schoolyard. After they jumped the gate, they see a door ahead of them that goes into the school.

"So, what's the plan now?" Bret said. "We just take this place for ourselves?"

"We should check the cafeteria to see if there's any food left over." Lucas said. "It can come in handy for us."

Before they could reach the door, it opened. The group takes a few steps back, but Lucas stands his guard. Coming out of the door is an middle-aged man carrying a shotgun, behind him are two young women and a young man, all of whom carrying weapons ranging from knives to handguns.

"Who are you people and why are you here?" The middle-aged man said.

"We're here to see if this place was secure from those things." Lucas replied. "We don't want any trouble at all."

The middle-aged man looked at the group from their heads to their feet. He placed his eyes back on Lucas.

"None of you were bitten, were you?"

"No bite marks or scratches on us, sir."

The middle-aged man nodded and moved over to the side, allowing Lucas and the group to enter the school. The middle-aged man shut the door and locked it from the inside.

DAY 9

After entering the school, the group decided to look around for anything they could use for survival. They enter what appears to be a large office that might have been used for conference meetings.

"You can just call me the Custodian." the middle-aged man said. "These three are Pratt, Silica, and JiJi."

They greeted the three other survivors and sat with them at one of the conference tables. They looked over to another table and saw the large amount of food sitting on the tables with some bottles of water and soda.

"You may get something to eat and drink if you want." The Custodian said.

"You sure we can?" Bret said. "Only asking to be sure."

"By all means take as much as you can get."

They agreed and began to eat some of the food on the table and took some bottles of water for themselves. Lucas grabbed a bottle of water and approached the middle-aged man.

"I have to thank you for allowing us in this place."

"It's the least I could do. None of you had any bite marks or scratches and it appeared that you all were running nonstop through the woods. The amount of dirt and broken limbs on your clothing pretty much prove that point."

Lucas smiled as he took a sip from the bottled water.

"Been a while since I had a bottle of water."

"That long you say."

"I basically lost count of the days that have gone by since we all took off and left for safety."

"Follow me."

Lucas followed the middle-aged man into the nearby office where he seen a large calendar posted on the wall. The days were marked with an X except for one where it said, "The Dead Arose". Lucas pointed toward it, thinking to himself.

"It's only been that long?"

"Yeah. The outbreak started around six days ago and I've been trying to keep track of it ever since. I figured someone should keep counting the days."

"I can somewhat agree on that."

"Why don't you and your group take the rest of the day to settle up and we can continue on with our discussion tomorrow."

"I would highly appreciate that. Thank you."

"Don't thank me, good sir. Thank yourselves for finding this place and jumping over that fence to get here."

DAY 10

Right around the start of the next day, Lucas, Bret, and the Custodian decide to go out into the woods to hunt for some deer. Pratt decided to stay with Marylyn, Jeanette, Silica, and JiJi. Outside in the woods, they formed a sort of huddle structure to see all angles of their surroundings.

"I take it you've done this before?" Bret said.

"Back in my day and at my former home, I went out and hunted deer for dinner."

"Free food." Lucas said. "Smart strategy."

"It is. Not having to worry about if I was going to eat the next day or the next week."

"I couldn't do it. I need some fast food in my life to keep going."

"Do you see any fast food around now?"

"No. They're all closed down because of this outbreak. I will tell you that chaos does indeed ruin some things in life that are useful."

"Those fast food places only wanted your money and they surely received it gently."

"You have a point there, sir." Lucas said. "So, how many deer have you encountered in these woods because while we were running through here, we didn't run into any kind of animal."

"The deer sit in the quiet places of the wilderness. It is our duty to seek out those places in order to find them. Once we find them, we'll have them in our sights and soon on our dinner table."

After walking a couple of more feet, the Custodian encounters an adult male deer sitting in the woods eating off the bushes. He smiled and let out a small laugh.

"There's our food right there. Look at that thing of beauty."

"How can we catch that thing in a time like this when those things are running loose out here?" Bret said.

"Simple."

The custodian kneeled and moved a bag over to his side and revealed a bow and a pair of wooden arrows. He raised it up as he looked toward Bret.

"Bow and arrow, buddy. Useful for quiet kills and quick takedowns, if used correctly."

The Custodian placed one of the wooden arrows bow onto the bow and aimed closely toward the deer. He stayed quiet and so do both Lucas and Bret.

"I got this one." The Custodian said.

He released the bow and the arrow flew through the woods. The arrow hit the deer in the neck, piercing its hide. The deer moved around before falling onto its side. The Custodian smiled as he placed the bow onto his back and moved the arrow set.

"We got our kill."

Back at the school, Pratt seemed a bit uncomfortable being the only man in the room with four women. He found himself attracted toward Jeanette and he approached her. She glanced at him and he gave off a small smile.

"I don't know what you're doing, but its best if you stop." Jeanette said.

"Why should I stop."

Pratt placed his hand on Jeanette's shoulders and started moving his hand lower onto her breast and even lower onto her jeans. Jeanette grabbed his hand and placed it on his head. Pratt gave off a small sigh.

"I'm sorry, but Bret is my boyfriend."

"Oh, well then I truly apologize for my act of seduction toward you. I meant no harm."

Jeanette looked over toward Marylyn, who sat at the table reading a book. She looked over in the corner to see Silica and JiJi kissing each other passionately and shoving each other on the wall and back in the corner.

"I see why you're not with one of them."

"Yeah. You know why I made the moves on you. They should take that in the other office or classroom. I mean we're in a school after all."

Lucas, Bret, and the Custodian return to the school with the deer in their possession. Pratt smiled as he looked at the deer's body. Rubbing his hands together.

"Look at how much meat we have stocked up just with this one buck."

"Don't get too carried away, Pratt." The Custodian said. "We still have to skin it and do the other assumptions."

"You're right there and I will offer my hand in helping."

"Well, thank you."

DAY 11

The group ate the deer and had most of the deer meat left over to later consumption. Lucas and Marylyn sat in the other office to talk amongst themselves. The rest of the group stayed in the main office and talked among themselves.

"What do you think of this place?" Marylyn said.

"What do you mean?"

"I mean how do you feel about this place and about these new people?"

"They're good people and this place is starting to seem like our official stopping point."

"You're sure about that?"

"The whole school and the schoolyard are completely gated, and those things can't climb over the gates, otherwise they'll just pierce themselves on the top. Luckily none of us did."

Marylyn nodded and smiled. Lucas smiled also.

"I see your point there, Lucas."

"All you need to worry about is being safe and having me at your side. That's all that should be on your mind."

"We can't try our relationship in this new world. It just doesn't appear right to me."

"Don't worry about that. Once we're officially set up in a place, like this, we can discuss all of that."

"Ok"

Lucas leaned over and hugged Marylyn. She held him tightly as they both smiled over each other's shoulders.

DAY 12

Everybody sat in the main conference room and spoke with each other. Lucas and the Custodian made it official to everyone that they're officially staying at the school to live in and start a new life if possible.

"We're going to try this place out and see if it works to our advantage." Lucas said. "So, as of this day, we should at least have a small celebration for finding a safe haven and living this long in this apocalyptic time we currently dwell in."

"So, we shall." Pratt said. "To survival."

"TO SURVIVAL." Everyone said as they took a toast and drank the soda.

Everyone continued to talk, and they even had a small party amongst themselves. Lucas sat with Marylyn to discuss plans of their relationship. Bret and Jeanette decided to take one of the classrooms not far from the conference room for themselves to live in. Pratt stayed in the other office drinking cups of soda, and Silica and JiJi stayed in one of the nearby classrooms enjoying one another.

They continued to party for most of the day till nightfall and they still partied. Most of the group fell asleep except for Lucas, who was plotting out ideas as to how to kill the Dead with new techniques.

"This is only a plan in progress, and I will remember that." Lucas said.

In the woods behind the school, one of the gates have been knocked down by what seemed to be a tree. Cracking sounds are heard as the Dead begin to slowly enter the schoolyard. After three head through, seven walked through. After seven walked through nine walked through and the entire field was covered with the Dead all moaning and sliding their feet through the grass. One of the school's back doors is unlocked and one of the Dead rammed his head through the door, opening it slightly. Shoving against the door and walked through, allowing more of the Dead to enter the school without anyone realizing it.

DAY 13

A loud screech is heard as the group run to a nearby classroom and see Silica and JiJi being attacked and ripped apart by the Dead. Lucas screamed for everyone to grab their stuff and head out. The Custodian grabbed his shotgun.

"What are you doing?!" Lucas said.

"I'm clearing a way out of here and I can do that with this baby here."

The Custodian began firing at the Dead, but more seemed to appear. He continued firing as the rest of the group grabbed their stuff and began to head out. Bret opened the door leading out into the schoolyard and seen it to be overloaded with the Dead. The Dead lunged at Bret, ripping his neck apart. Jeanette screamed as she tried to pull Bret from the morbid hands of the Dead. More of the Dead came up behind Jeanette and started biting her on her head, neck, back, and legs. She went down screaming next to Bret as the Dead ate them both alive.

"We have to go!" Lucas yelled. "NOW!"

"You go!" the Custodian said. "I'll hold them off!"

"They'll kill you!" Pratt said.

"Just go."

Lucas, Marylyn, and Pratt ran out of the school and onto the other side facing the gate. They jumped over the gates as they can hear the shotgun going off several times before it went silent. They knew them that the Custodian was dead. While running, Lucas stumbled upon a vehicle that sat in the yard. He ran toward it and found it was unlocked.

"Get in here!" Lucas said.

They threw their bags in the car and they entered the vehicle. Lucas noticed that they couldn't find the key. Lucas looked around the car and couldn't find the key as the Dead inched closer toward the car.

"Come on!" Marylyn said.

"Where the hell is the damn key?!" Pratt panicked. "We're about to become breakfast for those biters!"

"Not if you stop screaming."

"Sure. We'll just be a pair of flesh omelets for them. All in different shapes and sizes to enjoy a wonderful meal."

Lucas checked underneath the seat and found the key. He kissed it and placed it in the ignition. The car starts and Lucas see it apparently has a full tank of gas.

"We're out of here." Lucas said.

He slammed his foot on the pedal and the car drove off, ramming the Dead that were in front of it. Lucas turned onto the road and drove off, leaving the school behind him as he took a glance in his rear-view mirror

THE HORDE

CHAPTER ONE

Interstate 5 in Washington state is completely packed. Many are trying to enter Seattle as other drivers try to find their way through. In the front, the drivers notice that a hazard sign has been placed on the interstate for anyone traveling through. No vehicles are moving, just sitting in their current places. One driver, a man, exits his vehicle and proceeds to walk to the front of the interstate. As drivers honk their horns at each other trying to get pass, the man continues walking through.

As he looked closer, he's yanked to the ground. He started to scream as his body is being ripped apart by unseen forces. They bite onto his neck and arms, draining the blood from his body. His screams are heard from the other drivers. As he screamed, other drivers walk out of their vehicles, only to be attacked by the forces as well. Now, the entire interstate is covered with abandoned cars and over a hundred scattered people running for their lives.

The people begin running toward the entrance into downtown Seattle. They continue to run and scream in horror as many of them are being knocked to the ground or yanked behind a vehicle. Many lie on the ground, being ripped apart and bitten in the neck, arms, and thighs. Many are reaching the entrance quickly, but the forces are moving at a faster pace, catching and killing anyone who's in their way.

Inside an office of a home sat Dr. Allan Desportan, a scientist who works on different species of animals and sometimes works on finding cures for diseases. As he sat at his desk, examining a file that contained information about Polio, he looked up at the TV in his office, he noticed it was CNN, which presented a broadcasting the instate event, Desportan leaned in and realized the running people were heading downtown in Seattle. As he watched the live footage, he seen the forces that were chasing and killing the people. Deep pale skin, some with red eyes, glowing from the reflections of light, others with clear eyes and long fanged teeth coming from their mouths.

Desportan stood up from his desk and goes for his white lab-style coat and someone's knocking on his door. He walked to the door and opened it. A Caucasian woman with long wavy black hair. She wore a buttoned-down shirt with blue jeans and looked to be in her late twenties.

"Dr. Seward." Desportan said. "What are you doing here?"

"I came to check to see if you just saw the footage of the interstate."

"I did." I was about to drive near it to examine the creatures."

"I think you shouldn't go." Seward said. "Its best that you stay indoors to avoid this. I'm sure we'll be involved with this tomorrow."

"You have a point there." Desportan said. "Thanks for warning me, Lucy."

"You're my colleague." Lucy said. "I have no choice but to watch out for you."

Lucy left Desportan's home. He walked back inside and sat in his office, still watching the live feed of the interstate. Now, there aren't many people running on the streets, they're just lying on the ground either dead or dying.

"What in God's name is going on."

CHAPTER TWO

In the morning, CNN reports that over one-hundred and fifty casualties were documented in the interstate massacre. Desportan arrives into the public science laboratory in Seattle. Seeing Lucy again, he walked toward her, entering her office.

"Good morning, Lucy."

"Same to you, Doctor."

"So, what's the current situation on the Interstate incident?"

"The bodies have been taken to the morgue. I will contact them in a few about any unusual symptoms to the bodies."

"Very well."

Desportan walked into his office to find an envelope on his desk. He walked over and picked it up. He looked to see who it was from, which was his ex-wife, Eva Desportan. He opened the letter, which was a response about their divorce and what she would receive from it. The letter stated that she demands a BMW be brought to her. He picked up his cell phone and called her.

"Eva, yes its me. I just received your letter about the car."

"What do you mean 'the car'? it's a BMW that you bought me and I want it immediately."

"There are more important things going on right now and I can't get to it at this time."

"You better get to it, because there's nothing more important than me receiving my BMW."

"It'll be a while before you receive it."

"Just bring it to me."

Eva hung up, which Desportan put the phone down.

"She'll never understand."

Lucy walked into Desportan's office. He looked up and seen her.

"Anything major?"

"The bodies at the morgue. They all have bites marks on their throats, arms, and legs."

"Bite marks?"

"The coroner's not sure as to what caused those bites."

In the Museum of History and Industry, a man is currently walking through. He is German doctor, a fellow historian and he's also a vampire hunter. He is known as Professor Abelard Ekkehardt. Abelard scans the aisle for anything related to vampirism or any source that connects to vampires. As he approaches the final set of aisles on the row, finding a book related to vampirism. He sits at a table in a corner as he scans through the book quickly. He stopped at one particular page, which showed an illustration of a horde of vampires.

Abelard squinted his eyes at the pack and thought back about the interstate incident. Abelard knows that vampires are the cause of the interstate disaster. Abelard leaves the museum. Abelard arrived at the hospital which has the bodies of the deceased in their morgue. He walked toward the receptionist's desk.

"Excuse me, I would like to speak with your coroner, please."

"I'm not sure if I can allow something like that."

"Please, madam. It's of a serious matter. The bodies are not safe to be examined on."

The receptionist cautiously points to the direction of the morgue. Abelard looked and thanked her. He moved quickly through the amount of people in the hallways. He turned two corners before reaching a door that says "Morgue" on its nameplate.

"Finally."

Abelard walked into the morgue and seen firsthand the number of bodies lying inside. He spotted the bite marks.

"Dear God."

The door opened behind him and it's the coroner. Abelard

walked up to him and pointed at the bodies.

"What are you doing in here, sir?"

"Please, you must listen to me. You need to rid of these bodies and burn them immediately! They're not safe to be around."

"Why don't I just call security to see if you're alright."

"I am alright! I've been doing this job for over thirty years. I know when a body should not be messed with and you're trailing on some thin ice here, young man."

Abelard walked to the door, before exiting the morgue, he turned to the coroner with a concerned look on his face.

"Please, burn the bodies. All of them."

Abelard walked out of the morgue and exited the hospital. The coroner walked out to see if Abelard left. As he stood at the door, a doctor passed by, looking the same direction.

"What was the problem?"

"Just some crazy old man, that's all."

After the moon set, a group of vampires, some with hair, others bald. All of them are pale and have clear eyes and razor sharp teeth. Others have some sort of ooze coming from their mouths. Over a dozen of them gathered at Crown Hill Cemetery. The dozen vampires move quickly to a grave site. The grave dug opened. The vampires sit or stand in an orderly fashion. They seem to be waiting for something or someone. A few begin to hear someone walking over to them. A tall force, wearing all black with black hair and pale eyes. He even had a pair of sharp teeth of his own with sharp nails. He stood above the dozen vampires as they bowed before him. The tall force raised his arms.

"My children. I am Dunkan, The Dark One. Your lord and master."

The vampires cheer at Dunkan. Praising him as their God.

"I have gathered you all here on this night to pass down a message of The Fated Ones. We shall transform this city into our homeland. The interstate was just the beginning as we much kill as many as we can. Whether they're man, woman, or child, we must make a stand here and claim it as our own. Once we claim this city, we'll travel south to claim more. After a few months, we'll have this entire country and within a year, we'll have the whole world at our disposal."

The vampires cheer with sounds of snarls and growls. Dunkan smiled down at them, loving the attention he was receiving.

"We must fully take command and give praise to The Fated Ones. For if not for them, I would not be standing in front of you today to give you this message. We must stand tall and we must conquer all!"

All the vampires screech in praise. Dunkan walked away, looking back one time with a huge smile on his face.

CHAPTER THREE

The next day, as Abelard and Lucy were sitting in the office, discussing the bodies in the morgue, Abelard appeared immediately and approached Desportan's office. Desportan and Lucy get up from their chairs and stood up, facing Abelard.

"Excuse me, doctor. I need to deliver a very important message here."

"What would that message be? If I may ask?" Desportan said.

"Burn the bodies that are lying in the morgue. They're not safe."

"What do you mean they're not safe?" Lucy said.

"The bite marks on the bodies from the interstate. They're not what they seem to be. An animal did no such thing. You're dealing with a much threatening force."

"What are you talking about, sir?"

"I sense that you wouldn't believe me even if I told you."

Desportan sits at his desk, Lucy sat back down. They allow Abelard to sit in front of the desk.

"Please, tell us."

"What you're dealing with, they're cold-blooded, threatening, terrifying, and bloodthirsty. I'll just tell you that they're vampires."

Desportan turned to Lucy. No word from his mouth.

"Vampires?" Lucy said.

"Yes ma'am. Vampires. I know it seems hard to believe, but I am telling you the truth. Those bodies must be burned immediately. They only have one more night before they fully turn."

"I don't fully understand." Desportan said.

"I am aware of that, doctor. So, what are the two of you going to do about it?"

Desportan turned to Lucy. Not knowing what they could do. He paused and looked at Abelard. He nodded his head.

"Could you tell us more about these vampires, as you call them."

"I sure can."

Abelard pulled out a book from his coat and opened it. He turned from page to page. He stopped at one page and handed the book to Desportan. He put on his reading glasses and looked at the book. Lucy stood up behind him, looking in the book as well. Desportan is confused as to what he's currently reading.

"This cannot be possible to exist." Desportan said.

"They do, sir. They exist among us."

"How did you discover all of this?" Lucy said.

"Because I am a vampire hunter from a land far away. I'll tell you more about that later. But, for right now, we must focus on what is here in Seattle."

Desportan read the book and noticed the title *"v12 Virus"*. He looked at Abelard, turning the book around for Abelard to see. Abelard sees it and smiled. He could tell the doctor was interested.

"What the hell is a v12 virus?"

"The v12 virus. That particular strain is what created the vampires in today's time. They appeared to be a mixture of certain viruses that are commonly spoken of across vampire folklore. Noteworthy are the *v5* and *Blood Fire* viruses. After some thought and examinations, it appears the v12 virus is the strongest and most contagious out of the three virus strains. However, it takes a much longer time span for the virus to fully spread throughout the human body."

"I've heard of those two viruses." Desportan said. "I'm fully aware of those two."

CHAPTER FOUR

Desportan handed the book back to Abelard. Abelard takes the book and places it back into his coat pocket.

"So, what are you going to do about those bodies?"

"I'll talk with Lucy about it and we'll come up with a decision." Abelard smiled.

"That's fortunate enough to hear."

"Though, I would like for you to leave this office. Don't want to have security come up here asking questions."

"Fair enough."

Abelard walked out of the office. Desportan called Abelard back into the office. Abelard stood by the door, waiting for Desportan's response.

"We can talk at lunch. At the café. Once there, you can tell me everything."

"Very well. I'll meet you there, doctor."

Abelard left the office. Lucy turned to Desportan as she sat in the chair in front of the desk. Desportan sits quietly thinking to himself of what he just read and what he heard from Abelard.

"You're not seriously taking this all in."

"What if that man was telling the truth. The bite marks had to come from something and there were no animals reported at the interstate that night."

"Animals could've been there. The interstate was right next to an opening where dogs or cats could've came over. I can't take this vampire tale seriously enough to believe it."

"I understand where you're coming from, Lucy. I get the whole picture here."

Desportan stood up from his chair and stood by the window, looking out over Seattle.

"I'll meet with him at the café to see what else he has to say. I have to be sure on this one."

Later that day, Desportan meets with Abelard at the café. They shake hands as Desportan sits at the table.

"I never got your name." Desportan said.

"I am Professor Abelard Ekkehardt. I'm from Romania."

"I'm Dr. Allan Desportan. So, what are you doing in America?"

"I was doing some research about the country and I was about to leave the country until the interstate incident."

"What more could you tell me about these vampires?"

Abelard pulled out more books, a map, and medical reports containing information about the vampires. Desportan looked at the books. They appeared to be a century year old.

He scanned the map that showed locations where vampires have been throughout the world, and he started to read the medical reports.

"If I may ask, where did you get all of these?"

"While I am a professor, I am also a vampire hunter. I did most of my hunting across Romania and parts of Germany."

Desportan continued reading the medical files. He is stunned by its accuracy and how they also give references to the v5 and Blood Fire viruses.

"The v5 and Blood Fire viruses exist, according to these reports."

"Yes they do. Apparently, the theory says that when both viruses are combined, they create the v12 virus."

"That's hard enough to hear. I'm still believing that vampires don't exist. Yet, I'm reading files that contain concrete references to their existence."

"It's hard for a first-time believer to accept these things. It happens a lot in my field."

"That's good enough to hear."

Desportan's cell phone rings. He looked and saw Lucy. He answered it.

"Lucy, what is it?"

"The bodies that were in the morgue are gone. Every last one of them that were from the interstate."

"What of the coroners?"

"They're dead. Bites marks on them as well in all the same places. Maybe that doctor wasn't crazy after all."

"That's exactly what I was thinking. Keep me updated."

Desportan put his phone back into his pocket. Abelard looked at him, wondering what the call was about.

"So, what did she tell you?"

"The bodies are gone and the coroners are dead."

"Already? It can't be. They only had one more night before they fully turned."

"Maybe, that virus has been updated to spread faster."

"We must get prepared, immediately."

Desportan stared at Abelard. He can't even think.

"What do you mean prepared? Prepare for what?"

"This is a sign of a war. A war is coming and we must get prepared."

"What kind of war?"

"The End War. The war that is slated to end all humanity on this planet, so vampires can have it for themselves."

Abelard stood up and packed his bag. Desportan looked at him, concerned about what to say or do.

"What should I do if its as bad as you're saying it is?"

"Pack all of your gear. Your medicines, your tools and find some weapons that you can use. Because you're going to need them very soon to defend yourself."

Abelard left the café as Desportan drinks the last of his coffee.

CHAPTER FIVE

A group of drug dealers sit within an alleyway in the midlevel areas of Seattle. They're discussing the drug trade of shipments that haven't arrived at the proposed due date. One of the dealers began to threaten the others, demanding that he have his shipment in by the morning. As they talked, a man, wearing a black jacket and jeans with a hood over his head, covering his face, walked in between them. The dealers stare at him intensely, believing he's a spy for another dealer or a cop.

"Hey, what's your problem here?"

The man continued to walk past them. One dealers jerks the man by his jacket and slammed him into the brick wall. Looking him in the face, he asked the man the same question again and he received no response. They notice they can't see the man's face due to the hood. The dealer reached for the hood. Above them are a group of vampires, sitting quietly on the roof, watching the dealers in the alley. The dealer placed his hand on the hood and pulled it off.

"What the hell."

The dealer stared in the eyes of the man. His skin pale, eyes a clear gray, and sharp fangs. The man screeches at the dealer before lunging on his neck, biting into him. The other dealers try to run out of the alley but surrounded by more of the vampires. The vampires snarl and screech before attacking the other dealers. Killing them instantly their fangs went into their throats. The blood draining from the bodies as water would drain from a pipe.

In the morning, Desportan reads a newspaper on his desk. The front cover of the newspaper reveals the dealers that were killed in the alley. The most focused detail within the article are the bites marks that were seen on the dealers' throats, arms, and legs. He placed the newspaper on his desk, looking outside his window. As he turned around, Abelard entered his office.

"So, I take it you heard about those drug dealers in the alley."

"It doesn't prove anything except they were murdered."

"By vampires. The bites marks confirm that theory. We must warn the citizens, get them prepared and protected."

"We can't do that, it would start a panic in the city, causing more harm than good."

Abelard nodded before walking towards the door. He turned back, looking at Desportan. He smiled.

"I have a suggestion."

"Name it."

"What if you and I head out to that alley this very night. Look for sources and traces ourselves. That way, if we do stumble upon something, it will prove to you that everything I've told you and telling you is true."

"I'm not allowed to go to the crime scene. Let alone take someone who's not a member of the force."

"Just take my word this one time, doctor. Let me prove to you that vampires exist."

Desportan gets up from his desk and walked over to Abelard.

"Very well, I'll tag along with you tonight to investigate. But, don't cause any damage to the crime scene."

Abelard walked out of the office. Desportan sits back at his desk as Lucy looks on toward him. She knows that he won't listen to her about ignoring the possibility of vampires living in Seattle. So, she returned to her office and stayed quiet.

Meanwhile, inside an abandoned tunnel of a railway station, Dunkan gathered the vampires among him into the railway. He looked at each of the vampires, smiling at how animalistic and vicious they have become recently. Some of the vampires are in fact victims of the interstate incident, clothes torn and dirty. Others with their clothing drenched with blood. Theirs and others.

"Our time is not far away as the humans believe. Once, we take this city by surprise, we'll take the country and the world. We must achieve the goal of The Fated Ones, no matter the sacrifices or mistakes. The Fated Ones must be worshipped and after we've taken over this decadent land, The Fated Ones will rise again to reclaim this world as their own. With you as their soldiers, they will be unstoppable at their cause to reshape Earth into a shadowed land."

CHAPTER SIX

As night fell, Desportan and Abelard travel to the interstate to look for any other signs of vampires. While they search, Desportan stared to ask Abelard questions concerning the vampires' existence and how he's well known of it.

"I'm well aware of vampires because they mainly appeared in across decades. For example, during the end of the World Wars, mostly World War II, vampire sightings were increased expediently in small villages. Quieter. Less noise. Frightening many Europeans across the country more than those of Stalin or Hitler would have done. I took it upon myself to fight off those dreadful creatures and save my homeland. Not for the duty of the War, only to do my part in protecting my people."

"So, were they involved with many world events? Possible experimentations?"

"They weren't experiments. The war was more talked about than the vampires. Even though the vampires would feed on the desperate people within the concentration camps and villages. I fought as many as I possibly could to save as many as possible. All of the land was polluted by the evil which lurked."

"Sorry to hear about that."

"Funny thing is after the war ended, the vampires disappeared. Ever since, any war that was started in any corner of the world, the vampires would be there. Whether the wars were civil or global, the vampires were there. It seemed they were attracted to warfare or even conjured up somehow through possible occults."

After finding no traces to vampires on the interstate, they travel to the alleyway. Within the alleyway there were no signs of the murdered drug dealers. As they proceeded to enter the alleyway. Abelard started to feel uncomfortable, which caught Desportan's attention.

"Are you alright, professor?"

"I'm well. I sense a presence among us and it isn't a friendly one. We must hurry this quickly."

Abelard reached into his coat pocket and pulled out two standard revolvers. He handed one to Desportan, who took it slowly.

"You ever use one of these before, Desportan?"

"I've used a gun before, but never a revolver."

"Their filled with silver bullets. So, watch your every move as possible."

"You're telling me that silver bullets are the only thing that can kill a vampire?"

"You ask so many questions for a novice in this field, doctor. There are other things that can kill a vampire, I only have those bullets currently."

"Good to know."

They entered the alleyway. Its darker than it was before with only a few inches of light shining in from the buildings nearby or the moon above. While, walking through the alleyway, Abelard looked down at his feet and noticed a large amount of dried blood. He gets Desportan's attention and points down at the blood.

"We need to take some of this blood. Could be some traces of vampire venom within it. Just to make sure."

As light shined through the alley, it touched the blood, causing it to glow a greenish color. Abelard pulled out a cloth and rubbed it against the pavement. Getting much of the blood onto the cloth, Desportan takes out a plastic bag as Abelard placed it inside.

"I'm sure you and your lady friend can do some tests on that blood. It could definitely be a key to the vampires."

Desportan placed the bag in his pocket. Suddenly, they hear something scurrying in front of them at the other side of the alley. Desportan slowly reached into his pocket for the revolver as Abelard pulled out a flashlight. He points toward the end of the alleyway. They moved closer and Abelard hears the sound coming from a trashcan nearby. They move towards the trashcan to only reveal a possum. It runs past them and out of the alleyway, moving left into the sidewalks.

"We had to be sure."

They prepare to leave the alleyway since there was no hard sign of a vampire. As Abelard turned around, a vampire jumped in front of them. Pale skin, red eyes, and an extensive amount of hair loss. He snarls at Abelard and Desportan, revealing its elongated fangs.

"Desportan, shoot it!"

Desportan fired a shot at the vampire, it dodges the bullet quickly, moving in a pace to which Desportan and Abelard moved very slowly. The vampire jumped onto the wall, snarling at Abelard. Abelard pulled out his revolver and fired at the vampire three consecutive times. The first two shots were dodged by the vampire, but the third shot hit's the vampire through its head. The vampire's body falls to the ground, motionless.

"Nice shot."

"I had to do something because you missed."

Desportan kneeled down by the body, beginning to examine it. Abelard noticed Desportan's reaction and behavior concerning the vampire. He's seen such responses in the past. Much in similar detail. He never surprises him. Desportan was in total focus, looking at the body.

"I suggest we take this back to your lab so you can examine it there instead of in a crime spot. Unless you want the police to find us here and bring us in for questioning. Just a thought."

"Good idea." Desportan replied. "Lucy can help us with this."

"Will she?"

"We'll see."

They pick up the vampire's corpse and place it inside Desportan's car, heading to the lab for the study.

CHAPTER SEVEN

Desportan and Abelard enter the lab with only Lucy inside. They're carrying the vampire corpse with them. Lucy watched as they brought the body into the morgue area of the lab.

Inside the morgue, Lucy slowly moved toward the body and noticed its pale skin and elongated fangs. She turned to Desportan with an uncertain look upon her face. She started to shake her head in disbelief.

"This can't be real."

"Well, it is." Desportan said.

"Now, do you truly believe, doctor?" Abelard asked.

Desportan only gave a nod. Abelard nodded back.

"I see. This means you will continue in your efforts to end this before Seattle is fully consumed?"

"Consumed?" Lucy said. "What do you mean?"

"He means before everyone in the city is turned into whatever these things are."

Looking closer, Lucy realized the body was dehydrated, pointing toward the veins and the arteries. Desportan approached the table, staring at the dried veins. Abelard sighed.

"What is this?" Desportan asked.

"There's no blood flowing through the body." Lucy answered. "None. Not even an inch. Somehow, this body was drained prior to the transformation."

"Because another vampire drank from this poor soul." Abelard said.

"Drink?" Desportan asked. "Like drink-drink?"

"How else do vampires consume the blood of their victims."

"Then, how did this person become one of them?" Lucy questioned. "I'm not understanding any of this."

"When the vampire bites into the victim, not only does it drain the blood, but it injects a parasite, if you will, a venomous parasite which travels from the neck to the heart. From there, the blood is fully drained, and the transformation begins. Sometimes quick and other times slow. It all depends on the health of the victim's body."

"And you've seen this before?" Desportan asked. "All of it?"

"Yes. Why else would I be here talking to either of you."

Desportan sighed, walking toward one of the seats, sitting down, holding his head.

"I see the woof you have some adjustments to do on your beliefs as to what's real and what isn't." Abelard spoke. "However, now isn't the time. By this rate after what we encountered, there has to be around a dozen of them already in the city. Underground most likely and we need to find them now. Before they come up and scatter through the city like rats."

"How far could they be underground?" Desportan asked. "Maybe they're hiding out in the sewers."

"Not if sunlight is beaming through the tops." Abelard replied. "They go deeper. They always do."

Lucy walked over toward the desk, digging through the drawers. In the second one, she pulled out a map and laid it out. Gazing across the map of the city and its underground layers, she pointed toward a particular spot. She called Desportan and Abelard over to the table where they came and saw.

"Perhaps here." She pointed. "The Central Link Station."

Desportan nodded.

"Let's give it a shot."

"Ready when you are." Abelard said.

"Then let's get going." Desportan replied. "Lucy, myself and Abelard will head out. I would like for you to stay here."

"Stay here? You need as many hands if you come across any

trouble. Much less anything else.”

“It’s better you stay here. You can learn more about their biology. That way, you can find a way for us to face them head-on.”

“Silver is for that.” Abelard said.

Desportan gave Abelard a look. Abelard nodded with a grin.

“Just stay here, keep yourself safe. Me and Abelard will be fine.”

“We will.” Abelard said. “Trust us.”

Lucy sighed with a slow nod.

“Go. See what you can find.”

“We won’t be long.” Desportan replied.

They left the lab as Lucy returned to the table, continuing the study of the body.

CHAPTER EIGHT

Desportan and Abelard walked through the Line 1 Light Rail Station, moving through the crowds. Desportan found it strange to have so many people crowded in the station at the time of night. Abelard didn't mind it, the people were enough of a shield in case a vampire had emerged from around them. The crowd would give Abelard the opportunity to strike unseen.

"See anything?" Desportan asked.

"Only the people in front of us, behind us, and all around." Abelard replied. "What of your end?"

"Same."

Both move through the corridors, continuing to bump into the civilians. Desportan is still processing the amount of people moving through the area as Abelard moved with haste, searching throughout the corridors. He stopped, staring toward one and pointed. Desportan walked over to him, seeing Abelard pointing at a sign.

"This corridor is abandoned. Out of use."

"You think this may be the spot?" Desportan questioned. "Perhaps, they're dwelling in there."

"Only way to find out is to walk in ourselves."

They step forward, heading towards the corridor. Yet, in their path arrive two police officers. The officers stand in front of them, blocking their path into the corridor. The officers look at them, searching them. Desportan nodded as he pulled out his ID. Abelard stood steady. Calm. Collective.

"Sorry gentlemen, but this area is closed off to the public."

"Are you sure?" Abelard asked. "Because, me and my associate here have some business to attend to in this particular corridor.”

“I’m afraid you or your colleague have no entry into this section of the station. Otherwise, you’ll have to talk to services.”

“Look, I understand you cannot let civilians pass through, but this is an emergency. I’m a scientist and what we’re working on may have some significant inside that corridor. It’s hard to explain, but you have to trust us. We’re not here to cause any harm. Just looking for answers.”

The officer turned and looked at his partner, who only nodded his head with a smirk. The officer looked back to Desportan and Abelard and nodded.

“Sorry. Can’t let you pass.”

“I’m telling you, we have to go in there and search for answers. What’s going on in this city is a hazard to everyone. Potentially the entire country and you’re blocking our path to find a source to the cause?”

“I don’t follow your orders, sir. Now turn around and walk away.”

“Just let us pass and we’ll be gone before you can count to fifty.”

“No can do.” The other officer said. “Now, you heard my partner. Turn around and head on home.”

Desportan nodded, putting his ID back in his pocket. He nodded again and shook his head, turning around to walk away. Abelard watched Desportan leave and he looked back at the two officers and sighed.

“I understand he’s keen on getting to the problem to save the people. However, you have orders of your own to follow and I respect an honest man. Yet, what is happening in this city is beyond either of our hands. By declining us entry into that corridor, you may have let loose a terror this world hasn’t seen since the Middle Ages. Now, what comes over this city will be on your hands and yours alone.”

The officers paused, giving one another a confused, twisted look. Abelard nodded as he turned away.

“Good night to you both.”

CHAPTER NINE

Several days had passed with no signs of vampire sightings, which all seemed a bit strange for Abelard to comprehend. Meanwhile, the news began to release reports of a woman moving throughout Seattle claiming to have been killing vampires within the city. The woman was described as a dark-haired sword-wielding huntress who's sole goal was to eradicate the vampires from the city. Abelard and Desportan were inside the lab alongside Lucy as the saw the news on the TV. Abelard nodded with a smirk.

"Seems we're not the only ones out here doing the work."

"I take it you want to find her?" Desportan asked. "Have her join us in this endeavor."

"Exactly. What else will she be of sue besides slaughtering vampires."

"So, how do we contact her? Send out a signal only she will understand? Hopefully."

"We call her out."

"No one knows who she is." Lucy said. "Not even her name."

"That is something we'll discover ourselves." Abelard replied. "No need to wait on the news to inform us of details we surely need."

"Still doesn't answer how we'll track her down."

"I have one." Abelard said. "It'll be a simple task."

"How simple?" Desportan questioned.

Abelard and Desportan traveled out to the City Park. There, Abelard sat down as Desportan gazed the surroundings. Seeing people casually out during the day. No fear in the air nor any paranoia. Desportan found it comforting, however Abelard felt sadness as to what may come.

"I'm not certain as to what we're supposed to be looking for."

"Give it a minute." Abelard said. "You'll catch someone acting strange within a second."

"How strange?"

"Strange enough to get some eyes on them."

Desportan nodded with uncertainty. He continue looking around. Abelard kept his eyes focused on the field in front of him. Checking his pocket, Abelard caught a glimpse of something in the corner of his eye. He grinned. Looking to his right side, seeing a woman sitting next to him.

"Good to see you noticed." Abelard said.

Desportan turned around to see who Abelard was speaking to and saw the woman sitting beside him.

"You looked strange just sitting out here." She said. "As did your friend standing there gawking around like a stalker."

"I'm not a stalker. I'm a scientist."

"You look like one."

"I take it you're the woman who was on the news today. Going around slaughtering vampires?"

"Truth be told, I did what had to be done."

"So it is you?" Desportan asked. "You're the huntress."

"Huntress? Funny. Never thought of myself as one."

"Good to finally meet you. Abelard Ekkehardt."

"Anna Ilario."

Desportan looked at Anna's attire. Seeing it's mostly all leather with violet highlights layered throughout. Her long dark hair is what strikes the most from her appearance as did her blue eyes.

"Why seek me out?"

"Because we share a similar goal. I've spent most of my life hunting down vampires and sometimes other nasty creatures. After seeing the news and hearing about your work, I must ask if you will aid us."

"Aid you in taking out the vamps? I'm sure you two can handle them yourselves. I'll just continue to do what I do."

"Do you know that these vampires have a master? That it is he who sends them out to do his bidding?"

"Like some kind of warlord vampire?"

"More so." Abelard nodded. "I get going around the city killing any vampire in your sights is doing swift justice. I know. But, there is more to their existence and to this work. Much more."

Anna nodded. She looked at Abelard's side, seeing he's holding onto something tightly.

"What's under the coat?"

"My choice of weaponry." Abelard answered, showing his blade.

"Not bad." Anna smiled.

"No need to show me yours. I'm aware of your sword-wielding achievements."

"By achievements, you mean kills."

"Precisely. So, will you be joining us on this hunt?"

"If it means protecting the innocent in this city, then I'm all in."

"Good. But, remember this. It's not only Seattle you're fighting to save. It's the entire world."

Anna nodded slightly. She let out a sigh, gazing at the park.

"Are we going to be enough?"

Abelard cocked his head. He let out a faint grin.

"Time will tell. Right now, we need to find out where they're keeping themselves hidden."

"Well, I know a place." Anna said.

Desportan stepped forward. His ears were keen to her next words.

"Where is this place?" Abelard asked.

"First Hill is where I came across them. Still, I see them roaming through the area during the night. Perhaps, they're coming from the hospital. Maybe underground."

"What hospital do you speak of?"

"She's talking about Harborview." Desportan replied. "Harborview is the place."

Abelard stood up from the seat, Anna followed.

"Very well. Let's head to this hospital."

"Wait." Desportan said. "You just want to go there now and do what? Slay the vampires you come across?”

“If it comes to pass, yes.”

“But, it’s noon. Nightfall isn’t here for a few hours.”

“Better we head to the hospital and warn the people. That way, the place can be clear for us to continue our work.”

“What if they don’t believe us?” Anna wondered. “What then?”

“Then we give them a farewell and leave them to their fates. Otherwise, we’ll intercede at the proper time.”

They agreed and headed on out to Harborview Medical Center. Abelard rushed inside with Anna stepping beside him. Desportan walked in afterwards, greeting the people as Abelard stood in the middle of the lobby, gathering everyone’s attention with a yell. The doctors turned to him, making their way toward him Anna stood back, but steady.

“Is something wrong, sir?”

“Yes. You and your colleagues need to evacuate this hospital immediately.”

“Why would we do that?”

Abelard sighed, looking over to Anna. She nodded.

“There’s a plague somewhere around this place. In order for you not to get caught, you must leave. Return home or wherever you go. Protect yourselves.”

“Listen, we’re doctors. I’m sure we can handle this matter ourselves.”

“This is beyond natural remedies. Only swift justice can cure the world of this plague.”

The doctor closed her eyes and turned to Anna.

“Is he ok?”

“I know it’s difficult to fathom. But, he’s telling the truth. Everyone needs to leave this hospital before dark.”

“What of the patients?”

“Take them to another hospital. I know you can transfer them.”

“I’m afraid we can’t. many rooms are already full. This is the only place to keep them.”

“By staying here, you are putting yourselves in serious danger.” Abelard said. “I get my words sound like a horror’s tale. However, it is the truth. All of it. Creatures beyond human understanding have settled themselves in this city and many have been seen around this hospital. Hence why we're here today."

The doctor nodded and walked over to the desk, speaking to the receptionist. Their voices were low. Desportan remained by the door, watching all who passed by and walked through the lobby. Anna kept her eyes on the desk, seeing the eyes gazing around from the receptionist.

"We need to leave."

"Why?" Abelard asked.

"Because they're calling security. We have to go."

Abelard grunted, approaching the desk. Coming closer, he slammed his hand on the desk, startling the doctor and receptionist. Hearing footsteps from the hall in front of him, Abelard saw three security guards.

"This is what you do. Call security on those who are trying to save your lives?!"

"Sir, you need to leave. Now."

"I'm trying to warn you of the danger which lurks here!"

"Either you leave on your own or by taken in by security. Your choice."

Abelard sighed, looking at the doctors sanding in the lobby as the security arrived. Abelard held his hands up and turned back toward the door. Making his leave. Anna followed him with Desportan last to leave.

Elsewhere, back at the Link Station, one of the tracks had been placed into construction after an apparent faulty track. The construction workers arrived at the station and went quickly into the work of replacing the track. While working, one of the workers caught the sound of a creaking in the distance. He looked into the direction of the sound as it lowered itself. From the creaking came the screeches. Curiosity grew in the worker's mind as he made his way into the corridor. Finding it in a deep darkness. He turned on the flashlight attached to his helmet and turned around to call his collogues, yet the screeches grew louder. The worker went deeper into the corridor and eventually found nothing. Sighing to himself.

"What is that?" He asked.

Turning around to return to the work, the screech echoed through the dark corridor once again. Only this one came from above. The worker stopped in his steps and raised his head to the ceiling, only to find a strange pale-like fluid dripping down on his helmet and shoulders. He wiped it off and as he did, the screech clicked above. The worker looked up and saw a figure latched onto the ceiling. The quickening of fear grew in him as the glowing red eyes froze him. The creature snarled and leaped onto the worker, taking a bite out of his neck and drinking the flowing blood. The worker's cry for help muted into the darkness of the corridor. Turning into silence.

CHAPTER TEN

Desportan and Abelard bring Anna back with them to the office where she is greeted by Lucy while glancing over at the operation room next door, seeing the vampire body. She pointed.

"You guys caught one?"

"Not exactly." Desportan answered. "Just an opportunistic event."

"So, what have you found so far?" Lucy asked.

"Anna here has told us she's come into contact with the vampires around Harborview." Abelard said.

"Did you guys head over there? Just to see for yourself?"

"We did." Desportan answered. "However, the doctors there didn't take our words seriously."

"They wanted us out." Abelard added. "Went as far as calling security to escort us."

"But, that's not going to stop us." Anna said. "I have an idea."

"And what might that idea be?" Desportan questioned.

"Yes." Abelard said. "I am eager to know."

"We, could, you know, head out there by nightfall. Once the vamps make themselves known, we take them out. All in one swoop."

Desportan scoffed, Lucy shook her head, and Abelard nodded silently.

"That's suicide." Desportan said.

"Do you have a death wish or something?" Lucy wondered.

"Straightforward." Abelard said. "I like it. But, it's too much of a risk. Can't take it."

"It's a start at least." Anna sighed.

While they continued speaking, Lucy looked over toward the shelf toward the TV, seeing the news broadcast speaking about the Link Station. She stopped the conversation, pointing towards the TV. Desportan and Abelard looked on as the news unveiled the mysterious murder of one of the construction workers. Abelard knew what killed the worker. He looked over toward Desportan. He knew too. Lucy turned off the TV after the broadcast was finished. She sighed. Anna took a moment to think and snapped her fingers.

"We should go there."

"Been there already." Desportan said.

"Looks like we're going back." Abelard said. "Won't we?"

Desportan stared, rubbing his head.

"We have no choice. We can find the source ourselves. Even though the police might try to block us again."

"No. Don't worry about them. They can't tell us anything after this. No chance."

"Wait, you two went there already?" Anna asked.

"Before the murder." Abelard answered. "We tried to tell the police. They didn't listen."

"I'm tagging along." Anna said. "You'll need another member to join you."

"Then I'm going too." Lucy said.

"Lucy," Desportan replied. "It's better you stay here."

"And why is that?"

"Because if you discover something else related to these things, you can give us an advantage."

"It's better we head there by nightfall." Abelard said.

"What? Why?" Desportan questioned. "We can go there now while there's still sunlight."

"If we do, we won't be able to track down the vampires correctly."

"Correctly? You're sounding like Anna now."

"It's a start at least." Anna responded.

"Very well." Abelard said, standing up from his seat. "I'm ready whoever you are."

"You know what?" Desportan said. "You two go and look. I'll

stay here with Lucy."

Abelard stood by the door as Anna walked through. Abelard stepped one foot out as he turned back to Desportan. Looking to be sure he made his decision. Desportan simply nodded and it was all Abelard needed and he exited the office. Desportan turned toward Lucy and she only looked back between the door and Desportan.

"Allan, are you sure you want to stay here?"

"Abelard and Anna can take care of themselves. Right now, it's best we stay here and see what more we can learn. Now, what have you discovered so far?"

"Nothing besides what we already know."

Desportan grinned with a nod.

"So far, it's all we know about these things."

"Yes."

Desportan reached into his pocket, pulling out his phone. What he saw was a text. He opened and read the message and shook his head. Lucy noticed it bothered him.

"What is it?"

"It's Eva. She wants to meet with me at the bookstore."

"Right now? During all of this?"

"Don't worry. I'll get through it smoothly." Desportan walked toward the exit door. "I'll be back."

"Be safe."

Abelard and Anna arrived at the station, finding it covered with police and forensic scientists. Abelard liked the scenery as Anna was hesitant to make the move forward. Abelard calmed her as they entered the station. Seeing officers speaking to one another as well as several civilians going about through the station. Abelard walked with Anna, pointing toward the corridor.

"That's the one."

"Yes. We have ourselves a little problem." Anna said, seeing two officers standing by the corridor entry.

Abelard remembered the previous encounter, yet, it didn't bother him as he moved forward, approaching the officers. Anna stood with him as the officers looked, seeing them approaching.

"I thought we already told you no entry."

"Yes. You did. However this isn't the time to hold someone back. I have knowledge as to what's dwelling inside that corridor. I know what killed the worker."

"You do?" the officer said. "Then, elaborate for us what killed him?"

Abelard sighed.

"He was killed by a vampire."

"A vampire? Where are you getting this from? Silly stories?"

"He's telling the truth." Anna said. "The man's not fucking around with this."

"Ma'am, lower your tone."

"I'll lower it when you let us pass."

"I will not allow you to enter. This perimeter is cut from the public."

"You said that last time. I let that slide. Now, since my theory is correct, there is a vampire lurking within the corridor. Maybe even more."

The second officer receives a call and wanders off from the area. Abelard saw it as an opportunity. He made a move forward and the officer placed his hand on Abelard's chest. Anna raised up her sword, holding it near the officer's throat.

"Raise up your gun and you'll be bleeding to death."

"You people are crazy."

"No officer." Abelard replied. "Only the naysayers are crazy."

The officer had no other words to speak. Abelard took the silence as permission, walking past the officer into the corridor. Anna lowered the sword and smirked, bumping the officer as she walked past him. Inside the corridor, they found it covered with more forensic scientists, Anna ducked herself behind several crates. Abelard looked ahead, seeing a strange liquid on the ground. He knelt down to get a closer look. Anna saw him as she peaked from behind the crates.

"What is it?"

Abelard sighed bitterly as he saw the liquid.

"They're here."

Abelard stood up and moved with haste from the corridor, returning near Anna. She could see the fear in his eyes as he moved quickly, even his hands began to shiver.

"What's wrong?" Anna asked. "What is it?"

"We need to get everyone and I mean everyone out of this station right now!"

CHAPTER ELEVEN

Abelard and Anna exited the corridor, seeing the officers and forensics continuing their work. Abelard yelled at them to leave the station. The officers glanced at Abelard and Anna, questioning their business in the station.

"Please listen to me." Abelard said. "This place is not safe. You all need to leave this station now."

"We'll leave once our job is done." The officer replied. "Right now, the work continues."

"No. you're not understanding. The danger is within that corridor. An ancient evil killed the worker and it's coming out to kill more. You must heed my words. Leave this station now!"

Anna looked outside the windows, seeing the night sky looming. She turned to Abelard, who also noticed the sunset. He shook his head, pushing himself from the officers who had surrounded him and Anna. One officer jerked Abelard's arm.

"You seem unsettled."

"Because there is danger here. This young lady and I are leaving before it gets dark. You should do the same. All of you."

"Sir, we need you to calm down."

"I'm calm enough to be aware of my senses."

"We didn't do anything." Anna said. "We're just on our way out."

"Right now, you'll stay put. Both of you."

Abelard stomped his foot, showing his eagerness to escape the station. The officers weren't moved. Anna kept her eyes on the exit as one of the officers took out handcuffs from his pocket.

"These won't do any good." Abelard said. "We all need to leave this place now!"

The sunset had come, far quicker than Abelard anticipated. It was there he knew something was changing. Both in the city of Seattle and the atmosphere above it. The officer went to place the cuffs on them both, but was caught by the sudden sound of screams echoing from the corridor. The officer paused and looked over to the others. They nodded. The officer removed the first cuff from Abelard's wrist as they reached for their firearms and made their way toward the corridor.

"We need to go!" Anna said.

"Save yourselves!" Abelard yelled to the officers. "Do not enter the corridor! Do not!"

Abelard and Anna made it out of the station, moving toward the car. Once they entered, gunfire streaked through the air, coming from within the station. Abelard looked on, seeing several officers running toward the doors as were the scientists. Behind them, Abelard saw three moving figures. Their speed was far more enhanced. He knew.

"We need to return to the office immediately!"

Anna drove from the station as the night sky covered the city and from the station doors came the vampires. The first three caught the car driving away and they quickly ran after it. Abelard looked at the mirror, seeing the vampires making their way toward them.

"Step on it!" Abelard said.

Anna drove faster as two of the vampires lunged in the air, only to scratch the trunk of the car. The third one managed to leap atop the car and began starching its way on the roof and on the windows. Abelard pulled out his revolver.

"What am I supposed to do?" Anna wondered.

"Keep your eyes on the road. No need to get us killed or wrecked."

Abelard rolled down the window, starling Anna as the vampires lowered its head directly in front of Abelard's revolver. He pulled the trigger, blowing the head off of the vampire as its body fell from the top of the car to the road. Abelard rolled up the window, wiping the blood from his face with a towel. He nodded while Anna did her best to keep her eyes on the road.

"Problem solved." Abelard said. "For now."

"What now?" Anna questioned.

"Now, we return to the office. Tell Dr. Desportan and Dr. Seward about what we've discovered. Do what we can to warn everyone in the city of the coming days. Because, those days might be this city's last."

Anna drove down the street, entering a small traffic stop. The cars covered the streets. Lines of them. Abelard sighed as he glanced around the area for other vampires. Anna also took a look herself just to be sure. The car had stopped with only other cars in front, beside, and behind them. Abelard looked out of the window, catching what he saw was a shadow. Dodging through the traffic. He sighed slowly.

"We need to move and fast."

Desportan had entered the bookstore where he saw Eva sitting at one of the table with a cup of coffee. He greeted her and sat down. She saw he had other things on his mind. However, she did not care and Desportan already could tell.

"Why did you want to meet me?"

"Because we need to talk about the materialistic things."

"Materialistic things? What are you talking about?"

"I need to know what I'll be taking and what you'll be keeping."

"You contacted me for this? In the middle of all that's going on in the city with the interstate and the findings?"

"Now is the important time to discuss these matters, don't you think?"

"I think not, Eva." Desportan sighed. "What do you want?"

"The car."

"The car? Which car?"

"You know the one. I told you to bring it do me. You haven't"

Desportan shook his head and tossed his hands up in the air.

"You called me to come here just because you want the BMW?"

"Yes. What other reason do we have to meet like this? I want the car. Simple."

"Fine. It's yours."

"Where is it?"

"At the house in the garage."

"Then how'd you get here?"

"My work vehicle. What else would I be driving during a time like this."

Eva nodded.

"Fair point. So, how will I be getting the car?"

Desportan stared, reached into his pocket and handed her the keys to the car. He stood up from the table.

"Contact your friend to take you to the house. You can pick up the car."

Eva looked at the keys while Desportan walked out of the bookstore.

Desportan had returned to the office, seeing Abelard and Anna speaking with Lucy. Abelard turned around as Desportan entered through the door.

"Doctor, you've returned."

"I have. Good to see you two aren't dead."

"It was a matter of our speed over suggestion." Abelard replied. "Anyhow, we were telling Dr. Seward what we learned concerning the station corridor."

'What is it?"

"The vampires are there." Anna said. "Not sure how many to be exact. But, we were chased down by three of them."

"Three?" Desportan said. "Out in the open?"

"As soon as the sun sets, yes." Abelard answered. "Even that is a mystery to me."

"The sunset? How?"

"It set faster than it usual does. As if something or someone was manipulating the clouds or the atmosphere. I'm not sure if it happened but the Dark One is known to possess such abilities."

"By the corridor, you're saying you got through."

"We did." Anna said. "Yet, some of the officers weren't so lucky."

"The three vampires killed them. Right before they chased us down the road. We lost two. I killed the third one."

Desportan nodded.

"That's a good start. So, where do we go from here?"

"We need to warn everyone in the city to evacuate as soon as possible."

"I'm sorry, Mr. Ekkehardt, but we cannot put these innocent people in danger by having another traffic hap on the interstate. Not again."

"You are not aware as to how this began. The interstate was only a ploy for them to enter into the city. They were already heading this direction anyhow. If Interstate 5 was not jammed, the vampires would've arrived possibly yesterday or even today. In total, we would all be in this same place regardless.

"And what are we supposed to do?" Lucy wondered. "Go out there and hunt down any vampires we find?"

Abelard stared.

"Yes."

Back at the station, the electricity is out and from the corridor stepped forward the vampires. Approximately over a dozen. In two single-filed lines. In the middle of them walked out Dunkan the Dark One. He looked out through the windows and grinned.

"This night is the moment. The city shall be ours."

CHAPTER TWELVE

"What did you mean by 'The Dark One'?" Anna questioned.

"The Dark One. Known by the name Dunkan. He is the one responsible for all of this. Every bit of it."

"Is he like a god or something?"

"He believes himself to be. I've only ran into him once. Many, many years ago."

"How long has he been around?"

"A very, very, very long time." Abelard said. "Right now isn't the time for a history lesson. We need to bring the fight to him and end this now."

Desportan and Lucy walked toward the table where Abelard and Anna were sitting.

"So, what's the plan?" Desportan asked.

"We take the battle to them. Find the Dark One and end this."

"And how will we find the vampires?" Lucy questioned. "And this Dark One you've spoken about?"

"We make a return trip to the station. We know they're in there. Perhaps, their leader is dwelling within the corridor along with them."

"Hold on." Desportan said. "I'm not sure that's such a good idea. First, you and Anna say you went there and saw several vampires. Attack the police and even managed to chase you down the road. I'm sorry, but that place is not an option. Choose another."

Abelard nodded, glaring toward Anna, who shrugged.

"Very well. What other alternatives do you have, Doctor?"

"Let's head over to Crown Hill. Find out what we can there.

Maybe the vampires travel when necessary. Possibly pertaining to the sunlight directions. If we can find something in that cemetery, it may lead us toward this Dark One."

"I stand by your choice." Abelard said, standing up. "Let's get moving."

The four of them had traveled out to Crown Hill Cemetery, discovering many of the graves were not touched. Yet, while searching Anna looked around and discovered over a dozen graves were opened. The coffins were broken into and the bodies were gone. Desportan nodded as he looked down into the graves.

"So, they've come back from the dead."

"Not as their past selves." Abelard said. "They've become something else."

"This is all the openings we've found out here?" Lucy asked.

"Yes." Anna said. "The other graves are covered. Not even a pile of dirt above them."

"Looks like we hit a dead-end of sorts." Desportan said.

"Indeed. What is the proposed next place?"

"Next place? What other places d you think they may operate?"

"I have an idea." Anna said. "The University."

"Are you sure?" Desportan questioned.

"Yes."

Abelard grinned.

"Only one way to find out. Besides, the guards will be busy with what they discover lurking around in the dark."

Desportan with a hint of hesitance decided to go along with them to the University of Washington. Anna detailed them with several instances regarding the university. She described a sighting of a vampire which occurred the day before the Interstate Incident. The students were told to leave the campus grounds the day after the incident, which caused a stir amongst the university.

Once they arrived at the university, they recognized a strangeness in the air surrounding the university grounds. Finding a way inside, they stumbled upon the interior and immediately find a rugged man dressed in jeans and a brown leather jacket walking through with a shotgun. Anna raised her sword as Desportan and Abelard held up the revolvers.

"Put those things down." The man said. "I'm not one of them."

They lowered the weapons as the man walked into the light from the ceiling.

"Who are you?" Anna asked.

"Brant Wade. Who the hell are you guys?"

"We're on business." Abelard said. "What did you mean by 'one of them'?"

"Those creatures. They're in this university. Moving all throughout it. Ran into several of them back there."

"Any survivors?" Desportan asked.

"None so far. Not in here."

"You should join us. Help us in this fight against them."

"What fight?"

"There's more to all this than many know."

A scurrying sound moved through the hallway, causing them to raise their weapons. From the hallway where Brant came from, rushed out three vampires. They lunged in the air toward them, only to be blown in parts by Brant's shotgun.

"We need to move fast." Abelard said. "They know we're here."

They made their move toward the library. However, standing at the other end was a shifting figure, yet its eyes were red as blood and glowing through the darkness. Abelard paused, aiming his revolver forward.

"What is that?" Desportan said.

"A familiar face."

"It is good to see you still living and breathing, Romanian."

"Same goes to you, Viril."

Viril?" Desportan said. "Who the hell is that?"

"Who am I? I do the bidding for the Dark One. I am his right-hand. Before you stand before him, you must first come before me."

"I've dealt with your wickedness for a far too long." Abelard replied. "This day shall be your last."

"I believe it not to be the case. My lord, Dunkan will decide such a fate. See you around."

Viril warped into the darkness, unable to be found. Abelard stomped his foot and fired several rounds into the shadows in anger. Desportan walked toward Abelard, who sighed before sitting down at one of the nearby tables.

"Tell me, who is this Dunkan?"

"He's, he's far beyond the vampires we've encountered. He is one of the progenitors of their existence. Dunkan is a member of the Fated Ones, a species of vampiric begins who were eliminated during the Great Flood. Few survived the waters as did the Nephilim. Afterwards, the Fated Ones scattered themselves across the world and disappeared into the shadows. Only to reappear during major events. The Trojan War, the Roman Empire, the Babylonian-Persian war, and many others."

"That explains the World Wars connection."

"Yes. To my knowledge, Dunkan is one of the last ones to remain. The others were killed off centuries ago by other hunters in their own regions."

Lucy approached the table, pointing toward the windows, seeing a hint of sunlight peeking through the clouds.

"We need to get moving."

"Of course." Abelard said. "But, I believe we need to prepare ourselves right now. Because this day we're living in, is truly the beginning of the end."

They exited the university with Brant alongside them and as the doors closed, all of the electricity shut down. Not just in the university but throughout the entire city of Seattle. Streetlights, public locations, all electricity was out. An entire blackout filled Seattle.

"What's happening?" Desportan wondered.

"Dunkan has made his move." Abelard answered. "There are no more delays. This is the day."

CHAPTER THIRTEEN

The sunlight above Seattle suddenly turned into darkness, startling everyone on the city. Abelard looked above as they stood outside of the university. Desportan glared up, seeing the eclipse. He pointed with confusion.

"What's happening?"

"This is all part of his plan." Abelard said. "We have no more time to waste. We must find the Dark One and finish him for good."

"Where will he show up?" Brant asked.

"He'll make himself known for us to find him. This eclipse will bring him out in the open. Alongside his soldiers."

Entering the car, they drove through the streets of Seattle, witnessing many of the civilians being attacked by the roaming vampires. Desportan couldn't believe anything he was seeing. Abelard was focused. Lucy shook her head in pity for the people. Anna wanted to help them, even Brant.

"We can't help them." Abelard said. "Only with the Dark One defeated, may those who live be spared."

"Well, in order to end this Dark One, we have to find out where he is." Desportan said.

"I have an idea." Anna said. "Worth a shot."

"What is it?" Abelard wondered.

Anna told them the idea and without haste, they made the move through the city. Arriving back at Harborview. The car had stopped as they glanced out toward the building. No sign of doctors anywhere. Nor vampires.

"You're sure about this?" Desportan asked.

"I am." Anna replied. "This has to be the spot."

Stepping into the hospital lobby, they see the bodies of doctors and patients on the floor. Desportan shook his head. Abelard walked through, stepping over the bodies and the blood which was splattered throughout the lobby across the floor, walls, and ceiling. Abelard paused as he caught the faint sound of a screech deeper into the hospital hallway. Holding his revolver steady, he signaled the others to follow him. They walked down the hallway, leading toward the cafeteria where they found themselves staring at a dozen vampires.

"The hell is going on here." Brant said, loading the shotgun.

In the midst of the vampires, stood a much taller one. Abelard raised the revolver as the Dark One.

"The Romanian."

"You remember me." Abelard said. "How interesting."

"This is the day you've been waiting for. To face me like a warrior. As where the many have failed, you seek to be the one."

"And I will be the one. Wicked One!"

Abelard fired a shot, hitting Dunkan in the chest. The Dark One wiped off the blow and disappeared into the shadows of the cafeteria. The vampires snarled as their eyes glowed and their teeth glistened. The team was ready for the fight. Abelard searched through the darkness for Dunkan, shouting his name.

"Abelard, where are you going?!" Desportan yelled.

"He's going to the roof! I must face him!"

Abelard moved through the vampires, shooting them in the heads as he made way for the stairs. Desportan, Lucy, Anna, and Brant took out the remaining vampires as they followed Abelard toward the stairs. He reached them and made his way to the ceiling. Once he stepped foot on the ceiling, he saw Dunkan standing before him, gazing up toward the eclipse and orange burning sky. Abelard reloaded the revolver, clicking it to gain the Dark One's attention.

"Are you ready to fall?" Abelard said.

"Fall? Oh no, Romanian. This day, many will fall. yet, I will not."

Abelard fired another shot, Dunkan dodged the round, swiping the revolver from Abelard's hand. Desportan and the others bolted from the door, seeing Dunkan. Desportan fired a shot, getting the Dark One's attention.

"The Doctor."

Brant moved into the fight, blasting the shotgun across Dunkan's chest. The Dark One stumbled as his robe torn from the shot. Anna and Lucy rushed toward Dunkan, slashing him in the arms with their blades. Desportan picked up Abelard's revolver, handing it back to him. All of them combined used their tools against Dunkan, pushing him further toward the edge of the roof. Abelard turned toward Lucy.

"Do it!" Abelard yelled.

Lucy moved and speared the blade into Dunkan's chest. The Dark One froze in place as his arms grabbed the blade. Abelard looked over to Anna.

"Give me the sword!"

Anna tossed the sword to Abelard as he ran over and severed Dunkan's left arm from his body. The Dark One screeched in pain and Desportan fired one shot, hitting the Dark One in the forehead, causing him to collapse and fall off the roof to the pavement. They moved toward the edge, gazing down as they noticed Dunkan's body was not found. Abelard sighed with anger, placing his revolver into its holster. He returned the sword to Anna. Desportan was lost for words.

"I shot him in the head. He should be dead."

"No. He's not dead as you clearly saw. There's more to all of this. We must find out quickly."

Brant looked out toward the city of Seattle and shook his head. He couldn't believe what he was seeing.

"Hey, guys, what's happening?"

They turned, seeing what Brant was watching. Looking out in the distance, they saw flames and smoke growing from Seattle as the eclipse remained. Desportan turned toward Abelard with fear in his eyes. None of them could explain what was happening, only that the city was in chaos and was slowly burning.

"It all makes sense now." Abelard said.

"What makes sense?" Desportan questioned.

"His return. The vampires. The eclipse. The city burning. This isn't the execution. This is the start of his plan."

"So, what do we do?" Anna asked. "What's next?"

"The prophecy has begun." Abelard answered.

"So, it has begun." Desportan said.

Abelard nodded.

"Prepare yourselves. The fight for our lives, everyone's lives is now at stake. We need more fighters to join us. Now, let's go and find them before everyone in this city is either dead or turned."

THE PASSOVER: A SHORT STORY

An uproar has been ongoing in a small county concerning the event known as Easter. Two men appeared before a crowd of the county's residents, stating the truth of Easter and exposing its pagan history and roots. The two men speak to the crowd about the word Easter and how it refers back to the pagan goddess known as Astarte or Ishtar. They even went into detail of how the rabbit and eggs came into the pagan holiday.

"The rabbit is an unclean animal. Why would you people entertain such an abomination." One man said.

"The rabbit is also a symbol for fertility and the eggs deal with fertility rights as well. In the ancient days, the eggs would be colored with blood and placed on grounds concerning their worship toward their pagan goddess."

A middle-aged man in the crowd approached the two men speaking. He appeared angry at their words and couldn't hold in his emotions toward them.

"You two are just trying to ruin our traditions! We didn't ask for you to come here and talk to us about its history."

"If you are were true believers as you say, you would be partaking in the Passover. The first of the Most High's feasts and the beginning of the new year. Exiting the dead season and coming into the season of life."

"January is the beginning of the new year!" A woman yelled. "What are you talking about?!"

"To you and this world, yes. But to the Yahweh's people,

Passover is the beginning of the year."

"What are you guys talking about? We praise the name of Jesus every Easter. We eat lamb every Easter. We know what we're doing and the Lord knows our hearts."

"That they're desperately wicked and who can know them but the Father." The men said.

"We know why we partake in Easter. We've been doing it since the time of our parents, grandparents, and so on! Leave us be!"

The two men turned to one another. They agreed to leave, but decided to give the crowd one last warning that concerns themselves and their partaking of Easter.

"We leave this last message. For those of you who will not be partaking in the pagan day of Easter, leave this county before dark and find shelter in the wilderness. As for those of you who will be partaking in worship your pagan goddess. You all will be slaughtered before sunrise by what we've grown to call, an Overseer. We leave you, Shalom."

The two men walked away and left the county. Only a few in the crowd took the two men's warning seriously and left the county. Most of the people stayed in the county and partook in the worship of Astarte. Later that night, a full moon shined down upon the county as the people partook in the celebration of Easter. Some even presented carved images of Astarte.

"I will say those men were telling the truth." One man said to the people. "But we love our traditions."

The people partied and drank for most of the night. They later ate a table full of lamb, swine, and even shrimp. They ate until they could not even lift a spoon or fork to put in their mouths. They were drunk off of the wine and beer they drank. Some of the men swapped wives and laid with them that night in their homes.

While they partied and worshipped Astarte, walking in the wilderness nearby was a figure that carried a hybrid weapon of a machete and axe. The figure paused as it look out to toward the county, hearing the reveling and partying of the people. The figure proceeded to enter the county. The figure looked like a human, but from its presence, through discernment of spirit, you could tell it wasn't a human being.

People ran out of their houses and into the streets, dancing and partying. Bringing the party to the outside. But, when they turned and looked, they seen the figure slowly walking toward them. Believing it to be some form of a joke being played by someone who lived in the county. They laughed it off and walked toward it.

"What are you doing dressed like that?!" A man said. "Who are you playing a joke on?"

The figure raised its arm and swiped the weapon toward the man, slashing his neck. As he falls to the ground, the figure walks over his body and proceeds to slaughter everyone else in its sights. From that night until sunrise, the figure slaughtered and killed every man, woman, and child that was dwelling in the county and even destroyed their Easter images and smashed the carved images of Astarte. Leaving most of it in the streets. As the sun began to rise, the figure vanished into the wilderness.

Within a few hours after sunrise, the residents that fled the county returned to see the streets filled with the dead and their blood flowing. The county still stood, but its Easter images and artifacts were destroyed. A man looked down and seen the smashed Astarte statue. He looked up and turned to his wife.

"Those men were right. The Overseer came and cleansed this place."

"We were warned and they were warned." His wife said.

"Yes. Honey. We have to thank God for it. Greatly."

After cleaning up the county, the remaining residents removed all the images of Easter within their homes and burned them. They later decided to partake in Passover rather than the pagan day of Easter. During the night, a young boy living in the county had a dream where he seen the two men appear to the county again, proclaiming that the Overseer would return if they continue to keep their traditions rather than converting to the Laws of Yahweh and keeping his holy feast days. In the dream were images concerning Halloween, Christmas, Valentine's Day, St. Patrick's Day, Sunday Worship, and even their birthday celebrations.

In the morning, the boy awoke and told his mother and father about the dream. They rubbed it off, saying that it was only a dream and nothing more. Within a few months, the two men returned and gave warnings concerning the other pagan holidays and declaring the Overseer would return.

DARK TITAN
OMNIBUS
VOLUME I
TY'RON W. C. ROBINSON II

DARK TITAN
OMNIBUS
VOLUME II
TY'RON W. C. ROBINSON II

THE
EXTENDED
AGE
OMNIBUS
TY'RON W. C. ROBINSON II

ABOUT THE AUTHOR

Ty'Ron W. C. Robinson II is the author of several works of fiction. Including the *Dark Titan Universe Saga, The Haunted City Saga, EverWar Universe, Symbolum Venatores, Frightened!, Instincts, Chevah Mythos, The Horde, Argoron, The Supreme Pursuer, Vanok, Dark Titan's The Dead Days,* and *Agent Trevor.*

Also of other books (*The Book of The Elect, etc.*) and One-Shot short stories.

More information pertaining to the author and stories can be found at darktitanentertainment.com.

Twitter: @TyRonRobinsonII
Vero: @tyronrobinsonii

Twitter: @DarkTitan_
Instagram: @darktitanentertainment
Facebook: @DarkTitanEnt